Missing Soluch

MAHMOUD DOWLATABADI

Missing Soluch

Translated by Kamran Rastegar

MELVILLEHOUSE
HOBOKEN, NEW JERSEY

Missing Soluch was first published by Nashr-i Chishmih-yi
Farhang-i Mu'asir as *Ja-yi khali-i Suluch* in 1979.

Melville House Publishing
300 Observer Highway
Third Floor
Hoboken, NJ 07030

www.mhpbooks.com

First Melville House Printing: May 2007

Library of Congress Catloging-in-Publication Data

Dawlatabadi, Mahmud.
  [Ja-yi khali-i Suluch. English]
  Missing Soluch / Mahmoud Dowlatabadi ; translated by
Kamran Rastegar.
    p. cm.
  Novel.
  Translated from Persian.
  ISBN-13: 978-1-933633-11-4
  ISBN-10: 1-933633-11-5
  I. Rastegar, Kamran. II. Title.
PK6561.D39J313 2007
891'.5533—dc22
                        2006101686

Printed in Canada @ WEBCOM

BOOK 1

1.

Mergan raised her head from the pillow. Soluch was gone. Her children were still asleep—Abbas, Abrau, and Hajer. Mergan tied the loose curls around her face into a scarf, rose, and stepped through the doorway into the small yard. She walked straight to the bread oven. Soluch was not there. Lately, at night, Soluch had been sleeping outside next to the oven. Mergan didn't know why. She would just see him sleeping out beside the oven. He had been coming back home late at night, very late. He would go straight to the awning over the oven and curl up beneath it. He had a tiny body. He would fold himself, pull his knees to his belly, and fit his hands between his thighs, which were hardly more than two bones. He would rest his head against the edge of the wall, draw up his donkey-skin blanket—

made from the skin of the same donkey that got sick and died the last spring—and go to sleep. Or, perhaps he wouldn't sleep. Who knows? Maybe he stayed up until dawn, muttering and mumbling to himself. He'd grown less talkative of late. He'd come and go without a word. In the mornings, Mergan would stand over him, and Soluch would rise in silence. Not looking at his wife, he would sneak out before the children were up, exiting through the opening in the wall. Mergan would only hear her husband's cough as he walked away down the alleyway. And then Soluch would be gone. Soluch and his cough would be gone. He didn't even own shoes or slippers for Mergan to hear his footsteps as he left. But where would he go? Mergan could never understand. Where could he go? Where would he lose himself? It wasn't clear—no one knew. Or, no one would say. People kept to themselves. People were preoccupied with their own lives and hid their faces inside upturned collars. They wouldn't show their faces. No one would see anyone. It was as if the residents of the village of Zaminej were hidden beneath a dry layer of ice. The boundless, insistent cold would fill the empty and winding alleys of Zaminej. Ragged Soluch would head out and disappear, wearing no shoes and no hat, barely protected by the hide of his old donkey thrown over his shoulders, in a cold that was so cold even a stray dog wouldn't linger for a moment outside. And Mergan had no idea where her husband had gone. At first, she was curious where, but she eventually lost interest. So he'd go. So let him!

Mergan no longer felt close to her husband. Her attraction to him had faded long ago, and now only habit remained. Lately, even the habit was becoming weaker and weaker... and soon, it seemed, it would be gone altogether. All of the visible and the hidden things that bind a husband and wife together no longer existed between Mergan and Soluch. They shared neither their work nor their intimate lives. Without work there's no pleasure, and without pleasure, no love. Without love, there's no speaking, and without speaking, there is no shouting and arguing, no laughter and joy. Both the heart and the tongue grow old, breath dies on the lips. The face loses life when devoid of light in the eyes. Hands grow idle from boredom, and the shovel and hoe and spade and scythe lie unused in the empty shed, hidden under a heavy layer of dust. What else? Once things are so bad that even the donkey has died, and if the winter's so dry and cold that the body tries to press up under the animal's cold, black body, with sorrow overflowing from the very pit of the soul... Under these circumstances, what is left to bind two people together? What is left to feel or to say?

Of late, Soluch had grown confused, silent. He wouldn't talk, and it was as if he couldn't hear either. It wasn't as if Mergan had very much left to say to see if he could hear her or not. Was there anything left, even one small thing, that they still shared to give Mergan an excuse for speaking to him? When everything has been buried in a sickly and silent dust, what good is there in opening one's lips to speak? Mergan's lips had been sewn shut by invisible hands. Only her eyes remained open. Her eyes were wide open as if she were in shock. As if even the very walls astonished her. Or the air. Or day and night. As if she were astonished by her very being, her walking, her breathing, her feeling the cold to the very marrow of her bones. As if the fact that she had a mother who had given birth to her, suckled her, and had raised her was astonishing and terrifying. Was it true? Could it be possible? What a strange, incredible world.

Everything was strange. For Mergan, everything was strange, and the strangest of all was Soluch's empty place. But never before had his absence provoked such a reaction in her. This wasn't fear; this was terror. A new terror, sudden and unfamiliar. Without realizing it, her eyes were wide open, her mouth left gaping. Soluch's empty place seemed emptier today than ever before. It seemed like a sign to Mergan. Something both visible and hidden, like what the village women called "the spirit," a sort of myth. It was possible that Soluch had really gone. This was becoming clearer to Mergan. She began to realize that Soluch's removing himself from everything, his avoiding Mergan and the house, was not just a sign of something else, but rather revealed the heart of the matter. Soluch had separated himself, cast himself off far away. Like the tip of a finger cut off, tossed aside. How many long nights had Soluch passed alone going to Kelenjar? How many heavy days had he spent forlorn and weak in some ruins or a field or in shelters...? What thoughts had he had, what had he imagined? He had—no doubt—painfully torn the children from his heart, one by one, and cast them away. And in the same manner, he had hidden Mergan away in the folds of his memories. Nothing was left for him to leave behind—certainly not his regrets. He'd taken those along with him. Apparently he did. It's not easy to tear regret from one's heart and to cast it away. And it's not easy to leave it in someone else's care. No, he must have gone with a heavier burden on his heart. He must have gone. So let him go. Let him go!

Let him go?

This seemed easy for Mergan to say to herself. But only to herself. Because she had never before felt as at one with Soluch as she did at this moment. She sensed she had suddenly lost something, and she didn't know what it was. She knew its name, which was Soluch, but she didn't know its essence... It felt like something else. Was it possible to say that Mergan had, in fact, lost part of herself? She didn't know. It wasn't her hand or an eye or her heart. No, her spirit, her sensation, her *self* had been lost. It felt as if the ceiling was torn off above her, her walls, brought down. She felt naked. Naked inside, naked and lying on ice. As if her arms were bound behind her. Just as if she had been thrown naked and bound and speechless onto the surface of ice that formed in the gutter beside the public baths. Naked, yet without a shadow. Is it possible for any object to lack a shadow? This was what Mergan felt of herself: exposed, bound, shadowless, cold, threatened. Her heart beat as a lump of burning coal in the cold of midnight. It burned quickly. Something was alight. The old ashes that covered everything in Mergan's life had suddenly been blown off from her heart. Something lost, voiceless, and forgotten had raised its head inside her chest. Soluch, an ancient love, covered with rust. A kindness mixed with pain, a sudden sensation; she suddenly realized how much she wanted Soluch.

As long as you still have your eyes, everything looks normal. But if somehow suddenly you're blinded—say, by a hot iron or by a beast's cold claw—all at once you can no longer see the fire in the fireplace that you had stoked for all your life. For the first time, you realize what you've given up, what a dear thing it is you've lost: Soluch.

Has Soluch really gone? Where to? What about me? And Hajer? And the boys—Abbas and Abrau? Soluch has gone! Where the hell has he gone to? Who does he think will protect us now?

Mergan was slowly coming to. Her eyes were slowly opening and comprehending what had happened. Once again, the pressure from a wild force was building up within her. Her eyes became themselves again. They apprehended what was around her clearly. Everything was alive, as if new. In the dry, cold heart of the winter, life was once again boiling up. It was as if everything had come back to life. It felt as if the field of ice that had surrounded and imprisoned Mergan for months was cracking. Mergan could move again. She'd gone from ice to fire. She was burning, and she wanted to burn. Covered in flames, like a cat drenched in gasoline and set alight. She felt the melting of all the ice in the world within herself. She was burning, so much so that she felt she could melt the head of winter itself. Speechless, silent. Silent and unresisting. The heart beating in Mergan's chest was no heart. It was a furnace. A furnace of anger.

She came to. Despite these feelings, something drew her to keep her eyes on Soluch's empty place. In Mergan's eyes, Soluch's empty spot sank slowly into the ground, deeper and deeper. It was a womb. It had the shape of one. With a place for a head, two legs pressed together, a bent back. Had Soluch really been so small as to fit inside that space?

Mergan turned away. Soluch's granary was still in the middle of the yard, next to the pit. A granary only half-built. It had stands and the first level was finished; its walls were cracked and dried out. The intensity of the cold had left cracks in it. Soluch had left it there incomplete. He left it there half-built, in disgust. It had been a month that the clay oven had just been sitting there unfinished. No one had asked Soluch to build it. He'd just started building it one day, apparently out of boredom. And then a few days later he abandoned it just as suddenly. Why shouldn't he have abandoned it? When there are no goods, no grain? What's the point of a granary? And why build a clay oven? For whom? For which bread, which dough from what basin? What a waste, all the dirt that Soluch had carried on his back. What a waste, the clay that he used in the structure. What a waste, the sweat on his brow. What a waste, Soluch! He would kneed the clay, kneed it and shape it so much that he'd give it life. No baker could fashion his dough like that. Soluch worked like an alchemist—all the granaries, those full of flour and grains, all the new clay ovens of Zaminej had been shaped by the slim hands and gaunt fingers of Soluch. As long as they needed him, everyone considered Soluch an artisan. They saw him as someone with a different skill in each finger of his hand: Soluch the clay-oven maker, Soluch the pit digger, Soluch the dredger, Soluch the reaper, Soluch the room plasterer, Soluch the porter, Soluch the blacksmith... They even came from surrounding villages to take him to build their clay ovens. In Soluch's fingers, mud became as pliable as wax.

May those fingers be adorned with flowers.

Now, Soluch's legacy was only this unfinished, cracked granary. Was there a skilled granary builder in the place where Soluch had gone?

Abrau, Mergan's second son, with his big ears and his wide and sleepy eyes stepped across the doorway into the yard and went straight to the ditch beside the wall. His mother passed him and disappeared inside the stable. To Abrau, his mother's coming and going was different than it usually was. Today she was aimless, erratic. She couldn't stay still. She came out the door and went to the porch, beside the clay oven. She seemed uneasy. Unconsciously, she made circles around herself, poked her head into this hole and that one, mumbling to herself.

"Gone. Fine! Gone...Gone. Ha! Let him go! Let him go to hell and back! Go. So what? What do I care? Go!"

Abrau looked at his mother and asked, "Who's gone? Whom are you talking to?"

"He's gone to hell. Gone to find his father there. Where that bastard came from. He's gone to stop by his mother's gravestone. What do I know? Gone. Just gone. Don't you see? He's not here. Before, when he'd leave, there'd be something of his left here. Somewhere around here. But today, there's no sign, nothing!"

"What did he have to leave here every day? What could he take? Just his donkey skin, which he had with himself every day."

Mergan was silent and confused. Anxiety was winning her over. She shook her hands uncontrollably, flapping them like a hen with its head cut off. She said to herself—and in response to her son, "I don't know, myself. I don't know. But it seems to me he'd always leave something of himself, something, behind. Didn't he?"

"Like what?"

Mergan screamed at her son, "What do I know? What do I know? I don't know. Maybe his cloak. His cloak!"

Abrau washed his hands and rose from the edge of the ditch. The cold water dripped from his fingers; he slid his hands under his armpits and went to continue talking to his mother. But Mergan was already leaving. She exited through the gap in the wall and walked up the alley facing the dry wind. Where should she go? Where was she going? The alley outside was empty, as all the alleys in the village were. The dry cold rose from the open fields and scraped its rough body against the walls and doorways of the village of Zaminej. The dogs, and only the dogs, were wandering the alleys. Skinny, sickly dogs. Pell-mell, barefoot, with only a thin shirt to warm her, Mergan made her way toward the house of the Kadkhoda, the village headman.

When she reached the central square, she saw Karbalai-Safi, the old father of the Kadkhoda, who was leaving the baths and sauntering up the alley. Karbalai-Safi was one of the white-beards of Zaminej. Seeing him, Mergan had to stop and wait. She stood by the wall and said hello. Karbalai-Safi came forward, holding his side with one hand, caught his breath, and said, "Ah Mergan! Where to this early...? Afraid of something?"

Mergan suddenly realized she was shaking, so she hid her slim and drawn hands beneath her armpits while shuffling her feet. She said, "Soluch's gone, Karbalai. He's not here. Gone. Lost. Gone."

Karbalai-Safi, not looking at Mergan, passed her while saying, "Wherever he's gone, he'll come back by himself. Where is that fool to go? Where could his feet take him to, anyway?"

Mergan followed along with Karbalai-Safi, and continued, "He's not here! Not here, Karbalai. I know in my heart he's gone. He leaves every morning early on, but today it was different. It's as if he were never there."

Karbalai-Safi stroked his beard for a moment without speaking and then pressed his thick and twisted fingers against the large, termite-marked door. The door opened with a dry, cold sound, and Karbalai-Safi entered the stone-floored vestibule, crossing to the courtyard with silent footsteps.

Mergan wasn't sure what to do. She stood there, looking at the back of Karbalai-Safi's head. He put one foot onto the brick stairs, lifting his rather heavy body carefully before disappearing across the veranda into the house. Mergan waited for a moment and then quietly entered the yard, sitting in a corner by the threshold of the doorway. The thought that the Kadkhoda was likely still asleep, and that she would have to wait there for him to wake up, stung at her. Despite this, she saw no other way. She'd have to stay where she was until something happened. Eventually someone came out, and a voice called out, "God is great."

The sound of Karbalai-Safi's prayer arose in the air. After that, Moslemeh, the Kadkhoda's wife, began to make sounds as she did her chores. There were sounds of pots and pans and the clang of a basin. The sounds of plates and copper placemats scraping, mixed with the grumbling of Moslemeh, clashed against the tenor of Karbalai-Safi's words.

When Moslemeh woke up every morning she'd begin to grumble to herself, and her furrowed brow wouldn't let up for even a second. She'd speak to no one, instead acting as if she were angry with everyone. Some would say, "It's like telling your own tail, 'Don't follow me because you smell!' She's so full of herself she can hardly fit in her own skin!"

The people of Zaminej came to understand Moslemeh's nature and slowly began to look at her with a more jaundiced eye, as if she were different from everyone else, like a kind of crazy woman. And they found the evidence for this in her brother and father. Moslem, her brother, who was in fact mad. Moslemeh's father, Hajj Salem, was himself considered to be nearly so by the villagers.

"Ay! What are you sitting there for, girl?"

It was Moslemeh. She had a pot in one hand and was standing facing Mergan at the bottom of the steps. Mergan rose from the corner of the yard and said hello. Moslemeh went in the direction of the stable, saying, "Come and help me. Come! Let's get this calf to take a few pecks at his mother's teats. Come. The cow won't give us any milk until she's licked the tail of her calf. Stingy cow!"

Mergan followed Moslemeh into the stable. It was still dark inside. The outline of the cow was only barely visible at the other end of the stable. Its glassy eyes glistened; its head was tilted to one side. The cow was at ease, and as the door opened, it took a step forward.

As their eyes grew accustomed to the darkness, Moslemeh slid her pot across the smooth and worn floor of the stable and directed Mergan. "Grab its neck and bring it here!"

Mergan brought the cow over and turned the animal so that the pot was positioned beneath its swollen teats. Moslemeh brought a decrepit stool forward from the edge of the stall. Her shoulder leaning against the cow's belly, she sat on the stool and began playing with the engorged tips of the cow's teats. She smacked her lips and began milking.

"Don't be stingy, now. Don't be stingy. Ah, that's it. Ah...Ah...Ah...Give us a little, stingy! Give us, my dear. Give us some. Ah...Praise God...Give a bit...Give some...Give a bit more."

The cow was dry. Teats that size should be pouring milk like a spring shower, and each nipple should be streaming milk like a fountain into the pot. But the cow's milk wouldn't come out. Its large head was still tilted and its glassy eyes were looking toward the other end of the stable, at the eyes of its henna-colored calf held behind two pieces of railing. The delicate and beautiful ginger-hued calf was stretching itself over the railing toward its mother and braying softly, a call its mother responded to with her own half moan. Moslemeh was slowly losing her patience.

"Nothing. You could kill yourself just to get a cup of milk out of her. Let the calf out, so it can come over here and eat me up!"

Mergan opened the latch on the gate, and the calf brought its head over to the underbelly of the cow, nuzzling at the full teats of the mother. Moslemeh wasted no time putting her fingers to work at milking.

The cow's milk was now flowing, and the pot was slowly filling. Moslemeh, who had propped her head against the belly of the cow and was hard at work with her nimble fingers, shouted, "Get it, the bastard! It's like it's lapping milk from the spout of a watering can! Grab it! What's wrong with you!"

Mergan placed the head of the calf beneath one arm and struggled to detach the calf from its mother's teats, but the calf wouldn't let go. Helpless and ashamed, Mergan said, "It's stronger than me—somehow it's grabbed a nipple and..."

"You can't handle it? Haven't you been raised on bread? Grab that muzzle from that nail and put it on the calf. It's there. In the corner. Next to the lantern."

Mergan took the muzzle from the nail and brought it over. Moslemeh stopped milking the cow and together they wrested the head of the calf from under the cow, and Moslemeh tied the muzzle on the calf's snout.

"Now let it go!"

Mergan let go of the animal's neck, and the calf headed back to its mother's underbelly. Moslemeh returned to the old stool and went back to milking. Now Mergan had nothing to do. She sat on the edge of the stall watching the calf as it rubbed its nose against its mother's teats in vain, while the cow licked the calf's tail. The work was going smoothly now. Now that Moslemeh was no longer distracted by the calf, she asked, "So, what's brought you here at the break of dawn?"

Mergan, jolted as if she'd been awoken from sleep, said, "He's gone. My children's father is gone."

Moslemeh said, "Gone? So what if he has! He won't find anywhere better; he'll come back himself. Where's he going to go to?"

Mergan didn't say anything else. Speaking was pointless. Moslemeh didn't continue the conversation either. She was busy with milking and used various techniques for drawing the milk out from the cow's teats. When the pan was one finger's measure before overfilling, she rose, tired and satisfied, and pushed aside the old stool. She carefully raised the pan, and as she left by the stable's door she said, "Take the muzzle off the calf."

Mergan took the muzzle off and returned it to its place on the nail and left through the doorway. Moslemeh had set the milk on the ground and was waiting for her outside. Mergan picked up the pan and carefully and gracefully placed it on her head. She adjusted the pot on her head and evenly walked to a door leading to a room beneath the stairs. The room was a pantry, where Moslemeh made yogurt from milk. Mergan had worked for Moslemeh many times before and was familiar with this room and all of the nooks and crannies of the house. As she reached the doorway, she lowered the pot from her head, set it in a space in the wall, and straightened her back. Moslemeh placed a cover over the pot and left. She said, "By the time you take a water jug and fill it from the water cistern, the Kadkhoda will be up. It's over in the corner of the veranda over there. I'm always worried that the jugs will crack, so I cover them with rags."

Mergan took a jug and left the house.

The alleys were still deserted, as if people hadn't even begun to think about leaving their houses. A cold wind licked at her, winding its way around her body through the holes in her dress. Her dry fingers were sticking to the handle of the water jug. She held it fast against her shoulder, so the wind would not catch at it and lift it. The wind and its coldness brought tears to her eyes. But she was still not thinking about herself, as her eyes involuntarily darted back and forth in case Soluch, or some sign of him—whatever it could be—would appear. But the alley, the doorways, and the ruined houses along the way were all so lonely that Mergan's hopes were not to be raised. Despite this, she went along peeking into this ruin or glancing over that wall. When she reached the cistern, she walked around the domed structure, looking at all the corners and crevices. But it was clear that Soluch was not to be found there either. She then descended the stairs to the water, filled the jug, and began to return back to Kadkhoda Norouz's house, walking with her back to the wind. As it was blowing in the direction she was walking, she walked a little more easily, putting less effort into it. Yet she still struggled to keep the jug even on her shoulders. The wind blew in gusts, as if aiming to dislodge the jug from its place. The most difficult span was the open square that separated the cistern from the alley where the Kadkhoda's house was. As soon as she made it across and reached the alley, she sought cover against the wall, dropping the jug from her shoulders. She propped the belly of the jug against her thighs and for the first time registered the pain that was coursing through her fingers. She held her hands under her arms and squeezed her elbows, then brought her hands out and rubbed them against each other. But her dry and frozen fingers would not be warmed so easily. But it was enough that she could still open and close her fist. So she grasped the handle of the jug, threw it back on her shoulder, and set out again across the cold ground.

On the way, she saw Hajj Salem and his son, Moslem, as they walked toward her. Hajj Salem had still preserved his mind and sanity enough to expect a greeting from anyone of a lesser standing than him. Mergan, her head bowed, offered a salutation, and Hajj Salem responded with a grunt from the depths of his throat. Meanwhile, Moslem fixed his wide white eyes on Mergan and said to his father, "Water. Water! Papa, I want water!"

Mergan did not falter. She had no patience to tarry with the father and son. She turned a corner and moved away, while Hajj Salem's old voice echoed around the wall, saying, "Manners! Learn your manners, boy! You haven't even eaten your morning bread, so how are you thirsty? Whatever you happen to see, you want, foolish boy! Even if it was on the shoulder of a stranger, you'd still want it? Manners!"

Moslem responded, "So, I'm hungry. Bread, bread! I want some. I'm hungry!"

Hajj Salem said, "Manners! You beast, learn some manners!"

They moved out of Mergan's range of hearing. She arrived at the house and placed the jug on the porch. The Kadkhoda had just washed his hands and was walking up the steps. Mergan adjusted the jug's position, then turned and said hello. The Kadkhoda raised the edge of his cloak, mumbled a greeting to her, and stepped into the room. Then he said, "Come on in. Let me hear what your business is, Mergan."

Mergan followed the Kadkhoda inside, standing by the door. Kadkhoda Norouz dried his wooly hands on the edge of the curtain, then went over to the hearth and sat down, covering his legs with a blanket. He called out to one of his sons, who was still sleeping beside the hearth, "Wake up and get yourself out of the way! Come sit and warm your hands, Mergan. Come, you're shaking."

Mergan approached and sat by the feet of his son. She placed her own feet beside the hearth and warmed her face with the blanket. Her back was bent over, and her spinal column was clearly visible through her shirt. Just bones—you could count each vertebra. She couldn't stop the shaking in her shoulders and her back. The soothing and pleasant warmth of the hearth spread through her body and began to calm her. Now her shaking came only in spells. The Kadkhoda's middle son came in bearing the tea samovar.

Mergan knew her role. She rose and took the tray from the wall, placing it beside the hearth. She chose a cup and saucer, washed them, and brought them over. She knew that Moslemeh rarely ate breakfast or supper with her husband and children. She would prepare bread and stew and then sit in another room to eat her bread and tea alone. Didn't they say she was mad? Moslemeh handed yogurt and bread to Mergan to set out by the tray for the Kadkhoda. Then Moslemeh saw Safiullah, her oldest son, setting a saddle on their white donkey in the yard. She said, "Where are you going to? You can't plow frozen land now—at least let the sun rise!"

The Kadkhoda's sons usually didn't bother responding to their mother. Safiullah tied the saddle while Mergan took the bread and yogurt into the room and set it before the Kadkhoda. He placed one foot on his sleeping son's hand and leaned on it. The boy, Nasrullah, half-asleep, screamed out, and father said, "Get up and get going; go wash your hands and your mug!"

Nasrullah held his hand, got up from under the blanket, and left the room, dizzy and staggering. Kadkhoda Norouz reached for the bread and took a piece. Mergan dropped her head. She didn't want to look at the bread or the Kadkhoda's hairy hands. She swallowed, but didn't want to pay mind to her stomach. She was afraid of looking at the bread; she didn't want to be drawn to it. She busied herself with the samovar, pouring tea for Kadkhoda Norouz, washing the cups, pouring hot water, and then diluting the tea.

"Pour a cup for yourself; let it warm your bones. You must be freezing."

"I've had my bread and tea. Thank you."

Kadkhoda Norouz knew Mergan was lying. Mergan also knew; she knew that he knew she was lying. Despite this, the Kadkhoda didn't insist. Mergan was waiting for the Kadkhoda to begin by saying something. Something that might untie the knot around her heart. Even if just to loosen it a little. Despite this, just as she was waiting for him to say something, she began to lose hope in this path. She felt a hopelessness that was descending upon her like night and enveloping her. This spurred questions in Mergan's mind. Why had she come at all? What did she expect them to do? Why seek useless consultations? A man who spent untold nights beside the bread oven alone and quiet, why would he tell anyone where he was going?! And others weren't blessed with powers of foresight to be able to tell her something she didn't know but wanted to know. What for? To gain useless sympathy? Even if heartfelt, what could sympathy change? Who could lift such a burden from her heart simply with empathy and talking? So why had she hurried from the house and headed straight for Kadkhoda Norouz's home? Why had she not held out a bit longer? Why? Habit! This was simply a habit, to seek out those in a higher standing to discuss her problems with. Also, worrying; this too was a habit.

So she rose and exited the room. As she was about to descend the front stairs, she took a look into Moslemeh's room and asked if she could do anything else for her. Again, habit!

Moslemeh, who was so often wordless, signaled no with a silent motion of her head. As Mergan reached the courtyard, she heard Norouz asking Moslemeh, "So what did that woman want?"

Mergan didn't wait to hear her the reply. She left quickly and turned up the alley.

Three men—Zabihollah, Mirza Hassan, and Salar Abdullah's father, Karbalai Doshanbeh—were walking toward the Kadkhoda's house. Mergan moved to the side, lowered her head, and said hello. Zabihollah replied and continued what he had been saying. "Some things just stick you in the eye like a thorn. No matter what you do, they just stick in your eye like a thorn. Now say what you want, but I say this canal system is on its last legs. I've said so to both Salar Abdullah and Kadkhoda Norouz. We need to think of something before we're left helpless when the water dries up. I've put all my hopes in God's Land."

When Mergan reached her house, Abbas was awake and was looking for his belt. At just over fifteen, Abbas was already a young man. Large ears, a lank and drawn face, wide dark eyes, and an overall coloring that ranged from light to bruised. When his father was around, he insisted that the boy have his hair cut close to the scalp. But, by struggling and putting his foot down, Abbas had been able to convince Soluch to let him grow a foppish tuft of hair on the front of his head. So it was that now a thick and curly tuft of hair stuck out from under his cloth cap. He was wearing a jacket that was too small for him, wornout at the elbows and shoulders. A rope was tied around his waist; his pants legs were hemmed up. He had removed the heels from his cloth shoes and had tied the shoes up with a bit of string. If he hadn't done so, the shoes wouldn't stay on his feet; the shoes were tattered and falling apart.

Mergan pulled the sheet from her daughter, Hajer, and nudged Abrau with her foot, saying, "Don't you want to get up? You were up at dawn already. And you, my daughter, wake up! You've drowned yourselves in sleep!"

Mergan ignored the groans and grumbling of the children. She left and was about to step into the alley when Abbas emerged from behind the stable. Wiping his nose and upper lip with his jacket sleeve, he said to his mother, "Mama, bread!"

Mergan didn't want to hear this. She left through the space in the wall. But Abbas insisted. He stretched himself over the wall and said, "Didn't you hear me? Bread! I want to go gather some wood."

Mergan turned around and said, "There was some bread left in the bread basket!"

"Well I ate it."

"You ate it? All of it? What about your brother and sister? Are they supposed to eat each other?"

Abbas bellowed, "How much was there anyway? Not even enough to feed a baby goat!"

Mergan replied, "So what do you want me to do? Turn myself into bread? There's none left! Can't you see?"

"Well, go borrow some from the neighbors. Go get some from Ali Genav. Can't you walk?"

Mergan's lips and eyelids began shaking from rage. She came closer, controlled the anger in her voice, and spoke directly at Abbas. "I can walk. But I can't beg. Do you hear me?"

She began to walk away. Abbas shouted after her, "So I'll sell my corkwood myself. I'll take it to the market and sell it!"

Mergan, as she left, shouted, "Wake up your brother, Abrau. Take him with you. Drag him out from under his blanket!"

Abbas shouted after his mother, "I won't give a single penny of what I get from selling the wood to anyone else. I'll buy bread and eat it all myself!"

Mergan didn't listen to him. She stood straight in the wind and made her way toward the outskirts of Zaminej.

No one had left their homes yet. Only Hajj Salem and Moslem were out and about. The two were leaning against a wall and were waiting for the sunshine to emerge. Moslem had his hands between his legs, and every now and then would raise and lower one or the other of his large bare feet. He was muttering to himself, "Ah...ah...the sun's late! The sun's late...It's not coming out! Not coming. Ah? Papa? Isn't the sun coming out?"

Hajj Salem replied, "Take it easy, you. Don't blaspheme! God will be angry. Take it easy!"

Mergan walked past the father and his disheveled son and set out on the road. Outside Zaminej, the path that crossed the foothills of Boluk met with another road and extended to the city. Mergan walked away from the village. The sun was lost in the dry and lifeless cloud cover, clouds that could offer no hope to any villager. The only use of these clouds was to cover the sun. Their quality was only the intensity they gave to the cold, the edge they lent to the wind, making everything around feel forlorn. Beneath the clouds' cold belly, the sand hills and salty wasteland were laid out; the surface of the land was seemingly sealed by a layer of ice. The face of the land was frozen into a scowl, as if an enemy of everyone. A grim-faced father, a dead child. Why could it not be reborn, remade? Why not a cloudburst, at least!

The road was scratched into the body of the wasteland, set in place like a shed snakeskin in the dry cold. The expanse was empty; all that remained from last year's bushes were solitary tumbleweeds. Little clusters here and there that served to illustrate the wind's blowing. Wind and wasteland, wasteland and wind. The road, wind, and wasteland. Loneliness and despair. Mergan's bare feet and toes were lamenting the cold. Something more profound than pain coursed through her feet.

Mergan reached the edge of the salt river. The river flowed in seven streams, and each stream flowed softly and quietly like an ancient serpent. The water was low, almost nonexistent. The surface of the water was covered by ice. The ice was so thick, one could stand on it without breaking it. But to what end? On the other side of the river, there was nothing moving to distract her from her thoughts of Soluch. Nothing and nothing more. As if the land were evacuated of life. Nothing grazed, or even slithered. So where could Soluch have gone? And where was Mergan to go? Why had she come here? Why? What for? And even if she did see Soluch...

See him? See him! There he was. He was coming! Was it Soluch? He had appeared out of the ruins of the old mill and was coming! He had wrapped his cloak around himself and he was coming! It was him! Was it him? Or a dream? No! It was daytime. Clear as day. It was him. A small man's frame, with a satchel.

She wiped her eyes with the backs of her hands. No! It was him. The sunken eyes, the drawn face, his heavy brow, his locked lips. The darkness of his face, and his threadbare cap. He'd come! He was coming closer. His bare feet bore his cloak-wrapped body closer and closer. He came softly. Like a shadow.

His eyes were fixed on the dry ground before his feet as he came closer. He reached Mergan. Quietly. Wordlessly. As if she were not standing there, as if Mergan were not right there in front of him, as if she were no one to him. Nothing and more nothing. A shadow! He passed by Mergan's dry eyes and walked toward the river. He rolled up his trousers. Silently and without a word, in the same manner as he had come. The shadow placed one foot on the ice. He walked lightly. As if he were floating. He moved, not step by step, but as if floating. The slow-moving shadow grew more distant. His cloak was blowing in the wind. He was growing distant, moving farther and farther away. Across the river, across the ice. A bed of ice now separated Mergan and Soluch, just a bed of ice. If only he would turn his head and look...but no. A shadow has no head. It kept going. A weary flight, made in the shortest distance. The last flicker of the floating shadow played upon the ground. It was far away. Far. Farther. Lightly, shapelessly, and without a form. Farther. A small shadow. A dot. It was about to disappear. It was gone. A wisp. Nothing.

Wasteland and wind. Wind and wasteland. Thoughts. Thoughts and the river.

Was it him?

Mergan opened her lips. She began to feel that the dryness of her eye sockets was giving way to moisture. Perhaps from the cold wind. What should she do? Should she stay? Should she wait? Go? Stay now and come back later? Let her eyes go and stay herself? Close her eyes? Yes, that would be better. Move her arms and shoulders? To shake off the layer of ice that had covered her? Yes. The cold. The cold moved her. She shook. She felt she'd just had a nightmare. A nightmare that had left her shocked rather than terrified. As if life had hesitated for a moment inside her. Sight, all that remained was her sight. Shock. Is it really possible to see all this with these two simple eyes? Is it? Now she had seen that Soluch had gone, just as the water beneath the layer of ice flows. The water flows and is gone.

I saw him. I saw Soluch leaving.

Mergan shook herself. Her body was wrapped in a lining of cold. She had to leave. She had to go. But not to look for Soluch. She turned her back to Soluch and faced Zaminej. She headed back, speeding the pace of her steps. You can't acknowledge the cold. If you stay still too long, it will attack you. So, you can't stay still. You have to move; it's all that can protect you. In the outer fields, the cold is a ruthless adversary.

Tears filled Mergan's eyes. She preferred to think they were from the cold. She didn't want to admit to herself that she was crying. She didn't have the heart. What's crying anyway? Her eyes had been dry for years. And now... now she had no patience for it. She didn't have the patience for it. What point was there crying?

Let him go. He can go to hell. Has no other woman ever been struck by misfortune? As if no other man ever just up and left. No... No point in crying. To each his own. Let each make his home wherever he beds. He can go to hell!

Mergan appeared to believe what she was saying. But this sentiment was not the flame that was burning in her heart. That was a flame not easily extinguished. Mergan didn't want to allow the flame to escape out from her eyes, her throat, her hands, or her mouth. She wouldn't allow it. So the flame flickered inside her, burning. It stung and consumed her. Fire poured within her. A silent clamor. A rough farmer was ploughing her heart with his ploughshare. To the very roots! The roots that had grown deep these many years were being ploughed and upturned from their ancient place in her heart. Being and nothingness were upended, turned upside down. Her heart was no longer that small, quiet bird, that tame and obedient sparrow. The wings of the bird had been torn out. Naked and featherless. The hawks, yes, the hawks had set out to flight. And where were the vultures? Mergan felt the cold sharp blade of the plow cut into her guts, as if the sedimentary skin of the soil was scraped off. What was being unearthed in this long-forgotten land opened her eyes: Mergan was in love with her man! She sensed this clearly now. She loved Soluch! She remembered the love she had for him. A forgotten love. She began to realize how much she had forgotten her love for him. Her love was for a man whose absence from her side, even if he were to sleep alone out by the clay oven for a thousand nights, was unthinkable for Mergan.

This man whose very presence and absence was uncertain of late suddenly rose again in Mergan's heart. Mergan just realized that she truly loved Soluch. That she had loved him. But what was this feeling? Where had it come from? How had it been awakened in her? So he'd gone—yes, and he could go to hell! But why had he left this trace, this echo of himself inside of her? As of today, nearly seventeen springtimes had gone by since they had married. Seventeen springs, and Abbas, their oldest, was now nearly a man for himself. His upper lip had sprouted peach fuzz. And with that mouth and those big teeth, he could really swear up a storm...

Seventeen years! Is it possible for something to be lost inside you for years without your knowing of it? To have loved and to have forgotten it? Where would these words lead to?

With every step Mergan took, with each breath that took her farther from Soluch, she felt she was instead rushing closer and closer to him. How far, how distant had they been from one another in enduring the passing days and nights? Oh...How a lifetime is wasted!

People were slowly emerging and leaving Zaminej. It was the season for ploughing. But not for dry farming. The dry farmers were still waiting for the rains. They were still sitting in their homes, praying in their hearts, and looking to the skies. Here and there a man and a cow would walk out of Zaminej, heading for the higher grounds. Hajj Salem and his son Moslem were still sitting beside the wall. Moslem had stopped stomping his feet, but his hands were still hidden between his legs.

"Papa...Papa..."

Hajj Salem was unresponsive, and his gaze was transfixed to a spot in the gray cloud cover, as if his eyes were caught on something.

"Papa...Papa..."

The old man came to.

"Damn it! What's gotten into you now?"

Moslem showed his thick, yellow teeth from satisfaction.

"The sun...the sun's come out!"

"So...what am I to do?"

"Warm yourself! Warm yourself!"

Hajj Salem looked at his son, was silent for a spell, and then said, "The fool!"

Mergan passed by the father and son like the wind. Blue from the cold, she reached her home and rushed into the room. Salar Abdullah was sitting on the earthen floor. He had a scarf tied tightly around his head and had wrapped the edges of his robe around his knees.

Mergan entered without greeting him and passed him without a second glance. She went to the far side of the room and sat quietly in the darkness of the corner of the house. She lifted her hands, which were numb from the cold, and her contorted fingers hung limply. Pain shot through her fingers, and only modesty prevented her from crying. Despite everything, she could still hold herself back from crying. Pain raced through her fingers, just as the stifled cries were caught inside her throat.

Salar Abdullah berated Hajer, "Why are you just sitting there and pouting, girl? Get up and put on some water to boil. Get up and bring some hot water!"

Hajer arose and lit the stove. Abrau entered the room with a broken sickle. His pockmarked face was twisted, and he was chewing on his thick lower lip. Not looking at anyone, he said, "You can't uproot corkwood with this sickle!"

Mergan, whose voice was deadened by the cold, said, "What happened to your upstart brother? Where's he gone to?"

Abrau said, "He's fixing his shoes. His sickle's not broken. With this broken sickle that's fallen into my hands, do you expect me to bring back a bundle of corkwood as big as his?"

"Go borrow another one from someone. There's no one here who can fix that one."

Abrau groaned and walked out, saying, "'Borrow one, borrow one'—who's going to lend me one? Everyone's using their own."

"So what do you want me to do about it? Make you one myself? Hey...Abbas!"

Abbas came to the doorway, holding a shoe in one hand. Mergan said, "Why won't you lend your brother a hand?"

Abbas chewed on a bit of string, saying, "How? Am I a metalsmith?"

"Well go scare one up for him; you can speak, can't you? Go get one from someone for him."

"What am I supposed to get? Is this the metal-works market? Tell him to use a shovel instead. You can uproot corkwood with something other than a sickle, you know!"

Salar Abdullah interrupted the banter and told Abrau, "Go to our house and tell Alireza's mother to give you the short-handled sickle from the shed. Go. Say, last night we had roasted watermelon seeds—that way she'll know I sent you. Go."

Abrau stood shifting his feet. Abbas grabbed his brother's collar and dragged him to the alley and pushed him off. Abrau set out down the alley, complaining as he went. Abbas returned to the doorway, sat on the ground, and busied himself with putting his shoes on. Smoke was filling the house. Salar Abdullah went to the stove and stuck a finger in the water in the bowl and said, "That's fine. It doesn't need to be boiling."

He took the bowl of warm water and walked over to Mergan, placing it in front of her.

"Put your hands in the water. Put them in, and you'll see what good it does you!"

Mergan placed her hands in the warm water. "God bless you and your father, Salar Abdullah. Ah... Why hadn't I thought of this myself? I'm losing my mind!"

Salar Abdullah sat at the edge of the wall.

"Each living being, Mergan, finds its own special talent in some way. A man has his, and a woman has hers. When we traveled to Mashhad, one of our traveling companions, a man from Anarak, was frostbitten. It's not right to say, I'm ashamed to even mention this, but it struck him in his manhood. So we took him to the closest coffeehouse. There was an old man, also a traveler, who took care of that poor man from Anarak. As soon as he saw him, he went and poured all the hot water from the kettles that had been prepared in the coffeehouse into a basin. He added some cold water as well, and he told us to strip down the poor man. We did so, and then we put him into the water up to his waist. After just half an hour, he had all but recovered. Thank God there was no lasting damage to him either...It was after this journey that I sold off my camels and came and bought a few hours' worth of water from the canals. I was rescued from my waywardness and roaming, and I began to preoccupy myself with working a few handfuls of dirt here with a few drops of water...Anyway, now where is our master Soluch? Is he around?"

Mergan said, "He's gone to hell!"

"What? Are you back at each other's throats like cats and dogs? Yes? What happened? You seem in a bad way. Where's he gone to so early this morning?"

"He's gone!"

"But where?"

"God knows. I don't know. When I got up this morning, I saw he'd gone. That is, last night...I don't know. I'm confused. Every night he'd come and spend the night by the clay oven, but last night he left. I don't know where. That's all I know."

Salar Abdullah sat a moment and then involuntarily said, "I spit on the father's grave of any robbing thief! Just yesterday he swore a holy oath on the saint's shrine that I should come by this morning to pick up those five pieces of copper."

"Which five pieces of copper?"

"The same ones he bartered for fifteen measures of wheat from me."

Mergan said, "Well, he's not here right now."

"So what if he's not here? He made a promise. There were witnesses. Kadkhoda Norouz was the guarantor of the deal."

"So go ask the Kadkhoda for it."

"I should get it from the Kadkhoda? I gave Soluch the grain, so I should get the copper from the Kadkhoda?"

"The copper isn't Soluch's property to barter. Do you think Soluch inherited these pieces of copper from his abject father? These few bits of copper were a trousseau from my brother to me! Now I'm supposed to put them up for a barter made by my husband who is God knows where?"

Salar Abdullah sat silently, dumbstruck, then asked, "So? What about my payment, then? Soluch took my wheat, which you've all eaten, and what about me? Am I guilty that I have to suffer at the hands of his wife and children this winter?"

Mergan said, "I didn't eat bread from your wheat, his children did. Go tear open their bellies if you want and take back your wheat."

Salar Abdullah was losing his patience. His anger flared as he said, "What are you saying, woman?! You think you're speaking to a fool? Do you think I'm joking with you that you would answer me in this way? I've sold my wheat, and now I want the payment in money or in property. Just yesterday Soluch swore an oath."

"So go find him! He's not flown away to the heavens. He's probably gone off hiding somewhere in these ruins."

"So you're not willing to give me the copper?"

"I don't have any to give anyone."

Salar Abdullah leaned over and brought his face close to Mergan.

"Look at me. Why are you looking at the backs of your hands? Open your ears! I want the copper."

Mergan removed her hands from the bowl and shook them.

"So if you were to demand my children's heads, I would have to give them to you?"

"I'm not asking for your children. I am owed these."

"So collect what you're owed from the one who you did business with. What do I know about all of this? Did I buy the wheat from you?"

"Your husband did. Didn't that same son of yours pick up the canvas bag and bring the wheat to your house? Wasn't it you, Abbas? Didn't you bring it?"

Abbas looked at his mother. Mergan said, "He's not of age yet. When he's old enough, he'll take the winds of the desert that he's inherited from his father and sell them to pay off what's due you!"

Salar Abdullah suddenly leapt forward and furiously shouted, "So all you know is how to talk high and mighty? You're quite a sweet-talking, rag-wearing one; you think you're equal to me and that I have to go head-to-head in playing games with you? What's wrong with you? You think I'll let someone get away with taking what's mine? If I have to tear it from the belly of a wolf, I'll get what's rightfully mine. So I'm not worried about you!"

"Well fine, kill me if you can. I'm tired of this life already."

"To hell with your feeling tired of life. I'm just here for what's mine."

Mergan's heart was racing, and the blood was rushing through her hands and feet. She leapt up and screamed, "Get up and get out of here, you bastard! What a song and dance you've put on for me, you hyena! I have no food for my own children, and here you are trying to drag the last few pieces of copper I own away from me. You think you're up against a weakling?"

Salar Abdullah, who had also jumped to his feet, said, "I should leave? Fine, I'm going. But I'm taking the five measures of copper that are owed me before I leave this house."

He rushed into the pantry of the house and emerged a moment later carrying a tray, a vase, a bathing pitcher, and a pot. Mergan threw herself onto him, grabbed his hands, and cried out, "Put them down. Put them down, you merciless bastard!"

Salar Abdullah reached out and also took a skillet set beside the doorjamb. Mergan grabbed onto his arms and hung on.

"Put them down, you bastard... Leave them!"

With a single motion, Salar Abdullah threw Mergan to one side. Mergan rebounded and shouted, "Children! Abbas, Abrau, my girl, block the door. Don't let him take what's yours. Get him!"

Abrau had just returned with the short-handled sickle, and he stood shoulder-to-shoulder with Abbas in the doorway. Salar Abdullah rushed the door with his hands full of the items. Mergan leapt onto him from behind, tore his scarf from his head, and threw it to the edge of the room. She grabbed the cloth of his robe, and he had to let go and drop the pot, vase, and pitcher to try to disentangle himself from her. Hajer quickly grabbed the copper pieces and hid them in a chest. Mergan slid down to Salar Abdullah's feet and grabbed him between the legs. Shouting, he kept trying to free himself, but

Mergan would not let go. She dragged on him, pulling him down. Salar Abdullah's wailing filled the air. Then he kneed Mergan in the shoulder violently, sending her tumbling.

Salar Abdullah had lost any sense of restraint and unleashed a stream of whatever insults came to his lips. The boys rushed in, Abrau with the sickle and Abbas with a cord of rope. Mergan, short of breath from the pain in her shoulder, dragged herself back to the center of the room, grabbed Salar Abdullah's leg, and sank her teeth into his heel. He screamed and kicked Mergan away. Reaching the door, Salar Abdullah was entangled with three people at once, swearing and swinging. Abbas and Abrau didn't back down either, insulting his wife, children, father, and mother in return. He finally freed himself of Mergan and her sons and rushed back toward the chest, opened the door, and threw the copper pieces out. Abbas and Abrau threw their bodies on the copper. Salar Abdullah flayed at them, trying in vain to pull them off. Mergan dashed to the door shouting, "Thief, help! Thief...Help me! In broad daylight, he's emptying my home!"

Somehow she rushed to the stable and grabbed Soluch's shovel and was back inside the house in seconds, like the wind. She raised the shovel and with wild eyes and foam at her lips said, "Salar Abdullah...your life is in your hands. I'll kill you. I'll kill you and one of these children as well. I'll kill you with God's blessing. I'm done with living! Done. Do you hear me, man?"

Under Mergan's shovel, Salar Abdullah slid up against the wall and, with wide eyes, stared at her. Mergan's eyes were also tinged with dread. Kill him? Could she really kill him? Salar Abdullah, with an uncovered head, raised himself from the ground and threw himself out the door of the house, where, met by the frightened faces of the neighbors, he broke his silence. "That woman...that bitch...she's crazy! She tried to kill me! Ay...Ay...Honest to God, she wanted to kill me! I swear...I swear on the Prophet, she wanted to kill me! Kadkhoda...Norouz...She wanted to kill me. She almost smashed my head in with a shovel!"

The neighbors gathered one by one in the alley and joined the arena. Ali Genav took the role of the mediator. Sanam's son, Murad, went back to calm Mergan. In the midst of this, Kadkhoda Norouz arrived. With him were Mirza Hassan, Zabihollah, and Karbalai Doshanbeh, who entered from the alleyway. But Zabihollah hadn't realized that a woman had fought with his cousin. So, before Zabihollah could make a move, Kadkhoda Norouz passed by the side of Salar Abdullah and entered the room. Mergan was standing with the shovel in her hands, her eyes wide open. The boys, Abbas and Abrau, were on either side, leaning against the walls. Hajer was shaking. The Kadkhoda took the shovel from Mergan's hands and laid a backhanded slap against her face.

"Troublemaker! Stirring up things?"

He left the room, tossed the shovel to one side, and handed Salar Abdullah his headscarf. Then he shouted at the crowd, "So what are you all standing here for? Is there something to see here?"

Salar Abdullah tied the scarf around his head. Agha Malak's son-in-law grabbed him under the arms, and along with the others—Zabihollah, Karbalai Doshanbeh, and Kadkhoda Norouz—he left.

Mergan fell to her knees in the doorway of the house. She covered her face with her hands and, with a wail, let go of a cry that had been locked away inside of her heart until that moment.

2.

The moist earth was frozen beneath the boys' feet. The icy soil sent painful jabs through their bare soles, as if they were walking on crushed glass. For all their effort, they had little to show for it. The sun was already climbing into the sky but Abrau and Abbas had gathered less than a bushel of corkwood each. The roots of the plants had frozen in the soil, and the tendrils of the roots were thoroughly entwined in the earth, making it as if the plants were rooted in stone. Pulling out each root required more effort than it otherwise should have, straining and hurting their backs and shoulders. At times, it felt as if a snake had twisted itself around Abrau's waist. His face was contorted—his eyes squinted, lines emerged in the corners of his eyes, and his eyelashes would press together—expressing his pain in a thousand different signs. But Abrau couldn't dare to let even a quiet cry escape through his lips. This was because Abbas was heartless, always competing at work. Because of this, he would goad Abrau constantly and incessantly. He did so both for the excuse of driving him on as well as to ensure that Abrau didn't manage to sneak off with a few of the roots that Abbas had himself collected and set aside.

While working, Abbas did his best to make Abrau jealous. If Abrau's bundle of wood was smaller than Abbas'—which it always was—he would sting his brother with sharp and mocking jibes. He would do his best to poison his mood. Not infrequently, this would lead to pushing and shoving between them. Their argument would become a fight, and they'd go at each other. Abrau was the one who was always eventually hurt and would end the contest by crying. On this day, his pain came from the stubbornness of the earth, but also from Salar's short-handled sickle, which was unfamiliar to his hands. This added to Abrau's frustration, because if the blade of the sickle passed over a stalk of corkwood once without hooking it, then pulling it out afterward was a hundred times more difficult. This was because a first swing would scrape off the rough-hewn outer skin of the stalk, only exposing the smooth and moist inner core, which was much more difficult to hook with the blade of the instrument. And no self-respecting man would allow himself to just leave the uncut stalks standing there, surrounded by the others that had been cut. This is why the work required a sharp-edged sickle and strong upper arms—neither of which Abrau possessed—so that the stalks could be pulled right out of the heart of the compressed earth. Neither did he have a decent tool to work with, nor hands with strength to speak of. His bones hadn't set yet. His muscles were loose, like water. Even though in his short life his fingers had grown thick and calloused, Abrau had still not achieved the high and proud station of being considered a young man. He was even short for his age. But in the work itself, he obtained a certain substance and depth. When he focused on the task he was given, he became as one with it. While stooped over a stalk of corkwood, he was like a bee sitting on a flower sucking out the flower's nectar. He would suckle and suckle. He'd suck out the essence of the work as if it were the essence of a flower. The sickle became like a fingernail, and the stalk of corkwood felt like a thorn caught in his foot. Rather than pulling a stalk out from the earth, he felt as if he were pulling a thorn out of his heel. He moved quickly, strongly. He would not straighten his back, for fear of falling behind his brother. For fear that at the end of the day, his bundle would be smaller and less significant.

The fierce and nimble wind had left the boy's hands raw; his fingers were as dry as a goat's hoof. His nose was running and tears were streaming out of the corners of his eyes. His big ears felt frozen. The icy metal handle of the sickle burned in the palms of his hands. Still, he went from stalk to stalk, stooped over like a baby gazelle, following from one root to another.

Needing to warm his hands with his breath, Abrau paused from his work for a moment. He straightened his back, raised his hands to his mouth, exhaled a "ha" into his hands and rubbed them together angrily, as if the fault were his hands' for freezing. He once again took the sickle in his palm, but before he stooped his body over the stalks, his eyes passed over the fields before him. Others like him, both younger and older, were scattered across them and were gathering corkwood here and there. A short way up and over, only about a shout's distance away, four or five children had started a fire. Abrau watched them gather around the fire as they lifted their hands or feet to the flames to warm them. A single word passed through his lips.

"Fire!"

Abbas turned his head without straightening his body, fixing his large eyes on him. Under his brother's glare, Abrau came to himself again. Abbas said, "Sooner or later the sun will come out from behind the clouds; keep working!"

He went right back to the task of pulling up the stalks. Abrau saw there was no point in him saying anything, so he bent over and went back to work, struggling with stalks and with himself. Abrau knew that his brother was aware of how he was doing. But there was an unspoken agreement between the brothers not to speak during work, as if they had both come to know from experience that what needed to be done would eventually be done. It could happen with crying and complaining, or it could happen quietly and stoically. And yet, the unspoken agreement between the two brothers would inevitably fall apart, because the pressure from their pain and hunger would seek a way to be let out. And neither of them could control this. When a calf is branded, it brays, stomps, scratches, and rubs its head on the ground. All that the boys could do was hold out for as long as they could. And when they lost the battle against their pain and hunger, a single gesture or sound would signal their defeat. And this signal indicated their loss of self-control.

Abbas planted the handle of his sickle inside his belt and

turned to gather and arrange the loose stalks he had just pulled from the ground. He went to work picking up the stalks, one by one, two by two.

"Why are you taking my stalks?"

"Which stalks of yours?"

"Those with the thick roots—I sweat like a pig to get those out of the ground."

"Look at your scrawny self. How can you claim you pulled out stalks with roots this thick from soil this heavy?"

"You're blind if you think I can't! Toss them over here. Those are my tracks anyway. Can't you see my footprints over there? Hand them over to me!"

The thick and knotted root of the corkwood remained in Abbas' hand. Abrau nimbly grabbed his brother's wrist and Abbas tried in every way possible to free himself, in vain. He had no choice but to resort to insults and abuse. Exasperated, he said, "You're such a liar, Abrau. I should smash you with this very stalk!"

Abrau knew Abbas' nature and disposition. He couldn't let the situation end in a fight, because he knew better than the back of his own hand how badly he would be beaten by Abbas. So instead he said, "Do you swear that you pulled up this stalk?"

"You, why don't you swear?"

"Okay, I swear!"

"No sir! No need. I swear first—what do you want me to swear on?"

As he quickly tucked the thick and knotted stalk under one arm, Abbas said, "I swear on the Qibleh of Mecca that I pulled up this stalk."

"Which Qibleh? You're pointing at Hajj Habib's pool and

saying, 'To the Qibleh of Mecca.' Mecca's in that direction, toward that hill!"

Abbas turned toward the hill and said, "To the Qibleh. Is that enough?"

Abrau said, "'To the Qibleh' what?"

"I swear on the Qibleh of Mecca that I pulled up this stalk!"

"May the liar get his due!"

"May you get yours, then!"

Abrau said, "Fine. From now on we'll draw a line. You stay on one side, and I stay on the other."

Abbas had busied himself with piling up his new stalks and said, "You know, you should just go to the next field over. All of this is God's Land in any case."

"Why should I go? You go yourself!"

"I should go? You think I take orders from a pip-squeak like you?"

"And I should take orders from you?"

"Yeah, from who else?"

"I take orders from myself. I want to gather corkwood stalks right here in this field. What's it to anyone? Do you own this land?"

"Don't get caught up with just answering everything with another question! I'll beat you till you're sorry!"

Abrau said no more. He put his sickle to work on the stalks in front of his feet and grumbled beneath his breath. Abbas turned and said, "Now you're swearing and calling me names? I'll hit you so hard your teeth will fill your mouth!"

Abrau mockingly said, "So, you did great work this morning, to eat all the bread yourself!"

"I ate the bread? Of course I did. I didn't eat anything that was yours!"

"Oh, so whose did you eat? We're not good enough to eat as well? You think you're the only one with teeth to chew bread? This isn't the first time either. It's always the same thing. Eating everything yourself. The last time you took the dates out of the chest and ate them yourself. And those dates were for alms!"

"Of course I'll eat them. You'd rather I brought them and gave them to you to eat?"

"At least just eat your own portion."

"Oh, you'd not said that before!"

"So now I'm saying it."

Abbas placed the handful of stalks next to the bundle and, crouching on his hands, suddenly flared up. "Lower your voice to me, Abrau. You'll regret it otherwise!"

"Fine!"

Abbas bellowed with anger, "And stop grumbling under your breath. I'll bury you right here!"

"Yeah, fine. I'll just go dumb then. Is that what you want?"

"I wish you would!"

The heavy shadow of Salar Abdullah filled the space between the two boys. Abbas and Abrau had not noticed him approaching at all. Both were dumbstruck before the man. Abrau raised his foot and took a step closer to Abbas. Abbas also moved a step toward Abrau. Now, only a walking-stick's distance apart, the brothers stood in an even line. Salar Abdullah faced them. He bore no sign of anger, but a rough sort of dryness filled the expanse of his face. This field was worked by Salar Abdullah, but the custom was anyone could gather corkwood stalks from any of the village's land. This is good for the soil, since ploughs cannot dig up the stalks from the root unless the plough was run by a tractor. And it does no good to the new crop for a farmer to leave the stalk roots in the soil. So not only is the work of gathering the stalks not a detriment to the land, it actually benefits the landowner. So what could Salar Abdullah complain about?

"Gather your things, you sons of bitches! Pick up your bundles and rags and get off this land!"

Abrau looked at Abbas. Abbas was silent; his lips trembled softly.

Salar continued, "And hand over the sickle you borrowed from my house this morning. I need it for something."

Abrau again looked at Abbas, who reached over and took Salar Abdullah's sickle from Abrau's hand and tucked it into his belt. Then he turned away from the man and went toward the pile of stalks he'd picked.

Salar Abdullah glared at Abrau. "Didn't I tell you to bring the sickle and give it to me? Are you deaf?"

"He has it!"

Salar looked at Abbas and said, "Hey...you, idiot! Bring the sickle and give it to me."

Abbas, who had just finished piling the stalks onto his bundle, said, "I didn't borrow a sickle from you."

"Didn't you just take it from Abrau?"

"I borrowed it from Abrau, not from you. Call an apple an apple. Get it back from him!"

"It's tucked in your belt and you want me to get it from him?"

"That's not my problem!"

"So you want me to straighten you out with a few swift

kicks, eh?"

"Let's see if you can!"

"You think I'm worried about you? Your mama's not here to throw her skirt over her head and raise a ruckus! You bastard son of a bitch, I'm telling you to hand over that sickle right now! Are you deaf?"

Abbas had already tied up his bundle of stalks. Ignoring Salar Abdullah, he raised his half-full bundle to his back and said to Abrau, "Don't you want to take all those stalks you spent so much time and effort digging up? Well, get on with it!"

Abrau quickly devoted himself to gathering up his loose stalks. Salar Abdullah strode toward Abbas, saying, "I'm talking to you, idiot! Hand over the sickle! It's mine!"

Abbas started walking away with his back to Salar Abdullah, saying, "Get it from him. What's it to me? I didn't borrow it from you!"

He spoke quietly, and walked quickly.

The man set out after him, saying, "Don't make me angrier than I already am today, you bastard's child! Hand over the sickle and go back to whatever hell you're from!"

Abbas picked up his pace and threw a quick look over his shoulder. Salar Abdullah's strides grew longer. Abbas sped up, just waiting for the right moment to begin running. Salar Abdullah bent over and picked up a stone. Abbas began running. Salar Abdullah began to run after him and threw the stone in his direction. The stone hit Abbas in the buttocks, but despite the pain he showed no reaction. He ran. Faster and faster. Abbas was light on his feet, while Salar Abdullah lumbered. Abbas outran him for a distance. Salar Abdullah stopped and let out a stream of insults. Abbas also stopped. They were now far from each other. Each insult that Salar Abdullah shouted landed squarely on Abbas' heart, so Abbas let his own tongue loose, eventually adding invectives involving the man's wife and children as well. Hearing his wife being named, and by a nobody who wasn't mature enough to have had a woman, made the insults a hundred times more denigrating for Salar Abdullah. Even in a passing joke it would be impossible for a young, inexperienced man to assume the right to speak of women to a man with a wife. And of course, that was quite apart from the other kinds of insults about his ancestors and so on.

Salar Abdullah began running again. Only a beating could even the score now. But Abbas was still faster on his feet, and quicker. He ran farther away, with fear giving him an extra incentive to run even faster than before. Running from one field to another, leaping from one ditch to another. Hopeless, Salar Abdullah stopped once again. He stood for a moment and suddenly turned around. Abrau was just placing the last stalk onto his bundle. Salar Abdullah began undoing the buckle of his belt as he strode quickly toward him. He had to undo all of the humiliation he'd seen that day. Abrau did his best to tie up the bundle before Salar Abdullah reached him, but he was too late. Just as he had lifted the bundle to his back and was beginning to escape, Salar Abdullah reached him and threw him to the ground.

"And you're from the same stuff as that other son-of-a-whore!"

Abrau's cries and pleading had no effect. Salar Abdullah, lost in the long folds of his cloak, circled around him like a hawk, landing blows from the left and right. His belt was thick

and heavy, and Abrau's small and emaciated body was only covered by his pants, a shirt, and a loose jacket. Salar had lost his
mind, and he clearly had forgotten that Abrau was not even fifteen years old. He bruised the boy with an endless rain of blows
from his belt, kicks, and punches. When he finally stopped, as
he was buckling his belt back up, he said, "Now get up. Get up
and take the good news to your mama, so she knows whom she's
dealing with! And tell that rat brother of yours to keep his eyes
open until we settle accounts. I'll see him again unless he leaves
this village for good. So get out of here!"

Abrau, whose old shirt and pants had been torn in different
places under Salar's blows, picked up his bundle. Sobbing with
a sound like a calf's braying, he left, limping unevenly.

Exhausted, his face and hands smeared with dirt, Abrau
reached the refuge of the old fort. Abbas had gone behind the
ruins to rest. The sound of uneven steps, and Abrau's last vestiges of sobbing and sniffling, drew Abbas out from behind
the ruins. Ignoring his brother, Abrau continued on his way
back to the house. He only wanted to find some corner to
crawl into and to burrow his head inside an old quilt. He'd
taken a beating unjustly, and he was angry with Abbas. He
didn't want to see his ugly face. It always ended this way.
When it came to pay the price for something, Abbas was first
to run away. He'd set the fire, and then disappear. Despite all
of this, Abbas could be even more impudent than his brother
had realized. He stode alongside Abrau and began asking him,
"Is he gone? Where's Salar Abdullah? Which way did he go?
Hey are you deaf? I'm with you, stupid!"

Abrau was stopped by Abbas' rough, furious hands. He

stood still. Spittle gathered at the edges of Abbas' mouth as he stared at his brother, saying, "Where the hell did he go? Didn't you notice?"

"No."

"Did he beat you badly? What did he use?"

"His belt. His feet. His fists. He just beat me!"

"A lot?"

Abrau didn't answer. Abbas lifted the bundle of corkwood off of his brother's shoulders and set it alongside his own bundle. He sat and told his brother to also sit down. Abrau dragged himself over to the wall but didn't sit down. He leaned standing against the wall and flexed his hands.

Abbas squatted on his feet. He scraped the earth with his broken root-cutter, swore a storm of insults directed at Salar Abdullah.

"That bully! Some day I'll settle up with him right. Just because of a bit of land and his thirty, forty sheep he thinks he's someone. His head's so big he can't even fit into his clothes. Even if I only have one day to live, I'll make him pay. I'll cut his ankle tendons!"

Abrau listened to what Abbas was saying, but didn't believe a word of it. His tongue was always braver than his actions. He'd puff his chest and open his mouth. What a liar! They were only lies. He'd stand up and act angry, but he'd never deliver when it counted. He always looked out for himself first. Even now, Abrau couldn't understand why he was telling him all of this. Was his motivation to win over his brother's feelings? Did he want to make up for the fight with a few meaningless words? What was it?

Abbas spoke up again. "You...Wouldn't you be embarrassed

to take this tiny bundle into the village for people to see you?"

Abrau was silent. He had closed his eyes under the soft rays of the sun; his lips were firmly shut. Abbas continued with what he was saying. "Well, for me I'd be embarrassed. Even girls gather more than this to bring home. What would people say if they saw us with these pathetic bundles?"

Abrau said, "If we had a decent sickle, I'd go to another field and just fill up my bundle."

Abbas said, "You narrow-minded little bastard! Look at how he's willing to waste himself on work, you son of a bitch! So what are we supposed to do? I for one can't bear the thought of walking through the village with this little bundle of wood."

Abrau said, "Well, you have a decent sickle. Go find another field and fill your bundle."

"Salar Abdullah's still out in the fields. I'm afraid. I'm afraid I'll have to beat him and finish him off! Also, my belly's eating itself from hunger. My insides are all tied up!"

"Well, this morning you ate up all we had."

"What was there to eat anyway? Take a look!"

Abbas thrust a hand into his pocket, brought out bread crumbs mixed with dirt and dust, and held it out before his brother.

"Here! Eat this. To your heart's content."

Abrau hesitated and then unwillingly reached out and took the bread bits, poured them onto his tongue, shut his large mouth, and set to chewing. It was half a mouthful. He swallowed.

Abbas said, "If we were to put our bundles together, we could sell the lot by this afternoon. I'll sell it, get us some bread, and bring it home."

Abrau considered his brother's intentions. Abbas wanted

to finish the day's work by taking all the credit for himself. Not to mention bringing home the bread. So Abrau responded, "I'll sell it myself."

Abbas leapt at him like a dog. "What fool do you think would take this bundle of wood off your hands? Each bundle is supposed to be enough to heat a bread oven, no? Your little pile would hardly be enough for a stove! Would it?"

Abrau said, "And you? Your little bundle? Is your pile any more than mine?"

"No!"

"So why are you shouting at me?"

"I'm not shouting at you. Listen to me for a second and you'll see that what I'm saying makes sense. I'm saying, let's put these two bundles together and make them one full pile. Then we'll take it over to the old fort's gate and find someone who'll buy it."

Abrau said, "Agreed. We'll put them together, but I'll put the full bundle on my back and I'll take it."

"You? You'll take it? Am I nothing here? I'm your older brother! You want me to let you take the bundle on your back? What will people say? You don't think they'll just spit in my way? They'll say, look at this worthless fool who's making his little brother do all the work. Don't you see how stupid what you're saying is?"

Abrau said, "I...I'll take it on my back. What's wrong with that?"

"It's wrong for a thousand and one reasons! What will others think? They'll think I'm getting you to do all the work. Your bones aren't even firm yet, and you want me to put a big bundle of corkwood onto your back to carry? Am I nothing here? And if you're injured? What then? Who will be responsible? Like Karbalai Doshanbeh, Salar's own father, who's been injured and now has to spend all day sitting in a corner somewhere. Your back's not at full strength yet. I won't let my own brother be hurt!"

Despite all this, Abrau said, "I'll take the load."

The veins on Abbas' neck stood out as he screamed, "Stop being a fool, you idiot! I'm taking the load!"

Abrau, calmly and evenly answered, saying, "I'll take the bundle up by the mosque, and you go home by the back alleys. I'll sell it, and I'll take the money to get bread to bring home."

"You'll sell it? You think you can buy and sell goods? I've traveled three times with Uncle Aman and have bought and sold goods myself, and now you think you should go and sell the wood? Who'll come and buy this from a pip-squeak like you? You want to waste all the work we've done today? Don't you care? I've scraped with my own hands and fingernails to unearth each one of these stalks of wood, and now you're just going to go and give it all away for nothing?"

By now Abrau only had one card to play. "I'll take and sell the wood. When you were traveling with Uncle Aman, you were only riding the donkey. You don't think I know that? And if you were any good at that, he'd still be taking you with him. I'll take the bundle and sell it. If you like it, fine; if not, we each can take our own. You have a sickle; if you don't like it, go and fill up your own bundle."

"Fine, I'll give you the sickle!"

"Forever?"

"No! Just for today. Go and gather a decent bundle for yourself and bring it. What else do you want?"

Abrau replied, "Agreed. Give me the sickle. I have half a bundle. I'll gather another equal pile and have a full bundle then."

"So now you want to turn around and go to the fields carrying a bundle of corkwood? Won't you be embarrassed? Who have you ever seen walking from the village to the fields carrying kindling wood? You want everyone to laugh at you?"

"So let them laugh. Are they giving me bread to eat that I should care if they laugh?"

Abbas ground his teeth and said, "Just stop this game playing, you fool. I'll beat you senseless! The hungry man has no fear of God. I'll just shut my eyes and choke you. Don't think that just because you're my brother, I'll show you mercy. No! My belly's aching from hunger. I could rip the meat from your bones just with my teeth! So come on, don't fool around. I'm not going to go and eat all the bread this bundle will buy; you'll have your share, too. I swear on the honor of our brotherhood. Why do you want to bother me so much? I'm at the end of my rope with you. Don't you respect your faith and religion? Don't you believe in God? I'm your own brother, your older brother! Aren't you embarrassed...? You little nothing! Why do I have to talk myself hoarse to make you understand? Can't you show a little mercy to me? You want me to lose my voice with all of this shouting? My body's shaking all day and night from the evil you do to me. Why do you act like I'm your enemy? You want me to go mad and head out for the wastelands because of you?"

Abrau said, "I'll take the bundle."

"You'll take it? Are you mocking me, you son of a bitch little nothing! You'll take it? I'll show you!"

In one way or another, Abbas leapt like a rabbit onto Abrau's pile of wood and grabbed the cloth of the bundle. Abrau also, in one leap, threw himself onto his pile and wrapped his body around it. Abbas lost control. His blood rushed to his eyes, and he saw nothing more. He only wanted to peel Abrau, who was stuck onto the pile of wood like a leech, off of the bundle and to put the two piles of wood together. He opened his arms wide and picked up the bundle—which had become one with Abrau—lifted it to his chest, and smashed it to the ground. But Abrau still clung onto his small bundle and wouldn't let go. Abbas lifted his foot and brought a heavy blow down on Abrau's back, so that he let out a cry. Despite this, he didn't let go of the bundle. He was screaming and holding on. Abbas was like a mad dog. His anger was overflowing. With a struggle, despite scratching the backs of his hands badly, he managed to get his arms under Abrau's belly and hold him in a tight embrace. He fell on one knee and pulled Abrau to his chest and stomach. But Abrau wouldn't let go. Abbas stuck himself to his brother's back, put his knee in the small of his back, and took his dirt-covered ear between his teeth and bit.

As a result of the pressure from Abbas' knee, the tight hold around his body, and the pain of his brother's teeth biting his ear, Abrau lost consciousness and, like a bit of cargo that has fallen from a load, with a quick kick, he fell onto the clods of earth beside the wall of the ruins.

Abbas' mouth was full of blood. He spit. The blood was salty. He rolled his brother's head on the earth and looked at his injured ear. The left side of Abrau's face was covered in blood. The rays of the sun glittered in the crimson blood. Abbas sat on a pile of dirt and put his head in his hands. He couldn't even cry. It was as if he could only cry in blood-tears. He rose and gathered Abrau's woodpile and added it to his own. He left Abrau's cloth next to where he had fallen. He sat next to the new bundle and set it against his back.

Now that's what you call a bundle of wood!

He set his back against the bundle and set one knee into the ground, and with an effort lifted it from the ground. He stayed bent and adjusted the heavy bundle on his back. Abrau was there, fallen before him. He passed by Abrau and stepped into the road. His shadow fell before him, and he walked with an eye to the shadow cast by the bundle. He wished it looked bigger. But it didn't look very big from this angle. The sun was shining from behind him. So he turned and stood with his side to the sun. Now the shadow looked bigger. It gave Abbas a sense of satisfaction. He set back out on his way, going up another alley. The sound of Abrau's heavy breaths stopped him. He turned. Abrau was running up from behind him. He stood. Abrau's eyes looked like two hot coals. Two hot coals and smoke. Abbas felt sorry for him. Despite this, he snapped at him, "Well, now what do you want? Wasn't what you got enough for you!"

Abrau replied, "The sickle. I want your sickle."

3.

Abrau returned as the sun was setting. He had a bundle of wood on his back, and sweat was dripping from the tip of his nose. His face was white in the moonlight. His lips and cheeks were trembling from weakness. His heart felt empty. The sweat that covered his face and ears was not the sweat of fatigue; more than that, it was a sweat of weakness. Of fragility. He felt as if the very fabric of his body was coming apart. He had heard the saying "If a man's knees begin to tremble, he will eventually fall." However, Abrau refused to fall. He conjured up the last reservoir of strength within him and took another step toward the awning of the bread oven. Gasping, he arrived and leaned the bundle against the wall, and his knees began to fold under him. The wood stalks scraped against the wall as they slid to the ground. He sat down, leaning his back against the bundle of wood. His legs extended out beneath him, and his eyelashes, heavy with sweat, slowly shut as his arms stretched out naturally to each side. But he didn't remove the bundle's strap from his chest. It was as if his body was melting. His head was spinning and he felt like a kite lost in the air, fluttering along. It felt as if his body's weight was dissipating. It felt like coming apart at the seams, like breaking apart, and transforming into the tiniest speck. Like being torn off like a meteor is torn off a star. Hanging, suspended, and abandoned. Hanging in a moment's hesitation between being and nothingness. Selfless, blowing in the wind, swinging. It seemed to him as if nothing was tethered to its place. Dust filled the air, blowing around everything. Blowing onto the millstone, mixing with the grains of wheat. Swinging, like on a swing. Soluch once took the family on a New Year's picnic. On that day, he hung a swing from a tree for the children. A rope hung between two willows.

Abrau became dizzy, nauseous. Abrau was torn from his place by the bile that was pushing up from his intestines. Rising, the bundle of wood was lifted along with him. He knelt over, and the wood slid over and on him. Bile. Abrau vomited and fell on the ground chin first. The bundle slid to one side on top of him. The pressure in his intestines was not quelled. It kept throbbing. Wind blew within his empty intestines. He had no strength left in him to move. But the pressure inside compelled him to do something. The notion occurred to him to rid himself of the bundle of wood, so he grasped the knot on his chest and with a motion opened it. The bundle loosened and fell to one side. Abrau became lighter. More vomit. Not just bile, this time also some blood. He quickly lifted a finger to his ear. No, the blood on his ear was caked dry. He didn't want to believe that he had brought up blood. Drenched in sweat, he crawled on all fours into the house and dragged himself to the foot of the stove. The extinguished stove.

In no time, a cold—the cold that he had, in his feverish state, forgotten—took hold of him, shaking him like an electric shock. Every part of his body shook. No one was there. No one was home: "Is there anybody here? Anybody?" His broken voice echoed back at him. He had to get up. He rose. With one hand on the wall, he stood, still shaking. Like a willow sapling in the wind. As if an earthquake was shaking him. His knees, shoulders, and waist all shook. It took a great effort to hold himself up against the wall. The house was dark, or...were his eyes going dark? He looked at the door. The night had filled the doorway. No, the house itself was dark. Nonetheless, he had to do something. The blankets were in a far corner. Staggering and groping, he made his way to them and, trembling, lifted one blanket over him. No, one wasn't enough. Another. And one more. All of them, every blanket. But the sound of his chattering teeth continued. His teeth made the sound of hard candy shaking inside a tin. Something even he didn't understand compelled him to let out a wail. A cry. Something to open the way for the pain. To open the narrow passage that any person in pain must keep open. Otherwise, if the pain cannot escape, it explodes. A cry, a drawn-out cry. As it ploughs through the heart. A cry that sounds as if it's one hundred years of age, drawn from the veins and arteries, from the marrow of the bone. No, it is the veins and arteries, the marrow itself, that has transformed itself into this sound, this call, now pouring up through the throat. It is life itself. Life, pouring over the tongue, getting caught within the chattering teeth, seeking a way to ask for help, to seek succor.

"Oh... mother..."

These words, now being lost within the chattering teeth of this son, of Abrau, must be the first words a human ever uttered as a result of pain.

Abbas arrived. Bread in hand, a morsel in his mouth. As he chewed, his eyes were stretched open more than even usual for him. He took the empty bundle from his shoulder and tossed it to one corner. With the loud voice of a man bringing home bread, he shouted, "Isn't anyone home in this ruin?"

Only Abrau's trembling body shook the darkness of the room.

"Why didn't you light the goddamned lamp?!"

Abrau couldn't respond. Words lost their form beneath his teeth. Abbas grasped the wick of the lamp and a weak light broke the blackness of the room. Abbas still had the bread in his hand. He turned around and his eyes fell on his brother's broken face that was visible wrapped among the blankets, and his sickly and fear-stricken eyes that were darting to and fro. Whatever blankets there were in the house were piled upon him, and with his small face and frightened eyes he looked like a vulnerable animal. Abbas, not thinking of what he was seeing, walked over to Abrau and, with a tone not bereft of violence, said, "So what's happened? Why'd you go and dig yourself a grave like that?"

Abrau didn't respond. He couldn't. He didn't try, either. Abbas wasn't blind; he could figure it out. He came closer and asked, "Why are your lips bloody? Did Salar get his hands on you again?"

Abrau trembled and his teeth continued to chatter. Abbas indignantly fell to one knee in front of his brother and said, "So you're deaf and dumb? What's wrong with you?"

Abrau responded in fits, "Fever and chills. My bones are coming apart; my veins are being ripped apart. Help me!"

"What should I do? You've gone and thrown every rag and scrap on top of yourself already!"

"Yourself, yourself! I can't stop shaking!"

Abbas stood and lay on top of the blankets, belly down. The motion of Abrau's body also shook him.

"What'd you bring on yourself this time?"

"My belly, my insides..."

"What shit did you eat?"

Abrau didn't respond. He only moaned. Abbas slid off the blankets and brought over the bread.

"Maybe because you've not eaten anything, huh? Here, here!"

He took a piece of the edge of the bread and fed Abrau.

"Chew it well. Chew it. I'll give you some more. I'll give you more. Chew it."

"Cold. Cold. Warm me somehow. My bones are cracking. Cold!"

Abbas went straight to work. He tore his shoes from his feet, slid under the blankets, and grabbed his brother tightly. Abrau's shaking body shook him as well. But Abbas, like a harness on a bouncing ball, kept Abrau snug in his arms.

"Eat some bread. Eat more; eat as much as you want! Your belly's empty; that's why you can't shake this fever. Eat!"

Abrau swallowed piece after piece of the bread. Slowly, more and more of the bread was being consumed. Like a hedgehog that has grabbed onto the tail of a snake, slowly, slowly swallowing more of it. If Abbas had remained generous, the whole bread would have been eaten. But he came to all of a sudden, grabbing the last piece from Abrau's teeth. "You two-timing bastard! I didn't say eat the whole thing! You ate most of it already!"

Abrau wailed, "You'd eaten the larger part already!"

"Oh, so now you're complaining, too! I shouldn't have...Well, anyway, you seem better, no?"

"A little."

Abbas' shirt was soaked in the belly from Abrau's sweat. He let go of his brother's body and dragged himself out from under the blankets, saying, "Don't let air get to you. You're soaked with sweat."

Fever. A moment later, Abrau's body was in an oven. He was burning in his sweat. Sticky, slick sweat. He was in a bad way, and bit by bit felt more and more as if he was suffocating. As if he was trapped beneath a mountain's weight.

"Take these old rags off me. I'm suffocating"

Abbas would not agree. "You're having the sweats. The last thing you want now is air blowing on you."

"Then lighten what's on me. I can't breathe!"

"No. Hold out a bit."

Abrau began swearing before his brother. "I swear to God, to the Imam, on the life of anyone you love, I feel I'm going to die under all this. Please do something!"

Abbas stopped his restiveness, and he slid the last piece of bread into his shirt, swallowed the morsel he was chewing, and said, "Fine, very well, now that you're swearing all over the place, I'll take one of these off of you."

He removed a sackcloth.

Abrau continued pleading. "Another, just take another. I beg you on Papa's life!"

Abbas hesitated a moment.

"That reminds me; why has he not been around for the last few nights? What do you think, Abrau? Is he really, really gone, or is Mama just acting in front of that bastard, Salar Abdullah?"

Abrau kept pleading, "God, it's like I'm in an oven! Take another off me."

Abbas replied, "But where is she? I mean Mama. Don't say she's also taken off in a different direction."

Abrau screamed, "Abbas...Abbas...Have mercy, I can't breathe! Take the mattress off me!"

Abbas dragged the mattress that he had laid on Abrau off and placed the last piece of bread in his mouth. "Better? That's the mattress."

Abrau said no more. It was as if he was losing consciousness. He laid one side of his face on the ground, brought together his heavy eyelids, and emitted a plaintive cry, "My bundle...bring my bundle over here...leave it here by me."

He was sleeptalking—Abbas had heard that feverish people sometimes hallucinate. So there was nothing to worry about. He wanted to go and take a look at the bundle of wood Abrau had gathered. He went outside and set the wood straight. The bundle seemed heavy to him. He became curious. He sat next to the bundle; it made him worried. He set his back against the bundle. He drew the rope over his shoulder and pulled it. The loop on the rope tightened against his chest. He tied the end of the rope back to the bundle. It was now set tightly against his back. He gathered strength and pulled. The bundle would not rise from the ground. The load was heavy, but Abbas couldn't accept this. He convinced himself it was due to the wetness of the wood. Again he pulled with all his might. The bundle rose, but before falling into place on his back, it fell back on the ground.

How did that half-pint kid carry this?

He decided that it was because Abrau's legs were shorter than his, and so could fit beneath the bundle more gracefully, and only had a short distance to be lifted before fitting on Abrau's back. Despite all of this, it was too much to accept that he couldn't lift a bundle that Abrau had carried. He summoned the last of his will and strength, and with two pulls, lifted himself with the bundle on his back. The weight made his knees tremble, and his legs could not steady him. He involuntarily made a half-circle in place, but before becoming dizzy, he managed to stop. He stood straight in his place. A sensation deriving from arrogance made the weight easier to bear. If it had been otherwise, if he'd not been able to lift the bundle of wood, he would have been ashamed of himself. He wanted to set the bundle back down on the ground. But something prevented him. He shifted the bundle on his back, set out to the alley, and was lost in the night.

Abbas sensed the sound of Mergan's way of walking. Then he could make out the outline of her body. Abbas' sister, Hajer, was walking beside their mother. Abbas leaned the bundle against a wall and remained stooped over under the weight of the load.

"Where the hell have you two been?"

Mergan, who was swallowing a sensation of rage, instantly said, "At your daddy's grave!"

She was about to pass by her son when she slowed her step and asked, "Are you coming or going?"

Abbas raised the bundle back off wall. He set out with his back to his mother, saying, "I'm heading to the bread seller."

Mergan ground her teeth and continued on.

Mergan and Hajer were lost in the house, and Abbas in the darkness.

Abrau continued his moaning. "My bundle. My bundle. My wood. Bring it here. Right here. Next to me. They're taking them."

Mergan was drawn to her son. She paid no mind to what he was saying. Abrau's moaning made clear that he was unwell. Fever. Mergan lightened what was piled above him. Abrau's eyelashes and eyebrows were awash in sweat. She dried his forehead and his eyelids with the edge of her scarf and sat beside him and ran her fingers through his hair. His hair was dripping wet.

Hajer was left there standing. She was still considered too insignificant to be able to have a role in such matters, much more than to become saddened by her brother's plight. Hajer stood, waiting for an order or instruction, for someone to want something, to demand something. She'd not yet found enough of her own place to be able to go, of her own volition, to take a jug to get water. She was able to carry the jug on her shoulders. But she only did so when her mother asked her to. The little girl, the baby of the house. All this made Hajer seem insignificant. Her small face continually shifted between doubt and anticipation. Between weakness and irresolution. In this face, there was not yet a sign of her as herself—it was like a pool of water. Sometimes it sparkled, as if the sun was shining on it. Other times it was dark, as if a sandstorm was brewing. Sometimes it was frozen over, as if winter had set in. Sometimes it was gray, as if clouds were accumulating. If on this night she seemed dark and sullen, it was because the house was dark and sullen. Hajer reflected her surroundings.

"Girl, go put the kettle on."

Following her mother's instructions, Hajer went to light the stove.

Disturbed and upset by her son's moaning, steadfast and unbending in the face of what had been happening, anger coursing through her, Mergan was in turmoil, yet struggling to control herself. She had to do something. The only release was to take a step forward. She took a lantern from the cupboard and went to the pantry, rummaging in the corners of the house that only a mother would know of. She returned with two or three dried herbs, which she crumbled up into the kettle to boil and to give to Abrau. She replaced the lantern and unconsciously walked around herself in a circle, returning to kneel beside Abrau.

For Mergan, illness was nothing new, nothing that could be cleansed from life and forgotten. She had grown up with it, and she believed she would grow old with it as well, stepping into her grave hand-in-hand with it. She had already seen untold numbers of young and old who at one time or another had entered death's embrace. She had also seen many who had returned from the edge of the grave and had once again rejoined the living, who walked step-by-step with the march of the days. Mergan's memories, seen and heard—her mind was filled with these memories. But who can calmly set aside her motherly instincts when her own child is burning with a fever, even a simple fever?

Mergan appeared calm, but was in turmoil inside. Abrau's sleeptalking hallucinations elicited such waves of sorrow in her that pain rose from her heart like smoke, burning the lining of her nostrils. The extent of what she must do in this situation was simply to give him boiled herbs, which she was already in the process of doing. What else? She consoled herself by the fact that he was sweating, which was a good sign. Now she only needed to keep watch over him so that the cold would not do him in. She had to keep watch so that after improving he wouldn't relapse. But this was all she could do.

"Has it started boiling?"

Hajer didn't say no. She said, "Almost."

Mergan, speaking to herself as well as Hajer, said, "When was the oven lit today?"

Hajer had spent all day with her mother, so the question wasn't one she could answer. But by giving voice to this, Mergan was seeking a degree of healing. Just to say this warmed her heart. Somehow, it was meant to convince both her and the children that she was looking to the issue of heating that night. With a few words, she was showing her children that her duty every night—to find a bit of kindling from other ovens—was still on her mind. Somehow she would bring a little hope to Abrau's hallucinations, Hajer's worried eyes, and her own troubled heart.

Hajer brought the kettle and cups and then returned to the side of the oven, sitting at the edge of the wall. Mergan filled a cup with the boiled herbs and told Abrau to sit up straight.

Abrau struggled to lift himself, using his arms like pillars, sitting up like a cat. Mergan had heard that heavy nausea brings on a fever. She had also heard that these herbs, when boiled, relieve nausea. So she let the boiled herbs cool a little, then poured some in Abrau's mouth. She did just what she knew to do. No less, no more. With her heart and soul, and hopes for his better health, she poured a mix of boiled herbs, with violets and cassia herbs, into her son's mouth, when her arm brushed against his injured ear, causing him to cry out in pain. Mergan had only just noticed that someone had bitten his ear.

"Who? What son of a bitch? Who? Well? Now I see why my son has a fever! Tell me. Who was it? What bastard? Tell me. Whoever it was, I don't care. I'll make him pay. Tell me. I'll beat him with a stick. The sons of bitches have found an orphan to attack? Hasn't God done enough to this poor child, that now you also do this to him, you heartless bastards?"

Mergan was no longer asking her son who had given him the beating. She wasn't speaking to him at all. She was speaking to everything. To the air. To the walls and the doors. For ears that could hear and those that couldn't. She placed Abrau back in the blankets and rose. She tied her robe to her waist and was walking in circles around the room, around herself. Hajer remained frozen in her corner against the wall, and Abrau had set his dizzy and confused head back down. Mergan would walk, then stop, stop and then begin walking, all the while speaking to herself. She spoke out loud. To herself. To the house. To the night. To what is and is not. What she was speaking of wasn't simple speech. It was more like poetic recitation. She would speak, and then go silent. She would be silent, and then suddenly it would boil over, her voice rising and calling out.

"Which one should I take care of? Which one should I cover with my wing? In which one's mouth shall I put a few seeds? Whoever can comes and pecks at one of them. Whoever can comes and pecks at the head of one of them. So just come all at once and take us all! Come and toss us all in a pot of boiling water! Come, come on!"

"I hope no one's head is uncovered. We're coming in!"

The heavy sound of Kadkhoda Norouz' footsteps, accompanied by a short cough, brought Mergan back to herself. The shoulders of two men filled the entryway of the room. Kadkhoda Norouz had a cloak thrown over his shoulders, and Salar Abdullah was wearing a long tunic. Both had head scarves tied around their heads. Kadkhoda's scarf was tied with greater care, and the tail end of Salar Abdullah's scarf trailed down onto his chest.

The men brought the cold into the house with them. Until this moment, the cold had been forgotten. It was only Hajer who had suffered the cold and had stuck herself to the stove. Mergan and Abrau were each burning with their own fevers; Abrau of illness, Mergan of rage. On seeing the men, Mergan went silent and retreated to sit in a corner. Not that she wasn't expecting their visit; she was. She had even prepared for it. All the same, their arrival was a shock. Seeing the men, she was frozen in her place.

The men sat, Salar at the doorway, and the Kadkhoda by the stove. Hajer slid away from the Kadkhoda, who sat beside the stove in such a way as to position his crotch close to the faltering heat of the fire. Because of this, in order to look at Mergan so as to speak directly to her, he had to twist his large head on his shoulders, straining to face her.

"Go bring those four bits of copper work!"

Mergan stayed just as she had been, with her back to the wall, hugging her knees silently.

The Kadkhoda repeated, "Get up. Get up and go bring those four pieces of copper work!"

Mergan still did not respond. Did not move. Salar was eyeing her. Her parched cheeks and drawn profile were discernible in the flickering light of the tallow-burner. A stubborn silence had her frozen in her place as if she were not alive, like the outline of a woman cut from stone. But Salar was agitated. His spleen held more than a few things that he wanted to bestow on Mergan and her boys. But since Kadkhoda Norouz had come to mediate, it would not have been to his advantage to let loose at this time. The Kadkhoda turned his head again and shouted at Mergan, "Have you gone deaf? I told you get up and get those four bits of copper work! Do I have to become rude with you?"

Mergan, staring ahead at the floor, said, "You go get them yourself. You know where they are."

The Kadkhoda replied, "If you don't go get them yourself, that's what we'll have to do. I've not come here just to sit and look at you!"

Mergan replied, "May God repay you for your kindness!"

The Kadkhoda smarted from the sting of the remark, and said, "A deal is a deal. Brotherhood has its own place—one brings wheat, and leaves with apricots. Salar, you go yourself. Get up and go get the copper pieces from their place and bring them here. Get up—while I'm here, it isn't against the law."

Salar Abdullah was ready and he rose to enter the pantry. The others in the room—Mergan, the Kadkhoda, Hajer, and

Abrau—each remained silent in their own way. The clanging sounds of copper could be heard on the other side of the curtain. Salar Abdullah drew the curtain back, placing the copper pieces outside one by one. Finally, he exited the pantry, a goblet in one hand, and said to Kadkhoda Norouz, "The copper's less than half of what it was, Kadkhoda! Come and see for yourself!"

The Kadkhoda rose, went to the doorway of the pantry, and fell into thought while looking at the copper work set out there.

"Ten *seers*, half a *man*...Fifteen *seers*. Estimate this one piece at seven *seer*; all together it comes to...ten, thirty, fifteen, and seven—my guess is this is, all together, about one *man* and two *seer*. So we're short four *man* and two more *seer*. So...?"

Before anything further could be said, Salar Abdullah removed the tallow-burner from the shelf, went back into the pantry and looked in all the nooks and crannies, came out and replaced the tallow-burner to its place, and said, "Nothing. They're not here. They've melted into thin air!"

Mergan remained silent, looking at a spot in front of her feet. But she could sense the sharp glare of Salar and the Kadkhoda on her. She was ready for a fight. She'd made all of the calculations. Perhaps that was why she was so firmly frozen in her place. Like a dragon protecting treasure. She had no choice. The earth itself was the only thing giving her support. She had no desire to rise, to stand. She didn't want to have her knees begin shaking from the Kadkhoda's and Salar's accusations and quarreling. She wanted to hold her own. That was why she was firmly fixed to her seat on the earth.

Salar said, "Thief! She's taken a hand to the copper. I'd seen them myself! A pot, a bathing pitcher, a tray, the vase, and a set of pieces coming to thirty *seer*. It wasn't just these four worthless bits of copper. She's taken a hand to my property!"

Your property?

It would have been natural for Mergan to say this, but she didn't. She only thought it. The Kadkhoda approached her with wide strides and stood beside her and asked, "So what's happened to the rest? Where did you put them?"

Mergan's mouth remained firmly shut. The Kadkhoda repeated, "I'm with you! Where did you put them?"

Kadkhoda Norouz's voice was shaking. Mergan couldn't remain silent any longer, so she said, "Just where they were before!"

Salar cut her off, saying, "They're not! All there is are these four worthless bits of copper work! Where are the valuable pieces?"

Mergan replied, "They've gone to hell—where are they? What do I know where they are? He himself, his own cursed self, he'd come and take one piece every night to melt down. So what do I know? He'd come and go to the nearby villages— maybe he's left them with a friend of his. God burn his cursed soul for absconding holy Zaynab's rights!"

Salar began shouting out of control, "It's a lie! A lie! She's lying while swearing on the purity of Zaynab! It was your own dishonorable self who absconded with the coppers!"

Mergan stared at Salar a moment and said, "Me? May my hands dry up if I've even touched these copper pieces. May my children wither and waste before me if my soul had any idea of what happened to them. Soluch, that son of a bitch himself, was the one who's made off with my bathing pitcher, my vase and tray, and the rest of them, and has sold them!"

"You're lying, you and your seven backs, you witch! That man wouldn't touch the property of others. Soluch wasn't the kind of man to steal something from his own property!"

"His own property! How could he have gave gotten it? Oh, maybe he inherited it from his father, a mud-plasterer! Do you remember when his old man died what he left for him? A plastering spade. That was all. His property, his property! It's as if you think I was the wife of the son of a nobleman and I didn't even know it!"

Salar said, "Will you swear on the Qur'an?"

"Swear what on the Qur'an?"

"That you didn't steal the copper work yourself!"

Mergan ran toward Hajer, embraced her daughter, slapped her head, and said, "May I bury my own daughter! May I bury her with my own bare hands, if...if I should know anything about this. Kadkhoda! At least say something to this man!"

Kadkhoda Norouz knew Mergan well. Not just Mergan, but also he knew most of the people in Zaminej better than anyone else did. And that was why he was the Kadkhoda, and not Salar Abdullah. So he knew that if the matter should be drawn out any further, Mergan would not hesitate to even lift Hajer up and smash her into Salar's head, and Kadkhoda Norouz didn't want this to happen. He didn't want something like this to happen while he was there. Mergan's attack on Salar Abdullah earlier was a consequence of a similar situation. So the Kadkhoda wisely realized he would have to take a moderating position. To step on Mergan's tail more than this would be unwise. Mergan was that kind of person that the Kadkhoda and Salar Abdullah termed "headless and footless"—out of control. From one standpoint, they were right, since Mergan had never had an opportunity to distinguish her head from her feet. In a sense, her head had never benefited from a strong neck; her feet had never had shoes. But if they meant "headless and footless" to signify something else, then it was up to the Kadkhoda to know what that was. Because Mergan exemplified the working woman of Zaminej. She was perhaps the hardest-working woman of the village. She was like a sharp sword. She never rested. Once she began, she could do the work of two men. Strong and obstinate. And so the Kadkhoda estimated that Mergan would not back down. He turned to Salar and said, "Leave it. Just take these four pieces, and we'll later deal with the remainder."

Mergan rose and said, "There is no remainder, Kadkhoda. I can't go on having to look away when I happen to cross paths with someone who claims I'm in his debt! Either take these copper pieces and settle the business, or I'll stop you from trying to take even a cup from this house. Blood will have to flow!"

"That's enough from you. Don't shout yourself hoarse with all that."

"Enough is enough. Just don't leave me at the mercy of every nobody who's around. But I'll leave the rest to you."

The Kadkhoda looked at Salar Abdullah and said, "So, what do you say?"

Salar stooped and gathered the pieces and then shot a hurt and angry glance at Mergan, saying, "Oh, I'll have the rest. You'll see!"

Mergan grabbed Salar's hands and said, "There is no more. Do you understand? Either we are even, or you leave these behind."

The Kadkhoda separated Mergan from Salar's hands and said, "Get going, Salar. Get a move on, you! Soluch isn't dead. Who knows, he might return."

Salar cradled the copper work and exited by the door. Then Kadkhoda Norouz released Mergan, picked up his overcoat that had fallen to the floor, and left, following Salar Abdullah. Mergan sat on the ground.

From inside the doorway of the stable, Abbas was taking in the sight of Salar Abdullah and Kadkhoda Norouz leaving. After eavesdropping on what they were saying as they walked by the wall, he quietly slipped out the door. The possibility of Salar's return frightened him. So from the edge of the wall his eyes followed the two men as they left down the alley, before he quietly entered the room. He found Mergan in tears. Hajer was frightened and cowering in a corner silently. Abrau was still lost under the blankets, more or less still moaning as before.

Abbas kneeled by the stove and said, "Mama, where did you hide the copper?"

Mergan, whose frustration had been building up inside her, shouted, "In hell! What are you starting up for now? Let me die in peace!"

Abbas kept at the subject, saying, "I heard everything. You've hidden the copper somewhere."

Mergan was about to launch into an argument when she instead wiped her nose with the edge of her scarf and asked, "When did you get back that I didn't notice? So where's the bread? I thought you were taking your bundle of wood to the baker, weren't you?"

Abbas answered, "The bastard didn't take it. He doesn't want any more tonight. And what he needs tomorrow he'll only buy tomorrow. I nearly killed myself bringing the load back to the house!"

Mergan suddenly thought of something.

"Did their bread oven still have embers burning?"

"I don't know. They'd already shut the door of their house."

Mergan hurried, taking a tin container from beside the stove. Abbas grabbed his mother's wrist.

"You still didn't say where you hid the copper? What are you hiding? What were you thinking? That I'd be fooled? That copper belongs to me, too. It's not all just yours!"

Mergan pulled her hand from her son and said, "You'd better shut your mouth, you. So now you think you've become a grown-up for me! Let's wait till your piss froths, then I'll let you puff out your chest a bit!

However it was, and from wherever she could get it, Mergan needed to bring embers back to the house. For this reason, she couldn't wait around and argue with her son. She grabbed the edge of the tin and rushed out of the door like a wolf. Abbas, stung by his mother's treatment, felt he was weak, a nothing. Such a nothing that he wasn't even worth fighting with; exactly the sort of sentiment that no young man can bear. The fact that he didn't have facial hair yet was acceptable, as long as he was taken seriously, treated like a person, like a man. Mergan, in the state she was in, had no chance to perceive the nuance of this. So Abbas was left to bemoan his mother's insult. An insult, no matter how off-handed. He wished for the day that he could take a place above his mother. To be the master. But this was not all. Someday...? When? Where to find the patience to wait for that day? Now. He had to make up for his humiliation right now. If no one had been there, then that would have been different. But this had happened in front of his little sister. So, just as Hajer was staring at him, he glared back at her.

"What? What are you looking at? You've never seen a human?"

Hajer looked away.

Abbas said, "Very well! So if you don't want me to make you pay for it, tell me, where did you go with Mama today?"

Hajer replied quietly, "We went to get some sun."

"What else? After that?"

"After? After..."

"Stop hemming and hawing! Speak up. Where did you hide the copper?"

Hajer began to cry, half from fright and half on purpose.

"I swear...I don't know. I wasn't there, I swear! I swear on my father's grave!"

"Watch what you're saying, you! Has our father died for you to be swearing on his grave?"

Hajer began to sob, saying, "Mama said. She said today he was dead!"

"She's talking out the side of her mouth! Dead? Ha! Just wait till she comes back. I'll show her how dead our father is. She'll see!"

Hajer let out a cry. But Abbas wasn't so weakhearted as to let her off so easily.

"Fine. Let's forget about this. Let's imagine our father's dead. Tell me, where did you two hide the copper work?"

Hajer again evaded the question and set to stalling. Abbas began removing his belt and rose.

"So, are you going to talk, or do I need to make you?"

Hajer slid to the corner of the room. Abbas pursued her, stood before her, and cracked his belt against the floor.

"Get up! Start talking! Or do you want me to make you black-and-blue with this belt?"

Hajer shut her eyes and lifted her small hands to protect her face, still crying. Abbas bellowed, "I swear to Imam Abbas I'll make you sorry! Have some mercy on your own skin and bones and start speaking!"

Hajer just kept crying. She was crying from her heart. Not only from fear, but from everything. Everything she'd seen and heard weighed upon her heart, and since she had no other way of relieving herself, she could only cry and cry. And perhaps if Abbas hadn't also jumped on her, she would have still had plenty to cry about. But now that Abbas had set into her, her tears flowed from her heart. It was like a boil ready to be lanced, as if it were ready to burst. She had to cry, so as to loosen the knot around her heart. Even if she did not want to, she had to. These tears were ready to flow. These tears only made Abbas angrier, these tears and her locked lips. And the suspicion that Hajer was hiding something beneath her tears only made him angrier. He began to lose control. Perhaps he was looking for an excuse as well. He raised the belt above his head and brought it down. Hajer flickered like a lantern. Abbas showed no mercy. He brought it down again. And again.

The sound of the belt falling on Hajer's body brought Abrau around. He opened his eyes with difficulty and saw his sister backed into a corner while Abbas' merciless blows fell upon her. He leapt up, throwing aside the blanket. He did it unself-consciously. Still hot with fever. From behind, he was able to throw his hands around Abbas' throat and pull him back. They both fell over backward. Hajer ran. She escaped through the door shrieking. But she didn't go far. A moment later, she returned to watch her brothers grappling from the doorway. Like a mongoose and a snake. They twisted and struggled in the dust. Hajer didn't dare come closer. With one movement, Abbas was able to release himself from Abrau's grip and to position himself on his chest. Now he placed his hands around Abrau's throat.

"So, you little rat, should I suffocate you? You're too weak to even stand on your feet, so why are you throwing yourself into the arena? Now go get lost!"

Abbas rose from Abrau's chest, threw a blanket over him, and then turned toward Hajer. She ran and reached the alley. She screamed and ran toward the house of Ali Genav's mother. Abbas decided not to start a commotion in the night. He turned back and sat in the doorway.

Now it was Abrau who had disappeared. He wasn't to be found anywhere. Maybe he had slid away, ashamed of himself. That is what Abbas presumed. He wanted to find him to explain why he hadn't whipped Hajer unjustifiably.

He said, "Mother and daughter, they're working together. Just when our attention was elsewhere, they went and hid the copper somewhere. Do you see? Are you listening? They took four pieces of good copper work and have lost them somewhere. Somewhere only they know. Just themselves! The little one is working with Mama. She won't open her lips for a second. But you..."

Abrau didn't respond. He didn't have the heart. He didn't want to show his face. He hid himself under a blanket. But Abbas was worked up. He couldn't let go. He rose, stuck his head outside the door, and shouted, "Hey...if you don't want me to give you a beating, come back to the house yourself. Get up and come back. I won't do anything...Where the hell are you? Hey...I'm speaking to you. Come on, where are you?"

There was no reply from Hajer. Abbas left the house. He investigated the bread oven and the stables. Hajer was nowhere. He went to the alley. The alley was dark. She was like a cricket, lost in the night; she could be hidden in any corner. So Abbas decided to try to use sweet talk.

"Hey, you little devil! You think I don't know where you've hidden yourself? I can find you, but I'd rather you came out yourself. So come on! I was just kidding around with you, girl! Don't you know what a joke is? So come on out...Hajer... Hajer...Where are you? Eh? I'm with you, girl!"

Abbas began to worry again. Hajer was stoking his anger. Her sudden silence in the dark night struck his heart with a kind of fear. There was no clear reason for him to worry; nonetheless, for some reason his heart was filled with dread. Something unclear frightened him. Something like the image of Hajer falling into a ditch or a well. So Abbas began to zigzag the cold, hard soil of the alleyway, in bare feet, winding up and then loosening the belt that was still in his hand.

"Where are you, you foolish girl? You want to drive me mad tonight? Come out from whatever hellhole you've hidden in. Come out! Why are you all trying to torment me like this? Come out, you daughter of a beast! Hajer...Hajer!"

Hajer was nowhere to be found. It was as if she'd melted into the earth. Abbas, tired and angry, like an injured dog, returned to the room and sat by the stove. Abrau had still not emerged from beneath the blanket. Disconsolate and irritated, Abbas shouted, "Now you're pretending to be a dead mouse! Get up and let's see where the hell this girl's gone off to! Get up!"

Abrau didn't respond. He didn't want to reply to his brother. Abbas cut short his fury, wrapped a blanket around his shoulders, and left the house again, saying, "Damn you all. You can all go to hell. Go to hell!"

He went straight toward the bread oven and climbed onto the roof of the structure. He slid over to the edge of the wall and leaned against it. He propped his elbows on his knees and his chin in his hands, and he sat there. He felt like crying. But it was as if his penetrating eyes could only cry blood. So silent and despondent, with sorrow in his throat, he remained in his place with the blanket wrapped tightly around himself.

The dark night and its cold cut like a double-edged knife. He tucked his feet in and wrapped them with the blanket, wiping his nose with the palm of his hand. Pointless anger. Why was he so wound up? He felt something deeper than this commotion was bothering him. Something voiceless had softly pricked his heart. Like a thorn, slowly it cut in, opening a wound more and more as it went. It wasn't painful; it irritated. He knew it wasn't deadly, but it was wearing down on him. He could see very clearly that it had made him out of sorts. He'd become rabid, like a dog. His father always used to call him a flame, and said that if he was left in a forest, he'd set the place afire. His father had put all of his efforts into raising Abbas as a mud-plasterer for bread ovens, but Abbas refused to learn. He would always escape. He'd escape and get a beating when he came back at night. Abbas' grandfather was a reputable mud-plasterer who, in his later years, suffered from a bad back. He couldn't stand straight. When he walked, he had to keep himself steady by holding onto his knees. He walked in a way that made Abbas think he was just about hit the ground with his face. He wobbled like a broken wheel on a cart.

Abbas didn't want to follow in his father's steps. The crooked back of his grandfather—Samad the Plasterer, as he was called—was always in his mind. But he'd thrown himself more into the work of well digging. When Soluch would pick up his spade and pick and go to dig a well in someone's house, or if he went to open a blocked canal, Abbas would tag along. This work was more interesting to him. Soluch would position Abbas at the top of the well and would descend to the pit of the well himself. Abbas would send down the tools Soluch needed in a bucket. He'd also send down the tallow-burning lantern, the water jug, and bread when the time came. Abbas would lie on an incline of dirt around the well and watch the birds flying in the sky, waiting for Soluch to fill a bucket with dirt. He would sing songs to himself, or toss stones at the reeds. He could stare at the distant wastelands, or watch the road that traversed the surface of the highlands.

"Hooooy..."

This was Soluch's call rising up from the well. Abbas had to grab the rope and slowly raise the bucket of earth to the surface, empty it, and send it back down to the bottom.

"Hooooy...coming down!"

This was different from the work of replastering bread ovens. Mud-plastering required someone who was dedicated to the job. Someone with patience for hard work. From morning until dusk. It was detailed and careful work, needing full attention and patient dedication. All of which Soluch possessed. In the same way that Soluch was dedicated to this kind of work, Abbas was disheartened by it. During working, Soluch would never say a word. His eyes and hands worked as if he were weaving silk. Abbas, who couldn't sit still for a moment, didn't have the patience.

Abbas preferred well digging to plastering, and preferred working as an itinerant salesman to well digging. Traveling with his uncle, buying and selling goods, wandering from place to place. Molla Aman would buy four blocks of sugar, four boxes of tea, ten boxes of safety pins, ten boxes of sewing needles, two *mans* of hard candy, forty or fifty pieces of *gaz* candy, and a couple of packs of rice bangles from town, pack them onto the back of his donkey, and head out to the mountainside villages around Mount Kuhsurkh. Once or twice, Abbas went along for the trip on the coattails of his uncle. Afterward, Molla Aman had told his sister Mergan that Abbas wasn't trustworthy. But Abbas knew there was another reason—Molla Aman couldn't countenance sharing his life with the son of his sister. Abbas actually respected the fact that his uncle had blamed Abbas for this decision.

Molla Aman had told his sister, "I can't look away for a moment before your son pockets a couple of *seer* of hard candy and hides the take in his bag. And he's got a thing for deal making...and worse, he'd take a few hair clips or bangles and give them away to girls for free. All it would take is for one to smile at him, and he loses his wits. The goods aren't safe in his hands. He'd even try to steal the sand from the desert! It's as if I didn't sweat blood to get those goods in the first place. But my biggest fear was that one day he'd lay a hand on some girl and start a scandal, and a hundred men with sticks and clubs would descend on me in some distant hilltop village. Now that would be just perfect!"

Uncle Aman wasn't far from the truth. The girls in the hilltop villages weren't modest at all. They didn't even wear *chadors*. They were quick to laugh. They'd gather in groups and come to buy things. They'd gather around the display and beguile Abbas with their natural and pleasant laughter. Abbas would lose his bearings and the girls would pocket pins, hair clasps, and bangles, trading them for a flirtatious wink.

One time, Uncle Aman and Abbas had begun to argue, in the middle of nowhere. The uncle's blood began to boil, and he threw Abbas onto the parched cracked earth, and said, "I'm going to search you all over, even in your nostrils! You've wasted just the few coins I have. You're bankrupting me, you thief! What the hell am I supposed to do with you?"

Then he stripped Abbas bare. Naked. He looked in every fold of Abbas' clothes until, out of the hem of his pants, he managed to find a two-*toman* note. Still naked, with his clothes in his arms, he ran alongside his uncle, pleading, "I swear to God, on the blood of Imam Hussein, these two *tomans* are my own. I won it gambling!"

But his uncle didn't believe him. He simply set new rules for Abbas to obey.

"If you even think of doing this again, I'll tie up your hands and feet and toss you right here on the cracked earth so that vultures can have a go at your eyes!"

After that, Abbas kept his mouth shut and quietly followed behind Uncle Aman and his donkey. Later, while he was working on plastering a bread oven, Soluch, who had never gotten along well with Uncle Aman, said, "So are you satisfied now? Did you learn a trade from your uncle? If you've hit your head on a stone, come and take on the work of your ancestors and buy bread with an honest wage!"

Abbas had never gone back, and he didn't feel a moment's regret. Now that he thought about it, he realized that the girls in hilltop villages were beautiful and pleasant. "They were like milk-drunk lambs nudging for more!"

Mergan arrived, carrying with one hand the tin of embers, and with the other, holding Hajer's hand. Abbas could make out their outlines in the night. Hajer had just begun to cry again. Not loudly, her sobs were stifled. Her mother was pulling her behind her; Hajer was dragging her feet. Some sort of terror, a terror of her older brother, made her knees tremble. Although she had found her mother's protection, she was still uneasy. She dragged her feet and looked anxious. This only stoked Mergan's anger, and even before reaching the house, she was swearing a storm over Abbas and addressing him with whatever insult came to mind as she walked.

"So where is he, the son of a bastard? In what hell is he hiding? So he thinks he's a young lion, eh? I'll show him! As soon as the arena's empty, he attacks, does he...? So where is that brother of yours?"

Abrau emerged from under the blanket.

"I don't know. He's the one who attacked me and chewed my ear this morning."

This lit a fire beneath Mergan's feet. It compelled her to increase the volume of her swearing. Abbas was becoming a challenge in Mergan's closed life. She couldn't let him go any further in his impudence—she'd have to take care of him very soon. In this house, there was only room for one lord, either Mergan or Abbas. She had to make clear who held the reins in the household. She couldn't let her son become a threat, even a hollow one. The boy had become a lion for himself. Now he was threatening Mergan's children.

Mergan placed the tin next to the stove. She went to the pantry and returned with fire tongs. She went to the stables, searched the nooks and crannies, came out, and shouted, "Where have you hid yourself, lion heart? If you're such a man, why not show yourself to me?"

Abbas scrambled and climbed up to the yard wall around the house, but Mergan made out his dark outline as he did so. Mergan ran, but before she could reach him, Abbas was on the wall and shuffling away. Mergan went to the foot of the wall and said angrily, "You! If you so much as touch one of my children again, I'll ruin you! Take these words and hang them on your ears!"

Abbas didn't reply and leapt to the neighboring roof. Up there, the cold air had more of a bite, but just that he was out of Mergan's reach was enough for him. Mergan grabbed the blanket he had left by the bread oven and began walking back to the room.

"Tonight you can wander the streets and rooftops like a stray dog—that should teach you a lesson!"

Mergan entered the room and closed the door behind her, sliding the heavy lock into place. Hajer was still trembling. Mergan set the blanket on her daughter's lean shoulders and, using the tongs, stirred the embers in the tin beside the stove. Then she tossed the tongs to one side and busied herself with setting out the places for sleep. The beds needed to be set around the tin of embers, as they were every night. Mergan set a heater cover over the tin and placed a blanket over the contraption. She laid out Hajer in the place she had been sitting and covered her entire body, as much as was possible. Then she pulled on Abrau's feet and positioned him close to the heater as well. Then she blew out the lamp and lay down in her own place.

Beneath the arched ceiling of the room, the night was pitch black. Since during the winters they covered the opening in the roof, there were neither doors nor windows to allow the eye to pass through the darkness to catch a glimpse of the open and starry night.

Under the weight of the night, Mergan was trembling. Her feet, her hands, and her heart, all trembling. She could not calm herself. She ran her fingers through the smooth hair of her daughter and cooed, "Did he hit you hard?"

Hajer answered, "I didn't say. I didn't tell him anything!"

Mergan pressed the girl's face to her chest and felt something like smoke escaping from her heart and passing through her entire body, eventually escaping through her eyes and throat. Her lips and eyelids began to shake, but Mergan held back the clamorous wave. She didn't want to worry her daughter by sobbing. She herself hated mourning ceremonies. So she let Hajer go and she rose, took a handful of wheat grain from the pantry, and put half of it into her daughter's hand.

"Tomorrow we'll get flour. We'll light the bread oven."

She was left to calm herself. But peace of mind escaped from her. Her heart beat. Her thoughts went in a thousand directions. More than anything, Abbas was the object of her irritation. It was cold outside, the dry cold of the desert. A wolf could hardly survive in this climate. So what could that baby grasshopper do? There was no sign from him! Mergan was waiting for Abbas to let out a cry. To scream. To swear and throw himself against the door. But Abbas had not done this. What would he do? Why was there no sign of him? Mergan wanted to get up and go out, grab his wrist, and bring him home. But something unclear prevented her from doing this. Perhaps because she didn't want to go against herself? She didn't want what she had said to be worthless. She didn't want her threats to seem without substance. She was stuck. She had trapped herself. Pangs shot through her heart. She didn't want to torment her son, but she did. She couldn't bear the pain of this, but she did. This itself was the worst. That she was able to bear something that her heart did not want to bear. So she was hurting herself twice. Once, from her son's pain; second, from the pain of bearing this pain. She didn't know what she could do. If she called out and told him to come home, Abbas would never again pay mind to her instructions or threats, and would never take her seriously again. But this way, she would have to stay up worried about him until the dawn, grinding her teeth and feeling vinegar boil inside her. If she sent Hajer out to him, she knew he was clever enough to see that this would be a ruse arranged by their mother. Then the only outcome would be a fruitless mendacity. So Mergan was confused. Her heart was on fire, and she couldn't lie still. She kept moving her weight from shoulder to shoulder, and she chewed on the blanket and pillow.

How could she stand it?

Mergan rose and tiptoed to the door. She opened the latch quietly and waited a second. There was no sign of Abbas. No footsteps. No breathing. She wanted to shout the boy's name out, but she couldn't. She didn't want to be able to. The cry was tied up inside her throat. She returned to her place, lay down, and fixed her eyes more intently than before upon the door. At this moment, Mergan had no other wish other than for the door to open and for Abbas to return. To return. To return swearing at her. To return and to turn the house upside down. To return and to set fire to the house. To return and to beat his mother. To give a beating. Return; just that he return!

Hajer asked, "Mama, where did you get the embers?"

"From hell!"

4.

On the domed roofs of Zaminej, the dry cold wind shook Abbas. The wind flapped his trousers as he stood straight as a skewer, his hands thrust beneath his arms. His teeth chattered from the trembling that had taken over his body. Tears were beginning to stream from the corners of his eyes.

He sat with his back to the wind in the sheltering area between two roof domes and gathered his composure. He had to do something; even this somewhat sheltered spot did not afford enough protection from the wind for him to spend the night there. He had to find somewhere else, somewhere warm. But whose door could someone like him knock on? Who would open their house to Abbas, the son of Mergan? He had to think of someone like himself. Aunt Sanam's house! But no. There was nowhere to sleep there. And more important, the people who came and went from Aunt Sanam's house were all either inveterate gamblers or opium addicts. It was no place for a boy like Abbas, especially on a night like this. If he could hold out until morning, perhaps then he could go to Ali Genav's bath-house to warm up a bit. But Ali Genav didn't open the baths until the dawn prayers—even if he was a stray dog, he wouldn't last outside that long. He then thought about finding a stable and warming himself with the heat of a cow's breath, or by lying among some sheep. But in this season of the year, and in a year like this, it was possible that someone could accuse someone like Abbas of stealing livestock at the drop of a hat. Was it worth the risk? No—that would be foolish as well. He could only think of one place to go: Hajj Salem's old crypt of a house, behind Ali Genav's house, adjoining Kadkhoda Norouz's stables.

Abbas half stood and climbed across the roofs on all fours, like a black cat. He tried to crawl quietly as he went. God forbid that someone below hear him on the roof, as that would surely end with a commotion: "What are you doing on my roof at this hour of the night, you son of a bitch! Don't you have any respect?"

Someone could raise a commotion just because of where he was. So he had to go as quietly as a cat, and he did. He paused on the roof of Ali Genav's house and looked around. Hajj Salem's tallow-burning lamp was still lit. Abbas knew the old man was up late most nights. And it wasn't that late, in any case.

As Abbas watched, the door latch of Kadkhoda Norouz's sitting room sounded, and a moment later the Kadkhoda exited, walking down the steps with a lantern in one hand and a walking stick set over his shoulder. Abbas heard Moslemeh's voice complaining, "Where to, at this hour of the night? Again, you've put on your overcoat and hat and are going? Where to?"

The Kadkhoda answered right away, "I'm going to Mirza Hassan's house, the son-in-law of Agha Malak."

Speaking now to the yard rather than to Moslemeh, he went on. "My voice's hoarse from bargaining with that woman...and in the end..."

The sound of the heavy outer doors of the house clanging drowned out Kadkhoda Norouz's grumbling. Abbas turned his head from the Kadkhoda's house and looked to the hovel of Hajj Salem, Moslemeh's father. The dying emanation from Hajj Salem's lamp flickered through the cracks of the door. Abbas looked directly down; at the bottom of the wall he was standing on, ash and dirt was collected in a pile. Abbas leapt onto the ash pile, half rolled, and then rose. He shook the ashes from his clothes and crouched by the wall.

The sound of Hajj Salem berating his son rose from inside the house.

"Beast! Tie up those pants of yours! Showing yourself nude is bad in the eyes of God, you oaf! Tie up that pants string! We have work tonight. Didn't you hear the gate of your sister's husband's house? The Kadkhoda's left. I have a premonition that he's going to the house of one of his partners. Tie up those pants, you bastard! How many hundreds of lice are hiding in the lining of your pants anyway?"

The unhappy sound of Moslem rose. "D...d...d...!"

Abbas moved himself from the edge of the wall where he was to the shelter of the crypt and backed up against its wall. If the father and son were about to leave, how could he make himself their guest?

Hajj Salem's voice kept up. "Tie it! Tie it, animal! That's enough, enough! And tomorrow is God's day. Let's go. We'll head toward a reward. Tonight, the big men are all gathering, and you have to collect a week's worth of bread from them all. Eh, I said tie it, you beast!"

"Okay...Okay...Don't hit me, Papa. Okay!"

Hajj Salem emerged from the crypt hunched over and covered by his tattered quilt, holding his crooked walking stick. He looked to the sky and said, "Dear God, my hopes are with you. If you've made me destitute, then bless others with your blessings! If you've tied my hands, then grant joy to the hearts of others...Come on out, you beast of God!"

Moslem exited, still holding the tie-string of his pants in one hand, saying, "It won't, Papa! It won't...I can't, Papa!"

Hajj Salem, with a curse on his lips, knelt at the large bare feet of his son. He took the string from Moslem's hands, and while he tied the pants, began to swear. "God give me compensation for how you torment me! May his hands be crippled, my little animal. He's spent thirty springs on the earth like an ass, and still can't tie his pants up...I swear to God! Get moving! Come on, let's go!"

Moslem set out behind his father and bellowed, "Very...Papa! Papa! Very..."

Hajj Salem turned. "God damn your 'Papa'! Very what?"

Moslem said, "Very...very...tight. Very tight...knot... knot..."

Hajj Salem set out again, saying, "Come on! It'll let itself out slowly. Haircloth string doesn't hold a knot well. Come on!"

"Yes! Okay, I'm coming. I'm coming!"

Father and son left the ruins, and Abbas, who was still stuck against the wall, had no choice but to follow them. It could have been possible for him to sneak into the old crypt and to warm himself in a nook or corner inside. But he was somehow drawn to follow them instead. In Abbas' estimation, Hajj Salem must have smelled a treat of some kind if he had dragged Moslem out tonight.

Hajj Salem and Moslem spent their days in their destitute crypt, under the collapsed roof of a half-destroyed stable just behind Kadkhoda Norouz—and Moslemeh's—house. They eked out a daily pittance from this and that person, with the kind of work that was preoccupying Hajj Salem right now.

No one had seen it, but it was rumored that Hajj Salem possessed a huge quantity of old books. Until quite recently, he would take a volume of the *Shahnameh* epic written in a large script, sit at the edge of the mosque, lean his old walking stick against the wall, and begin to read out for the villagers of Zaminej. But lately, his failing eyes were no longer of use for trying to read the *Shahnameh* or any other book. Because of this, his books were most likely gathering dust in the back of his hovel.

"Take my walking stick!"

"I'm taking it, Papa! Give me...give me..."

"Okay! Now help me from the edge of this wall. This night's so dark. God forbid I fall into a pit!"

"Yes, Papa. Okay!"

"Tonight, the night's like a ghost that has washed its face with tar!"

"Yes, Papa, dear. Okay! I'll take you. Where should I go?"

"Zabihollah's house. The new lords of the village should be gathered there!"

"Yes, Papa, dear. Zabihollah Khan's house. Zabihollah Khan's house."

Moslem was always with his father. Hajj Salem was also stuck to his fool of a son like a worn-out shirt. Each morning, when Hajj Salem would put on his worn, long robes, take his twisted old walking stick, and leave their crypt of a home, Moslem was like his shadow. The father and son would set out in Zaminej's alleys, chewing on a bit of bread—if there was one to be had—all the while bantering and bickering. Everyone's ears were drawn to this banter, because it was part of the fabric of the lives of all who heard it. And in the end, the bickering was always resolved peacefully.

When two people have no choice but to live with one another, a special kind of conflict binds them to one another. And after this, under no circumstances can they live without this conflict, whether they acknowledge it or not. It's as if a thread has been tied around their hands, their shoulders, their legs, and their necks, and each end of the thread is in the other's hands. They become each other's binding. In this inevitable conflict, if they draw too near, they will both choke, and if they draw apart, fear will bring them back together. If they both don't let go of the thread together, the conflict inevitably continues.

For Hajj Salem and his son, even walking together was fraught with conflict. The thread that bound them together, wove them to each other, was the conflict itself. In eating, sleeping, walking, and falling, they were perpetually at odds. Moslem always wanted to be seen by others as walking shoulder to shoulder with his father, their shadows falling beside one another. But Hajj Salem never wanted this. Moslem would try to stick himself to his father's shoulder, and Hajj Salem would use his walking stick to deliver a blow to his son's legs, driving him away from his side. Moslem would grab his legs with his large hands and furrow his brows, pursing his lips. His father, speaking in a contrived voice—that voice that he chose to speak in all the time—would order his son, "Two steps back, you fool!"

Moslem, trying to protest for the thousandth time, would say, "D...d...d...!"

And for the thousandth time, he would take two steps back, falling into step behind his father.

"So now you've done your deed, you son of a whore! You finally delivered your blow! You delivered your poison, you beast! Ah...my back!"

Just shy of Zabihollah's house, Hajj Salem had slipped and fallen into a ditch beside the wall. His walking stick was in Moslem's hand, and the old man was flailing around at the bottom of the ditch. Moslem extended the stick toward his father and was saying, "Papa...Papa...take it! Grab the end. Grab the end of the stick. Grab it."

"I can't see, you fool! I can't see! Are you blind that you can't see that I can't see?"

"Take it! It's here. The stick...stick...here...here..."

"Ah...Oh...You son of a whore...Why are you mixing me up with that stick? Don't hit me! Don't hit me, my son!"

Moslem began laughing out loud. The old man was at the bottom of the ditch grabbing at nothing and turning around in circles, swearing at the top of his voice. Moslem would tap the top of his father's head with the stick, occasionally grazing his beard and neck with it, laughing as he did. Hajj Salem was at the end of his wits, and began pleading, "Don't torture me, my son! Don't torture me! God won't forgive your sins. Don't torture me. I pray to you. I'll breathe my last breath in this ditch. Don't torture me. You'll become an orphan, Moslem! Ah...now you've lost your father, Moslem. You're fatherless!"

Hajj Salem sat at the edge of the wall on the edge of the ditch and covered his face with his hands, breaking into loud sobs. Moslem also sat at the top of the ditch and began crying along with his father, hitting his head with his hands. As the walking stick had fallen into the middle of the ditch, Abbas conjured the courage to jump down, handed the stick to the old man, and helped him climb out and shake the dirt off his clothes.

Hajj Salem said, "God did not forget me. An angel! God sent me a Gabriel! Gabriel! Who are you, boy? Who are you at this hour of this dark night? Who are you? And that foolish son of a bitch, that torturing degenerate, where did he go?"

"He's there sir; he's over there."

"I can't see him! I've been stuck with the night blindness, oh no! I'm night blind! Aren't you the son of Mergan?"

"Yes, sir."

"I recognize you from your voice. From your voice. May you have a perfect life. God sent you to rescue me, I know it. You...you're...Gabriel. But that son of a whore, where is he? Moslem!"

Moslem came forward crying and pleading.

"Don't punish me, Papa. Don't punish me. I beg you on your life, don't punish me."

"I won't punish you. Stop it. I just don't want you to embarrass me where we're going. Just stop it!"

"Okay...Okay...I'll stop it. Yes."

Abbas took the end of the stick and handed it to Moslem, who then set off in the direction of Zabihollah's house.

The sound of a cow's cry rose from the stables of Zabihollah's house. Moslem stopped his father at the edge of the wall. Hajj Salem ordered his son, "Knock on the door!"

Moslem pounded the door with his fist, and a moment later Zahra, Zabihollah's sister, opened the door.

"My daughter, I've come to see Zabihollah Khan."

"He's not here!"

"Where is he, child?"

"At the house of Mirza Hassan, Agha Malak's son-in-law."

Hajj Salem spoke to Moslem, "So get going then! Didn't you hear?"

Moslem pulled on the stick to lead Hajj Salem to Mirza Hassan's house.

Abbas remained at the door of Zabihollah's house. Zahra was about to shut the door when Abbas ran up to her.

"I heard your cow crying!"

"She's birthing."

"Do you want me to watch over her?"

"No! She'll do fine herself."

"Do you want me to go and call Zabihollah?"

The door shut and Abbas was left alone in the alley. He had no choice but to head to Mirza Hassan's house. So he went.

They hadn't let Moslem and Hajj Salem into the house. The father and son were sitting quietly by the wall. Abbas sat beside Hajj Salem. The yard was quiet and two beams of light shining from the kitchen and the sitting room struggled to break through the dark. It was clear that the wife and mother of Mirza

Hassan were busy in the kitchen. And Abbas could see that Hajj Salem was grasping Moslem's hand as he breathed in the air, smelling something.

The men—whose voices could be heard—were sitting around a hearth in the middle of the sitting room and discussing something. Abbas could easily tell who was speaking from their voices.

"I know, I know. It's clearer than day to me that the woman's gone and hid the copper. Wherever it is, she's really hid them. I know this witch's tricks already!"

"You should be hunting lions, Salar Abdullah! Why drive yourself mad for these bits of copper?"

"She's showing me up, Mirza! It's hard to take. It hurts less to have a loss of thousand *tomans* in a business deal than to misplace a single *toman* yourself. If only I had grabbed Soluch's collar right then on that day and hadn't shown him mercy...Ah! I'll be sure never to do another favor for ants like these people."

Kadkhoda Norouz spoke up. "Let's move on, Salar! We need to go the heart of the matter we're gathered here for. Right to the heart of it. Karbalai, please, tell us what's on your mind."

Karbalai Doshanbeh didn't respond. In his place, it was Mirza Hassan, who was heard saying, "Don't you know how Karbalai works by now, Kadkhoda? He takes a word, chews it in his mouth a hundred times before he spits it out. And by then he's swallowed half of it, after all!"

Salar Abdullah said, "My father has no interest for this kind of thing." He then continued, "I'm saying this in front of you all. He doesn't approve of this."

Mirza Hassan said, "Are you saying he doesn't want to contribute his money into this plan, even though he's not doing anything with it?"

Salar Abdullah replied, "That's right. It's not clear to him what the end of this is. Right from the beginning, after he sold those camels, he didn't buy a bit of land or any water. We all know this, don't we?"

Mirza Hassan asked, "How about you, Salar?"

In the silence that followed, Abbas crept to the edge of the sitting room's door. Salar Abdullah finally replied, "Me? I'm just a farmer. And that's all I do."

"So how much can you put into the pot?"

"I'll sell off forty of my sheep. Whatever I get from that, I'll put into this."

"How about you, Zabihollah?"

Zabihollah chewed on his lips and said, "I'll see what I have around. Maybe I can put in something like twenty. Twenty thousand *toman*. Honestly, I had set aside half of it for my wedding and had planned to use the other half for a few deals, but I'll use it for whatever's best. So I'm in."

Now Abbas could see half of Mirza Hassan's pockmarked face and part of his slim black mustache in the light shining from a wax lamp. Mirza Hassan ashed the tip of his cigarette onto a tray by the hearth and said, "Kadkhoda...I'd guess...we can count on you for forty or so?"

Kadkhoda Norouz sipped at his cup of tea, placed a hard candy in his mouth, and said, "Maybe not that much. But...I have some ideas."

"It's just that at some point we have to determine how much each of us can offer. Because we need the money to go forward and get the loan from the Ministry of Agriculture."

Before addressing Mirza Hassan's comment, Kadkhoda Norouz asked, "Have you thought of the land yet? They have to send surveyors to look over the land. They have to determine if the soil is appropriate and if it will be suitable for pistachio farming or not. In this area, pistachios are an absolutely new crop. The government's not just going to throw its money away, you know?"

Mirza Hassan paused a second, then said, "It's just as you say. The surveyors will have to see if the land is right for this. The reason we're here is that in actuality our plots are all next to each other. And so our land may have a problem."

"Yes, I know. The problem is that we all still want to plant our usual crops and to harvest them from our own plots. We don't want to give up on planting wheat, barley, cotton, cumin, honeydew, and watermelon and use our precious land for pistachio planting, only to slap ourselves in the face in seven years and find ourselves sitting at the roots of some unripe pistachio saplings! Beyond this, pistachio plants need soft soil. You can't farm pistachios in dry, hard land!"

Mirza Hassan replied, "This is my view as well, Kadkhoda. That's why now I'm thinking about using God's Land"

"God's Land?"

Karbalai Doshanbeh smiled at Mirza Hassan as he spoke.

Mirza Hassan said, "You're laughing, Karbalai? Yes, God's Land. At the edge of our land and Zabihollah's. And one side of your son's lands extends up to it. We can easily stretch out into God's Land."

Karbalai Doshanbeh said, "God's Land is all that the poor people have to work with."

Mirza Hassan replied, "People work on it, but they don't own it!"

"So who owns it?"

"God does! That's why His name is on it!"

"Fine. And now some simple souls are working on it and they raise a few watermelons from it."

"What's a few watermelons worth to them? We'll pay them for the land!"

"What if they don't take the money?"

"We'll take it and register it. The more documentation we have, the more money we'll be able to get from the government for it. I've even laid the groundwork to do this."

"You don't say!"

"And why not, Karbalai? It seems you only have bad to say about all of this; you're jinxing us!"

"We'll see!"

Karbalai Doshanbeh rose from the hearth and went to put his shoes on.

Mirza Hassan said sarcastically, "Oh, now are you upset with us, Karbalai Doshanbeh?"

Karbalai, busy tying up his shoes, said, "No, no...Goodbye...Goodbye..."

Karbalai Doshanbeh was about to leave the room when Mirza Hassan delayed him by saying, "Karbalai, come on, and for once put your unused money to some good, why don't you!"

Karbalai Doshanbeh stepped outside the room and then said, "I didn't get this money from water, so why should I try to irrigate God's Land with it?"

Abbas hid himself in the shadows. Karbalai Doshanbeh came down from the porch steps and Hajj Salem rose before him. Looking at the father and son, Karbalai Doshanbeh said, "What's going on here? A funeral?"

He didn't wait for an answer, and set off. Moslem began following him, but Hajj Salem pulled him back. "Take it easy, fool! Don't you recognize him? He'd take the life from the angel of death himself!"

Abbas crept to the edge of the door. Mirza Hassan was lighting a new cigarette. Karbalai Doshanbeh had humiliated him. He had to recover by saying something.

"He's a coward!"

Zabihollah said, "From the start, I didn't have high hopes for my uncle. If he doesn't have his money near himself, he can't even sleep at night. He's a person who for twenty years has eyed the alms hungry beggars collect, just to figure out how he can get a cut of it. How could we imagine that he'd come here and put his precious money into something like this?"

Salar Abdullah said, "Any older person, my cousin, and not just him, eventually loses his nerve and ambition. It's not just about him."

Kadkhoda Norouz said, "Good. So let's go the heart of the matter. Mirza Hassan Khan, you think you can register God's Land somehow? You say you've already started the process?"

Mirza Hassan replied, "Don't worry, I'll register it!"

"In your own name?"

"No. In all our names. I've already made the request. In Zaminej, we only need a water pump and a tractor. That's all! Once we're all in agreement, I'll set out for Gorgan City. There, I can find a used tractor in good shape. I know people there."

Salar Abdullah said, "So Mirza Khan, how much will you be able to put in yourself?"

Mirza Hassan replied, "My mother, Bibi, and I can put in fifty. If necessary, more."

His mother's voice sounded from the kitchen. "Mirza Khan, dinner's ready."

He rose and said, "Bibi, bring the embers from the kitchen and put them on the hearth here."

Zabihollah and Salar Abdullah rose and made to put on their shoes.

"What about dinner? Aren't you staying?"

Zabihollah said, "I need to leave. My cow is about to give birth. I think she's overdue."

"What about you, Salar?"

"I'm going to go to work on convincing Karbalai Doshanbeh. After all, what's he doing sleeping on all that money and not using it?"

Mirza Hassan said, "Don't push him too hard. He's already said no. Anyone who's going to be a partner on this needs to be committed."

"Let's see what happens."

Salar and Zabihollah left the house, and Abbas drew himself back. Kadkhoda Norouz shouted after them, joking, "Don't let the old man go and convince you instead, Salar!"

"Don't be worried, Kadkhoda!"

Hajj Salem and Moslem rose before the men. Hajj Salem invoked a prayer. "May God bring good to you. May God will you good and happiness."

Mirza Hassan came out to accompany Zabihollah and Salar to the outer gate. Moslem pulled away from his father's grip to follow the men. But Hajj Salem grabbed him and growled, "Beast! Can't you smell the rice? We're due for a portion!"

At the gate, Mirza Hassan looked into the alley and said, "See you on Friday night, when we'll all discuss how things stand."

Zabihollah said, "My money's ready."

"I'll go and see what I can get for my sheep."

Mirza Hassan said, "In any case, Friday night, we'll meet here again!"

"Friday night."

Mirza Hassan returned and climbed the steps of the porch. His mother, Bibi, brought out some bread and a bowl of rice for Hajj Salem and his son, saying, "Take this outside and go eat it. Go on then! I want to shut the door."

"Yes...Yes, Bibi."

Bibi returned to the kitchen and Abbas crept to the gate and slid out.

Zabihollah and Salar Abdullah were still in the alley. Zabihollah was saying, "This Mirza Khan really talks up a game, doesn't he? He makes it seem he has one hand in this world and another in the other, what with his fancy hair! But we need to watch out that there's not something going on under the table!"

"Well, but we're not negotiating the deal with him. We're negotiating with the government. We'll use our land titles as a collateral to borrow money and pay it off month to month. Over here, we need to deal with a few poor farmers who use God's Land. We'll toss a few scraps to them to satisfy them."

"All I'm saying is that I hope he won't take our few coins and waste it on his scheme!"

Zahra, Zabihollah's sister, came running from the end of the alley, a lantern in one hand. With a trembling voice she angrily said, "Where the hell have you been? The cow's about to die...and you...you..."

"What? It's dying?"

"The calf won't birth. The poor animal's on her last legs!"

"What do you mean it won't birth?"

"It's a breech birth. It's stuck!"

"What?"

"Feet first, it's stuck!"

Zabihollah took the lantern from his sister and set out running. Zahra followed him. Abbas stepped out beside Salar Abdullah and said, "I had come to give him the same news, Salar!"

Salar turned and looked at Abbas.

"You have some nerve to even speak to me, you! God damn the devil's black heart, and curse you!"

Abbas didn't back away—instead, following Salar, he went along to Zabihollah's stable. Entering the stable, the air was warm. The cow was sprawled on one side, its eyes fixed and staring into space. Zabihollah said to Salar, "What should we do, cousin?"

Salar Abdullah removed his overcoat, rolled up his sleeves, and said, "Nothing. We have to pull it out. Girl, go and prepare a pot of hot water! And you, bring the lantern over here!"

Abbas followed Zahra out of the stable, and the cow's cries began to slowly intensify.

By the time they had prepared the hot water, Salar Abdullah had extricated the stillborn calf and tossed it to one side. They brought the warm water and Salar busied himself with washing his hands. Zabihollah was kneeling over the dead calf's body, clasping his forehead in his hands. Zahra leaned on the wall. Abbas drew himself to the corner of the stable, hiding in the dark. The cow was still on the ground, panting.

Salar Abdullah rose, grabbed the stillborn calf's legs, and dragged it out of the stable to the alley. The sound of a pack of stray dogs could be heard. Salar Abdullah returned and grabbed his cousin under the arms, lifting him.

"Up! Thank God the cow's still okay!"

Zabihollah rose and said, "This is a bad omen, cousin. It bodes badly for what we're getting into."

Salar said, "Don't speak ill, man! These things happen all the time. Now let's go."

"No. No! I have to stay with the cow. I'll stay out here tonight."

Abbas stepped forward. "If you'd like, I'll stay here as well. Right here, in the manger."

"No need. I'll stay here myself."

Zabihollah sat at the edge of the manger, and Salar Abdullah sat beside him. Zahra left to get a blanket for her brother. There was no need for Abbas here. He walked slowly and left the stable.

The alley was still dark and cold. Hajj Salem and Moslem were struggling in the middle of the alleyway. Moslem was pulling his father with the walking stick, while Hajj Salem from time to time would say, "Beast! Beast!"

And Moslem would reply from time to time, "D...d...d...!"

Abbas set out following Hajj Salem and Moslem.

BOOK 2

1.

The winter was passing. A slow and static winter. Like a mule stuck in mud, it toiled and pushed on. But it had become back-breaking. Cold! Cold was all there was. A dry, forsaken cold. And then the snow! That night, it snowed. A heavy snow. It was, as they say, one waist of snow. But if it wasn't actually waist-high, it was more than knee-deep. The baked-mud domes and cupolas on the roofs of the village were smothered beneath the weight. Silent. Exhausted. Like camels weighed down with their loads. It still was snowing. But not heavily. At dawn's break, the blow softened, and it fell more lightly. By then, it was as light as pigeon feathers. It spiraled and settled. For Mergan, the snow only brought affliction. But for the fields, and for most people in Zaminej, for those who had at least a bit of land and a cow at the trough, the snow was as precious as gold. A few flakes of snow were equal to a thousand grains of wheat. Or a watermelon. Or a handful of cumin seeds. Or forty cotton pods. Not only for the folk of Zaminej, but also for all the people of the plains, snow meant bread. It was bread that was snowing, and how pleasingly did it snow. It made the sharp coldness bearable, and the dwindling winter provisions seemed less worrying. These worries became ephemeral. Dreams of spring and verdure lifted the spirits. Mergan knew this, as she had endured such times before. When tables are full, there would always be a little extra for her and her children to eat, but when they are empty, what but dust may come to fill them? The precarious nature of life had taught her this much. Thus, even if Mergan was hungry—which she was—she wasn't hopeless.

Mergan was no longer a young woman. In her time, she had seen everything. She was nearly forty years old, although her drawn face was stony, cracked, and tired, and this made her seem older than her age. But her dusky hair had only recently begun to show hints of white in a few places. It was as if the serrated edge of her hair had carved wrinkles on the hard and taut skin of her forehead. Fine crow's-feet emanated from the edges of her eyes. Her cheeks were deep and hollow. As her face aged, her wide white teeth had begun to push aside her thin and jagged lips. On either side of her mouth and chin were two deep lines. The veins on her neck stood out, and at the base of her neck, just where she fastened the safety pin to hold together the corners of her headscarf, a deep recess had set in. Her jaws were prominent, and when she bit down, her teeth were visible beneath the skin. In essence, the flesh on Mergan's face had melted away, and it was as if nothing lay beneath the skin itself. Taut skin, drawn over rough, persistent bones, with visible inclines and peaks. Despite all this, her eyes were beautiful. Sorrowful and beautiful. Although deeply set, her gaze had a certain brilliance. And although her bones seemed poured into her skin, her stature was not broken. She stood straight and tall.

A pained soul resided inside this worn body. But it was not defeated. This injured soul masked a hidden fight, not a pained lament. This was why Mergan's eyes had retained their beauty. Hers was a stubborn radiance shining from an abyss of despair. Like a trembling light flickering from a lantern held in the depths of the night. Mergan was strong-boned. Not like her brother, who had a skull like a horse. But among the other women, she looked broader of shoulder, even if her bones were somewhat diminished. Destitution and constant hunger had not worn her down as they might have.

Mergan was looking outside. With the snow, the dawn seemed lighter than usual. A pleasant light, with a color that was rarely seen. It was a color that could not be seen just visually. One had to also see it with one's soul. How does the ailing person sense a panacea? The thirsty, water? This is how Mergan perceived the color of the snow. If you were to look at her face carefully, you would see the reflection of the dawn snow within it, and with it a transformation, a new perspective. You could sense that she imagined something was about to change. Imagine that the snow that had settled on the ground was instead a bed of colorful grass seedlings just sprouted from the dirt. Imagine the movement of those seeds beneath the earth that had imprisoned them for the cold, dry, and unhappy winter; imagine this earth was transforming; imagine the sun that will shine after the snow; imagine the plough share, the land just ploughed, the farmers; imagine the fields with their wide arms extended once again; imagine the braying of the cattle, the calls of the shepherds; imagine the smoke rising from people's bread ovens; imagine the people's furrowed brows vanquished by charging waves of laughter.

In imagining all this, Mergan had been renewed with new sensations. The kind of sensations that adolescent girls overflow with, the same ones that Mergan herself had while crossing the wasteland of puberty, drunken and confused, some twenty years ago. Those days when she felt she could wrap all the men in the world into a single embrace, when Mergan had spring fever. She felt it in her laughter, her jokes, her dancing and drumming, her idleness, her breadmaking, and her ginning, with her gleaning with the men at harvest. It was in her cotton spinning, and when she spent long winter nights spindling with the other girls, gatherings that culminated in waves of laughter and giggling. It was in the songs and poetry recitals; the whispers about what the men, the young men, were saying; in breasts heaving and hearts filled with joy; the flow of blood in the veins and the occasional taste of love; a love that was hidden, not yet emerging. It was in just being. In being at work, in the home, in bed, in the fields. Being in love. A tie in a stalk. In having children, in becoming pregnant. In breast-feeding. Singing a cradlesong. In swaddling the child. Washing the child in lukewarm water, under the mild midday sun. In the sensation of desire. He's ticklish! Laughter. Laughter. Water. Sun. Laughing. The pure laughter of the child. The flowering of the bud. A feeling in between laughter and crying. In loving everything. The man's firm shoulders. The sweet scent of underarm sweat. Soluch's shirt, a mix of sweat and dust. The boy playing in the water of the water pot. Kisses. Kisses on the head and feet of the boy, whose teeth have not come out yet, but who is ticklish. How he laughs, the little bud! He flowers. Ah...

The fields are brimming with wheat. The fields are golden, raining gold. The summer sunlight. The sounds of people calling. The gossip of the gleaners: girls, women, children. Bringing water jugs to the shelter of the haystacks, sleeping on the banks of the brook, a shade made from a saddle from the landowner's horse. Bread and tea and dates. Young men. The men. A silk handkerchief. The young men tie a silk handkerchief around their necks, with hair styled high with no hat. Sweat pours down under the handkerchief, passing the space between the shoulders to be caught on the tight belt, then spreads to each side. Wheat chaff the color of sugar, adhering to the sweat of a body, on a shirt. Shirts drenched with sweat. The mix of sweat and dust, and shirts in between. Sweat and dust, dust and sweat. The upper arms, the shoulders in motion. The forearm and hands in action. The scythes and sickles shine in the sun. The threshers gather handfuls to make bushels, and bushels to make stacks. The women and girls follow the threshers, gathering the stalks that have fallen aside while the wheat stalks grow into armfuls, and then bushels, and when they are placed onto a bushel bearer to be taken to where the stacks are gathered.

Mergan was among the threshers. She was sitting on the edge of the fields watching Soluch harvesting. Soluch had made a name for himself as a harvester. He was neither tall nor strong, nor particularly audacious, but he worked honestly and vigorously. Compact and capable, Soluch crouched on his heels and pivoted, clearing the land of the long and leaning stalks of wheat. An efficient harvester, Soluch enjoyed making an extra effort to clear a wider berth of wheat than was usual. The landowner of the field approved of this, even though he knew that Soluch was clearing the extra stalks for Mergan to gather. This was a kind of ritual. It was a secret agreement between the harvester, the landowner, and the woman gleaner. If a young man who was working as a harvester liked a woman, it was his right to employ his scythe in such a way as to leave more of the dry, soft stalks on the ground behind him. The pouch tied around the woman's waist had to be filled. As a sign of his love, Mergan had to return from the fields with her arms full of wheat. And so she did. So what of the gossip, the innuendoes? Let them say what they want! Mergan paid no mind. The talk only showed what was in their hearts. And so what if some hearts were not on Mergan's side?! There are always people who will use gossip to express their own frustrations. They don't realize that rather than seeming clever they seem two-faced. They lack the courage to be sincere. And what would be said at the end? That Mergan of the camel herder's family and Soluch of the mud-plasterer's desire one another? Let them gossip! What harm could come of it? What sin? Let everyone in the village climb on their roofs and sweeten their mouths by telling each other the news. Who could stop them from being engaged? No one. Mergan only had one brother. Her father was dead, and her mother was housebound. What would Aman say? He himself was under the spell of Gisou. Yes, Molla Aman! He was even more deeply ensnared by his own love. He was infatuated with her. He would walk aimlessly, composing vers-es of poetry for her. He had one foot in the stars. The fable of Molla Aman and Gisou gained renown with everyone. What's a brother like this say to Mergan? After all, Mergan was drunk with Soluch, with only him. What could Molla Aman, who was infatuated with Gisou, say about this? And even if he did?! If he resorted to threats and kicks and beatings? What could he do? Mergan couldn't be killed by kicking and whipping; only being apart from Soluch could kill her, being apart from the mud-plaster's son.

Where are you, Mergan?

She came to. The cold overwhelmed her. How far she had gone from the present! Where was she? Memories...remembrance. She turned. Her children were still asleep. The embers had burned to cold ashes in the hearth. The children had gathered themselves into a ball beneath the dozens of blankets that covered them. Mergan went and took a handful of corkwood to the stove and lit a flame beneath the kettle. Hajer turned her head. She had to get up earlier than the boys. Abbas and Abrau would rise shortly after her. Eventually they all were awake.

"What a snow!"

Abbas ran to the door. Abrau followed, standing shoulder to shoulder with his brother, and both stared out at the snow that had gathered on the wall around their house, and farther away at what had accumulated on the roofs of Zaminej. They stood transfixed. From a distance, crows were approaching: caw, caw. The brothers wanted to stay home today. The thought made them euphoric. On a day like this, no one would leave Zaminej. An idea entered Abbas' mind suddenly—gambling! He could arrange a game today. The other children would be idle, gathering at the shop to buy sweets. Sweets with nuts. Then the older ones of them, those with money in their pockets, would quietly sneak to the storeroom to gamble. Recently, Agha Sadegh had brought a pack of playing cards from town. The older ones would play with the cards and the youngsters would play *bajal* pieces. Since the time he'd brought the playing cards, Agha Sadegh didn't like them to play with the *bajal* pieces in his storeroom. The racket it caused interfered with his business. And he didn't just let anyone into the storeroom.

"What are you doing here, my dear child? You're still too young!" he would say.

So now the younger children had nowhere to go. It had snowed, and it wasn't any good trying to play *bajal* games in some ruins. Someone had to come up with a dry, warm, and empty place. A stable. And what stable better than the empty one by Soluch's house? Abbas thought that maybe he could snare three or four of these two-bit players and arrange a game or two. And maybe even Ali Genav would join as well.

This thought drew Abbas toward the pantry. He found a tin box containing his *bajal* pieces under some bric-a-brac and returned to the door of the pantry gleaming. He poured the pieces from the box and gathered two sets of them, one set of three, and another of four. The set of three would be used for the game with three pieces, and the four would be used for the game they called wolf. He wrapped each set inside a handkerchief and hid them under the waistband of his trousers, and then went back into the room.

Abrau was standing before the stove. Mergan was pouring herbs in the kettle while Hajer busied herself with the task of folding up the blankets before coming to her mother's side. Abbas positioned himself beside Abrau and held his hands over the flames that were choking in a cloud of smoke. The burning wet wood poured smoke and brought tears to their eyes. Because of this, although mother and children had gathered around the stove to warm themselves, they were forced to bid a retreat with eyes tightly shut and noses sniffling. The house was filling with smoke. Abrau fell to his knees, placed his hands on the ground, and began blowing inside the stove. He blew with all his strength, but it wasn't enough to bring a flame to the wet kindling. Self-loathing and hunger filled him; he felt abject and wretched. He kept trying, but he was unable bring the flame to life. He felt broken. His mouth protruded so that his teeth looked bigger and his lips seemed larger than usual. His trumpet-shaped lips began to darken, and his eyes flickered inside their sockets. Eventually, he lost his breath and fell back. Now Abbas leaned before the stove and directed his breath powerfully toward the source of the smoke in the wet kindling. Now the smoke blew upward, and a tiny flicker of a flame licked at the wood inside the belly of the stove. Mergan told Hajer to bring the cups, and she gathered two clay goblets from the cupboard, placing them before her mother. Mergan then told the girl to bring the oleander seeds. Hajer knew where the oleander was and brought back a small bag. Mergan divided the seeds, apportioning each person two. Then she filled the cups with hot herbal tea from the kettle. Abbas took one cup for himself—the fact that Abbas would take the first sip or bite of each meal had become an accepted fact within the family, regardless of whether they each approved of this or not. He saw it as his right, since he always reached for the food or drink before the others.

Mergan rose and went to the pantry while Abbas and Abrau drank their concoctions. When Mergan returned, Abrau was still looking out the door at the snow.

"I wish we could eat sugar-ice today!"

Mergan brought out a snow shovel and Soluch's old dirt shovel and placed them by the door, saying, "If you're men, you'll go get sugar-ice for us. I'll get the bread. Here's a snow shovel, and here's a shovel. If you clear snow from four roofs, you can buy ten *seer* of molasses for us."

Abbas said, "Today we don't have to go to the fields, but instead we have to shovel snow?"

"I'm saying, go for yourselves. You don't have to go. Get some fresh air."

"For one day, we can take a break from gathering wood stalks and you want us to get fresh air?"

Abrau said, "What if I get sick again?"

"You won't get sick. You're not a little chickadee, now! You can take my chador and wrap it around your shoulders."

Abbas said, "What about shoes? You can't wade into waist-deep snow with tattered shoes! My feet will go black from the cold!"

"So your shoes are good enough for getting up to tomfoolery in the snow, but not for work? Anyway, I'll wrap your feet up myself, and by the time you get back, I'll have built up a nice, big fire. The house will be as warm as an oven. What else do you want?"

Abbas said, "Everyone clears their own roof—who would pay to have us shovel their roof for them?"

"Plenty of people! Like the widow of Agha Malek. Who does she have to clear her roof?"

"Her gardener! She has a gardener—Karbalai Habib."

"You expect Karbalai Habib to be able to shovel snow on a day like this? If you held his nose for a second he'd fall down dead, the poor thing!"

"So if I clear Agha Malek's house, where will Abrau work?"

"Bibi Abdel's roof. Abdel's not around. He's gone to town to buy a motorized miller. Abrau can clear that roof, and he'll make a little from that."

They could come up with no other excuses. Abbas said, "How about our own house? Are we just going to wait until there's so much snow it collapses?"

Mergan said, "I'm here. I'll clear our roof myself."

"With what shovel?"

"Don't worry about that! Go tend to your own work!"

That was that. Abbas rose and took the snow shovel. Not surprisingly, Abrau was left with the old dirt shovel. This was Abbas' way, to take the best implement for himself. Despite this, Abrau complained, "Who's ever seen someone clearing snow with a regular shovel?"

Abbas ignored him. He had already claimed the snow shovel and was now wrapping his feet in rags. Abrau looked up at Mergan, who said, "Any house with a roof should have a snow shovel you can use. Stop complaining; get up and get yourself wrapped up!"

Abrau was not lazy; he was tired. All of a sudden he was tired. His heart wasn't in the task. His eyes showed his worries about the work ahead; he was even frightened. The cold and the misery of hunger had watered down his enthusiasm, replacing it with disappointment. Uncertain, deep down, he didn't want to set foot outside the house in this snow! A kind of terror set in and fixed him to the floor of the house. Mergan tossed her night chador next to Abrau and said, "Take that and wrap it around you. Especially around your waist. And take some old rags and wrap up your feet. Don't nod off there like an opium addict! Let's go!"

Forlorn, Abrau shook off his paralysis and rose. He had no other choice. He folded his mother's night chador. Mergan told Hajer, "Take the other end and help him, girl! Why are you just standing there like a stalk of grass?"

Hajer went to help tie the chador around her brother's waist. Abbas pulled on his canvas shoes, wrapped a piece of cloth around his ears, and took the snow shovel before leaving. Abrau was left with his mother and sister to help him prepare for going out into the snowy alleys. Mergan wrapped the chador around Abrau's shoulders and his sides.

Abrau said, "The cloth satchel—cover my back with the satchel, Hajer!"

Hajer looked at her mother, who said, "Get it. Let's use the satchel to cover his back and shoulders. It's as if we were sending the warrior Ali Akbar to the arena!"

Abrau said, "What about my feet? You want me to go out in the snow with bare feet?"

"We'll wrap up your feet. And stop needling me with your complaints!"

Abrau pulled the satchel over his back and tied it across his chest. Now Mergan was tying the ends of Abrau's pant legs shut with a piece of rag. Then it was time for the feet themselves. Abrau sat at the edge of the wall, leaning against it with his legs outstretched. Mergan took one of his feet onto her knee and Hajer took the other, and both busied themselves with wrapping cloth and rags around them. They tied the last knot around the back of his feet, and then Mergan tossed his canvas shoes over to him. She said, "Okay, now get yourself up off the ground. It's not as if you're a pregnant woman."

Abrau put his shoes on while still seated. He still had doubts about this all. Because of this, his hands took their time putting on the shoes. Mergan decided not to bother herself with him any longer. She went to the stove and called Hajer to her and both busied themselves with drinking their tea. Finally, Abrau rose—he had used up all of his delaying excuses now—and he took the shovel and walked out the door.

The snowfall was slowing. The sky was shaking out the last of the precipitation. The snow fell more and more lightly. Mergan took the tin tray in her hands. She told Hajer to take the container for carrying embers and to clean out the ashes and to come to help her. They both went outside. The first task was to clear a footpath. They began working. The snow was heavy, but Mergan had seen snow like this many times before in her life. She would scoop up the snow with the tray, and then place the snow into the tin container for Hajer to take to the alley to pour in a ditch. Once the steps were clear, Mergan cleared the path to the roof and then climbed up onto it.

The snow had stopped. The sky was silent, overcast, and quiet. A heavy, solid cloud covered the entire sky. The roofs of Zaminej, whether domed or flat, were all white, covered with snow. The crows cut black lines with their wings against the flat white. Caw, caw. A few people were up on the roofs. A spot here, another there. The dark spots—they were the people, wearing dark clothes. They carried snow shovels in hands wearing gloves. Their feet were covered in pieces of canvas, and for undercoats they wore old sheets. Their heads were covered in hats or caps; their waists were tied with a cloth or a belt or an old rope. Here and there a woman was among them. Smoke rose from burning wet kindling and blew across the white snowy landscape. The braying of a child from the other side of the village could be heard—the silence, broken. Sounds cut across other sounds. From one rooftop to another. Loud voices lay on the bed of steam made from their breath. Ali Genav was on the bathhouse roof. "What a snow! What a blessing!" Happy were those who worked the fields. The moist air still lay heavy over everything, like a thick woven carpet. Feeling alive, blood flowing, hearts awoke. As if everyone had found a sack of gold coins beside their pillow when they woke up. Bodies shook off their torpor. People moved their bruised bodies joyfully across the pure bed of snow. The measured gestures of arms and shoulders moving. Snow shovels swinging as if choreographed. Waists bent. An ancient illustration of the labor of humanity. Hanging on the white cheeks of the rooftops, clumps of snow clung to pants and leggings. Breath emerged from mouths in handfuls, and clouds rose in the cold. The snow on the roofs slowly disappeared. The color of the roofs slowly emerged, like a body rising out of the snow, coming to view, beginning to breathe. A man wiped the sweat from his brow. A woman held a broomstick with both hands. Whatever escaped the shovel was instead swept away. Balls of snow flew from one rooftop to another. The children grew excited, and snow games began. Angels' wings, the open wings of angels. Jumping from one high point to another, in one leap. There were only a few trees in the village, one pine and a few oleaster trees. Black wings against the white background. The flight of the crows, their calls. As if they were made to fly in the snow. Why do they appear so soon after the snowfall? Where were they before, and where will they go to afterward? What drew them here? What were they seeking?

The crows' cawing tells Mergan that the coming night will be very cold.

Mergan's underarms are sweating, but her feet are freezing. The roof has been slowly cleared. She tells Hajer to light a fire and expends her last energy to clear the last of the snow off the roof. She asks Hajer to throw the broom up, but the girl is unable to. So she brings it up the steps and gives it to her mother, returning quickly to light the fire. Mergan sweeps the roof and looks around, worried. Worried for her sons. What if they're not working? She cranes her neck from time to time, hoping to catch a sight of them. Abbas! Finally she makes out his outline. But there's no sign of Abrau. She bends over to finish cleaning the roof. The cleared snow piles up against the wall. She pauses to consider if she should take it out to the alley. The roof was now clean.

Suddenly the cries of women rise from the far end of the alley. The roof of the house where Ali Genav's mother lives has collapsed. The women scream. They had just been speaking of her! Mother Genav had separated from her son and his wife at the beginning of the winter and had made a nest at the end of the alley in an old abandoned house. The roof apparently collapsed in the middle of the night, the night before. Now the alley is full of the neighbors, and more are coming. The roof hasn't completely collapsed. Some raw scraps of the ceiling are still hanging. People shout.

"Her son! Tell her son!"

"Where the hell is Ali Genav!?"

"He was clearing snow from the roof of the bathhouse!"

The women, one by one, began to curse Ali Genav's bride. It was she who put her foot down at the beginning of the winter that his mother should live apart from them. Mergan arrives on the scene. Everyone waits for Ali Genav to arrive and help bring his mother out from under the rubble. Mergan rushes to the ruins, climbs onto the remains of the house, and grabs onto the remaining section of the roof. Mother Genav's head had been at the edge of the wall, and for this reason she's covered only up to her ribcage. Mergan conjures the courage to go into the area where the roof has half-collapsed, standing under the open sky. Then she turns and goes back toward the crowd. Two or three of the younger spectators swagger up, along with the wife of Kalati. They scrape away the snow and begin removing the dirt and rubble. Half of Mother Genav's body has been battered and crushed, like ground meat. Her face is also bruised, the color of smoke. It's not clear if she's still alive. First, they have to remove her from the rubble; then, they wrap her in a blanket and bring her out. A handful of bystanders clear the snow from part of the alley. Mergan and Kalati's wife, along with a few others, bring Mother Genav to the edge of the alley. Ali Genav finally arrives running, his jacket and the scarf under his hat snapping in the wind, his wife Raghiyeh just behind him. Ali Genav tosses the snow shovel to one side and falls beside his mother. He doesn't cry; he screams. The men pull him aside and lift Mother Genav's body. Ali Genav puts a hand on his face and lets it slide down. His eyes fall on his wife who is crying by the wall. He grabs the shovel—it is in his hands. He falls upon his wife, insults pouring from his mouth. He accuses her of driving his mother from his house. Raghiyeh doesn't respond; instead, she tries to run. Ali Genav runs after her. Raghiyeh's legs give out, and she slips on the snow. She falls on the snow on all fours, slides on her belly. Ali Genav reaches her. The shovel handle! He swings at her with the shovel handle. Raghiyeh is unconscious. She is senseless after the first blow. She stops breathing. Blood rushes into Ali Genav's eyes. He has no awareness that the bag of skin and bones beneath him is breaking. He is deranged. The men rush to encircle him and grab the shovel from his hands, throwing it to one side.

"You fool! You'll kill her, the poor woman!"

The women lift Raghiyeh from where she's fallen in the snow. The snow is red with blood. The blood still pours from her head. Her shoulder and ankle are also broken. She can't even cry. Two women, Mergan and Kalati's wife, take the limp body to Ali Genav's house. Ali sits on the snow and watches his wife with red eyes. What has happened? It's as if he is only just realizing what has happened. He cries out all at once, hitting himself in the face and head, and breaks into sobs.

Ali Genav has broken down.

Abbas arrived on the scene; he had been busy gambling with Ali Genav. Often, Abbas and two or three others would start up a game at Ali's hearth. Ali Genav was one of those people who love gambling. He had brought a set of cards to Zaminej shortly after Agha Sadegh, the shopkeeper. Now, sitting at the edge of the bloody snow, he looked as if he'd lost a round. His dark and broad face, his bruised and thick lips, were yellowing and defeated. His eyes were red, the color of blood. When he saw Abbas, he screamed, "I'm ruined, Abbas!"

Abbas grabbed him under the arms and lifted him from where he had fallen in the snow. Hajer was standing beside the wall. Abbas tossed the shovel beside his sister and said, "Did you light the fire? Go get one ready, as my hands and feet are freezing!"

Hajer took the shovel over her shoulder, and Abbas helped Ali Genav along to Ali's home. Hajer had already set a fire in the hearth of the home, but the wet kindling still was difficult to light. So the house was again filled with smoke. She arrived first and leaned the shovel against the wall. She sat beside the hearth, leaned onto her hands, closed her eyes, and began blowing. Again, the wood would not catch and nothing but smoke came from the fireplace. Smoke. Smoke. But despite this, there was nothing she could do, she had to blow, because at least the smoke dried the wood a little. If just one spark caught, Hajer could take the tray and fan so much that the fire would spread to all the wood. But there was still not even a spark, so Hajer had to keep blowing. The smoke drew tears to Hajer's eyes, and it set her nose running. Her lungs filled with smoke, but she still kept blowing. She knew her brothers well enough; if the fire wasn't ready when they arrived, there was no knowing what might happen. But she understood why, as she could imagine what it would feel like to work for one or two hours in the snow with only tattered shoes and rags wrapped around their feet. Their feet would first sense the coldness, and then they'd begin to freeze. They'd become numb, and then throb with pain. And toes, like babies, can cry—her own toes were also crying right then. Fear—what was stronger in Hajer than anything else was her fear of everyone, and most of all, of her brothers. Not that her mother was less of a worry, far from it. If the fire wasn't ready, Mergan was unlikely to be more merciful. At the very least, she'd give her a few slaps. So Hajer blew and blew. Either until the fire would catch, or until she collapsed trying.

Abrau threw himself into the house. He was shaking; his teeth were chattering. He tossed his shovel to one side and then sat down. He took off his shoes and unwrapped his feet and brought himself over to the hearth, saying, "It's not lit yet?"

Hajer kept blowing. Abrau sank his feet into the kindling, but nothing worked. He took his feet out and knelt by his sister with his hands on the ground, blowing alongside her. Finally, in the center of the kindling, slowly a fire was catching. Brother and sister together blew at the spot that was catching. The fire was rising just as Mergan and Abbas arrived. Mergan came straight to the hearth and knelt beside the children. Abbas took his shoes off and joined them. The flames were spreading. There was nothing to say. Abbas knelt beside his mother and blew into the fire. Now all four were blowing without pause. The flame kept rising. The twigs and sticks had dried in the smoke and now were sacrificing themselves in the fire. The warmth of the flames began to spread, and mother and children began to sense it on their faces. The fire had caught, but still they continued blowing. The fire must catch well. A feeling of satisfaction spread; they had defeated the smoke. Once the fire was strong, they drew themselves back. They lifted their hands from the floor, wiped their noses and the edges of their eyes, and sat around the fire. Abrau had his feet up to the flames, so close that the edge of his trousers caught on fire. Mergan threw his legs to one side and smothered the flames. Abbas had a piece of wood in one hand and used it to stoke the fire whenever it weakened. Hajer set the kettle to the side of the hearth.

It was time to find out what Abbas and Abrau had brought home. Mergan wiped the tin tray with the edge of her shirt and set it before Abbas, who undid his belt. He opened his pockets—he had tightened his belt over the top of his pockets. He leaned over to his mother and said, "Empty them!"

Mergan thrust her long fingers into Abbas' pocket and brought out handfuls of wheat grain. It wasn't bad. There was about half a *man* all together. When his pockets were nearly empty, Abbas put his knees on the ground and rose calmly. He looked like a dignified mother cow standing over a milk bucket while being milked; his face was marked with a pleasure approaching arrogance. His face was measured. His eyes were lost in the flames of the fire. His lips were shut, covering his teeth. Abrau's head was lowered while he glanced at his brother. Hajer, out of Abbas' view, looked at her brother with an expression full of veneration. Mergan tried to conceal her happiness, but her quick hand gestures and racing heart made it difficult to hide. She scraped the depths of Abbas' pockets with extraordinary care, extracting from their folds the last grains of wheat. Then she pulled each pocket out and shook it over the tray before neatly reinserting it. She wanted to grab her son's arms out of happiness and clasp him, but held herself back. Instead, he gave him a little squeeze on his shoulder and said to Hajer, "Bring him a cup of tea."

Now it was Abrau's turn. He put his hand beneath his arm and took out a flat cut of bread, placing it on top of the wheat grains on the tray.

"This. . . is from Bibi Malek."

After that, he removed a few small coins from the pouch he wore around his neck and said, "And her son Mirza Hassan gave me these."

Abbas and Mergan both stretched their hands out to Abrau, who placed the coins in his mother's palm. Abbas' eyes sparked from the sight of the coins, then went dark. He brought his hand back and said, "I thought I was supposed to buy us molasses!"

Abrau said, "I'll buy it myself!"

"With your shaking hands? Can't you see your feet are as red as beet root from the cold?!"

Abbas didn't continue arguing. He rose and took a container from a cupboard shelf. He put his shoes on and stood over his mother. Mergan couldn't say no. She couldn't look at him— he stood so firmly it was as if the coins were already in his pocket. Mergan, who was in the process of wrapping the coins in a piece of cloth, forlornly handed them to Abbas, saying, "Just promise me on your life that you won't skim any of the money for yourself."

Abbas walked out the door. The jingle jangle of the coins gave him light feet. Abrau had observed his brother's exit and then looked at where he had been sitting, then said, "It's impossible he won't steal some of it! Abbas would even bite off his mother's nipple to get a bit more milk!"

Mergan didn't reply. What could she say? She poured a cup of tea for Abrau and went to bring some oleander seeds. Abrau took the cup of tea, and then looked at the snow that was still piled against the outside wall. He barked at Hajer, "Go clear up that snow from the wall!"

Abrau spit out his oleander seed into the fire and asked, "No news from him?"

Mergan looked at him and said, "No."

Abrau wanted to ask something about his father, but Mergan cut him off before he could speak.

"Drink up your tea!"

He gulped the rest of the cup of tea and sat silently. It was obvious that Mergan didn't want to speak of Soluch. She never would allow them to speak of him. Forget him! She made every effort to forget her husband. Soluch was gone, and Mergan had already wrestled with his absence and had vanquished it. Perhaps her feelings were different from those of her children. No matter what the context or what the reason, she was heartless on one matter: she refused to allow his name to be spoken. The children simply did not have the right to speak of their father before her. So Abrau bit his tongue and said no more.

Hajer brought some snow in a handkerchief, which her mother took from her. Mergan placed the snow in a pan and then returned to the hearth.

"Will Mother Genav die, Mama?"

Mergan answered her daughter's question, "Everyone dies, my dear."

Mergan remembered that she still had a bit of sheep's lard in her stores, so she rose and brought it. She scraped some lard off into the pan, which she placed on the fire. Then she took the tray of wheat grain to the pantry to put it away. By the time she was finished, Abbas had returned. Mergan took the cup of molasses from Abbas' hand and poured it into the pan and then asked Hajer to lay out the tablecloth. Hajer brought the cloth while Abbas sat down by the hearth.

"In Agha Sadegh's shop, everyone was talking about Mother Genav. They say she's going to die!"

Abrau asked, "Did the syrup cost you all the money you took?"

Abbas replied without looking at his brother. "How much money do you think there was?"

Abrau said, "May it be more dirty than dog's shit if you skimmed even a penny of my money!"

Abbas carelessly answered, "Fine!"

It was clear to Abrau that the syrup hadn't cost what Abbas took. He even could guess, or almost be certain, that Abbas had mixed the syrup with water. But he had no grounds on which to make his claim. And Agha Sadegh wasn't the type to talk; he saw himself as everyone's confidant. Since he himself traded in stolen goods, he kept everything a secret. Abrau knew that he'd not be able to get information from Agha Sadegh. Since he refused to speak about his business in general, it was inconceivable that he'd give himself any trouble about a matter concerning a few coins, and that for a child like Abrau. Abrau decided he would prove Abbas' theft. He began to pay close attention to everything he did. One thing was that Abbas seemed nervous; he couldn't hide his awkwardness. Another was that suddenly he was acting like a dead mouse, refusing to speak or answer Abrau. In addition, he was half hiding his face in his collar, as if he were protecting a secret. Once the food was laid out, Abbas quickly gulped down a few mouthfuls of food and grabbed a piece of bread. He then began putting his shoes on and left the house. It was as if he'd grown wings and flew away! There must be a reason for his wanting to leave so quickly; it was clear he was up to something.

Abrau said to himself, "I'll get him eventually!"

Abrau licked the bowl clean, slid to one side, and leaned against the wall.

"Put down the fire a bit and let's set up a Kurdish hearth!"

Hajer set up a covering over the fire and placed a heavy blanket over it. Abrau crawled to the edge of the blanket and then slid under it, pulling it up to his nose. If Abbas hadn't worried him as he had, he would have been able to spend the rest of the day in bliss beneath the heated blanket. But his mind was racing. He couldn't imagine that Abbas had just gone to Ali Genav's house for a game. No matter what he thought of Ali Genav, Abrau couldn't imagine that on such a day—with his wife beaten and broken, and his mother breathing her final breaths—he would sit down with the usual low-lifes to play cards. But Agha Sadegh wouldn't give Abbas the time of day in his games; he wouldn't even let him into the back storeroom. This was because Abbas didn't have the money to play and wasn't of the same level and standing as those who came to play in Agha Sadegh's storeroom. His players were respectable people. One was the accountant for Hajj Ali's affairs. Another was Murad Dashtban. Another was Agha Vaseghi, one of the respectable landowners of Zaminej. There were one or two others who had only recently joined this circle; Khodadad and Hamdullah, the latter of whom self-admittedly was involved in theft and rustling. So it was likely Abbas had gathered up a few people and was this moment in a stable or in the storeroom of some abandoned house busy with his *bajal* pieces! There was a reason for his sorting through his collection of game pieces in the morning; he'd been planning this all along. Who knows if he might not have sold half of the wheat grains he'd earned and was at Agha Sadegh's shop on the way home? Anything was possible with him.

"Mama, do you think the wheat Abbas brought was all of the grain he earned?"

Mergan, who was still licking her fingers, said, "You're such a pessimist, boy! Of course it was all he earned. You think that woman would be able to pay him more than that?"

Abrau didn't say anything further. Mergan said, "Lay down a bit and take a nap. The hearth is so nice and warm!"

Abrau stuttered, "I don't believe it! Even if Abbas were to say that yogurt's white, I wouldn't believe it!"

Mergan didn't reply. She made herself busy undoing the knots in Hajer's hair. Abrau slid farther beneath the blanket and stretched his feet. The warmth of the hearth banished the fatigue and cold, and despite Abrau's restlessness, his body slowly surrendered to pleasure. His eyelids grew heavy and sleep beckoned. For this moment, the world was nothing but a comforting crib.

Abrau's gentle snoring brought peace of mind to Mergan. She unconsciously stared at her son's face. His eyelids and eyelashes had closed, and his face was calm. The canker sore at the corner of his mouth had nearly healed. His short hair was clinging to his forehead and framed his wide face. His expression was pure and calm like the surface of water. Mergan's heart wanted to go and sneak a kiss on her son's cheek. But something like an invisible barrier prohibited her. She was ashamed to show her affection for him; that was her nature. She simply couldn't be open with her kindness; she didn't know how. Perhaps, as with showing your love to a beloved, it simply needed the right opportunity to occur. Sometimes, if Mergan felt affectionate, a hostile weight erected a barrier, blocking her from acting on it. So expressing her affection had become the most alien impulse to her. In its place, she acted with roughness and hostility. She used her claws and teeth and anger. This became a habit, her way of reacting harshly to everything. She had been dispossessed—one could say plundered—of the ability to express kindness. And so only in her most calm moments could Mergan feel it once again, with tenderness. Then, it was as if a calm sea had handed her a pearl—the pearl of kindness.

Mergan was now at ease; her face was calm. Along with her daughter, she slid under the blanket, leaning on one elbow and playing with Hajer's hair with her free hand. Hajer was lying relaxed and satisfied next to her mother, as if nothing bad had ever happened and would never happen. Her mother was beside her—what could ever disturb her? Mergan sang a lullaby in her ear, with a gentle voice. Soft and gentle, pleasant to both the ear and the heart.

"The times change. We have both day and night. There's both lightness and dark. Heights and depths, times of plenty and need. Winter's nearly over; it's ending. Spring will soon arrive. And the air will be warmer. People will be generous, and we will work. Scarcity will be gone. We'll set out to the fields and prairies. God's fields will be all green. Milk and yogurt will be plentiful. Even if we don't have any sheep. Others may have more, or less. We'll have a bit of buttermilk to wet our bread. Your brothers will grow up. Day by day, growing, working. You'll grow older, taller. Become beautiful, become a woman. Your breasts and body will fill in. You'll become your own girl, when you breathe the air of spring. What don't you have that other girls have? You'll be good for the rest of your life. Thank God you're healthy and strong. You're not deaf or dumb or blind. If you find yourself just skin and bones, it'll only be because of winter. But in the winter everyone suffers, and in the spring a bit of water flows beneath your skin. But there's no hurry. There's two years till you're fourteen. In this time, I'll feed you the bread from my own mouth. I won't let hunger whiten your eyes. I won't let you be hurt. I'll endure hard times, but will raise you day to day. I won't let you go hungry. I'll protect you, raise you. And eventually someone will come to ask for your hand, and take you to his house, and spend his days with you. Not today, tomorrow. And let them dream of the day. My daughter's like a bouquet of flowers. Her father's traveling for work, like so many others do. A man is built to travel, all men do. All men suffer danger."

Mergan was lying, and she was well aware of her lies. But why? How was it that she began telling these lies about Soluch? She didn't know. Why had she been lying and saying there was word from their father? Perhaps she wanted her children to sense that he was supporting them, no matter how near or far he was. Because of this, she would think of new lies to weave before the children, and these lies spread to the ears of others all around.

"He's sent me money. From Tehran!"

"I've heard he's bought a cart, knock on wood!"

"He wants to come and take us as well. But who wants to go? He's deluded himself to think I'll be running after him—ha!"

After these lies, she would make a meatless stew, sprinkle some dry bran onto it, and let the smoke from the fire billow out into the alley.

"You know, my dear, why should I let my children go hungry? Now that their father's sent money to me, I'm going to buy two *seer* of meat and store it for them. After all, a believer is supposed to eat meat at least every forty days or he'll be considered an unbeliever! No, thank God I am generous with my children."

But of everyone, at least Shamsollah the butcher knew that Mergan hadn't bought meat from him for a very long time.

Let him know. This lie did no harm to him, or to anyone else. But at any price and in any case, Mergan didn't want her husband to be considered lost. At least for now... come what may.

Hajer had fallen asleep. The house was filled with the sounds of sleep. Only Mergan was still awake and was looking at the door. She was quiet, and in the gaps of her children's snoring, her silence seemed even more pronounced. She was looking outside. In the yard, snow had been piled up next to the short wall around the house. It seemed the weather was growing lighter. It seemed the clouds were lifting. The sun might even shine, soon. The snow becomes beautiful in the sunshine. And so Mergan's expression also shone, staring at the snow, in anticipation of the sunshine. She wanted to go and find out how Mother Genav was doing. But she didn't know why she was slow to do so. She felt lazy. The hearth was warm, the house was calm, and her daydreams were enchanting her. But as soon as she thought of Mother Genav's health, and the path to Ali Genav's house, she felt uneasy. Something was nipping at her calm state. She couldn't hold out. She rose from under the blanket, put on her shoes, put her chador over her head, and was about to leave the house when Ali Genav's broad shoulders filled the doorway. Ali Genav was knitting winter wear, as he always did as he went about his business. Wool socks, hats, scarves. He stood silently by the door and glanced at Mergan.

"I was about to go to your house. How is your mother?"

Ali Genav moved his thick and dark lips slowly, speaking with a sonorous and deep voice.

"It doesn't look good. I don't think she'll make it. I want to send someone to Dah-Bidi to get a bonesetter."

"You want someone for Raghiyeh?"

"Yeah, for Raghiyeh. My mother's a lost cause. Raghiyeh, that foolish woman, finally ruined my life! She pestered me so much that I sent the poor old woman to live in that ruin, and in the end you see what's happened. And I just lost my mind this morning... I beat her and destroyed her. I think she's got three or four broken bones. Now they're saying I need to send some-one to find a bonesetter. Raghiyeh's mother's cousin was about to set out to go, but his mother stopped him. She says she does-n't want her son leaving the village on a day like this. She wants someone to go with him. I thought of sending one of your sons with him—I'll pay a good wage for it."

Mergan said, "Abbas isn't home, and Abrau is asleep. You know yourself..."

Ali Genav said, "They can go with my donkey. They'll ride it there both together, and on the way back, they can have the man from Dah-Bidi ride on it. I'll give them sticks and bats in case they run across some beast on the way."

Mergan half-heartedly turned and looked at Abrau.

"I don't know! Which one do you want to go?"

Ali Genav said, "Abbas is more experienced, but Abrau is more reliable. But whichever wants to go, it makes no difference to me. Whoever brings the man will get five *toman* from me. I need to watch the two women, otherwise I'd go myself. The weather's becoming sunny. Coming and going can't take more than three, four hours. If they set out now, they'll be back before the next prayer. And these days, five *toman* isn't a little bit of money, you know!"

Mergan didn't want to wake Abrau, but she couldn't ignore the five *toman* offer by Ali Genav. That money would feed her children with bread for several days. Where could a job like this be found these days? It was just luck. Something like this comes up once a year or so. So Mergan couldn't let Ali Genav pass this task on to someone else. But which one should go? Mergan's heart leaned toward Abbas. Abbas was stronger, bigger-boned. In addition to being smaller, Abrau had been affected by the vicissitudes of winter. Mergan was uncertain whether to allow Abrau to go out of the village on a day like this, in the middle of the snow. She was afraid he'd not be able to take care of himself. Abbas wasn't around, though. And if he were, she would expect him not to give the household all of his pay. So Mergan remained torn.

"You won't pay more than five *tomans*, Ali?"

It was Abrau, who had raised his bony head and chest from beneath the blanket. As he looked at him, Ali Genav stepped into the house.

"So you're awake?"

Abrau pulled himself out from beneath the blankets and said, "Your voice woke me. Do I have to go alone?"

"No! Gholi Jahromi will come with you, and I'll give you my donkey to ride on."

Abrau said, "If you lend me your boots and your leggings, and your winter cloak, I'll go."

Ali Genav said, "My boots are too big for you!"

"What do you care? I'll wrap my feet first."

"So get up and come to my house, then. I'll put a piece of bread for you in a bundle. Come to my house and have a tea before going."

Ali Genav then stepped out the door and left. Abrau rose and told his mother, "I'm going to keep five *qeran* from the pay."

Mergan said nothing. Abrau put on his shoes. Ali Genav's voice could be heard from behind the wall.

"But Abrau is already putting on shoes and getting ready to go."

Abbas responded, "What shoes? With those torn and ripped-up foot covers, you think he's going to make it far in the snow?"

Ali Genav said, "He's going to borrow my boots and leggings. I'll give him a cloak to pull over his head as well."

Abbas said, "In that case, I'd go myself!"

"I would have liked for you to go, but I already spoke to Abrau. If you go and make some arrangement with him, you can go in his place. What are you doing gathering all of these kids?"

Ali Genav was pointing to one of the Kadkhoda's sons, the only son of Salar Abdullah, and two others of the older boys of Zaminej, who were standing with Abbas.

"They can go home! They don't have to play! I'll go and bring back that doctor even if he's in the Black Hills! But how does that pip-squeak brother of mine think he's going to convince that old opium addict to leave his hearth in this snow to come all the way here?"

Abrau had by now come out to the alley and was standing by his mother. He said, "You'll see when I bring him here! Let's go, Ali, sir!"

Abrau set off, but Ali Genav remained behind. He had sensed a game in the offing. He looked at the kids and said, "Are you playing *bajal* or cards?"

Abbas looked at the boys and said, "Who here has cards? Would you lend us yours?"

Ali Genav turned to follow Abrau, saying, "Perhaps I'll bring them with me."

This was the final confirmation that he would send Abrau to go bring the bonesetter. If he were to send Abbas, the gambling circle would not be held, and that wasn't what Ali Genav wanted. Abbas led the other boys toward the house and shouted after Ali Genav, "So you're coming?"

Ali Genav said, "Ah...maybe!"

Abbas led the boys toward the house, but Mergan said, "No, not in the house. You can do what you want to in the stable."

To enter the stable meant they had to clear the snow in front of the door first. Abbas ran into the house, grabbed a shovel, and ran back to clear a path. Salar Abdullah's son, Jalil, and the Kadkhoda's son, Hamdullah, just stood there, shifting their weight from foot to foot and chewing on their lips. It was clear they were uneasy, uneasy because they didn't want to be seen there. But they didn't want their opponents, Abbas, Ghodrat, and Morad, to sense their anxiety. It would be humiliating if it were known how afraid they were of their fathers. Abbas had told them that no one was home, but so far they'd run into three people. Although they weren't strangers, it was very odd that they were there. On the other hand, Morad and Ghodrat had no worries. Ghodrat had learned how to play from his own father, Mohammad Gharib. He was a serious gambler himself and had no problems with his son also gambling; it was only if he lost that he would have to worry. If he came home empty-handed, Mohammad Gharib would pick up whatever was close to hand and run after him, chasing him even to the outskirts of the village. Eventually, with his sweat pouring from his head beneath his felt cap, onto his dry eyelashes and his thin beard, between his forced wheezing he would begin to lay out a set of curses that made Ghodrat responsible for all that was bad.

"...You reek of foot-sweat! Who told you to take my dear money and toss it down a well! So you had bad luck gambling? You tossed snake eyes? What good are you? When you set foot in the world, was it me who made your mother stop breathing? You've made me old before my time! My life is black because of you! You want to gamble but you keep playing the fool!"

On such occasions, which were not infrequent, it mattered little to Mohammad Gharib that his son Ghodrat was following behind him close enough to hear his curses, or that others might hear them as well. For him, in those moments, all that mattered was to say what he needed to say to lighten the weight on his heart, as if not saying them would lead to his heart exploding. Although this would lead to a shaking across his body that would only be quelled with his smoking three more seeds of opium than his usual ration. All this naturally meant that Ghodrat would rarely admit his gambling losses to his father.

Morad was a different case. He was his own boss. His mother and his older brother ran an opium den, and only Morad didn't help in running it. He was free to tell his mother and brother what he thought, without fear. His strength, his disposition were of a sort that led his older brother to conclude that it was not in his own interest to try to let things lead to fighting between them. Morad worked, and he paid for his own bread, thus he held his head high and—if he so chose—could gamble without having to answer to anyone for it.

"Give me that shovel! It's as if you've never eaten bread, you weakling!"

Morad grabbed the shovel from Abbas' hand and pointed at him, laughing.

"Look at him! Look, the sweat on his forehead would make you think he just dug up a mountain!"

Then he bent his body over the shovel and didn't straighten himself until all the snow was cleared and piled up in one spot by the wall. Then he took the shovel in one hand and pushed the door to the stable open with his shoulder. The stable was small, just big enough for ten or twelve sheep and a couple of lambs. Despite this, no one could remember Soluch ever owning any animals, save the one donkey of his that had died the previous year.

The boys ran into the stable. First among them, the sons of Salar Abdullah and the Kadkhoda, who sat on the edge of the trough in a dark corner. Morad, Ghodrat, and Abbas knelt and began to work at clearing a spot of the dirt and rubbish that carpeted the floor of the stable. The lighter dust rose in the air and floated in circles visible in a shaft of light that penetrated the space from a crack in the door. They stopped once a space was clear and an even surface was ready. Salar Abdullah's son shut the door and Abbas enthusiastically began taking out the *bajal* pieces from his pocket, tossing them into the playing surface.

"Come on! Gather around!"

Salar Abdullah's son, Jalil, sat back on the edge of the trough and was squinting with his left eye at the *bajal* pieces on the floor. He was hesitating and acting cautiously. But Hamdullah, who, with his big head and bulging eyes, bore a passing resemblance to his crazy Uncle Moslem, thought it would indicate weakness to act hesitantly before the others. So instead, he came forward more quickly than anyone else sitting at the edge of the prepared space and began tossing the *bajal* pieces casually into the air. The pieces would fall onto the soft soil of the stable, and Hamdullah made as if he was prepared to be the dealer of the game. He collected the pieces and said, "Okay?!"

Abbas looked at Jalil and said, "Get up and come here! Why are you dragging your feet?"

Jalil replied, "You play a round. I'll come."

Morad said, "Don't be a baby. Come over here! A man needs to be confident and sure of himself!"

Jalil said, "You guys play a round. Just start without me."

Hamdullah said, "I'll throw the pieces. Are we playing wolves?"

Ghodrat spoke as if from experience, "Or do you want to play a three-piece game?"

Abbas said, "It's up to you. You decide."

Morad said, "I don't mind. I'll play either."

Abbas looked at Hamdullah and said, "The three-piece game is pretty complicated. With two three-goats you're completely done for. The game can be over before it's even begun."

Jalil spoke up from beside the trough.

"Four-pieces. Let's play four. I won't play a three-piece game."

Morad said, with a laugh in his voice, "However we play, your hands will be shaking, o son-of-the-village-lord!"

Hamdullah looked back toward the trough and said, "You get up then! What are you dragging your feet for?"

Abbas collected the pieces from the dirt and said, "Let's play wolves then, okay? Here we go, one round of wolves. Everybody take a *bajal* piece and toss it. Whoever has the highest one will deal."

Each of the boys took a piece and flipped it in the air. Morad had the highest one, and Abbas collected the pieces and set them before him. Morad looked at Jalil and said, "If you want, you and I can do it over. You might get the higher one...eh? I don't want you complaining later! If you don't want us to do it over, then you have to sit and play a round and wait for the deal to go a full round."

Jalil said, "Now just deal, will you?"

Morad laid out the pieces before himself, lining them up in a row. He arranged them and then took the "wolf" piece in between his fingers, telling Abbas, "Ante in!"

Abbas changed his place with Hamdullah, saying, "I can't see a thing here. You sit with your back to the door. From here, I can only see outside."

Hamdullah jingled the coins that he was holding loosely between his two hands. He then separated his hands and made

them into fists, lowered his right fist into the circle, and said,
"I've anted in!"

The pieces fell into the circle. One had the wolf sign, and
three others fell blank side up. Morad again arranged the
pieces and said, "Ante in!"

"I've anted in!"

"Here, two signs showing. Now pay in."

Hamdullah tossed two two-*qeran* coins at Morad's feet.

"Ghodrat, your turn!"

Ghodrat lowered his fist into the circle, saying, "I've
anted in!"

Morad tossed the pieces in the air and slapped his hand
against his thigh. Ghodrat's fist was below the pieces as they fell.

"Foul, do it again!"

Morad grumbled and rearranged the pieces.

"Right from the beginning, you're messing things up!
You're a cheat like your cheating father. Okay, call it! You can't
shake me with your moves. Ante double!"

"I've anted in. My hand's in!"

"Ante double!"

"I've anted. Just toss the pieces!"

"Nice one! Three horses!"

The pieces were on the ground. A full wolf hand!

"Pay in double!"

Ghodrat tossed in two five-*qeran* coins.

Morad said, "Let's see the other hand."

Ghodrat opened his left fist; there was one five-*qeran* coin
stuck to his left thumb.

"Accepted?"

"Accepted."

Ghodrat said, "Don't go saying anything bad about me!"

Abbas held his fist into the circle, and Morad smiled as he said, "Well, well…watch as I give you a set of four pieces with signs!"

Abbas pursed his lips and squeezed them together, not saying anything. His face was pale, and as was usual, the corners of his lips were trembling. When Abbas joined a game, he would change entirely. A kind of terror would take hold of him. His heart would pound and his eyes would bulge. If he won, he would scream with joy, and if he lost he would still scream. He was clumsy and awkward. It seemed as if he were trying to eat the anted coins with his eyes. For Abbas, nothing seemed as exciting as when the money in play would be collected in his pocket. But since that never happened, he was always unsatisfied. Morad, who knew Abbas' nature well, tossed the pieces up once, called a foul, and set them out again just to wind him up.

"Okay, ante in!"

Abbas, whose fist had remained clenched at the edge of the circle, said in a trembling voice, "I've anted!"

Two pieces with signs came up, one of them a wolf.

Morad said, "You have to put in three times as much as your ante!"

Abbas opened his fist. It was empty! Morad clenched his teeth and sharpened his eyes.

"Are you trying to pull the rug out from under my victory? Fine. I'll still win if we do it hundred more times. Ante up! I'm not worried!"

Abbas rose and said, "I'll ante a ten *shahi*."

As Morad rearranged the pieces, Abbas looked at Jalil and said, "Take my place a second while I go splash some water on my face. Come on! I'm the one who arranged for a place for you guys to play. I didn't want to play in the first place!"

Morad said, "Come on. You ante for yourself, Jalil. Don't be such a baby about the game."

Jalil came over heavily and sat in Abbas place, saying, "Let me examine the pieces!"

Morad pushed the pieces over for him to test out. He separated the wolf piece.

"There's lead in this piece; replace it!"

Rising to leave the stable, Abbas took the piece in question and put another one before Jalil, saying, "Even a bride isn't so finicky before going out to her wedding! Is there anything else you would like from us?"

Jalil picked up the new piece and said, "I thought Ali Genav was going to bring his deck of cards over. So where are they?"

Abbas was just about out the door as he said, "I was just about to go and see where the hell he's hiding his dark head!"

Abbas didn't wait to hear anything more. He closed the door behind himself and entered the yard. He stuck his head into the room, but Mergan wasn't there. Hajer was alone, asleep and snoring. He turned and entered the alley, finding himself face-to-face with Hajj Salem and Moslem. He was surprised for a moment, but gathered his bearings, saying hello and moving on. It wasn't far to Ali Genav's house; it was at the end of the dead-end. One of the doors was always open. Abbas entered; the house was always open to visitors. Ali Genav was sitting by the clay oven, in the sun, mending his camel-hair shawl. He seemed oblivious to the fact that both his mother and wife were in bed, crying in pain. Perhaps he thought to himself that he couldn't do much for them other than what he had done already—to send Abrau to find the bonesetter. What else could he do? Beat himself? Cry out loud? No, Ali Genav was more thick-skinned than that. He was also cool-headed when playing cards. Although he was one of the most experienced card players in Zaminej, he had not once had a scuffle with another player. He was always cool and calm. And he rarely lost. When he did lose, all that he did was furrow his brow in anger, but he would stay as calm as he was before.

Abbas' shadow fell on Ali Genav's hands, and while he continued his sewing he looked up.

"Eh? Can I help you? You must be here for the cards, no?"

Abbas said, "No! How are they?"

"Fine!"

So as to follow up with what he had said, Abbas walked to the door and peeked inside the house. The two women, Raghiyeh and Mother Genav, were on two sides of the room, and Mergan was sitting between them. Abbas returned. Ali Genav was still busy with his sewing.

"So? What do you want? Get to the point!"

Abbas said, "I think Hamdullah and Jalil have full pockets today! But they really want to play cards."

Ali Genav replied, "That one boy's in love with cards. But I won't lend them to anyone."

Abbas said, "What I mean is that you should come yourself. It looks like a good group to play with."

Ali Genav said, "If I come, I'll bring my cards with me!"

Abbas walked back toward the door to the alley. Before reaching it, he slowed down and turned around. He wanted to say something, but couldn't bring himself to. Abbas knew Ali Genav's temperament. It would be counterproductive to push him any more than he already had. So he turned again and left. But as soon as he reached the stable, his eyes opened wide with amazement. He couldn't believe that Hajj Salem and Moslem were inside the stable. Where did they come from? He hoped that Hajj Salem hadn't come to teach a lesson to his nephew, Hamdullah! If he caused a commotion, what would Abbas do? He couldn't think of a way around it. He said hello, and slid down beside one of the walls. Hajj Salem and Moslem were both sitting quietly. The former was sitting on the edge of the trough, with his cane leaning against the center of his chest. His son was sitting beside Hamdullah in the circle and was watching the game over the shoulders of Hamdullah and Morad. The game had heated up. Hamdullah was dealing; he would cast the pieces and then tell his Uncle Moslem to move his head to the side.

"I told you to move your muzzle to the side, you!"

Moslem followed Hamdullah's every movement with his entire body, and at that moment had reached his head and neck over the gambling circle.

"Three donkeys!"

The pieces moved on from his hands; in the last hand, he lost fifteen *qerans* from his total winnings. Hamdullah shoved Moslem's chest with his forearm, bellowing, "I told you a hundred times, sit back, you cow! You shook my hand so much I ended up with three donkeys!"

Moslem pulled himself back and collected himself before saying, "Be generous! A little gift! A gift!"

Hamdullah was collecting the coins from before his feet, and replied, "Go on. Forget it! God'll give you gifts some other place! You idiot, you really think you're going to get something here?"

Moslem didn't listen to this and kept staring at the clenched fist of his nephew's hand. Hamdullah said to Abbas, "Why don't you throw him out?! What are we paying you to host us here for?"

Abbas spoke up, grabbing Moslem's thick wrist between his hands and shouting, "Okay! Get up! I'm not a fool to want to split the host's take, giving a payout to the likes of you. Get up. Open up this space, you!"

It was impossible to move Moslem from his place. He was like a block of stone. He didn't listen, and he wasn't easily moved. He kept staring firmly at his nephew's fist until Abbas was somehow able to pull him into a prone position on the floor of the stable. But that didn't end the problem; Moslem simply started bellowing loudly, sounding unlike any other living thing. If his familiar and unsettling cry was raised for too long, it was likely that all the neighbors would make their way to Soluch's stable to see what was happening, and then Abbas' work would be ruined. There was nothing he could do. He had to find a way to get Moslem out of there. So he began pulling at him with all his strength. Abbas and Moslem were slowly starting to scuffle, while Hajj Salem stayed where he was at the edge of the trough. The old man was like a cleric sitting inside a religious academy. With his long cloak, his scarf and cane, his thick beard.

"I'm not playing any more!"

This was Hamdullah who was pulling himself out of the circle.

Ghodrat replied sharply, "What? You're out? That's what kind of man you are? You win a round and then say you're not playing? That's incredible!"

Morad realized the game was about to fall apart at a time

when he was down twenty-five *qerans* himself. It wouldn't do. The money couldn't leave their circle. He had to do something. He rose. The cause of the problem, Moslem, had to be removed. He gestured to Ghodrat to help him. Hamdullah opened the door of the stable, and Abbas, now assisted by Ghodrat and Morad, dragged Moslem out and threw him out into the snow. They ran back to the stable, closed the door, and threw their bodies against it. Hajj Salem had just risen from his seat and was passing his cane from hand to hand. Moslem reached the other side of the door and began beating on it, crying as he shouted, "Papa...Papa...Come here, Papa...! Come here! I'm scared. Come! I...want Papa. My Papa..."

Hajj Salem gestured at the door with his cane,

"He's crazy! What can be done?"

Abbas said, "Tell him to calm down, Hajji Sir! If he keeps up, the neighbors will come running!"

A smile lit up in the midst of Hajj Salem's bushy beard, and his eyes shone.

"A sensible person would say that's it's worth five *qerans* in order to not have a scene here, no?"

He had stretched one palm out before even finishing his sentence. Abbas handed him five *qerans* and said to the group, "You all see! I'm paying five *qerans* for all of you! It's coming out of the general winnings. I don't want any arguments about it later!"

Hajj Salem took the money in his hand and hid it in his fingers, shaking his head.

Abbas said, "Well, tell him calm down, then!"

Hajj Salem tapped his cane against the door and said, "Calm! You dog! Calm down!"

Moslem calmed down. The boys were able to leave the door and opened it for Hajj Salem, who stepped out. A few moments later the scraping of the steps of the old man and his son could be heard as they walked past the snow piled by the wall. Abbas spit thickly at a spot against the wall of the stable and said, "The blood-sucking leeches!"

Then he looked at Hamdullah and said, "I paid up quietly because of you lot! It wasn't that I was too weak to take him on. I could take on a hundred like him. But I'm worried about the reputations of you two here!"

Morad tossed the pieces in the kitty and said, "Sit down!"

Ghodrat also sat and said, "Yes, sit down. It's all done and over now! Each of us will pay one *qeran* to Abbas. Let's shut him up and get on with it!"

Hamdullah tossed a coin next to Abbas, but Jalil hesitated, shifting on his feet and looking around himself. Morad shouted at him, "Get moving, then! It's not like you have to give up an eyeball! You can't believe he had to pay to get rid of that screaming fool? We're not the ones that are afraid of anything. It's the two of you that are afraid of your daddies. So pay up! Pay it, one *qeran*! And here's my one *qeran*!"

Jalil said, "I'm not playing!"

"You're not going to play?"

"No!"

The veins on Morad's neck were beginning to show themselves and spittle was collecting at the edge of his mouth. He leapt up and grabbed the collar of Jalil's shirt, shouting, "You think anyone can just dance in here like you and then take your winnings out of the circle without playing on? C'mon! You cheat!"

Jalil was struggling simply not to run away. First of all, because he didn't want a scene, and more important, because he was terrified of Morad. It was clear to him that if it ended up in a fight, he'd not only get a beating from Morad and the other two, but that he'd end up with his pockets cleaned out at the end of it. So he decided to compromise. His problem was that he knew that Morad didn't need to work in Zaminej for his living. Morad always left the village shortly after the beginning of spring, coming back to stay at home through the winter. So he was under the thumb of neither the Kadkhoda nor of Salar Abdullah. He could make his own bread from the heart of a stone, if he needed to.

Salar Abdullah's son grabbed Morad's fists in his hands and softly said, "Let go of my collar!"

Morad shook him and said, "So what's your decision? Are you going to take your winnings, or will you keep on playing?"

Jalil still couldn't decide. He just wanted to find a way to get out.

Morad shook him one more time and said, "So what'll it be? Eh? I'm leaving soon anyway. Don't do something that will make me have to give you a beating. Will you stay and play, or do you want to suck up the money?"

Jalil sat down. Morad also sat, and told Abbas, "Toss the pieces!"

Abbas said, "Whoever's won has to pay up to the house first, and then I'll begin!"

Ghodrat pointed to Hamdullah and Jalil, saying, "They're the winners so far. Pay the house."

Hamdullah and Jalil looked at one another. Hamdullah tossed one *qeran* over to Abbas, who then looked at Jalil, saying,

"One *qeran* for the house charge, and there's the other one you owe from before. That's two all together. Pay up!"

Jalil took out two one-*qeran* coins and placed them before Abbas despondently. Abbas took the coins and tossed the *bajal* pieces into the circle. Morad collected the pieces before himself. Abbas said to him, "You set what everyone should pay the house, just so there's no cheating later on."

Morad said, "When the game goes two rounds, the dealer pays the house one *qeran*."

Abbas wanted to bargain. "Why two rounds? Most places it's one round."

Morad said, "Okay, we'll base it on the winnings then. And don't be such a greedy host. For every twenty *qerans* won, the house gets one *qeran*. Okay! Ante up!"

Jalil was sitting to the right of Morad. He took out a ten-*shahi* piece from his pile of coins and tossed it into the circle.

"I've anted in!"

"So far, has anyone been anteing small change, like a ten-*shahi*, for you to start with that?"

"Here's another ten *shahis* on top of it!"

"Cheapskate! You have to bid at least five *qerans*!"

Jalil took another one-*qeran* coin and added it to the others.

"That's all!"

"It's not enough."

"That's it. That's my ante."

"Very nice...! Three horses! Pay up six *qeran*! Ghodrat, you're next?"

Ghodrat held his fist beside the circle. Morad warmed the pieces in his hand and said, "Ante up!"

Ghodrat spoke like an old hand.

"I'm in!"

Morad threw up the pieces and Ghodrat put his fist beneath them, ruining the round. Morad gathered the pieces, saying, "I'm doing well for myself, so you cheat! If you're afraid, then ante up less!"

Ghodrat said, "Just toss them. I'm putting in an extra two *qerans* now!"

Morad tossed the pieces up.

"It's so dark in here!"

It was Ali Genav. He swung the door open and entered the stable.

"Close the door!"

"Close it!"

"Shut the door!"

Ali Genav blinked, then shut the door. The game had picked up again. Ali Genav slowly pulled himself to the wall and stood watching over the game. Morad was still dealing, and he was dealing winning sets to himself, one after another. Jalil was upset. He had begun to lose. His fist was getting more and more empty. From time to time, he wiped his nose with his sleeve, and he kept his eyes on the pieces as they were thrown and as they fell. The coins, ranging from the small ten *shahi* to the valuable five *qerani*, were circulating around the gambling circle, going from hand to hand. Their palms were sweating. Eventually all the boys, including Jalil, had arranged all their coins in neat piles beside themselves. Each had constructed a little tower of coins—from large to small in value—in front of himself. The boys were caught up in the game. The game was moving along quickly; time passed without their noticing. Now, no one was anteing small change, like ten-*shahis* or one-*qeran* coins. Even

Jalil wasn't anteing less than two *qerans* against the others. The pieces would go up in the air and fall on the ground and eight or nine *qerans* would change hands. Everyone was focused on playing the game. Their lips were dry, their eyes staring, their bodies tense. Even Ali Genav, the most accomplished gambler there, had stopped the knitting he had brought with himself and was fixated on the game. No one made a sound.

"Where is that son of a bitch?"

Kadkhoda Norouz's angry voice echoed in the yard, followed by the sound of his feet stomping across the snow.

"Eh? Where is your pathetic excuse for a brother, girl?"

The game stopped. Abbas knew the Kadkhoda was looking for him. He froze in his place. Everyone froze. Only Ali Genav was able to do something; he picked up his knitting and busied himself with it. He somehow also managed to reposition himself back on the edge of the trough, to make it seem as if he had nothing to do with the disgrace going on in the center of the stable. Nonetheless, Ali Genav immediately wished he'd never come.

The door of the stable flew open with a body blow by the Kadkhoda. He filled the doorway with his worn camel-hair cloak, a scarf on his head, and leather boots on his feet. He glared at the boys. Abbas, like a sparrow in the sights of a hawk, braced himself with his back still to the door. Others, standing or half-standing, froze in their places and lowered their heads. The money was still on the ground, left in individual piles. The *bajal* pieces were scattered on the dirt where they'd fallen: a horse and three others. Everyone was frozen in place. In the dim light of the dusk, the Kadkhoda quickly recognized Abbas. He strode toward him and laid a boot kick into his back.

"You son of a dog! Now you've gone to lead my son astray as well? You're running a gambling circle here?"

Abbas was thrown face down into the playing circle, and the first idea that occurred to him, while absorbing the Kadkhoda's curses and kicks, was to grab one of the piles of coins. He reached out to the small tower of Jalil's coins, grasping them in his hand along with a fistful of dirt and mud. The Kadkhoda took Abbas by the collar, lifting him up to turn his face toward him. The fear that the Kadkhoda would take the money away from him terrified Abbas, and so before he had been turned to face him eye-to-eye, he stuffed the coins—along with the dirt, mud, and old straw he'd grabbed from the ground—into his mouth, filling his cheeks as if he they were filled by two walnuts. The Kadkhoda planted a slap across Abbas' face, and a few coins flew out from between his lips and teeth. Before the second slap could connect with his face, Abbas swallowed, and while the Kadkhoda watched him, his eyes bulged as if they would pop out of their sockets. The veins on his neck were visible, and the skin on his face reddened.

The Kadkhoda shouted, "Go bring some water! The fool's going choke himself!"

He let Abbas go and turned to find his son Hamdullah. He found him in the corner on the trough. He dragged him down and jerked him left and right. Ali Genav saw an opportunity to sneak out. But the Kadkhoda turned toward him.

"Aren't you ashamed of yourself, man? Your beard's getting white, your mother and wife are dying, and you've come here to gamble with a few boys who don't have hair on their lips yet! Ach!"

Meanwhile, Hamdullah managed to escape his father's grip and ran out into the alley, crying. Ghodrat, who until then had been standing on the edge of the action, also dashed out. Only Morad and Jalil remained. Morad had left to bring a bowl of water, and now was busy pouring water down Abbas' throat. It was as if Jalil hadn't realized that he had a chance to escape. The Kadkhoda was still busy talking to Ali Genav. So Jalil crept out the door and tried to forget about his coins that he had lost inside.

Abbas was still swallowing the coins, with the help of the water that Morad was pouring down his throat. Although Morad kept telling him to spit them out, he didn't listen to him. With his red face and bulging eyes and veins, he was swallowing the coins one by one. After the last one had gone down, he took a deep breath and leaned his shoulder against the wall. Because of the effort, sweat was pouring from his ears, his back, and under his arms. He felt like dying. He hoped that the Kadkhoda would have nothing more to do with him, but the Kadkhoda returned and stood above him.

Abbas cried out painfully, "Kadkhoda, I was wrong!"

The Kadkhoda then swung the door open and went outside. Ali Genav stood over Abbas for a moment, then stooped and walked out the doorway. Now that the Kadkhoda had left, Hajer came into the stable to see what had happened to her brother. Ali Genav looked her over as if she were goods he was about to buy, and then asked, "Your mother's not returned yet?"

Hajer said no, then she entered the stable. Ali Genav was about to enter the alley when he changed his mind and entered the house. He sat by the doorway in such a way as to catch the last of the sunlight for the shawl he was knitting, and he busied himself with it. Hajer returned from the stable and began to light the lamp.

Ali Genav asked, "No news from my house?"

Hajer replied, "No. It was still light when I went there and came back. My mother was there then."

Morad brought Abbas into the room and leaned him against the wall. Then he sat beside him and asked Hajer, "Don't you want to light your stove?"

Before Hajer was able to reply, Abbas said, "The lock! Get the lock from the cabinet and give it to me."

Hajer brought the lock. Abbas rose from his place with difficulty and as he was leaving told Hajer, "Go tell Mama to come and make me her herbal tea! The kind for your stomach! Get going! Ow..."

He reached the stable door, while bending over in pain. He put the lock on the door and returned the same way. He mumbled painfully through his teeth, "All I have is mixed in the dirt and mud in the stable. How am I supposed to find it all? That sneak Abrau, I don't trust him!"

Abbas, wrapped in his own pain and worries, didn't notice Abrau returning. He crept into a corner bent over, and he hid the key to the lock inside the hem of his pants.

"Castor oil! Strained oil! Girl, go get our mother!"

He said this and then collapsed against the wall beside the stove.

Wearing Ali Genav's long cloak and his big boots, Abrau looked like a dwarf. He had wrapped something around his head and his face. His face was purple and his lips were cracked. The cold had broken his weak body down. In the doorway, his body collapsed like an old wall crumbling, and he fell to his knees. Ali Genav slowly rose up, grabbed Abrau under his arms, and pulled him to the side of the room. Hajer didn't wait a moment longer and ran out to get Mergan. Ali Genav set aside his shawl and began massaging Abrau's frozen hand in between his own thick, dark hands. Abrau's eyes were open, but he couldn't speak. Ali Genav told Morad to light the stove. Morad left to bring back a stack of cottonwood from the oven outside. As he continued to massage Abrau's heart and neck, Ali Genav asked, "So what happened? Did you bring him? The bonesetter?"

Abrau still couldn't speak. He raised his head up. Ali Genav began to massage Abrau's ears with his hands.

"What happened? What did he say?"

Abrau finally replied, in broken speech, "Cold...too cold...didn't come!"

Abbas brayed from across the room, "Didn't I tell you to send me? I told you not to trust him with that job! If I'd have gone, he'd be here. I would have brought him. Even if he was sleeping with his wife, I'd have dragged him out and brought him. Castor oil! I need some castor oil...You should have had someone capable do it!"

Ali Genav removed his cloak from Abrau's body and loosened the laces on the boots, taking the boy's feet out of them. He rose and was about to leave when Mergan entered the door with Hajer behind her. Just then Morad stepped in the room with his arms full of cottonwood. Ali Genav looked at Mergan as if he had a question he didn't dare ask her. Mergan's eyes had a shadow across them. What could he do? Finally he opened his mouth.

"Yes? Well?"

Mergan said, "She passed...God have mercy on her."

"Who? Which one?"

"Your mother. Mother Genav!"

Ali Genav said with disbelief, "Now what the hell am I supposed to do? Night! It's already night!"

He said it quietly, not directing it at anyone. It just slipped out. He put his cloak under one arm and his boots in one hand and walked heavily out the door.

Abrau pointed to Ali Genav as he left, and said to his mother, "My pay! My pay!"

Mergan sat between her sons. Abbas said, "Mama, dear! I need some castor oil! I'm dying. My stomach, my insides. My insides hurt so much! Give me castor oil. My insides are full of coins! Mama!"

2.

Worried and anxious, in the mists of the morning, Abrau slid
out from where he was. His bones had warmed a bit, and he felt
as if he could walk. Quietly, he dressed and tiptoed out of the
house. Sounds were still coming from behind the closed door of
the stables. Abrau crept forward and listened. These were the
last emanations from Abbas' troubled stomach—he had locked
himself in the stables last night and now, at the break of morning, wrapped up in his own pain and his own concerns, Abbas
had locked off the stable. He had closed the door and would not
let anyone else inside. The last light from the lantern flickered
in the darkness of the stable. Abrau thought that Abbas must
finally have found some relief in there. But Abrau wasn't really
concerned about his brother. He tied up the edges of his over-

coat, drew the string around his waist into a knot, and then exited through the gap in the wall.

The alley was still dark. However, the snow's light was beginning to break through the darkness. The snow was now covered by a sheet of ice. It had become dry and impermeable. The coldness was spreading, that cold that follows every snow. As the saying goes, "Worry not for the day of snow; worry for the day after!" But Abrau was relieved that on the day after the snow, meaning on this day, he had no major chores to see to. He had already made his contribution with his work on the day before. Even on the short distance he had to go, the coldness burned him. His eyelids couldn't fight the harsh dawn wind, which rose off of the snow and cut through him. His hollow eyelids, which were pockmarked from childhood chicken pox, flickered open and shut. They couldn't stop blinking. His nose began to run. His face, bitten by the cold, began to look withdrawn and bruised. Abrau felt frostbite beginning to numb his chin and forehead while tears gathered at the edges of his eyes. He hid half of his face in the collar of his overcoat as he passed before the door of the mosque. The door was half open. Abrau peeked inside. A casket covered by an embroidered sheet was set onto the winter cover of the pool in the courtyard, which was frozen stuck. One of the stray bitches from Zaminej's wild packs had decamped beside the casket. Abrau guessed that Mother Genav was still lying inside the casket, since people aren't buried at nighttime. So, there was no time to waste. He continued on his way, entering the alley leading to the town's public pool. The pool was a solid square of ice. All around the pool, piles of snow were heaped on top of each other. The bath's boiler room was just a ways farther on, at the edge of one wall of the town baths, next to the drain to the pool. Abrau circled the pool and headed step by step down an embankment along a narrow path. The path twisted and turned like a snake's tail, leading to the low and broken doorway into the boiler room.

Abrau opened the door. Ali Genav was sitting on a slab of rock beside the water heater stoking the heart of the fire with a metal poker, occasionally tossing a handful or two of kindling into the fireplace. He has sensed Abrau's entrance, but Ali Genav was calmer and more deliberate than to be drawn out of his own thoughts by a sudden movement in his surroundings. So, he remained focused on his work, as if no one else were there. Abrau shut the door behind himself, approached Ali Genav, and sat quietly in the comfortable warmth of the fire. How the warmth entered his heart! Without looking at him, Ali Genav handed the poker to Abrau and extracted a crumpled packet of cigarettes from the pocket of his shirt. He took a cigarette out with his mouth, holding onto the end of it with his teeth. Then he took a burning branch from the fire, lit up, and exhaled a cloud of smoke from his nostrils. With a voice full of self-pity, he said, "I've not slept a wink since last night! The moaning and groaning of this damn woman stopped me from even shutting my eyes, damn her and her father and ancestors! She was swearing and moaning until the break of dawn. It's as if she thinks she's owed something. Infernal woman! She makes the world a salt-desert, bringing nothing good to it. If she'd die, I'd be free of her. Why should someone waste his wheat and bread on a woman who has nothing to offer and who brings no blessings! A female donkey would at least bear offspring once in a while, but this bitch won't even bear a thistle bush so that one can at least feel the satisfaction of having left something behind! May her father rot in hell. What is supposed to give me hope in life? When I die, what will carry my name, except for a slab of stone?! When I die, it'll be as if I never lived. So like some fool I came and went. So what? So I beat her once the first time she was pregnant and she lost the kid! Now what am I supposed to do with her? I lost my head and I beat her. Now what? She complained so much and harassed my father and mother so much that I couldn't have a say in the house. And then this happened to my poor mother. I swear on this fire before me, she was the cause of all these problems. Otherwise, I would never have thrown my own mother out of my house to go and live in a ruins and to meet this kind of an end. Didn't I suckle from my mother's breast? How will she ever forgive me for what I've done? How? After all, she's gone now!"

Abrau had come to raise the issue of his pay for his previous day's work. His worries now came from the fact that, after having awoken at dawn to come down to the water-boiler room, Ali Genav was clearly so self-involved that Abrau didn't have the heart to ask him for anything, much less for his money.

"And now my donkey has come down sick, too! The hairs on his body are all on end, and the poor thing is shaking like a leaf. What did you do to him yesterday?"

"A donkey that's put to work doesn't become sick, does it?! You must have let it get cold last night!"

Ali Genav replied, "No! He must have been sweating, and you must have had him stand somewhere for a while in the wind, and he caught a cold."

Abrau took a handful of kindling and pushed it into the fireplace with the poker. "We went straight there and came right back. And I've ended up sicker than your donkey!"

Ali Genav smoked the last bit of his cigarette and sighed, "I don't know what to do with this woman! She's become the greatest burden of my life."

Abrau carefully said, "Ali..."

Ali Genav looked at him. The pupils of his eyes shone in the light from the fire.

Abrau asked, "Do men who leave ever return?"

Ali Genav stared at the smoke rising from the fire, took the poker from Abrau, and said, "What do you know about the ways of the world? He might eventually come back. Some do. Your father could return one day."

Abrau said, "And do they all leave in this way?"

Ali said, "No, each one leaves in his own way."

Abrau said, "I just wish I knew where he'd gone. Why didn't he tell us where he was going?"

Ali said, "Do you think he knew where he was going himself? Some have left and have never been heard from again; while others send word after some ten or fifteen years. Morad Nim Mani left and we didn't hear from him for eighteen years, when we found out that he was in Bejnurd working as a prayer scribe. But once Muhammad Balachai left, it was as if he'd never existed! And we heard the news of the death of another fellow just recently—his children went up toward Sangsar to take his sheep, and they ended up staying out there. And then there's Ghuli, the father of our own Safdar...He left like a real bastard. He had three camels and worked as a porter on the road to Ghuchan. Out there, he did business among the Kurds, and the women there attracted his attention. Some say he'd fallen in love. He used to play the *dohul* drum and he was a good dancer. Anytime the Kurds had a wedding, he'd show up.

Eventually, he sold his camels and wasted away what little he had. Then one day he came back to Zaminej with his hands empty, begging. I remember it well. I had just shaved for the first time and I was going with some others to play *kolah qidj* when I saw that Ghuli Khan had shown up. His camel's saddle was on his back. Those days, if you were a camel owner, you could marry well. He had a fiancée here, Safdar's mother, who was then still really just a girl. He went to his fiancée's home and was acting the role of the husband-to-be. That night, he had his way with her. He planted the seed of our own Safdar that very night. Then next day, he sold the inheritance he had from his father—a copper cup and saucer set and some bits—to Karbalai Doshanbeh, the father of Salar Abdullah. He bought some rice with the money and made a rice dish and ate it with his fiancée. The next morning he left and no one would ever see him again. No one knows what hell he's gone to! Some say he's gone back to those same parts, around Darreh Gaz, that is, where the Kurds are. Some say Safdar knows about this. But any time talk of his father comes up, Safdar shakes his head and says, 'He can go to hell!' One time, I jokingly said to him, 'Go find your father; they say he's been seen up by Darreh Gaz.' He replied, 'I hope he goes even farther away, to Kalleh Khavajeh or farther!' And you've heard the story about my own uncle, no?"

Abrau said, "I just wish I knew where he'd gone!"

Ali Genav said, "Forget about it—if wanting to see him was like a tooth, I'd say you should pull it out and throw it away. Imagine he was never here. What do we know? Goats go where there's grass, don't they?"

Abrau replied, "I just wish I could forget about him!"

Ali Genav said, "Between you and me, your father had no choice. He was a respectable man. We need to give him his due; he had a strong sense of honor. He was hard-working. He was creative. He wouldn't let anyone speak down to him. He had a short temper. He just couldn't take much more. That's why he left! Soluch was entirely different from Safdar's father. I know that if Soluch is ever able to fill his pockets with something, he'll be sure not to forget you. He'll be sure to show up then. He was a reliable sort, Soluch. The poor guy!"

Abrau was stoking the fire. He said nothing. He was sitting on his legs before the fireplace, lost in thought. His lips were pressed together. It seemed as if he were unconscious of Ali Genav's presence. Ali Genav also decided to drop the subject. He was tired and sleepy. He yawned, punched his chest with his fist, and said while rising, "I'm going to go lie down and see if I can sleep. You keep an eye on the fire. The pots are already boiling, so take it easy with the kindling. Just take care the fire doesn't go out."

Abrau was silent. Ali Genav went to a corner of the room, lay down on an old blanket, and said, "Put the kettle by the edge of the fire so that it'll boil. I have so much to do today! I have to dig my own mother's grave, God rest her soul. That other poor woman—I don't know what to do about her. But if I can't get some sleep, I'll be useless."

Abrau put the handle of the kettle on the end of the poker and set it on the edge of the fire.

"You're like me. We have the same nature. You're good with any kind of work. But this Abbas, he takes after his worthless uncle! He's split right down the middle. Instead of focusing his mind on any particular work, his eyes are always looking around for something else. He's always trying to get at what someone else is holding or carrying. His eyes are like hungry thieves. He's like a dog that thinks someone will eventually come around to throw him a bone. His mind and eyes are always searching, like a stray dog. In a few days, he'll have a beard and mustache—I can't help but wonder how he'll fill the belly of a wife and children then?"

Soluch had told Abrau many times, "The only time a man can raise his head among people is when his shoulders have been drenched in sweat. A man is someone who, if you slap him on the back, dust rises from his shirt!"

On the rare occasions when Soluch spoke, he would generally speak in this vein. He'd say things like, "Work! Work! The bread you get from work is what gives you your essence, your honor. A man only has his work!"

But why did he leave all of a sudden?

There was no way that Abrau could digest this. However he looked at it, he couldn't comprehend it. He knew that need was at the heart of it. Could there be anything else? Yes, need—but so what? Was Soluch the only one who was in need? Only him? How could he be justified in leaving? Just leaving like that. Leaving behind his wife and daughter. One might consider the others, Abrau and Abbas, as nearly men. But what about Hajer? Didn't he consider the fact that by next spring Hajer would be nearly at the age of maturity? That she'd be stepping onto the ladder of adolescence? Had he even thought about these things? He must have. The Soluch that Abrau knew was a responsible man. He was practical, more bones than muscle. He couldn't have gone without thinking over all of these questions. But where could he have gone? After all, winter's not the season for working. If you had a special skill that used the different fingers of your hand, during the winter you'd never have to open your fist. To the extent that Abrau's experiences in life had taught him something about these things, he knew that no matter where they went to find work, all the men would return to their homes in the winter. There, they'd huddle under one roof with the rest of their families to wait out the season until spring. They'd make it through the winter in one way or another, surviving with very little. So where could Soluch have gone in the middle of the winter? What kind of work could have drawn him away?

The kinds of jobs that Abrau knew about could be counted on the fingers of his two hands. And the places outside the village that he knew of were also just as few. Setting aside the seasonal work in the fields, Abrau had heard that some years back the young and old men of Zaminej used to go for work on the road line. These were the years during which the road from Tehran to Mashhad was being rebuilt. He had heard much about this. But he couldn't imagine what this road line looked like. It was just a name in his head. He knew that in the summers, especially in years when the harvest was bad, the skilled harvesters would go out toward Ghuchan for work and each would return to Zaminej with ten or twenty *man* of wheat, storing it in their storehouses to make morning bread for their children. But this was all he was aware of when it came to the kinds of work that were available outside of the area. Morad, the son of Sanam, wasn't so friendly with Abrau to have told him what sort of work he did outside of Zaminej. If pressed, he would just say, "It's a wide world outside. Out there, a man can always make a living." That's all he'd say.

Once, when Abrau was a small child, perhaps even before he wore pants, one of those "city-room" minibuses showed up to transport pilgrims from Zaminej. The children gathered around the machine and looked at its windows, tires, and seats with eyes wide with amazement—their jaws simply fell open! Pilgrims from three villages in the area had collectively rented the bus to take them to the city of Mashhad and back. Just seeing that bus opened vistas in Abrau's imagination. For the first time, he realized that people could travel with something other than an animal and that it was possible to go very great distances with a vehicle such as this. Places far, far away. After that, Abrau had grown used to seeing automobiles, but seeing these had not affected him as much as that first experience had. Abrau thought to himself that Soluch was not the kind to travel in a car. More likely he'd gone by foot. But where and how far could one go traveling by foot? And how far are feet willing to travel if being directed by an empty belly? What if he had fallen while trying to make his way through the snow and ice? What if wolves had tracked and circled him? And if vultures had hovered in circles above him? Abrau had heard that vultures would first peck out the eyes of a corpse. The shepherds of Zaminej used to tell stories of vultures that would descend on sheep that had fallen, plucking out the eyes of the carrion before beginning to disembowel it. Each vulture had to be about the size of a house's roof archway. They would cover the carrion like a tent casting shadows over the body. What a terrifying sight! They could frighten someone to death if he wasn't dead already. Could he imagine Soluch resorting to begging, given his sense of honor? Could he even consider for a moment that Soluch might steal a cup or a water jug from the front door of someone's house? That Soluch could even stretch out his hand so as to take what was not his? Was it possible? No! Abrau would sooner die than to accept such a thing. No! Soluch, his own father, would never steal or resort to begging. Abrau could never think of Soluch in that way. Soluch was a man with strong arms and broad shoulders, not a wolf with sharp nails and teeth.

"Hayyu ala al-salat...Hayyu ala al-salat..."

The glassy air of the dawn was broken by the call to prayer by the Molla of Zaminej.

Ali Genav's kettle had begun to boil. Abrau didn't know where the tea was. Ali Genav turned over in his place, grumbling and swearing under his breath. He directed his anger at the Molla for waking him, despite the fact that it was clear that the call to prayer was to mark the death of Ali Genav's mother, calling the people to join a funerary prayer that morning. They had agreed to this the night before; it was the Molla himself who had suggested they leave the body in the mosque overnight. He had no choice; Ali Genav had to get up. He turned over again, scratched his side, and then opened his heavy, tired eyelids.

Abrau asked, "Where is your bag of tea?"

"It's hanging on that nail. Just look there, you'll see it."

Abrau busied himself with making tea. Ali Genav stretched, pounded his chest with his fists, and yawned like a camel, bringing himself over to the fire. Abrau poured tea and he quickly downed four cups before saying, "I have to go and tend to the burial, God have mercy on her soul."

He rose and placed his cloak over his shoulders. He handed the long key to the door of the public baths to Abrau, saying,

"Open your eyes and ears! Other than the farmers, who pay me by barter, everyone else pays in cash. Adults pay three *qerans*; the children pay thirty *shahis*. Don't let anyone try to fool you! Let's see how you do today. And when you leave, latch and chain the door. Those sons of bitches, as soon as they see I'm gone, they try to get in here to set up a gambling session. Since the water boiler's warm, they like it here."

Abrau listened idly to what Ali Genav was saying, but he wasn't following him closely. He knew more or less what he was saying. But his thoughts were far from this place and these matters. They were lost in other places. Places that were alien to him. He just knew that they were far from here. Confusing, confounding places that pulled Abrau in like a tiny speck lost in a vast sea. Abrau's mind had been brought to a standstill; he had no power over it. He stared intensely at the ashes in the fireplace, his thoughts fixed on something that words could not express. For a moment, it was as if he had retreated from the world entirely. He was light, empty, free of burden.

Ali Genav threw a quick glance at the bony shoulders of the child and then bent over to exit the room.

The morning air was freezing. Ali Genav tied the ends of his scarf around his chin and then climbed up the steep hill in front of him. The pool was frozen over. The call to prayer still echoed in the air. A streak of smoke tainted the pure dawn sky. "What does he want to prove? It's enough! God damn your prayers—everyone's heard you by now. They'll come out of their homes in small groups shortly, of course they will! Ha! See how he drags out the call!"

"Aren't you going in the wrong direction? Who's to open the bathhouse then?"

It was Karbalai-Safi, the father of the Kadkhoda. He had his bath supplies under one arm and was leaving his house with some difficulty. Ali Genav greeted him and said, "Mergan's son will be there, Karbalai. He has the key."

Karbalai-Safi tucked his chin in and headed for the baths. Ali Genav turned the corner and went straight to Mergan's house. The stove in her house was already lit and a pillar of smoke filled the house's doorway. He looked inside and said, "Where is that son of yours, Abbas?"

She looked up from the oven and looked at him with watery eyes. She lifted the edge of her scarf before her nostrils and asked, "What do you want him for?"

"I want to take him to help me dig the grave."

"He's had an upset stomach since last night. I don't know. He's still in the stable right now."

Ali Genav turned to look at the stable door. The door swung open on its hinges with a dry and old-sounding creak, and Abbas stood in the doorway. He had one hand on the wall and the other propped up against the door. He looked as if he would collapse if he let go of either. His eyes were sunken into their sockets, looking like two watermelon seeds. His cheeks were puffed and his skin was as yellow as hay.

Ali Genav went to him and said, "So what happened to you? I was going to take you to the graveyard with me!"

Abbas could hardly make a sound. He whispered with great difficulty, "I'm sick...Really, I'm in a bad way...I'm really sick."

"So why have you locked yourself into the stable then?"

Abbas began to slowly shut the door and said, "I can't...I can't stand up..."

Ali Genav kept looking at the door after it was shut, as Abbas' voice faded away. He didn't have a moment to spare. He didn't need to think about the situation, as he more or less understood what had happened. He'd seen how Abbas had stuffed the coins, along with the dirt, into his mouth. He was about to walk into the alley when Mergan's voice stopped him.

"Just a second. I'm coming."

Ali Genav waited until Mergan came out. She had Soluch's small well-digging shovel in one hand. She gave the shovel to Ali Genav and busied herself with tying the edges of her chador around her neck. Once she was ready, she took the shovel from him and set out following behind him. First, they went to his house. She wanted to check in on Raghiyeh. Ali Genav lowered his head, entered the room, and passed by Raghiyeh and pushed back the curtain to the pantry. Then he disappeared behind the curtain. Mergan stood by the door, on the steps, and asked Raghiyeh how she was doing. Raghiyeh cried out deeper than before, "I'm a goner too! Mergan, dear, I'm also dying, my sister!"

Ali Genav came out of the pantry with his pick and shovel and answered his wife.

"You're not going to die, don't worry. You won't die till you cause the end of me!"

He walked out the door, not listening to Raghiyeh's cries and curses. In the alley he told Mergan, "She won't let herself die before she's dragged me to the edge of death myself!"

The Molla of Zaminej was still standing on the broken wall of the mosque chanting the call to prayer. Mergan and Ali Genav stood before him. The Molla stopped for a minute.

Ali Genav said, "Why are you shouting yourself hoarse, Molla dear! Who wants to leave their homes on such a day with such weather? And just for poor Mother Genav? Come down. Come down and go have a cup of tea while I go and dig the grave. See how you're suffering in this cold! Give me your hand and come on down."

Ali Genav took his hand and brought him down off the wall. The old man was shaking and his lips were nearly frozen. Ali Genav again told him to go and warm himself by the hearth. Just then the sound of Qur'anic recitation was heard. "By God! Who is this now?" Ali Genav put his shovel and pick beside the wall and entered the mosque. The place in the middle of the court-yard where Mother Genav's casket had been placed was now empty. Where did they take the casket, then? Who had taken it? The sound of recitation was coming from the night-prayers niche. He entered the niche, trying to see in the darkness. There were dark shapes at the back of the room. He entered, and as he stepped forward the sound became louder. He kept going. It was Hajj Salem; he was sitting cross-legged above the casket and was reciting from the Qur'an. His son was lying at the other end of the casket, snoring as he slumbered.

"God curse the devil!"

Hajj Salem and his son and taken the casket from the courtyard into the niche for night-prayers, so that, sheltered from the sharp cold outside, one could recite and the other could sleep.

Mergan and the Molla were still standing in the courtyard of the mosque when Ali Genav came out, growling, "They're making work for themselves. They're crazy! Now I have to pay up for the recitation as well!"

He left from the broken door of the mosque and grabbed his shovel and pick, heading to the graveyard. Mergan walked along with him, step by step. The Molla dragged himself slowly behind them, saying, "But...the prayers for the deceased! The funerary prayers!"

Ali Genav turned around and said, "Molla, your lips can't even move because of the cold! Just go and warm yourself. When we're ready to take her to the grave, I'll come and get you."

The Molla didn't say anything, and if he had, Ali Genav would not have listened to him. He had picked up his pace and was walking through the alleys toward the graveyard. Mergan was following behind him. Ali Genav stood at the edge of the graveyard. The gravestones were poking through the deep layer of snow, seeming more quiet than usual. Ali Genav looked to find his father's gravestone. It was a tradition that members from each family be buried near one another. Despite the fact that Ali Genav was one of the men least mindful of such matters in the entire village, due to an impulse the heart of which he didn't understand, he still wanted to be certain to bury his mother beside his father. So he walked to and fro between the graves alongside Mergan. There was no other way to find the right location; he had to go from grave to grave. He found his father's grave and took forty steps in the direction of Mecca. Then he cut into the earth with his shovel and told Mergan, "This is it!"

Mergan stood beside him and hit the ground with her shovel, busying herself with cleaning the snow from the site. Ali Genav took off his cloak and threw it onto the handle of the pick. Then he grabbed the cold handle of the shovel between his two hands. The man and woman both went to work. All around them was white and cold. Cold and silent. There was no one other than those two, hacking at the moist soil and piling the snowy dirt on the edge of the grave.

The snow glimmered with the break of dawn. Snow covered the sleeping village like a blanket. The graveyard and the crumbling tombs were framed by a broken wall in one direction, a wide-open field in the other. Crows, black crows circled the graveyard. The ditch was dug knee-deep. Then Ali Genav set aside the shovel and picked up the pick. They had dug out the moist top-soil and had reached the firm layer beneath. Now he had to use the pick. He began working alone, as there was not enough room in the grave for the two of them. Mergan stood to one side until Ali Genav's work was done, then she entered the grave and dug out the loose soil with her shovel. Meanwhile, Ali Genav straightened his back and set the pick on the mound beside the grave.

"Hand me the shovel!"

"Take a break. I'll dig out this dirt."

Ali Genav was exhausted. His forehead and ears were covered in sweat. He came out of the grave and sat beside his cloak, lighting a cigarette and throwing the burnt match to one side.

"I want to free myself of the burden of this woman!"

Mergan listened to Ali Genav as she dug the dirt out, shovelful by shovelful. He continued.

"I wasted my youth on her, but it's enough, now! In the few days I have left to live, I want to have some peace of mind."

Mergan was still shoveling the dirt from the grave, and didn't say anything. He asked, "What do you think, Mergan?"

She replied while digging, "God wouldn't approve. Her legs are broken and she has no one to protect her but you. If you throw her out, where would she find a roof to sleep under?"

Ali Genav wiped his lips with one hand and said, "I've had it up to here, though, Mergan! I've not had a single happy day for the past few years, now. What am I guilty of? And my name shouldn't die out when they put me in my grave. As long as I can remember, this woman has done nothing but complain, cry, and complain some more. I've not had one happy night in my entire life. Now that her complaints are mixed with curses, I can't even sleep a wink! She's torturing me with her complaining, her cursing! Also, she's the one who brought on that poor old woman's death. She complained so much that I threw my own mother out of her house during her last days on earth, and the poor thing's finished her life like this! Oh, God!"

Mergan finished clearing the last bit of dirt and came out of the grave. Ali Genav finished smoking his cigarette and tossed it away. He took the pick in hand and jumped into the grave. The grave was now waist-deep. They had to dig deeper, at least to chest-level. Mergan put Ali Genav's cloak over her shoulders and sat to one side. Ali Genav bent his body and sank the pick into the earth.

He said, "She's barren, it's clear! I did it myself, I know. She had something in her belly and I kicked her with my boot right in the stomach, and the baby was done for. Now I wish I'd broken my foot! I was an animal. Shame! That was youth. But now... Now what? Now... Who knows? But I have some ideas. Ideas, Mergan! You're a smart woman. You've seen the world. You know what I'm saying. I make a good living. I have to think about myself. My work, my life. The more I think about it, I see I want a woman who can help me. Someone who's able to come to the baths on the women's days, sit and help the customers wash or dry themselves, and collect a couple of coins of admission from each person. But this woman's stuck at home, and the state she's in she won't be able to do anything for at least a whole year."

Mergan didn't know what to say to Ali Genav. She was silent. She didn't understand why he was telling her these things, or what his intention was. Why was he telling her all of this here? Why now? Her mind was racing, but she couldn't find an answer. She was captured by her own imagination, taken by it. The weather was still; it was just about dawn. All around, as far as she could see, was emptiness. Zaminej was silent, broken. There was still some time before the day's eyes would open. A sudden fright ran through her. Fear. A fear mixed with an element of a woman's nature. Of the nature of a man and a woman. Of one body before another. Something was flickering, something that was not under anyone's control. Mergan was overtaken by a feeling initiated by Ali Genav's words. But this light and baneful flickering was fleeting. It was now covered in layers of apprehension. Fear was overpowering nature. Now her fear had frozen her. She couldn't move. Sitting under his cloak beside the grave, she was paralyzed. She felt as if her heart had stopped. Her eyes were transfixed by his thick, dark hands. His wide shoulders, his heavy breathing as he worked, all scared her. She suddenly wished she could find an excuse to get up and leave the graveyard, but she couldn't. She had neither the skill nor the courage to find a way to get away. Her knees felt weak, as if she were trapped like a sparrow in a hawk's sight.

Ali Genav threw the pick out of the grave.

"Now hand me that shovel!"

Mergan rose with difficulty, stood by the grave, and held the shovel out for him. Before she knew it, he grabbed both the shovel and her wrist, and with one motion pulled both into the grave. He threw her against the wall of the grave, and between his heavy breaths, he stared at her wide and terrified eyes, speaking in a broken voice.

"Your daughter! Give me your daughter! Let me marry Hajer!"

Mergan felt as if she were about to die and Ali Genav had taken on the likeness of the angel of death. That was how he appeared to her; his eyes bulging, spittle around his lips. She began to shake visibly, flapping her wings like a pigeon in a well. Her mouth and throat were dry, and she felt as if her limbs had been stretched and were being torn apart in his hands. When he eventually loosened his grip on her wrist, she sat back and leaned her head against the wall of the grave. Gasping for air, she shut her eyes.

"Oh my God!"

Once Ali Genav had regained his composure he busied himself with the work of digging and said again, "Give me your daughter. I want to have a son with her. I want to keep my name alive."

"My daughter...isn't old enough to marry. She's not ready for a husband."

"She is! If you toss your hat up, by the time it hits the ground she'll be old enough. And she'll be ready for marriage!"

"Hajer's still a child. She's not mature enough. She's not of age."

"She'll mature. She'll come of age. Why are you worrying about these details? If I marry her, I'll be satisfied with her as she is."

"Because...but..."

Ali Genav poured out the contents of his shovel heavily.

"No buts and ifs! Promise me right here. Your family needs someone to look over them. I'll give your sons jobs. I'll have you work with your daughter at the baths. Until your daughter's old enough to do the work by herself, you can oversee her. I'll take Abrau under my own wing. I'll have him tend the water heaters and he can go and gather kindling for the boiler stove. I'll find something for Abbas as well. If nothing else, I'll get him work tending my cousin's camel herd. If nothing else, he'll be making a living for himself! Your life will improve; you'll be happy. You think these young fools who leave the village for six, seven months to run like dogs after a single morsel of bread, who then come back and sit bored by the hearth for the rest of the time...You think they're better than me? Think of Morad, Sanam's son! You think someone like that can provide for a wife? A woman needs a man to oversee her, not a fancy baby rooster! Think about it and convince her. In the first month of the New Year, after the forty-day mourning period for my mother, we'll go to town to buy the things we need. You, too— you need to be in your best."

"But what about Raghiyeh, then?"

"She can't be a wife any longer. I'll have her stay in the pantry for a while, and then I'll build a little hole for her in the pen. When I have a chance, I'll build a roof next to the clay oven and I'll put up walls. Then Hajer and I will move out into the new room, and Raghiyeh will stay in the place off the pen."

Their work was done. Ali Genav scraped the walls of the grave with his shovel and tossed out the last pile of dirt. He pulled himself out of the grave and then held a hand out for Mergan. She wrapped her hand in her chador and held onto his hand. He pulled his presumed mother-in-law out as if she were already family. Then he brushed the dust from his clothes, put his cloak on his shoulders, and picked up the shovel and pick.

"Why don't you leave the shovel here. We're going to have to cover her up afterward."

Ali Genav replied, "I'll bring it back with myself. Some person might come by and take it."

They walked back together.

"Do you know how to wash the corpse?"

Mergan replied, "Of course. But after that, I'll need to carry out a full ablution for myself."

Ali Genav replied, "Nothing to it! In the evening, I'll give you the key for the baths, and if you'd like, you can take Hajer as well and give her a good wash."

Mergan didn't say anything, neither yes nor no. Silent, and with a lowered head, she walked alongside him.

He continued, "You know that bit of rough land that Soluch used to work? We'll plant watermelons on it. With the snow we've just had, I'll wager each plant will give fifteen *mans* of melons. I'll bring you the seeds. The land is rough and doesn't need to be ploughed. You can do the work yourself with your sons. I think we could have two, three thousand plants take root there. And let me tell you something, since we're going to be related. If you don't watch out, this year you could lose that very bit of land you own. Mirza Hassan, Salar Abdullah, and a few others are thinking about trying to register all the land out by the valley to themselves. I hear they've already begun the process in town. If you're not working the land, you won't be considered its owner."

Mergan raised her head. "They want to register God's Land as their own?"

Only half-seriously, Ali Genav replied, "If it were the land of God's worshippers, it would already be registered with a deed! It's as if they've found a dead horse and they're trying to steal the horseshoes off of its hooves!"

"What about the fact that we've been working on that land for the past several years?"

"No doubt you'll have to get your compensation from God himself. You simple woman! Landless people go out to these rough lands, pick a bit at it with a shovel, plant on it for a year, and then leave it in the hands of God. Very few people have chosen a plot for themselves. Usually they go once a year, plant a few seeds, and then leave the village for work. Later, they gather a small harvest off the land, and if they didn't, the wind would simply blow the seeds. That's why there's no accounting or ownership. It's constant work, planting, ploughing, harvesting, that gives someone ownership of land. Open, unused land has no owners, since there are no plots on it. No one works the land, and so the owner will be whoever has the strength to take it. Whoever speaks more cleverly, who has more in his pocket. What they're saying is that from the valley on one side of the land, to the edge of the sands of the desert, they want to plant pistachios in a field of one *farsakh* by three *farsakhs*. That's what they're dreaming of. They want to bring in a water pump and to smooth out the land there. The ministry of agriculture will give loans for these kinds of projects. In any case, what I'm saying is that to keep your plot, you need to be sure to keep working it. If possible, you should outline the borders of the plot. From what I hear, Salar Abdullah, Zabihollah, and a few others are doing the work on this. Kadkhoda Norouz also has a hand in it. They need to come to agreement with a handful of the landless here, one of them being you. I don't have high expectations of the others. People like the sons of Sanam. And like Ghodrat, the son of that thief. And a poor and motley group of others, just like them."

Mergan said, "I'll take my shovel out on the first day and go to the land. They want to register it? Ha! What about all the work we've done to pull out the thorny weeds one by one, and to smooth the land so it's like the palm of my hand? I have to feed my children during the summer from the fruits of this land."

"That's exactly what I'm saying. Soluch was the first to think of doing something with these forsaken lands. I remember seven years back, it was after he had begun to work there that others also started to as well. For example, I myself have only been planting there for two years."

They had now reached the mosque. The Molla of Zaminej was sitting on the broken wall. Ali Genav told him that the grave was ready. The Molla rose and entered the mosque. Hajj Salem had stopped his recitation and was now napping beside the casket. Moslem was awake and was playing with bits and pieces he had gathered from the floor of the mosque. Hajj Salem's head was resting on the casket. Morad was also there, standing silently by the pillar in the night-prayers niche, like a shadow. The Molla went and asked them to help raise the coffin. Morad came over. Hajj Salem jolted awake, picked himself up, and placed the tattered Qur'an of the mosque onto the bookshelf, mumbling something under his breath, something like, "There's no strength and no ability without God!"

The Molla of Zaminej looked at Ali Genav, who strode over to the casket. Hajj Salem tapped Moslem with his cane and gestured at him to help before taking one corner of the coffin in his hands. They took the coffin into the courtyard of the mosque. The front of the coffin was held by Mergan and Ali Genav, and the back was held by Moslem and Morad. The Molla of Zaminej and Hajj Salem were walking behind the coffin, praying and reciting as they walked.

The cold, silent coffin traversed the empty alleys to its grave. The cold had entered the marrow of their bones. There was no sun. The snow broke beneath their steps. Outside the village, the coldness was even sharper.

They passed the edge of a stream just before reaching the graveyard.

A cold wind was blowing. Ghodrat's father was standing over the grave leaning on his shovel, his cloak's edges flapping in the wind. Ghodrat was with him, sitting by the gravestone of Ali Genav's father. When he saw the casket, he rose and walked forward along with his father, who resembled a broken twig.

Before they reached the group, Ghodrat's father said, "We'd come to lend a hand, Ali!"

"God give you life. There wasn't much to do."

Ghodrat took Mergan's place under the coffin, and his father put a finger on its side and said, "There's no God but God himself!"

The water in the stream gave off a pleasant steam in the coldness of the dawn. The water was not very warm, but it was warm enough. They set the casket down beside the running water. The men stood around and Mergan rolled up her sleeves and the bottoms of her pants legs. Ali Genav diverted the stream with a few shovels full of dirt and stones, so as to prevent the water from the corpse-washing from going downstream to the fields. The men turned their backs and sat farther down on the banks of the stream. Mergan and Ali Genav took the corpse out of the casket and set it flat on the stones. She instructed him to fetch the half-broken jug that was submerged in the stream, which he did. Mergan began to remove the shroud and told Ali Genav that there was nothing more for him to do. He joined the other men and sat with his back to the corpse. Sitting beside the Molla, he lit a cigarette.

"Death is truth, my son!"

So as to not be outdone by Hajj Salem, the village Molla said, "And inheritance is just!"

Ali Genav half-smiled as he said, "How am I to repay you for this? Here! Have a smoke. Take one each. You, too, father of Ghodrat. What? You want one, Moslem? Here! One for you as well!"

The village Molla told Moslem, "Don't look over there, my son!"

Hajj Salem rebuked his son, "You ass! Put your head down!"

Then he looked at Molla of Zaminej and said, "What may we ask God for, Molla?"

It wasn't always necessary for Mergan to have been trained in something for her to know how to do it. It was often good enough for her to have simply seen it done once. So, there was almost nothing that she could not do. She never was afraid of working, although she had no illusions about it. She never ran from it. Her steadfastness, and her hatred for avoiding work, gave her a strength and a confidence to take on any kind of task.

To carry out the ritual of cleansing a corpse—fine! That's not a difficult job. She could also cut an umbilical cord. She had bitten off the umbilical cord of Abrau with her own teeth. The birth was unexpected, at the break of dawn. Before anyone could be roused to assist her, she had already cut the child's cord and had tied it. She did it all, from labor to birth. Now, she replaced Mother Genav's shroud and tied it. Ali Genav came over and they put the corpse back into the casket.

The Molla of Zaminej rose. Hajj Salem was helped by Moslem. They raised the casket on their shoulders again and took it to the grave. Mergan also took on the task of fitting the body in the grave. But first they had to say the funerary prayer. The men took their places behind the Molla, despite Hajj Salem's desire to do otherwise. Ali Genav didn't know how to pray, and neither did Morad. Most of them simply moved their lips while Ali Genav wagged his loosely. He was too tired and impatient to take the task to heart. Before the prayer was done, he stepped to one side. Once the prayer was over, he went toward the coffin. Mergan joined him. Mother Genav was not very heavy; in fact, she was light like hay. With two quick motions, she was brought out of the casket and placed into the grave. Mergan came out of the grave. Ali Genav picked up his shovel. Ghodrat's father also helped. Mergan, Morad, and Ghodrat all used their hands to push the dirt into the grave. It had to be filled to the surface. Hajj Salem and the Molla both withdrew from the graveside. Moslem stood at the edge of the grave looking, with his bulging eyes and an air of confusion, at the body slowly being covered. The filling of the grave was finished before anyone's forehead was covered by sweat. There was no water on hand. Mergan took the shovel from Ali Genav, filled it with snow a few times, and poured it over the grave, tapping it with the implement. Now their work was done. Ali Genav took a deep breath. A burden was taken off his shoulders. Now he could relax. He filled his lungs with the clean morning air, put his cloak on his shoulders, took his shovel, and followed the others as they left.

"May you have a long life, Ali!"

Ali Genav didn't know what the proper reply to the Molla's statement was, so he said, "May God grant you a long life as well!"

Hajj Salem added, "May God give everyone the grace of patience!"

Ali Genav nodded his head and stole a glance at Mergan, who was walking alongside the men with her head lowered. He made his way beside her and said under his breath, "It seems they want something for their prayers, no?"

Mergan said, "You need to give the Molla and Hajj Salem something each. You should probably also offer Ghodrat's father something..."

"How much for each?"

"You know best."

Ali Genav put his hand in his jacket pocket and moved over alongside the village Molla. Mergan watched as he slid a bill into his hand, before approaching Hajj Salem, who took the money but also bargained to be able to visit the baths with his son. He kept up his prayers, saying, "May God have mercy on that poor woman. She was good and God-fearing. May light always shine on her grave. No one could match her in her desire for good. I saw her many times give half of her dinner bread to others less fortunate. May she be in heaven with Fatima, the daughter of the Prophet himself!"

"God willing. God willing."

"From God's enlightened view, no good deed will be hidden, Ali. Do you know that providing for the washing of this poor creature, my Moslem, is itself a deed that will be rewarded in the hereafter, my brother? He will pray for you. I'll tell him to also pray for your deceased mother. The prayers of the innocent are always answered. This creature of mine is himself sinless, Ali dear!"

Ali Genav replied, "Very well, tomorrow morning. Both of you come to the baths tomorrow."

They entered the village. The Molla approached Ali and said, "If there's to be a mourning ceremony..."

But Ali Genav didn't listen. Hajj Salem stood on the incline beside the alley and raised his cane in salutation of Ali Genav, saying, "Until tomorrow morning, then! May you stay young and have a long and blessed life!"

He waved his cane in the air and walked away. Moslem followed his father. The Molla also changed direction. Morad said goodbye and Ghodrat's father looked at Ali Genav, who said, "You also come to the baths, and bring Ghodrat with you."

"Goodbye!"

They left. Ali Genav walked shoulder to shoulder with Mergan.

"What cheek! They expect a mourning ceremony? I'm supposed to give my daily bread to this and that person for what? So they can say a prayer? Better if they don't! What sins had that poor old woman committed for us all to want to pray for her soul?"

Mergan didn't say much. She didn't feel close to Ali Genav, even though he had now adopted an intimate tone with her. But Mergan herself didn't sense any intimacy between them.

"Now I need to take that woman to town, put her in a hospital. I'm fed up with her crying. I'll find someone and get the papers. But this damn donkey's chosen a bad time to get sick!"

They reached their alley. Mergan turned to go toward her own home, but Ali Genav blocked her way, insisting that she come to his home first.

"If nothing else, let me give you a piece of bread after all. My home is yours as well. Come, let's go see how Raghiyeh is doing."

Raghiyeh was lying in the same place. Her eyes were shut and she was moaning softly. It seemed as if she'd fallen asleep just after dawn. Mergan sat by the door and Ali Genav brought a few pieces of bread, setting them on the edge of her chador.

"Dry your mouth with these. If you want, take them to share with your children. Today, I'll take Raghiyeh to the hospital, somehow."

Raghiyeh opened her eyes and, speaking in broken breaths between her dry lips, said, "No...No...I won't go...to that place...I'll die...I'll die!"

Ali Genav growled, "Damn you. The right place for a sick person is in the hospital. What do you mean, you're dying?"

"No! Leave me here. Let me die right here under my own roof."

Not listening to his wife any longer, Ali Genav filled the pockets of his cloak and jacket with dry bread, breaking some into small pieces and putting them in his mouth. He left the house and went directly to his donkey. The animal was still shaking and its muzzle was wet from its runny nostrils. He ran his hand across the patchy, dung-stained hide of the beast. He pulled off bits of manure that were clinging to the hairs on its hips and scratched its belly with his fingernails before saddling the animal and putting its bridle on. He suddenly remembered that he still needed to take the coffin and put it in its usual place in the corner of the mosque's courtyard. But it was too late to take care of that. He had to focus on this task first. The stable door caught his eye; he took the door off its hinges and set it on the ground by the wall in the yard. He swallowed the bread he had been chewing, and he put another piece in his mouth before re-entering the house. He took his mother's old mattress outside and laid it on the stable door. He stood over Raghiyeh and said, "If you have some old sheets, best wrap them around yourself!"

Raghiyeh didn't respond. Helped by Mergan, Ali Genav began wrapping his wife with sheets. They put a blanket around her body and he told Mergan to grab her under the arms. Raghiyeh was not heavy; she, too, was as light as a strand of hay. They took her outside and lay her on the detached stable door. Ali Genav ignored his wife as she moaned. He brought some cord out from the pantry room. He led the donkey out of the stable and into the alley. He went over to Raghiyeh and wrapped the cord around her and the door, and with Mergan's help he placed her and the door onto the back of the donkey. Then they tied Raghiyeh and the door to the animal. Mergan brought out Ali's cloak and held it in her hand. He ran back into the house and then returned a moment later. He handed the house key to Mergan, adjusted his wallet in his side pocket, took the cloak from Mergan's hand, and said, "Tell Abrau to keep an eye on the water boiler. You also keep an eye on his work. If I end up staying in town tonight, you can light the water boiler and have Abrau keep an eye on it tomorrow. This evening, you and Hajer both go and use the baths. Also, tell Abrau that when Hajj Salem and his son come to use the baths tomorrow, don't ask them to pay. I won't ask anything more of you. If I don't come back tonight, you can bring Hajer and sleep here. Did you take the bread?"

"I took it."

"Good. Goodbye then. I'll take her and somehow have her hospitalized!"

Ali Genav prompted the donkey, and Mergan turned to go home.

Abbas was sitting on the edge of a ditch by the house and was washing coins in a ceramic bowl. The bowl was full of water, and the coins had settled on the bottom, although Abbas was still fingering them. Mergan passed her son and entered the house. Hajer was napping by the oven. The fire in the oven had burned to ashes. Mergan sat by the oven and set a piece of bread on the ground. Abbas entered the room, still bent over by some residue of pain. His fist was full of coins, which he was counting. It seemed as if he had counted them several times already. When he reached the oven, his knees folded and he sat down. He took some bread and broke off a piece of it with his teeth.

"I think two five-*qeran* pieces are still inside me!"

BOOK 3

1.

Abbas had taken his father's old sack, Hajer had her mother's chador, and Abrau had a bag made of bits of rags sewn together.

The two brothers walked shoulder-to-shoulder, and their sister followed behind them. They were heading to the fields. It was nearly the holiday of Nowruz—the first day of the New Year and the first day of spring—and the fields were turning green. The sun's rays were growing warmer, warming people's hearts everywhere. Feet were no longer stung by the coldness of the earth. Faces were no longer clouded over, at least not as much as they once had been. The sky was wide and open, no longer low and imposing. The days felt light, the fields and prairies seemed wider—all of which imprinted itself onto the hearts of Soluch's children. Their hearts felt brighter. It was spring's luminous return. People walked with less fear, although not fearlessly. Heads were raised higher, raised in the wind. Spring and youth! The drunken air of spring, raising heads once worn raw. Eyes no longer seemed drawn in, expectant, but were open, brighter, shining. The playful games of spring flickered in people's eyes, just as gazelles frolicked in the spring-struck fields.

Soluch's children—if only for an interlude—no longer addressed each other with anger, insinuations, or insults. Even if not precisely generous in their kindness to each other, which perhaps was impossible to expect, they were at least no longer enemies. They no longer went about their chores wearily, begrudgingly. Motivated now by something other than compulsion, their steps were marked with a hint of enthusiasm. Their hearts were lit by something new: passing out of darkness. One could perceive this feeling budding forth in their every action. Winter's ramparts were crumbling to dust beneath their feet.

"Where are we going?"

"To the grass fields!"

Abbas had answered Hajer.

Abrau asked his sister, "Do you know how to boil *bilqast*?"

"Why shouldn't I know how to?"

Abrau paid little attention to Hajer's reply, distracted by a tiny lizard with ornate skin. He wanted to be careful so as not to crush it with his meandering steps, or to injure it with his scythe. He wanted to catch it alive. Around Zaminej, when children became bored and restless enough, they'd go in a group and chase a lizard. Once they caught it, they'd pinch its head so that it would open its mouth. Then they'd place a pinch of snuff on its tongue and let it go. The lizard would move in fits and starts, eventually becoming confused and staggering in circles around itself, losing its bearings. Finally, it would lie down and roll over. Its belly would expand. At this point, the most audacious of the children would take the sharpest stone at hand and pound it on the distended belly of the poor animal, freeing whatever contents had been inside. This diversion would then be over, save for a few children who stayed around to spit on the ground before leaving.

Abrau backed away from the lizard.

"Let it go to live its own life. Why bother it? It's not in anyone's way!"

Abbas' tone was kind and brotherly.

"Want to throw stones?"

Abbas bent over and took a hand-sized stone from the ground.

"What target?"

"Over there! Next to the stream. Throw it from right here."

"What's the prize?"

Abbas hesitated.

"It's...two bunches of dates!"

"Whoever loses pays!"

"Whoever loses pays."

"Who goes first?"

"First...you."

Abrau told Hajer to stand by the edge of the stream to watch over where the stones landed. Hajer ran ahead.

"Wherever a stone lands, mark it with a stick!"

Hajer stood by the edge of the stream.

"Go ahead!"

Abrau said, "Why don't you go first. From here."

"No. You go first."

Abrau stepped forward and stretched. He put his weight on his left foot and felt the stone in his right hand before launching it. As Hajer watched, the stone landed on the banks of the stream. Hajer marked the stone by pressing a stick into the earth beside it. It was Abbas' turn now. A smooth stone from his hand, passing over Hajer's head and landing in the earth on the far side of the stream. Abrau looked at his brother. Abbas smiled broadly, showing his thick teeth. They went up toward their sister—Hajer was looking through the overgrowth for some edible plants. She found something, a kind of barley leaf. She knelt and pulled a stalk from the moist earth. Clods still clung to the roots, as they always do. The leaves were covered with a layer of dust.

Hajer took the roots in her thin fingers and shook the plant, to shake the dust from the leaves, until the stalk was clean. She was about to place the plant in her mouth when Abrau, like a baby goat, snatched the plant from Hajer's hand and put it in his own mouth. With laughter in his eyes, he brought his bugle-shaped lips together and puffed out his cheeks. He ran away and Hajer ran after him. He ran laughing and, stepping onto a mouse hole, he stumbled. Hajer landed a few light blows on her brother's shoulder—not really from anger, but simply to register her complaint. Abrau, doubled over in laughter, sat on his heels and began to cough. Half-chewed bits of the barley leaf—perhaps the roughest of all edible plants—had stuck in his windpipe. He coughed and coughed. His eyes filled with tears and all he saw was red. Hajer slapped her brother on the back and then began pounding his back with her fist. She'd learned this from Mergan. His coughing eventually stopped. Abrau lay on the ground, leaning on his elbow, laughter still in his eyes. Despite this, Hajer had to give voice to her complaint to him.

"Shame, shame on you. May it be worse than dog meat!"

Abbas called out with excitement.

"Hey! Hey! *Jigriz* plants! A whole lot of them!"

Hajer stood beside Abbas. Abrau gathered himself and ran to them. Next to the stream, in a small ditch, Abbas had found a cluster of *jigriz* plants. All three sat down. Abbas with a scythe, Abrau with a hoe, and Hajer with the broken handle of a spoon; all three scraped up and gathered bunches of *jigriz*—each bunch looking very much like a piece of goat's liver. It goes without saying that their mouths were chewing as they worked and that their lips and mouths were stained with the color of grass. Abbas' sack was half-full of the plant when he said, "Now we have to find *bilqast* as well. You can't just have *jigriz* for dinner! Let's split up and go in different directions."

"Let's go!"

They left their bags and satchels beside the stream and each went in a different direction.

The field was thinly covered with greenery. The new overgrowth was here and there more thickly woven into a shrub. The color of the growth and the color of the earth washed into each other: date-brown and green. Here and there a shrub of *bilqast*; here and there some *jigriz*. Everywhere the fragrance of fresh rain on earth. Footprints leave marks on light earth. The earth was claylike. They focused their eyes, cutting down handfuls of thorny overgrowth, gathering it inside their shirt-tails. Occasionally they would look at each other with hidden glances. Looking, searching, moving more quickly. It was a secret competition. The competition was the natural essence of the work, an essence that occasionally became apparent and naked. Most often this competition manifests itself through animosity. But not this time; this time it was hidden. The two brothers and their sister, each wanted to have the bigger harvest of greens. At least, each one wanted to have no less than any of the others.

As they began to regroup, they realized how far from each other they'd gone.

A man was sitting next to their things on the edge of the stream handling a bundle of *jigriz*. As they came closer, they recognized him—it was Karbalai Doshanbeh, Salar Abdullah's short, barrel-bodied father. Sitting where he was by the stream, he looked like a large clod of earth. Despite his being short, he was thick-boned and strong. He had a round face, a prominent forehead, a long white beard, and eyes that had not yet lost a hint of youthfulness. In both winter and summer, he wore a woolen scarf that had once been white around his old skullcap. As far back as anyone in Zaminej could recall, Karbalai Doshanbeh wore this same scarf and the same skullcap. Whether for funerals or weddings, in snow or shine. The edges of the scarf had begun to fray and the ancient pattern in its weave had taken on the hue of gray mud. On the old man's face one could see tiny red capillaries—especially on his large round nose, which seemed like it was cracked with lines and shriveled in the sun. A white weave of chest hair burst from the neck of his dirty and collarless shirt, the edge of which looked like a dark rosary hung around his neck. Despite this, his face and hands were always well scrubbed, and he never missed a prayer.

Waiting for Mergan's children to arrive, Karbalai Doshanbeh took clods of earth in his hand and crushed them between his thick, stubby fingers. When they reached him, he was still looking at the ground, which was where he usually would be found to be looking. He generally spoke little and slowly, but to great effect. The sickle and the satchel were by his hand, and he held onto a string tied around the neck of his goat, which was feeding by the stream. Mergan's children one by one greeted him, and then went to set down what they had gathered. Karbalai Doshanbeh looked up at them, and in response to their greetings said, "So you're gathering greens to eat?"

"Yes, Karbalai."

Abbas and Abrau sat on the stream's banks beside Karbalai Doshanbeh, and Hajer disappeared farther down by the water. Karbalai Doshanbeh asked about Mergan. Abbas responded, "She's somehow getting by..."

Karbalai Doshanbeh's voice carried sympathy. "That poor woman; see how she's been left without protection or direction? What news is there of your disgrace of a father?"

Abrau looked down and began playing with the dirt. Abbas replied that they had no news from him yet. Karbalai Doshanbeh said, "You need to forget about him now. Whatever stories your mother's spinning for people about Soluch sending her money... it's not as if we live in the village of the blind! If there were news, we'd hear of it ourselves, no? Mergan's playing the partridge—she hides her head under the snow and figures others can't see her. She lies... She slaps her own face to make it seem red. What about your uncle, her brother? Molla Aman? Any news from him?"

"It's been a while; we've not heard from him either."

"Before all this, whenever he passed by these parts, he'd always come to see me! Now, he never comes by. Maybe he stays away and doesn't show his face because he still needs to settle some debts he has to me? He used to work as a camel driver for me. You're too young to remember this. But that was why I lent him some money. Those days he was in love...I didn't know he'd not hold up his word! But now, I guess he doesn't intend to pay. But he'll eventually show up here one day. He can't go and hide at the ends of the earth forever. He'll have to come himself and repay his debt. But if you see him sometime, give him a message from me. Tell him that Karbalai Doshanbeh says, 'I didn't give you money to steal from me, and it's not as if I don't have the intention to reclaim it. It's time for you to come and settle our accounts!' But Mergan...Mergan's different. Poor Mergan! She's been burned. She was trapped by this son of a bitch Soluch, and he burned her. She never enjoyed her youth, and now it's come to this. Tell her, from me, that if someday she needs any money or help, let me know. I won't ask her for collateral, and I won't charge much interest. Although...I'll come by your house myself soon."

Karbalai Doshanbeh rose from the ground. Mergan's children were covered in a heavy silence, and he didn't want to stay any longer. He could see that they hadn't forgotten that it was his son who had gone to their house to demand payment of his own debts, and that he had later chased Abbas and Abrau from the cottonwood field. The impression of the old man's words on their faces had also caused him to feel uneasy. Their eyes had not lit up with hope, in the way he'd expected them to. He shook the dust from his pants front and grabbed the collar of his sheep, threw its feedbag over one shoulder, and took his grass cutter in hand, and said, "There's no worry on my part. I'll come by your house sometime!"

Mergan's children silently watched Karbalai Doshanbeh leaving, walking slowly and heavily as he went. He walked with wide strides. Everyone in the village knew he was bad-tempered.

Abbas rose and gathered the loose grass into his satchel. "How about we go to God's Land?"

Abrau said, "You want us to carry these bags on our backs all the way there and back?"

"So what should we do? We can't leave them here."

Abrau looked at Hajer. "Will you take them?"

"Why shouldn't she? Why would she want to come along to God's Land?"

"So she'll take them...You take these bags of grass and we'll go to check the water on the land. If we can, we'll plant some *farazu*."

"When we're ready to seed the field, we'll also bring you to spread the watermelon seeds! Now go and bring these bags of greens to mother to cook, and we'll be back at sundown."

They piled the greens into Hajer's satchel. Abrau leaned a knee onto the pile of greens and, with Abbas' help, took up tying the edges of the satchel. Then they placed the bundle onto Hajer's head. She stumbled a little, but held her ground, steadying her steps as she carried the load. Abbas and Abrau, relieved to know the greens were being carried home on their sister's head, threw their own bags and satchels onto their backs, picked up their grass cutter and scythe, and headed out toward God's Land.

***

God's Land was where the sands gathered together; it was a sloping, sandy piece of earth. Smooth and soft as the belly of a mare. A fallow, windy place. Uncared for, abandoned. Perhaps this was why they called it God's Land. Soluch's plot was bordered by those of Morad, of Ghodrat's father, and that of Ali Genav. To the left of God's Land, the fallow lands continued on, while to its right a stream cut into the earth. Its upper limits bordered on the Kolghar valley, below which, as far as the eye could see, was land, land, and more land. This was God's Land. But working such a barren land was not work for an impatient person. It was hard work. Until now, the land had only been good for growing watermelons. But lately, whispering voices had begun to speak of pistachio cultivation, despite the fact that Zaminej's people had no background in the planting or harvesting of pistachios. But watermelons, yes, that was something they did well.

By the time the watermelon plants bore their fruits, a dusty wind would have covered them over. So one had to be patient so as to extricate the plants, leaf by leaf, from beneath the sands. And few were the people who were willing to do this hard work. Most would just sew their seeds at the beginning of spring and would leave the plants in God's care. They'd either grow or die, and most would die under the withering wind. The plant would either be buried in the sand or would dry out. One in a hundred would survive out of sheer luck. When it was time to harvest them, a few plants would perhaps have held on, despite the winds, and bore fruits. Then it was time to wet your mouth a bit. Ripe or unripe, they'd pick the melons and leave, just happy with what they had. However, Soluch was one of the few who would go and watch over each plant carefully with a shovel in one hand.

Until the plants bore melons, Soluch was constantly and tirelessly to be found on the path between Zaminej and God's Land. After preparing the land, he would tend the plants. This was all that was needed for the melon plants of God's Land: just some earth. Otherwise, you could build a windbreak. A windbreak with earth and straw. This land neither needed a clod crusher nor to have its cracks filled so as to prevent the sun from stealing the moisture from the spaces. There was no need for irrigation either. But it required a great deal of work nonetheless. One needed to constantly check between the plants, and if nothing else, to weed the scrub grass with the tip of one's shovel. This is what Soluch did. During the summer harvest, the children were his hostages. They would follow behind Mergan, treating the plants like their babies, raising them until they bore fruit, eyes full of pleasure from each and every melon.

It was a short ways to God's Land. The distance of a few arrow shots. On the way, the boys played leapfrog, a game that lent itself to running, jumping. One would lean over and the other would leap over his back, and then run four or five steps before leaning over so the first could leap over him. It was exciting tying up the feet of the players with the skill and agility involved, sending them into peals of laughter that made the distance seem shorter.

Playing a trick, Abbas leaned over but then suddenly leapt ahead, throwing himself on his belly like a lizard. Abrau came racing behind him expecting to leapfrog over his back, but he couldn't slow his footsteps once Abbas slipped out from under him. Stumbling, he fell and tumbled and rolled, with a bitter laugh and a wounded look in his eyes. Abbas doubled over himself with laughter, holding his sides with his hands. Abrau brushed the dust from his head and face and began walking away. Abbas chased him and caught up, saying, "Are you upset?"

"No! But you're nothing but a spoilsport."

Abbas picked up laughing again, saying, "Ali Genav's found me some work. Herding camels for his father's cousin."

Abbas replied, "Ali Genav? He keeps hanging around our house. He feels sorry for us ever since our father's left us... Do you think our father will ever return?"

"Let him go to hell! If he wants to, he can come back. Otherwise, he can stay away. What good was he when he was here, and what have we lost since he's gone?"

"At least he used to be here."

"It's better he's not here now! All he gave us was dry bread and beatings. Now we just have dry bread. What more could he do for us?"

"But at least he was our father. Just his shadow was a good thing for us."

"There are kids without fathers everywhere. It's not as if we're the first ones. And now we've picked ourselves up from the dirt ourselves—we can pay for our own bread. We're not going to starve."

"There's more than bread and being hungry, though. It hurts—just the way people look at us as orphans. Didn't you notice how Karbalai Doshanbeh treated us, the bastard?"

"It wouldn't be any different if Soluch were here!"

"In any case, I miss him sometimes."

"I don't."

"He used to take me to God's Land with him."

"He would take me to dig wells."

"In the spring, he'd prepare the soil and I'd plant the seeds."

"I'd wait at the top by the well wheel, and he'd go down into the well. He'd fill the bucket with dirt and I'd pull it up."

"Sometimes, just before he left, I'd prepare the clay for a bread oven he was working on. He told me I had good hands for spreading clay."

Abbas became angry. "Okay, that's enough reminiscing; if he wants to disappear on the other side of the world, let him!"

God's Land was covered with dark streaks of gravel that followed along the stretches of snow still unmelted. Abbas leapt up from the side of the stream and ended their conversation. They were on their own land. They left their sacks beside the stream and Abrau picked up the hoe. Abbas pointed to one spot of land and they walked over to it. They both busied themselves digging at the wet earth. The top layer of soil was muddy and stuck to their hands. The next layer was less so, and farther down, the soil only bore the darkened hue of moisture. Abbas rolled the cuff of his trousers up to his knees and stepped into the hole he had just dug. The hole was as deep as the top of his knee. The soil was such that it held the moisture, and a watermelon plant could easily spread its roots into it.

Abrau said, "Shall we dig somewhere else?"

"You're so confused all the time! In this kind of soil you don't have to dig in different places. It's not like those places where you have to see how deep the moisture is where the rain collects, and how deep it is elsewhere. This soil is sandy—if you don't believe me, go dig by the edge of the gravel there. It's not level ground, so the water won't gather there itself. But I'll bet you it's even more moist than over here, since its soil is softer."

From the wilderness beyond the gravel, Sanam's son, Morad, was approaching. He had a bundle of kindling on his back and with each step sank ankle-deep in the wet earth as he went, leaving a path of deep footsteps behind him. As soon as he noticed the brothers, he changed course and began walking toward them.

"Hey there!"

Morad set his bundle of kindling against the steep embankment of the stream.

The brothers headed toward him. Morad loosened the binding that held the bundle on his back, releasing it. "The reeds are all moist, damn them! They're heavy. I'm exhausted just trying to walk in this soil. I'm knee-deep in the mud. See how I'm covered in sweat!"

It was true. His entire back and the area under each arm was drenched in sweat. He took the edge of his shirt and wiped the sweat from his brow and ears. He sat back, leaning on the bank of the stream, and shut his eyes. Sweat had dripped into his eyes, which were now red and burning. Morad opened an eye and asked, "You were checking the moisture of the soil, no?"

"Yeah...that's right. What about you? Aren't you planning to plant this year?"

"Not me. But my brother won't give up. As for me, I'm not willing to throw myself on the bull's horns just for a handful of soil."

Abbas did not pick up on what Morad was referring to, so he asked, "What bull's horns?"

"They're registering all of this land. Mirza Hassan's leading them. Salar Abdullah and Kadkhoda Norouz and Zabihollah are all working together. They're talking about getting a tractor and a water pump. In addition to God's Land and Kalqar Valley, they've got designs on the fields of Bandsar as well. Salar Abdullah himself was at our house on Friday. But my brother won't accept their offer, even though my mother's knees went weak as soon as she heard the sounds of a few coins jingling. Although, if I know my brother, he'll eventually give in. Salar Abdullah will put an end to his indecision with a couple of red bills."

"Is Salar Abdullah laying claim to other people's property? That's theft, isn't it?"

Morad replied, "He doesn't recognize the land as belonging to other people. That's why it's called what it is—God's Land!"

"So what if it's called that? Right now, it's in the hands of God's servants."

"Salar claims that he'll make the land productive."

"Ha! Make it productive! So what are we doing, then? Ruining it?"

"What do I know?"

"So what is everyone else doing about this? What about Ghodrat's father, the others?"

"They're going to buy them all off one by one. They're giving them promises and presents."

Abbas' eye shone. "You mean they're handing out cash?"

"Maybe, I'm not sure."

Abbas was silent. It was clear he was trying to determine what the most profitable approach to the issue was. Morad leaned back on his bundle. Abrau raised his head and said, "What about you, Morad? What are you thinking of doing?"

"I'm leaving. I've never really cared about this place. So I want to go somewhere where I know that when I work from morning to night, I'll be paid that night for my work. I went to Gonbad last year. The year before, to Varamin. This year, if I have to, I'll go as far as Ahvaz even. Wherever my heart is happy. What about you? Are you sticking around?"

"We don't know!"

Morad shifted the bundle and began to tie the rope around his chest again. "I hear that Ali Genav's doing a favor for you."

It was clear what he was implying from the tone of his voice. Abbas said, "You mean shepherding his cousin's camels? That's not been settled yet."

"I suspect you'll settle it soon. It's not a permanent job; after a short while, they'll be sent for sale and you'll tie them all in a line and off they go!"

Abbas said, "Maybe he wants to graze them over the spring as well?"

"What an idea! I guess some people are so naïve they should never leave their homes, my brother! I really love these new foreign tractors though. Sardar Abdullah will have no choice but to get rid of his camels. It's not because he wants to. And you think you can make a living with people like this around, running things as they do...? So, are you guys staying here?"

"No. We'll come too."

Morad straightened his back beneath the kindling. The brothers took their bags and tools and headed out, walking alongside Morad.

"Many of the others are leaving too. Ghodrat's coming with me. We'll go work for six months and then spend the winter relaxing by the hearth. We'll take it easy. If we were to stay here, we'd never even be able to save up ten *tomans*. But what I'm surprised by is why you're not coming?"

Abbas replied, "We have our own problems, brother!"

"And no one else does?"

Abrau asked, "Morad, have you been in a car until now?"

"How could I not have been? How do you think I've been to all these places? It's no big deal!"

Abrau remained silent. Abbas said, "If it's really heavy, set down that bundle and I can help you take it."

Morad said, "What's difficult isn't the weight of this bundle; it's that in this place there's no value for the work you do. This kindling is one thing, because at least my mother will be able to heat up bread in the oven with it. But other work is useless. Outside, I can work for sixteen hours a day if I know I'll be paid my due. You need to have a purpose for your work. By the way...I hear you're going to be marrying off Hajer?"

Abbas and Abrau said nothing. They had no answer to Morad's question. Morad didn't push the matter any further.

When they reached the ramshackle homes of Zaminej, Morad said, "If you were to just wait a little while longer, you'd probably find a husband for Hajer who doesn't have another wife! Goodbye."

"Goodbye!"

Morad altered his course toward a path beside a fallow field toward his home, while the brothers continued along the high ridge along a ditch. Before they were very far from each other, Morad made a turn beneath his load and said in a half-audible voice, "In any case...if you wanted to leave...it's better if we all went together."

Abbas took the hoe in his hand and waved it. "Okay...We'll let you know."

Then they headed away down the slope of the ditch.

By the time the brothers reached Zaminej, the evening air brought a soothing cool with it. It was for a good reason that for the first month of spring, many of those who could afford to would not leave their places beside the hearth. Abrau held his sack tight against his back, raised his shoulders a little, and said to Abbas, "What do you say we should do? As the weather gets warmer, Ali Genav's bath will become less busy. I don't expect I'll really have a reason to keep working there over the summer. Even now I think he's keeping me there just out of politeness. He's in a bind; his wife's still unwell. But just as soon as he sorts things out, he'll get rid of me. And it's not as if I'm really earning much there. So if you want my opinion, I think we should join the others, going wherever they go. Something might come of it, no?"

Abbas said, "There's plenty of time now. If things don't go well, if we don't join this group, we will just go with the next one. It's not as if the roads will be closed!"

Abrau began to try to convince his brother with another line of reasoning, but in vain. They approached Salar Abdullah's son, who was leaning against a wall. He eyed the two brothers as they came, walked over, and blocked Abbas' path. "So what's happened to my money?"

"What money?"

"The money you took from me in your stables and swallowed. Why is it everytime you see me you head in the opposite direction? You think you're dealing with a bunch of blind fools?"

"So, you yourself say I swallowed it, and I did. So go where I've left it now and take it back! When you swallow something, where does it end up?"

Abbas said this and moved on. Abrau followed behind him. Salar Abdullah's son shouted at them as they left, "I'll tear those coins out of your throat!"

Abbas didn't reply, muttering, "One hundred *tomans* wouldn't be enough to pay me for what I went through! And now he wants to raise the dead!"

Salar's son continued, "I'll make you give birth to that money!"

Abbas answered, "If you do that, be sure to cut its umbilical cord!"

"You son of a bastard dog!"

Abbas turned into the safety of their home's doorway before answering, "The bastard's you, with your seven shit bastard ancestors!"

Mergan stuck her head out of the door of the house, saying, "Now, who is it this time? Why don't you let me be calm for just a minute, you?"

Not answering his mother, Abbas looked at the saddle pack set against the edge of the wall, paused a moment, and asked, "Who's here?"

"Your uncle!"

"What?"

It didn't matter who or what their maternal uncle was, but his appearance excited the boys. They ran into the house. Molla Aman was sitting at the far end of the room, leaning against a pile of bedding. He was sitting on one knee—as was his habit—and had his large boney hand on his kneecap. His wrists were loose and his fingers were each like the claws of a crane, hanging down over his knee. His large, wide nose and its well-shaped arching tip cast a shadow over half of his face. The sight of his nephews brought a smile to his penetrating eyes. He shifted a little and stretched his hands, like a crane's wings, out to the boys. They threw themselves into the embrace of their Uncle Aman as he kissed each of their faces and set them beside one another against the edge of the wall. Jokingly, he asked how they were, saying, "I'd have expected you to have grown beards by now!"

Suddenly, Abbas and Abrau realized that Ali Genav was in the room as well. They noticed their mother, as well as the absence of Hajer. Abbas realized what was going on.

Ali Genav finished the cup of tea, took the edges of his cloak in hand, and rose, saying, "So we're agreed. We'll go to the town on the seventh day of the new year."

Mergan said, "God willing. I still have to whitewash five or six other houses, but once I'm done with that, I'll have less to worry about."

"God willing!"

Molla Aman also rose. "May you be blessed."

Before Ali Genav set a foot outside the door, he turned to Abbas and said, "I've also discussed your work with my uncle. From tomorrow on, you can take the camels out to graze in the fields."

Molla Aman exited with Ali Genav, then returned to the door, stooped to enter, and said, "He's a good provider. And that wife of his is now useless. So this is all for the best! May God bring good for everyone."

Abrau noticed that the tip of his uncle's hat scraped against the ceiling of the room. Aman said, "So that's that. You can come out now, our bride-to-be! Come out, Hajer!"

Molla Aman wasn't concerned about what Hajer did or whether she came out; he was just speaking for the sake of it. It signaled the end of the ritual. He sat in his place and slid the empty teacup toward his sister Mergan, while saying to Abbas, "If you have any money to wager, go get your pieces and gather up a group to play. Get going! I've not had a game in Zaminej for over a year!"

Mergan filled the cup and placed it before her brother. Abbas rose quickly and selected a set of *bajal* pieces from his collection. Abrau drew himself into the shadows and leaned his head against the corner of the wall. As Abbas reached the side of the chest, he said, "Karbalai Doshanbeh was asking about you, Uncle!"

Molla Aman answered, just as the sound of his donkey braying rose from the stable outside. "He can go to hell! He thinks money can be skimmed off the top of water! Does he want me to go present myself to him and set a pile of bills before him just to pay the interest of his money? This time, if

God helps me, I'm thinking I'll just swallow the loan and its interest all at once. Go bring the pieces, now!"

Abbas brought his box of *bajal* pieces over and his uncle busied himself with setting up the game. Mergan was worried about her daughter, and she went to the pantry. She sat facing Hajer, who had stuffed the edge of the drape into her mouth to silence herself.

The pantry was dark, blacker than night.

2.

Everyone had work to do.

Abrau rose at dawn and went to the baths. Molla Aman had brought his small donkey to graze out by the door of the stables. Abbas was busy wrapping up his feet. Mergan had placed the tin cans and other bits and pieces she used in her whitewashing work in one corner and was waiting for everyone else to leave. Mergan was responsible for sending each of the others off first, and only then would leave herself. With the New Year came new work for Mergan: whitewashing houses.

Abbas was still running circles around himself and asking for things from Hajer from time to time—thread, a safety pin, a handkerchief and...In response, Hajer poked around in this hole or that one like an innocent kitten. As was usual, she went about her work without a word. Molla Aman entered the house and went to take the sack holding all his possessions outside. Hajer and Abbas helped him. Mergan took the bridle of his donkey and pulled the animal over to the doorway. They brought out the sack and loaded it on the donkey. As he was about to leave, Molla Aman put one hand into the sack and pulled out a handful of candy and wrapped it into the edge of Hajer's scarf.

"And these sweets are for your wedding!"

Mergan asked her brother, "Will your path bring you this way again?"

"Certainly, of course, I'll come again. If God wills it, the next time I may even bring Soluch back with me. People I know say that they saw someone who fits his description over near Shahrud. They've been building a factory there for the past year. And there are coalmines in the hills above Shahrud. Not just one, but several. Perhaps he's gone there to find work! In any case, wherever he is, I'm sure he'll eventually send word to you."

"If he had plans to return, he'd never have left!"

Mergan turned to Abbas and said, "No need for you to spread your pearls of wisdom here! Get back to your work! Your father's walking stick is over there—go take it and get on your way. Are you planning to wait till noon to take the camels out to graze?"

The Sardar was to provide bread for him to eat that day. Ali Genav had made the arrangements from before. Abbas took the walking stick from the house and prepared to leave. Hajer and Mergan stood beside him. Molla Aman embraced his sister and her children. Abbas stood beside the donkey, squeezing his hand around the walking stick. Molla Aman leaned over and kissed Abbas on the cheeks.

"You weren't bad gambling last night. Let's see how you do as a camel herder? And look at that amazing tuft of hair on the top of his head...aah!"

"Why 'aah!' Molla Aman? Are you just a fly-by-night friend? You don't want to stay in touch? Now you're just a stranger? You've forgotten all about us!"

It was Karbalai Doshanbeh. The news had reached him and he'd appeared like a genie. Trying to keep his wits in the presence of the man who he was in debt to, Molla Aman replied calmly, "So busy, no time, Karbalai! Running around looking for a bit of bread, I can't keep track of my days or nights. I'm taking some goods to sell in the villages near here. I was planning to come to visit you as soon as I'd turned a profit from these goods. In your kindness, you'll surely forgive a late visit from your former camel driver!"

Karbalai Doshanbeh straightened his bent neck, looked Molla Aman up and down, and said, "Looks like you're growing taller day by day! Where are you going up there? Are you planning...to reach the heavens! Either that or I'm getting closer to the earth each day?"

"Karbalai, I've just lost weight, so I look like I've gotten taller."

"Hmm...How can someone of your height and size come to Zaminej and escape the notice of my blind eyes?"

"Actually, I've hardly been here, Karbalai."

"Hmm...so you don't come from time to time? Then come more often!"

"Of course, Karbalai. Of course. But with your permission, I'll be on my way then?"

"Yes, of course. Let the roads be open and the paths be clear for you!"

Molla Aman entered the alleyway, while continuing to joke, and called his donkey. Karbalai Doshanbeh shot a quick glance at Mergan and stepped over to Molla Aman.

"Still no news from that worthless man Soluch?"

"I have some news, Karbalai."

Abbas was leading his uncle's donkey. Molla Aman turned to look back at Mergan and Hajer, who were standing by the wall looking at him. In the early morning sunshine, Molla Aman's shadow filled the alley. Next to Molla Aman, Karbalai Doshanbeh seemed tiny. Mergan could no longer hear the conversation between the two men. But it passed without incident; her heart began to calm.

"So go in peace, uncle. God speed. And hopefully you'll be back to visit us soon."

"God willing, I will."

Ali Genav approached, shook hands with Molla Aman, and kissed him on the cheeks. It was as if he could smell what was happening with Soluch's family from the distance of his home. Molla Aman rode his donkey away from Ali Genav, a smile still on his face. Ali Genav looked back at Soluch's house. As soon as she saw him, Hajer ran into the house, but Mergan remained out by the wall. Ali Genav approached Mergan, who slowly stepped into the yard. He followed her inside and, while looking around for Hajer, greeted Mergan. She replied, "She's just shy. Remember, she's still just a girl! But come into the house."

Hajer was nowhere to be found. Mergan sized up her work materials and, while looking at Ali Genav, asked, "So, girl, where are my shoes?"

There was no answer. Ali Genav asked, "Where are you working today?"

"Zabihollah's house. Karbalai Doshanbeh's nephew."

"It seems you've worked on the houses of quite a few people this year!"

"Not everyone's house. But anyone who has a bit of extra to go around can afford to spend a few *tomans* to whitewash their house."

Ali Genav looked around the smoke-stained ceiling and walls of Mergan's house and said, "You should do a quick run over this house as well."

"God willing. Once I'm done with all the other work."

Eventually, Hajer brought the sack of supplies from the pantry and set it beside her mother. Hajer's movements and her eyes were marked by fear. She acted anxious. With just a little attention, anyone could discern the torment she was suffering. Only Ali Genav didn't notice this. Not because he was in love with her, but rather out of greed. His greed to conquer her. So he could not see Hajer as she was, however she was feeling. He could only imagine her in his bed. Just as a vulture must see a dead animal. With his eyes, he was devouring the girl and Hajer had no idea of how to hold out. Her innocence and fear were one thing, but her ignorance also made her defenseless. She felt so confounded that she couldn't even move. She was paralyzed and could only bite her nails.

But Mergan was different. Although she perceived the minutiae of her daughter's state of mind deep in the recesses of her consciousness, she actively tried to ignore anything disturbing about the situation. All of this, the nervousness of a girl before the man she is betrothed to, seemed normal. It's possible to say that this was even based on a principle; otherwise, questions would have arisen. Because even if a girl consents to enter the home of a man, chaste behavior—although more as a performance—would have to be expected. And even if she has not consented to the marriage, as soon as her foot crosses his threshold, this kind of behavior would have to be quickly forgotten. At that point, the bride has no choice. So Hajer's anxiety may have troubled Mergan's heart, but it was not unexpected. And it would have to end in one way: as soon as she entered the bedroom, she'd have to give up her opposition. Hajer and Ali Genav were now technically betrothed to one another, and Mergan, in her role as a mother-in-law-to-be, found that she enjoyed it. She wanted to experiment with this pleasant feeling inside her, so she left the room.

Hajer and Ali Genav were alone. Hajer, frightened, stayed right where she was, standing against the wall. Then, desperate to escape, her fear was transformed into terror. She moved as if to hide herself in the pantry, but then froze again. Ali Genav laughed. The piece of bread in his mouth was dry. He didn't know what to do or what to say. Just as Hajer had been frozen with terror, Ali Genav was frozen with excitement. He was speechless and felt self-conscious. He wished he knew what to say, even just a few words. If only he hadn't lost his power to speak. But at this point, only his body was able to react, like an arrow set taught in a bow. It had to be released; it couldn't be kept this way forever.

At that moment, more than anything, Hajer wanted to escape from the house. She had to make it to the alley. She leapt away. But Ali Genav caught the girl in midair and dragged her to the wall, as if he intended to hide her somewhere. He may have wanted a kiss from her, but Hajer fluttered like a bird in his arms. She didn't make a sound, she only flapped and fluttered. It was as if her lips had been sealed with wax. Ali Genav also said nothing. He just held the girl within his coarse hands. He had not even noticed that he had lifted Hajer off the ground and was holding her against the wall, so much so that her feet were kicking in the air.

Mergan coughed. She had not gone far and was only sitting just outside the door. No doubt she wanted to break the ice between her daughter and her groom-to-be. In any case, with hearing Mergan's cough, Ali Genav's hands weakened and Hajer crumbled in the corner, breaking into fits of sobs. He felt as if his entire body was covered with sweat. He wiped his forehead with the edge of his robe and lowered his face, walking out just as Mergan stepped into the room.

Mergan acted as if nothing had happened. But she sensed that the girl could not accept her silence. Hajer had not yet reached that stage of maturity where a daughter can share an unspoken language with her mother. Between a mature daughter and her mother there are always things that are communicated and understood without recourse to words. However, although Mergan could have played the role of such a mother, Hajer was not yet ready to be such a daughter. She cried and complained to her mother with a tinge of fear still in her eyes and voice, "He...grabbed me...all of a sudden he grabbed me! He almost broke my arm!"

Mergan sat beside her daughter softly and tenderly.

"Ali Genav will marry you, my dear. In a short while, he'll be your husband. It's sanctioned for him. His name is upon you. You shouldn't be frightened by him. You have to get used to each other!"

"I'm scared! He scares me. I'm so frightened!"

Mergan stroked the locks of her daughter's hair, saying, "There's nothing to be frightened of, my girl. What's to be scared of? All girls marry; all men marry. So what's to be scared of?"

Hager, between seemingly endless sobs, said, "He's rough, too rough. He'll crush me under his hands and feet."

"You'll get used to him, dear. There's nothing wrong with a man being rough! A man needs to have thick bones. If not, that's bad!"

"I'm scared. I'm so scared!"

"It's just the beginning; it'll get better. You'll get used to it!"

"No! I won't. I'm scared to be his wife. I won't do it!"

"That's enough, you little mouse! Do you want to be stuck next to me forever? How many times do you think good luck knocks on one person's door? Don't cry an ocean for me. It's not for you to say what you want or don't want, do you understand?! It's not for you to choose. Do you want to wait for a prince on his horse to come for you from around the mountain? Here you have a man...at least he has all his bones in place. He has bread in the oven. He doesn't need anyone. He has work and, knock on wood, he's not without a sense of honor. And what else? You saw, even your uncle approves of him!"

Mergan's voice slowly became firmer. Hajer was trembling. Ever since Soluch had gone, Mergan had not scolded Hajer like this. Hajer began pleading, "Don't give me to Ali Genav, mother!"

"So whom am I supposed to give you to? Don't tell me you fancy that starving fool Morad, Sanam's son!"

"No, I swear!"

"So what then?"

"Just wait one or two years... Why can't we wait a little?"

"One or two years?! How am I supposed to feed you until then? You think your father's left you a nice inheritance? Can't you see how hard I work, and I can't even give you a full meal to fill your belly?"

"So...so...is that my fault? What I am to do?"

"Your fault is that you don't listen. You just make up your own mind. You're nothing special! I saw with my own eyes that they wed an eight-year-old girl to Karbalai Ghollam Sarban. She was eight then, and she's had six children since then. And she wasn't even as tall as your shoulder then."

Hajer said with difficulty, "You just want to get rid of me, otherwise..."

"Otherwise what? I should make you into a crown and put you on my head?"

"No! But I...I'm...I've not become...!"

"Become what? Girls are of age when they are nine. You're of age. You're almost thirteen now. So what's wrong with you? You've got such a good husband, where will you find someone better?"

"But...he has a wife!"

"A wife! That woman's on her last legs. She can't be a real wife! Haven't you seen her? She's just skin and bones. It's like the poor thing is speaking from the grave. She's shrunk in half since they took her to the hospital that day. Anyway, what was she before that? A storehouse of misery! When was Raghiyeh ever healthy?"

Hajer suddenly leapt up, screaming at the top of her voice, "Are you going to force me? I don't want to... I don't want to get married at all!"

"You don't want to? You little shrew, you don't take to kind words do you? I'll teach you to then!"

Mergan leapt up like a madwoman and threw herself on her daughter, grabbed her hair in one hand, and without hesitation made a fist of the other, raining blows on her head and body. Her fury had removed any sense of restraint, and she did not pause for a moment to consider what she was doing. She just kept hitting. The girl was almost unconscious when Mergan rose and released her, sat to one side, and began hitting herself with her fists instead, cursing herself until her sobs mixed with Hajer's. The girl was lying fixed to her spot on the ground, crying from pain. Mergan looked at her daughter and her heart felt as if it was torn open. She could do nothing but wail. It was as if she was mourning for her daughter. She didn't know what she could do to make up for what she had just done. There must be something she could do, but she could think of nothing but to beat and curse herself until she was exhausted. Mergan's wailing made Hajer aware of her mother, and she looked at her. Mergan's eyes were drenched in tears. Hajer dragged her battered body toward her mother, and Mergan embraced her daughter, pressing her head to her bosom. She moaned in unison with her daughter. "I wish I would die..."

Her sobbing prevented her from finishing the sentence. Hajer pleaded with her, "Don't cry, please. Whatever you want. Just don't cry, mother."

A short while later, the sound of footsteps separated the two of them—it was Morad. He stood by the door and said, "I'm looking for Abbas!"

"Abbas went to tend the camels."

Morad replied, "We're heading out—a group of us have decided go to Gonbad together this year. I wanted to let Abbas know that if he wants to join us, he should come to our house tomorrow night. The others will come there too..."

Mergan said nothing. Something was caught in her throat. Morad turned on his heel and left. Mergan looked at her daughter; Hajer had hidden in a corner. Mergan rose, took the sacks and tools from beside the wall, and stepped outside before saying to Hajer, "Let's get going to work; it's well past breakfast..."

**

This day's work would be whitewashing the dining room of Zabihollah's home. The first task was to brush the walls clean.

Mergan busied herself with the task. She removed her evening chador, tied her headscarf, and took the broom from Hajer, who brought it over for her and began brushing from the doorframe. With every brush, an area of dust was wiped clean from the wall, settling instead on the ground. As always, Mergan was focused on her work. She carried out her work with the mastery of a sculptor molding clay. This was not only because she needed the work, but also because her own nature allowed her to master any task quickly. For this reason, she slowly came to take on all sorts of odd jobs that needed doing in Zaminej:

"Mergan dear, could you come and repair our walls..."

"Mergan dear, there's a mourning wake at our house. My mother wants you to come and help pour tea for the visitors."

"Mergan dear, my brother's wedding..."

"Mergan dear, my father's funeral..."

"Mergan dear, could you come to our house to help clean our blankets..."

"Mergan dear, could you bring a jug of water for the circumcision ceremony..."

"Mergan dear..."

Slowly, Mergan had begun to take on the role of everyone's wife, everyone's sister. When she busied herself with her work, her face took on such a focus that invariably her employer was compelled to respect and even fear her. It would be impossible for someone else to be her master while she worked, and she would never allow it. Some women, it's true, were inclined to view Mergan as an indentured servant—women like Moslemeh. But Mergan would hardly countenance such sentiments, and much less so now than ever before. Although she could be good-natured, it was impossible to mistake it for obsequiousness. Mergan's passion in her work was not a sign of her wish to please her employer, but came from her desire to master the task at hand. Mergan had come to learn that if she approached her work without passion or determination, she would be overwhelmed and defeated by it. So she tackled each task with an open heart. The nature of any work is that it can break you down, eventually destroy you. But it's you who must resist, hold your own ground. And Mergan would not accept seeing herself as in servitude, or as abject before her work. She tackled and uprooted each task before her.

"Girl, go bring me the water sack and the gunny sack!"

Hajer took the broom from her mother and went to bring what her mother had asked for. Mergan loosened her head-scarf, stuck her head out the doorway, and spit out the dust that had collected in her mouth and throat. A coating of dust had settled on her eyelashes, eyebrows, and the band of her hair not covered by the headscarf. Dirt marked an outline on her teeth and caked around her nostrils. She felt as if her throat was tightening. She shouted, "Hajer...! Have you gone to bring the water from the Zamzam Spring in Mecca?"

The girl was dragging the water sack with both hands with difficulty. Mergan stepped outside and took the water sack from her daughter and brought it into the room. First, she plunged her hands into the water and brought up handfuls of the liquid, sprinkling it into the air. Slowly, the dust subsided. Then she used a cup to sprinkle water on the walls and roof of the room. Hajer also did the same, but her work did not meet Mergan's standards. So she took the cup from her daughter's hand and continued to splash water on the ceiling. While dissolving the remaining grime from the walls and ceiling, the water also prepared the surfaces for whitewashing, as wet surfaces were better suited for the application of the whitewash.

Zahra, the bitter homebody sister of Zabihollah, brought out a pot of tea, glared at Mergan, and said, "If you've not had a cup of tea in the morning, have one now!"

Mergan splashed the last cup of water at a dry spot on the wall.

"I had tea this morning, but put the teapot and cups on the ground by the wall. We'll have some more!"

Zahra put the cups and kettle down, grumbled under her breath, turned her thick buttocks around, and left the room.

Mergan looked at her daughter.

"What an oven of jealousy! She's so envious she's about to explode. She'd even be jealous of a desert bramble bush. Since she's so beautiful!"

Hajer asked, "Shall I wet the clay?"

"Not now. Let's have some tea first and let her stew over it. We'll do it later!"

They arranged the cups and sat down. They drank cup after cup. Each sip was accompanied by a disparagement of Zahra, and each insult was accompanied by the sound of Mergan's guffawing laughter. Mergan sensed that with each cup she was pricking Zahra's heart with a pin. In the end, Zahra couldn't hold back and she poked her head into the room.

"Not done having tea yet, are you?"

Mergan said, "Come and take this all away! There's a bit of tea left in the bottom of the teapot. Take a cup and have some yourself!"

Zahra took away the teapot and cups, grumbling, "As if they'd just escaped a famine!"

Mergan imitated her mockingly, saying to herself, "I hope you die from jealousy!"

Hajer rarely saw her mother so happy. She attributed this joy to the success of her work, and to the fact that during the New Year's season Mergan's prosperity meant that she had become accustomed to the sound of coins and the color of bills. Hajer had not thought that the blood of youth could still course through her mother's veins. Although Mergan appeared old and broken, inside she was not. Women of Mergan's age, those who did not have the worries and problems that she had, are usually just reaching the heights of their womanhood. But alas, some are destined to age more quickly than others; Mergan was one of these. But one should not expect that in these cases, the vestiges of youth are completely erased. No, youth remains, if only hidden. Like something that is shameful, hidden in the far corners of the soul. It does not show itself, yet nevertheless it remains. It remains, wound up tightly inside, and given an opportunity or a momentary respite, it may show itself in the light of day. It waits, and if by chance the veil of age falls from one's grim face, so does youth make a move and tear its own veil off without hesitation. Youth will not accept depression or anxiety; instead, it riots, crushing and destroying everything around it. It smashes all the walls that have risen around the soul, obliterating every barrier!

Perhaps it was because of this that Mergan, as she moved around and between her tasks, snapped her fingers in rhythms, strode around in characters, and like a blushing new bride, told jokes to Hajer. This may also explain why Mergan sang while she worked, calling out romantic lyrics to different songs without a second thought. Does love have to be evident and apparent for one to have the right to be called "in love"? Sometimes love is hidden, but it also still remains. It remains because it has not truly gone. What is love, after all? Is it only that which is evident? No, in fact, if love is evident, it is not truly love. When evident, it becomes knowledge, wisdom. Love, one might say, is actually only evident when it is not. It's not apparent but it can be discerned. It riles... overturns... leads to dancing and clapping. It brings tears... beats... runs. It drives the love-maddened lover into the desert!

At times, one may be love personified. One may personify love just by being. By coming and going, by looking at the world. Love can be in one's hands and heart, boil in you, without allowing you to recognize its footprints. Without your understanding where it entered into you, how it grew within you. At times, it's better not to know. Perhaps you would want to know, yet also don't want to, or can't know. Sometimes love is simply that washed-out memory of Soluch and your mud-covered hands as you whitewash the walls. Perhaps love is Mergan herself! Love is evident and hidden at once. At times it excites; at times its pain throws you into a well.

So, is it Soluch? Is he the well that Mergan's been thrown into? Where is Soluch? It's the New Year, the holiday. It's that time when people of all kinds and classes drag themselves back to their homes, sitting around the tablecloth and, with whatever means are available to them, making an effort to enjoy one moment as special and different from the rest of the year. And where's Soluch? Where could he be? In the foothills of Shahrud? What could he be doing in a coalmine?

Is Soluch in the mines of Shahrud?

Mergan knew her brother all too well. Molla Aman could tell a hundred stories without your knowing which of them was untrue. Could it be that he'd make up a lie to comfort Mergan? His own nature was that he couldn't thrive in an air of gloom or depression. Perhaps he didn't want to spend even one night at his sister's side commiserating and cradling her sorrow in vain. Maybe he only hoped to bring some fresh air into their dark, silent home.

But where is Soluch now?

"Ah, Madam Mergan, how are you?"

It was Karbalai Doshanbeh, Zahra's and Zabihollah's uncle. He filled the doorway with his stocky, short frame, holding himself up with a hand against the wall. He held a lamb's collar in one hand, while his self-satisfied smile brought creases to the edges of his eyes. Mergan recognized his voice and without turning—and not because she couldn't—greeted him back. He stepped into the room and placed his hands behind his lower back and looked at the walls and ceiling.

"It's truly the work of a genius! Never before have I seen a woman capable of this kind of hard work. Bravo...! May my neck break for having broken my own woman like a piece of glassware...Bravo, Mergan!"

The sound of Karbalai Doshanbeh was soft and melodious, with an edge of sarcasm mixed with his perpetual self-satisfaction. In the resonance of his words a kind of presumption rang out, and that was the superiority of Karbalai Doshanbeh and his family. He had a kind of tribal chauvinism, and so did all the members of his family. Even if hunger were to bring them to their last breath, still the arrogant echo would remain which, in and of itself, mocked and ridiculed all others. This was the case with all of them, both woman and man. They were demanding, insulting. It was as if each of them had hung a veil of arrogance on their faces beforehand, so that all of their deeds and sayings would be marked by it.

Mergan was well acquainted with Karbalai Doshanbeh's nature and disposition. So even when she was the subject of his admiration and esteem, she could not help but sense the poisonous barbs that effortlessly dripped from his tongue and that were wrapped into every word. But she didn't care. As far as Mergan was concerned, all this was old and unremarkable.

Mergan imagined herself as a hedgehog that as soon as it senses an attack turns into a ball made up entirely of sharp needles. No animal is able to penetrate its defense. Mergan was thus made up of several different personas, and whenever needed, a different one would appear and face the world. At this moment, Mergan was a hedgehog. And none of the other personas wanted to give any notice to Karbalai Doshanbeh, saying to herself, "He can go to hell! I'm working, earning a wage!"

But Karbalai Doshanbeh was not dissuaded. "I've heard the happy news that you're giving your daughter's hand in marriage?"

"Oh...we'll see what God wants."

"God only wants good. If the deed is good, God will place no obstacle before you. And praise Him, she's really grown up!"

"It's in your kind eyes, Karbalai. Hajer is like your own servant."

Karbalai Doshanbeh turned and made a semi-circle, looking for a spot to sit down. There was nowhere to sit but in the doorway. He lifted the hem of his cloak and sat on the ground, set a shoulder against a wall, and brought his worry beads out from his pocket. He fingered the tiny beads with his short, thick digits. His lamb had come closer to him and was chewing on a bit of cloth torn from his cloak's shoulder.

"Did Zahra bring you something to drink?"

"Yes, Karbalai. She brought us tea."

He extricated two raisins from his pocket and placed them on his tongue, saying, "Your children must have delivered my message to you, Mergan! I had said that if you have any needs, just let me know. After all, I have a bit of my own to share. We would come to terms easily. You'd be dealt with as a close friend. I don't need any collateral from you, since you yourself are worth a good hundred *ashrafis* to me!"

"May God not reduce your greatness, Karbalai. But with His help, we've survived the worst of the winter."

"Well, all I'm saying is that I'm not the kind to make hollow promises...No news from that worthless man of yours, Soluch, eh?"

"Oh yes, I have news from him. He's busy with work out near Shahrud. In the mines."

"It's a lie! All of it! They're putting you on. If you want my opinion, you should just consider Soluch as gone. He never had the strength and foundation to bear living away from here, much less so during the winter, with nothing to his name. He'd have gone mad, the poor fool. Who's heard of a sensible man doing such a thing? In the darkness of winter! To leave from here then! I lived far away for some time, even as a prisoner. Six terrible years; everyone here knows about it. But returning in one piece is not something just anyone can do. Not that poor wretched Soluch; he could barely survive even while here. He'd sucked the marrow from his life already, the pathetic soul. He could hardly walk. He was dragging his legs behind himself as he went!"

If the conversation had ended right here, and Karbalai Doshanbeh had descended off his podium to go take care of his own business, perhaps Mergan would have been able to just take in all he said and not react. But he couldn't give up there. He'd found a foil for himself. He was sitting in his nephew's house, preaching to a woman whose hands and hair and face were covered in mud. It was as if he was intending to reach in and empty Mergan's heart simply through his oration. Mergan was trapped and didn't know what to do. Should she respond? Of course, if she could...but how?

"Karbalai, it's never good to speak of one who's not present."

Karbalai Doshanbeh responded with a sincerity verging on insolence.

"You mean, to speak of the dead!"

Mergan softly and painfully said, "What in the world had Soluch ever done to you?"

"Oh, nothing, nothing. I never saw ill from him. He was always truthful in his business. But we didn't know he was planning to leave. But the day before he left, he came to our Salar Abdullah and told him to come and settle his accounts by taking some pieces of copper work. But no, he was always honest in his dealings."

"Good. So why do you speak ill of him, then?"

"So you want me to sing the praises of such a man? Hardly even a man! Ha! In whose care did he leave his young wife before going? In whose care? In the care of the wind of the plains? How am I to speak of such a person? Isn't this just what he deserves? Do you even know what this means?"

"What?"

"If a man disappears himself in this way and is gone for several months—I don't know how many exactly—and there's no word from him, his wife is considered to have been divorced. Just as if a Muslim does not eat meat for forty days and nights he is considered an unbeliever! Did you know this? You're a Muslim woman! A person without a spouse is cursed on the earth!"

Karbalai Doshanbeh had said his peace. He rose and said, "This is an important point, from religious law. So you should know about your own status and situation!"

Mergan looked at the broken frame of the old man in silence. Karbalai Doshanbeh led his lamb away and left. She stood quietly for a moment and then, as if something suddenly clicked in her head, she sharply returned to her work. She snapped at her daughter, "What are you doing just standing there? Pour water in the mud! Can't you see the clay is drying?"

Hajer leapt back to work.

Once again, the mother and daughter were swept away by the work. But now a thorn had pierced Mergan's heart. Her heart was burning. Karbalai Doshanbeh had released a bag of poison in Mergan's heart and left.

Was it true, that Mergan was now single, and her marriage was invalid? Was Soluch no longer legally hers? Had Molla Aman brought untrue news of Soluch for his sister for this reason? These questions all mixed in her mind and made Mergan more and more anxious. Mergan had not taken this possibility into account. Could Soluch have divorced her with this silent act, just by leaving? Strange...! But why? Mergan wanted nothing from Soluch. So why had he not just divorced her by handing her a religious writ, as was legal? No, perhaps Karbalai Doshanbeh had made all of this up himself! It's impossible. Mergan had to go in person and request a religious consultation. But what would people say? If Mergan went to request a decision for this question, the others in the village would say a thousand different things about her. It was impossible that they would not say, "The woman's drunk! Her husband's been gone for a short while to work and provide for her and their children, and she's been possessed! What people you'll find!"

And if they said this—which they certainly would—Mergan felt they would have a right to. After all, she would say the same thing were it another woman instead of her. Things like, "She's scrambling around trying to find a legal justification for herself!"

But what would happen to Mergan? To her sons and daughter?

So she needed information. The matter needed illumination. Mergan had the right to be worried for herself. The only path she could imagine taking was to go late one night to see the Molla of Zaminej. But how? His wife would certainly find out, and as soon as she'd heard what questions she'd brought to him, it would be spread all across the town. Any gossip from the Molla's wife's mouth had an audience of a thousand ears. So what to do?

"Fill the cup with clay, girl!"

Mergan took the clay-filled cup from Hajer. She wiped clay over a spot under a high shelf and stepped back from her work. She still had to go to the house of Mirza Hassan, Agha Malak's son-in-law, to do the same task there. She brought her implements out into the yard. She set out to wash up by the edge of a pit next to the olive tree. Hajer poured water onto her mother's hands and then sat so her mother could do the same for her. Zahra came out of the kitchen and looked at Mergan from the corner of her eyes before calling, "Zabiholla told me to tell you to be sure to do two coats. You know he..."

Mergan picked up some of her tools and said, "Tell him I'll send Abrau to come and collect the payment."

She didn't stick around for further conversation. She walked out the door and told her daughter to gather the remaining implements and to bring them.

* * *

In the house, bread and tea were consumed without a word. When dry bread is combined with water, it expands inside the stomach, and when combined with a hard day's work, it brings on sleep. But Mergan couldn't succumb to the heaviness of her eyelids. Before the exhaustion could set in, she rose and took her work tools and Hajer and headed to the house of Mirza Hassan.

They had just set the table and the fresh blood of a recently slaughtered lamb was still on the ground. Salar Abdullah, Zabihollah, and Mirza Hassan were sitting on a cloth out in the sun beside the yard pool while picking their teeth. Salar Abdullah was sitting with his back against the wall, leaning the back of his head against it. Although he was sitting on one knee, holding up his body with his left hand, he still looked taller than the others. Zabihollah, round and bruised-looking—not unlike his uncle Karbalai Doshanbeh—was sitting cross-legged by the throw-cloth, picking at the mud dried on the cuff of his trousers. Mirza Hassan, a petty landowner in Zaminej, had risen and was going to fetch a round of tea.

Mergan, observing tradition, offered her greetings to the men before heading to the room behind the porch.

Mirza Hassan had put colored glass in two of the small windows of the room. The room was already clean and didn't need to be swept and washed down. Just a little water splashed on the walls would be enough. Hajer, as a student who has begun to master her lesson, went out to fill the water sack from the yard pool and brought it back. Mergan then began sprinkling the room with water.

"You're working hard for the New Year's season. Bravo, Auntie Mergan!"

It was the sound of Salar Abdullah. He was sweet-talking her from where he had been sitting. Mergan didn't reply. From the moment when she learned that Zabihollah and Salar Abdullah and a couple of the others had designs on God's Land, she couldn't bear seeing any of them. She refused to look them in the face. But one has to separate the accounts between breadwinning and those reflecting personal preferences of good and bad in people. Sometimes, one has no choice but to accept work and pay from the devil himself. One can't use the same hand to accept one's wages and to ask for help. That's just how things are. Despite this, Mergan didn't have the heart to respond to Salar in a voice that feigned happiness. She didn't see the need to.

Let him go to hell!

So she preoccupied herself with her work. After all, at this moment, Mergan wasn't just a toy for Salar Abdullah!

Mergan had heard that Salar Abdullah had been speaking about buying a tractor. She had heard it said that Zabihollah and Mirza Hassan and Kadkhoda Norouz were all partners in this purchase. Then, talk of a water pump also arose, and of unifying different scraps of land into a single domain. Then, the gossip became complicated and Mergan couldn't quite follow all of it. So, she let her imagination take over. Based on things Ali Genav had said, and what she had more or less heard from others in the village, Mergan pieced together that the larger landowners were now in a partnership. According to Ali Genav, the Kadkhoda's interest in this was that in addition to what he already had, the parts of his farmland that would not be served by the water pump would be ploughed for two years by the communal tractor. But Mergan couldn't really believe that this could all be possible.

Mirza Hassan's voice rose.

"They've accepted the plan. Pistachio farming is a new trend across the country. If it catches on—and I hope it does— it'll turn the whole nation around. On paper, after eight years, the harvests will have us richer than we'd ever dreamed."

Mergan hadn't known of these details. She had only heard that Ghodrat's uncle had offered his land and, so they said, had received a promise that he would work minding the water pump. And Ghodrat's father, who was heavily in debt to Kadkhoda Norouz, had come to an agreement as well. He bought his opium from him and so had been compelled to give up his land. But at this point, Salar Abdullah and his partners had not yet been able to make deals with many of the others, people like Mergan and Sanam's sons, Morad and Asghar Ghazi.

Salar Abdullah had called for Sanam's sons, and they had now come and were sitting beside the pool. Asghar Ghazi had a long neck and bony shoulders, a thin upper body, and a mole on his chin. He looked at the ground and played with pebbles in his hand, saying, "No, no. I'm a farmer here. I'm not the kind to take any other work. I'm staying in Zaminej. I'm busy here with my plot here, and in the end, I keep a couple of the water-melons just to wet my dry mouth with."

"To repay you, we'll get the best opium from Kadkhoda Norouz to give you; that'll be your repayment. In the opium den you and your mother run, you can make a living from that."

"No, Salar! I'd rather buy the opium from the Kadkhoda with cash. You can count on it!"

"So why isn't Morad choosing to drag his feet like this?"

Morad looked at his brother.

Ghazi said, "No, my case is different from Morad's, Zabihollah. Morad isn't meant to stay in Zaminej. His heart isn't here. He wants to leave. He needs to pay for his travel. But as for me…where could I go? My mother and I aren't able to leave like him! Morad has wanderlust; he's young, he'll be fine anywhere he goes and whatever he does. But let a cold wind blow in my face and I'm sick in bed for a month. And my mother's worse. So we're both fated to stay here. We're stuck with this land, Salar!"

Zabihollah placed a cup of tea before Ghazi and said, "Drink. Your mouth must be dry like wood now! You're smoking a lot, man! You've become like a pipe yourself!"

Salar Abdullah looked at Mirza Hassan and said, "So, you'll pay Morad's way, yes?"

Mirza Hassan said, "Sure. I'll pay for his travel!"

Morad looked at his brother and said, "My voice has gone hoarse from telling you to lend me what I need for me to go! I'll give you my part of the land, and I'll repay you the money later. I'll go and work, and I'll send you the money. If I don't pay any of my other debts, I'll be certain to pay off my debt to you. But you're so cheap! Well…now what should I do? Will you lend me what I need or shall I sell my share of the land to these people?"

Ghazi sipped the tea and said, "You keep saying 'give me'! No one's at your neck with an axe, but all you want is to extort from me!"

"I want to extort from you? You poor little lamb, who are you for me to extort from you? All I want is a little money to pay for my travel, in exchange for giving you my share of the land. That's extortion?"

"What share of yours? You keep talking about this land! How many times in your life have you dug that land with a shovel? Tell me! I've worked that land myself. I've planted cottonwood around it. I've sweated over it, weeded it on hot summer days. I've had to struggle just to pick a handful of watermelons from the melon patch—where were you on those days? Just because we came from the same belly, you think everything I own is also yours?"

"Everything you have? Tell me again, what do you own, anyway?"

Others had begun to arrive. Those who worked on God's Land. Asghar Ghazi gave up. He could see the veins on his brother's neck beginning to bulge. Ghodrat's father also arrived, as did Ali Genav. Hajj Salem and Moslem also showed up. Salar Abdullah invited the new arrivals to sit beside the wall, which they did. Morad rose, along with Asghar Ghazi. Mirza Hassan removed his money pouch from his side pocket and took Morad to one side.

"Do you need anything other than just the cost of your travel? I'll pay your way directly—but why are you being such a loudmouth?"

Morad said, "Let's wait for now. Just let it be, Mirza. Later...I'll...I'll..."

"What do you care about the good or bad of it? Take this money and go. I'll make a deal with Ghazi myself—he has to listen to us!"

Mergan called from the doorway, "Hey...Asghar Ghazi! Pay your brother's travel costs so he can go! That is, if you don't want your land taken from your own hands!"

"If you're so worried about him, pay him yourself! The same way you wanted to give your daughter to him!"

"You fool! I'm thinking for you. You're going to lose your land. He's your partner in that land, you know."

"Don't mix up things! Morad's not my partner. If he takes money from Mirza Hassan, that's between them. It has nothing to do with the land. Hey...everyone here! You are my witnesses that Morad has no claim to my land!"

Mergan came out into the yard, her head and body covered with dust and plaster, looking for Asghar Ghazi, but he had just left. She turned and approached Morad, taking him to one side.

"If it's just money for your travel, I'll lend it to you. Don't sell the land!"

"What sweet nothings are you whispering in the ears of our young people, Mergan dear!"

Mergan ignored Salar Abdullah's interjection, walked to the porch, and then was lost in the room inside. Morad followed in his brother's footsteps. The partners began haggling over the plots on God's Land with those who had arrived. Mirza Hassan had written up a document already and had placed it aside for those who worked the land to sign. First of all, he showed the document to Hajj Salem.

"But I don't own any of God's Land!"

"But no one does, Hajj Salem. It's intended to be a petition for the whole village. Everyone has rights here and we want to respect them. So anyone can sign this, or put a fingerprint on it. Moslem, you come here, too!"

Mergan was focused on her own work, but she was monitoring the sounds outside. She could sense the quality of each sound: demanding, unsatisfied, flattering, browbeaten, noncommittal, or indifferent. All the smaller farmers had spread the word that Salar Abdullah and his partners were interested in paying for the land. So everyone was coming; those who worked on God's Land, as well as those who farmed elsewhere. They were practically begging. Others were lying, but they thought they could snap their fingers and get something. They had nothing to give, save the fingerprints they left on the petition. Shortly, only a few were left haggling with Salar Abdullah and his partners. But there was a solution for this, too. Mirza Hassan had the skills of a diplomat; he could sweet-talk almost anyone. So most, eventually, left satisfied.

Mirza Hassan's voice was strong and clear.

"What we're doing is different from when you see ten or twelve half-dying people who don't even have a shovel between them to dig up the land to try to farm. You can't even call that farming. It's more like keeping themselves busy. I've seen it; you all know what I'm talking about. Ten people without an ounce of energy or life. Scrambling like ants in different corners of God's Land, working the scrub for a few days each year, and eventually harvesting a handful of watermelons. And only watermelons! Why only watermelons? Because for a hundred years it hadn't even occurred to you to try to plant something other than watermelons. And so you'll go on teaching your children the same things you learned from your fathers. Have you ever thought for a minute that you can plant something other than watermelons on God's Land? Clearly, no! In any case... even if one of you had thought of it, where are the tools you'd need? How would you prepare the land for planting? You can't just use your bare hands. You need to spend money on the land! Without investment, it's useless. I'm saying this for everyone here. But I'm saying this especially to those of you here who have thought that they were sitting on a pot of gold! It'd be good if you listen carefully; land that has no legal deed is the property of whoever makes it bloom. Am I exhausting my voice for no good reason here? Those three or four who are still holding out had better know they have nothing to stand on. We want to move ahead with this in a way that makes everyone happy and satisfied. We have to live as neighbors, so it's best we're all in agreement and at peace. I don't want the outside authorities to be dragged into Zaminej. But I'm afraid some of my partners may be a little inflexible. And those who have deeds to other lands around here should really stop playing the beggar! How long are they expecting to graze donkeys or camels on their bits of land? They really either have to sell up or join our group and have their own part in the partnership. I'm not too polite to say this; my plans for the land have already been accepted by the authorities. Which means the government wants this to go ahead..."

Mergan hadn't noticed that she had stopped working and was frozen in her place listening closely to Mirza Hassan's speech. But now she couldn't make out what was being said. There was a muttering so quiet it was almost inaudible. Softly, the sound of one or two sets of feet leaving could be heard. Then Mirza Hassan said, "Say hello to those who didn't come to this meeting! Tell them that after the third time, I'll stop trying to make contact with them!"

Mergan sensed that the gist of what Mirza Hassan was say-ing was addressed to her and those like her. She began her work again. It was as if this issue rubbed her the wrong way and there was no chance to accommodate her. She had already developed a grudge over this issue, a grudge that came from the pain in her life. It was as if her entire life now depended on this one little bit of land. She didn't want to yield an inch, even though she wouldn't admit to herself that her steadfastness was at root a purely emotional response. If she was honest to herself, she knew better than anyone else that God's Land was no more than scrubland that couldn't provide much for her and her children's sustenance. But she felt her only choice was to stand her ground.

"Did you hear what was said, Mergan?"

Mergan turned. Ali Genav was standing by the door. "What do you think?"

Mergan said, "I have no intention of selling off my children's inheritance!"

Ali Genav said, "You think you can stand up to them on this? Mostly everyone else has taken what's been offered and has left. You know as well as I that that land isn't much for farming!"

"Everyone has to make their own choice."

"What shall I do?"

"That's up to you."

"No, depending on you...no! If you won't sell, then I won't. And if you want, I'll give the land to Hajer in our marriage contract."

Hajer had hidden herself in the corner. Ali Genav continued, "Will you have time today to go to the baths?"

Mergan replied, "If I have a chance to I'll come by and pick up the keys from you."

Ali Genav turned to go, but found Mirza Hassan face-to-face with him. He was stretching and strutting as he ascended the stairs to the room.

"So what do you say, Ali?"

Ali Genav looked at Mirza Hassan and said, "I think I need to sleep on it."

"So go and sleep on it then!"

At the door, Mirza Hassan greeted Mergan. "So now your Hajer's all grown up, Mergan! Now it's her time, and hopefully it's all for the best!"

Mergan didn't stop working and she mumbled something under her breath in response to his greeting. Mirza Hassan leaned against the doorway; he stretched his long neck and looked into the room. Mergan was covered from head to foot in muddy water from her work. Ali Genav exclaimed, "God give you strength in your work!"

Mergan tied an old shirt to a broomstick and plunged it into a bucket of whitewash. She straightened her back and said, "Thank you for coming by!"

Mirza Hassan pleasantly enquired about Mergan's health, to which she replied in dry monosyllables.

"So, are your sons thinking of leaving Zaminej for work, Mergan? Do they plan on going elsewhere?"

"What should I know?"

"I can give one of them work right here. Your Abrau is a clever boy, but the other one's not good for much."

"That's how it goes."

Mirza continued, "If I were in your shoes, I'd send Abbas off with the other young men who are leaving Zaminej; let him work in other areas and grow up a bit."

"We'll see."

"If you do want to send him off to work, I would be happy to pay for his travel for you."

"Should he want to go, I'll find the money for his travel from somewhere myself!"

"Yes, of course, you'll find it somewhere. But let me give you the money to settle my debt to you."

"What debt, Mirza?"

"I'm talking about God's Land. It wouldn't be proper for me to just evict everyone from the land and tell them to go. God wouldn't approve."

"Where would you want us to go, Mirza? Where?"

"Mergan, don't play games with me. We've already registered God's Land to our own names. We intend to work it and to plant pistachios on it. That's a suitable crop for this land. You know, if pistachios are a yielding crop, what benefits can it bring not just to Zaminej but to this entire area? The engineers say that the pistachios that grow here can be more valuable than the famous pistachios of Rafasanjan! We want to make this area bloom. How long can we keep on just planting watermelons?"

"So what will I gain from all of this?"

"What will you gain? This is good for everyone. And why should you be only thinking about what you get from it?"

"So why should I want to give up my land?"

"Your land? Ha! What land? God's Land! That's land that belongs to God!"

"If it belongs to God, well, I'm one of His servants. What difference does it make? His servants work His land. Are you saying I'm not His servant?"

"Of course you are. Why shouldn't you be? Who is a better servant than you? But in the end, we need to make God's Land bloom!"

"Yes, let's make it bloom. Am I saying anything other than that? But if you're going to evict me from this land, who will ensure my rights and those of my children? You think the three or four bills you want to put in the palm of my sons' hands will be enough?"

"What would you prefer? That I bequeath all my property to you?"

"When did I say that?"

"Well, in effect, that's what you're saying! What else are you saying?"

"I'm saying that in a few months when you've harvested the land, are you planning on sharing the profits with me? Of course not!"

"But why should you expect me to? In any case, by then, who knows who will still be here and who will be gone? Pistachios take seven years to yield; so it's seven years before anything will be harvested."

"But what will be my portion of this?"

"Your portion? That's brighter than day! I'm offering to hire one of your sons. What more could you want?"

"That's it?"

"What more do you expect?"

"Nothing!"

"Fine! Why am I even wasting my time with you, foolish woman?"

Zabihollah came to Mirza's side and said, "Mergan's stubborn as a mule, eh?"

Mirza Hassan said, "Let her play the mule. She'll be the loser because of it!"

Zabihollah went down from the porch, walking shoulder-to-shoulder with Mirza Hassan.

"It's better to try to come to terms with her son Abbas. If he sees the color of money, his mouth starts to water."

Mirza said, "She can go to hell. Who does she think I am?"

***

Mirza Hassan's yard was now empty. Zabihollah and Mirza began to leave, and Kadkhoda Nourouz accompanied them. Salar Abdullah caught up with them at the gate. Kadkhoda Norouz said, "She has no one to protect her, the poor woman. We have to come to terms with her somehow. Thirty, forty *tomans* here or there isn't much to spend. It's as if we're fulfilling our religious duty to charity with it."

Mirza sat on a bench silently and took out a cigarette. "It's just that she's stubborn and doesn't know what's good for her, the bitch; otherwise I agree. I want to come to terms with her, because among the villagers she has the aura of victimhood and righteousness. But you see how she is!"

Kadkhoda Norouz began walking and said, "I'll go and convince her."

Abrau arrived, short of breath. Salar Abdullah asked, "So, what did you find out?"

"The driver says the tractor's been delayed for tonight. They need to change its light. He says he'll bring it tomorrow."

Salar said, "Be ready and on the road at the break of dawn. Did you settle your accounts with Ali Genav yet?"

Abrau said, "I didn't really have any accounts with him."

Salar looked at his partners and said acidly, "They call minding the bath a job? Anyway...the weather's getting warm. No one will be using the baths for another six or seven months. Anyone can just go down to the stream and wash there."

Kadkhoda Norouz returned. Mergan and Hajer were with him. It seemed she had finished her work; the sack with her tools was on Hajer's back. As she passed by the men, she said to Zabihollah, "You can give Abrau what you owe me for the white-washing of your house to bring with himself!"

Mirza looked at the Kadkhoda, who shook his head.

"No...she won't reconsider!"

Mirza rose from the bench. "I'll make her reconsider! You, boy, go tell Abbas to come to Zabihollah's house tonight. We need to discuss something with him!"

Abrau said, "Okay."

Mirza, Zabihollah, and Salar Abdullah left as Abrau stood watching them. Haj Salem and Moslem came out from behind a wall and set out following the partners. The Kadkhoda walked out as well, but before he shut the gate he looked at Abrau.

"Your mother is truly impossible, you know?"

3.

Abbas felt rejuvenated as he left Zabihollah's house. He felt satisfaction mixed with anxiety. The fatigue had left his body, or
was lost inside his body. He grasped the bills of money he had
received from Mirza Hassan, knowing just what he intended to
do with them. He didn't want to keep them at hand nearby. He
never wanted his money to be in eyeshot. He never wished for
his affairs to be out in the open. There was always subterfuge to
his plans. He always wanted things to be partially hidden, especially his winnings or losses in gambling. If not all of it, at least
a few *qerans* of money. He loved to keep secrets. Even if the
secret was meaningless. The feeling of insecurity and his lack
of trust in others had taken such a root in him that he sometimes
tried to keep hidden the most obvious of things. Most of his lies

were exposed in the light of day, but he didn't care if others thought of him as a liar, or called him one. What was important to him was that others not know what he was really up to. Put simply, Abbas didn't want anyone to know what he was doing with even a single *qeran* of his money, or where he had stashed it. Of course, this inclination was not particular to Abbas but is shared by many others in similar circumstances.

Abbas' present problem was to figure out how he could cut short the inevitable argument he would have with his mother. He wanted to think of a way to keep a hold of half of the money and to avoid a fight by giving half of it to her for the house. He had just decided to look for a place to hide the other half that he would keep. He entered a deserted and ruined home and undid the tie on his pants. The hem of his pants was the safest spot on him. Shortly, he returned to the alley and tightened the tie on his pants. Now only two bills remained in his hand from what he'd been paid for his portion of the family's plot in God's Land. He had just handed over two *dang* of the six *dang* that had been Soluch's plot.

In the alley he encountered Ali Genav's wife, who was creeping along like a shadow in the dark. She moved very slowly, holding onto the wall with one hand and grasping her walking stick with the other. Her soft moaning sounded like the flutter of a moth's wings. Abbas was saved from himself for a moment—Raghiyeh distracted him from the troubled thoughts filling his mind.

Although Raghiyeh had spent a few mornings in a town hospital, there was no sign of improvement in her. Day by day, this broken woman deteriorated. It was as if she was melting, as if her bones were shrinking and the skin on her face was drying. She didn't have the energy to speak for long, and her legs couldn't even transport her skin and bones from one place to another.

Abbas approached her and with a loud voice—as if she had gone deaf—he said, "How are you doing? How are things?"

Raghiyeh leaned against the wall and caught her breath. It was as if she could die at any moment. Leaning on the wall, she slid into a seated position and stayed grasping the walking stick with both hands like a pillar. She sighed sadly. It was an effort for her to make any sound, and she could barely raise her voice to be heard by Abbas. She sounded very far away. It was as if she were speaking from behind hills of gravel, or from the center of a furious tempest. She no longer had the sound of a woman, a human. She sounded like a lamb that had strayed from the herd and had been caught in a wasteland alone. It was the sound of exhaustion, thirst, of the sadness of a life in the desert, near death. The sound was not the sound of Raghiyeh but the soft murmur of dry wheat in the wind. It was as if a thorny handful of barley were blocking her throat. The sound seemed to rise from beneath the earth, as if Raghiyeh had already died.

"No. I'm dying. I'm dying. I was going...I was going to go to your house...your house..."

"Yes?"

"I was going...to tell your mother...Oh God...! My breath...why can't...I catch my breath?"

"Yes? To tell her what?"

"To tell her...that...that...she could have waited...at least until...I died before..."

"Before what?"

"Before...before giving...her daughter...to my husband...but...but...I turned back...I didn't tell her...because...I realized...What good...? What good would it be?"

Raghiyeh leaned her head against the walking stick. She waited for a moment and then tried to lift herself up with all of her strength. But she couldn't, and she sat down again. Abbas grabbed her under the arm and helped her up. She stood and leaned against the wall with one hand. She caught her breath and then slowly began walking. She went slowly and calmly, like a turtle, only slower. Abbas thought to himself, "It will take her all night just to go the short distance back to her home. What if she dies on the way?" He heard her voice.

"It's not right...Oh God...! I pray on Zaynab's misery...I pray on Zaynab's sacrifice...Just don't let this happen..."

The sound of her voice was swallowed in the turns of the alley, and Abbas headed back to his home, walking more slowly than before.

On this night, the house had a strange atmosphere. There were no visitors to their home, but inside it seemed more alive than usual. Everyone in the house had broken the humdrum continuity of their nightly routines, and their actions had a new hue and color to them. It was like when the autumn morning light shines on the wheat harvest; the old dry husks that contained them had begun to open and fall away, letting them flutter individually in the way that was their nature. They blew in the wind, this way and that. Some even took to the wind, flying. Each had its own reason for joyfulness. In the midst of this, although he tried not to show it, Ali Genav was the happiest of all, while Mergan was also happy, in her own way. Her life had been shaken; the wedding of a daughter is always a point of pride for a mother, and seen from her perspective, Mergan was satisfied. Even Hajer was now more or less satisfied, because she was slowly approaching that stage that customarily most girls, more or less, anticipate: marriage.

Hajer had brought herself to believe that most marriages are only slightly desirable but become more acceptable with a bit of imagination. It's a human affair, after all! One can quite often just choose to overlook certain things. Like the fact that Hajer wasn't yet thirteen, or the fact that Ali Genav's beard was turning gray. And most of all, the fact that she was marrying a man who not only still smelled of his first wife, but who also lived with her. Also, this wife lived her life as a ghost, pacing around their little house with a cane. Raghiyeh...a woman transformed into anger and complaints, whose voice seemed to emanate from the mud-brick walls. She was a woman with eyes that watch the world from behind an inner curtain. Eyes covered by dust, tinted with the color of sleep, which watch you from the depths of their sockets. They keep looking at you and ask you something silently. They only say one thing; something wordless, something impossible to express. A thousand words could be said, but that one last one would be left unsaid, a word that keeps on bothering you. But it's a human affair, after all. Some things can just be overlooked. No doubt, Hajer would have to overlook many things.

Ali Genav said, "Hopefully, we'll just sign the marriage contract there. I know a certain Molla."

Mergan put a cup of tea before Ali Genav and said, "Hopefully!"

Abbas was in the doorway. Mergan looked at Abbas and asked, "So? What did he want?"

Abbas sat down right there in the doorway.

"He wanted the plot in God's Land. So I gave it to him."

"Gave it? What did you give?"

"That scrap of land!"

Mergan couldn't tell if her heart had suddenly frozen, or if it was her head that caught fire. She rose to her knees and said, "To Mirza Hassan?"

"To all of them!"

"With whose permission?"

"With my own permission!"

"But who are you? Who do you think you are?"

"I'm Soluch's oldest son. The oldest son. That's what they told me."

"Are you responsible for all of us? You can't speak for all of us! That piece of land belongs to the whole family!"

"I just sold my portion. Did you expect this to be like the coppers that you took and secreted away somewhere? Anyway, you're Soluch's wife and can't inherit the land. That's what they told me. A woman can only have a claim on the house and the household. That's what they said."

Mergan went limp, leaned her head and shoulders against the wall, and cried out, "Oh God! May God strike you down! You've ruined us! Ruined us! Now how am I going to hold my own in the face of those thieving, cunning men?"

Abbas said, "You're ruining us yourself! Everyone else is taking their offer and going; it's only you who's holding out like a stubborn mule!"

Mergan raised her head from the wall.

"If they gave everyone everything and a bit more, I wouldn't care! Why are you breaking away from your own family and joining those sons of bitches?"

"Because I wanted be done with this business! Why are you so shortsighted? It's clear that in the end they'll take the land, so why fight about it? Do you think I can fight them? When the game's up, you're better off giving in. Kicking and screaming at that point is of no use! And from now on we'll have to come to terms with them, so we'll be beholden to them. They'll have a hand in everything. Take a look; who's offering to hire your other son to work with the tractor?"

Mergan and Ali Genav both turned to look at Abrau, who, despite looking at the ground, felt the sharp, heavy glare of his mother's eyes on his forehead. He couldn't stay silent. He looked up and said, "Abbas is right. After tomorrow, I'm not working at the baths. I'm working with the tractor!"

Ali Genav asked, "What? You're going to work with the tractor? So what about your job at the baths? Now that winter's over, you're free to fly away? That's the customary way of behaving?"

Abrau didn't look at Ali Genav while he replied.

"I never promised to work at the baths till the end of my life. If something better comes up, you have to take it!"

Ali Genav gritted his teeth. "Fine, great! But I'll remember this, be sure of that!"

Abrau realized it would be better to speak his mind honestly, so he turned to Mergan.

"I'm thinking of selling my portion to Salar Abdullah and his partners as well. How long am I supposed to live in these tattered rags like a flea? I want to go to town and buy myself a decent pair of pants. You can't work on a tractor wearing torn, worn-out clothes!"

Abrau ended his statement by standing up, and began to get ready to leave. He didn't want to continue the discussion he had just started. Mergan wiped the edges of her eyes with her scarf and spoke with a trembling voice.

"He's talking about 'my portion' as well! He doesn't understand what's really important!"

Ali Genav said, "So tonight, I'll have to go to prepare the furnace for the baths myself."

Mergan didn't say anything. Ali Genav rose.

"So tomorrow, at dawn, I'll come to get you!"

Mergan only nodded her head. Ali Genav left.

In the alley, Ali Genav saw the two brothers walking shoulder-to-shoulder toward Zabihollah's house.

"May it be a blessing. Congratulations, Ali Akbar Khan! Congratulations!"

Hajj Salem and Moslem had materialized before Ali Genav. Moslem walked right up to him. Ali Genav said, "Wait until morning. Morning is better. I have nothing in my pockets right now. Hopefully in the morning."

Hajj Salem rubbed his son's neck with his walking stick. "You beast! Wait until morning. Every day is God's day. Now let's go to Auntie Mergan's house to offer our services. I'm sure that given it's the auspicious day of her daughter's wedding, she'll offer to whitewash our humble nest!"

Father and son began walking in the darkness toward Mergan's house.

Ali Genav waited for a moment, then turned away from his own home and began following Hajj Salem and his son.

Abbas and Abrau left from Zabihollah's home. Zabihollah had even paid Mergan's share to Abrau, who was worried about finding a place to hide his own portion without mixing it up with his mother's money. Abbas, playful and chummy, made circles around his brother, saying, "Zaminej is full of money! You know, everyone's rich now! Today, so much money has changed hands, so many have been paid by Mirza and his partners—they've been giving out money since the morning!"

Abrau said, "These guys mean business. Not like Ali Genav, with the pittance he pays! The source of his generosity is smaller than a rooster's asshole! When he agrees to pay you a couple of coins, he acts as if he's giving life to the angel of death! The cheap son of a bitch! You want to earn a real living with a man, but not with someone like that. It seems I really broke his heart, but I liked it! Now he has to get up in the middle of the night and work the furnace until morning, just to learn what it means to never sleep! It's as if he thought that by marrying into the family, he'd become our lord and master as well!"

Abbas said, "I'm not happy even about his marrying into the family. I'm afraid we'll get caught up with his wife and her problems."

"Tell me about it! His wife is constantly going around cursing everyone!"

"But it's too late now; everyone's heard all about it. What can we do? We have to let him take her! At least he'll give her a roof over her head. In a way we'll be freer, ourselves. To each his own destiny!"

The boys talked as they walked down the tightly woven alleys of Zaminej. They spoke of everything, even Soluch. It was so dark, they couldn't see each other's eyes. Perhaps this allowed them to speak more frankly. Their complaints of each other were lost in the darkness, and a natural feeling of fraternity took its place. Because of this, Abrau became worried about Abbas' plans and future.

"What are you planning to do? Would you go with the other guys, or do you want to stay?"

"I'll stay. There'll be work here during the spring. I'll herd the camels until the Sardar wants to take them out on a caravan. He may even want me to go out on the caravan with him. If the wages are good, I may just go. I like camel herding."

"That's not bad—camel herding's not bad. But what will come of it? In a single night, these cargo trucks can take the same load that forty camels used to take in forty days! Eventually, we're just going to have to fatten up all the camels and put them under the knife! In Zaminej, other than the Sardar, who has camels anyway? No one! Take Karbalai Doshanbeh. He used to have forty camels. But he got rid of them. He sold his camels and put what he got into money lending. Now he's sitting on a pot of treasure like a dragon. The heartless bastard! He's not even used ten *qerans* of his money for anything so that a few other people could possibly earn a bit of bread from it. That's why I've always liked Mirza Hassan. He eats well but he also helps others eat. He's like a lion, and Karbalai's like a jackal. The lion eats his fill and then backs off, but a jackal will hide the rest of a carcass where others can't find it."

Abbas said, "Well, to each his own. In any case, Mirza Hassan and his partners are some twenty or thirty years younger than Karbalai Doshanbeh. Some of them have seen other towns and cities. Mirza himself has been in contact with all sorts. He's even had relations with Arabs and other foreigners. These all make a difference."

"In any case, I think you have to pursue some kind of work that has a future. Not camel herding. Can you think of anyone here in Zaminej who's made a living from that?"

"No."

"So? And you want to spend your life with that work?"

"But what choice do I have?"

"You have a choice! Leave! Follow the other guys and leave here! Just do whatever they do. At least you're healthy; you can go and see the world, which is a good thing, in and of itself. If all I had to do was to work at the baths, I'd leave in an instant."

"I can't imagine leaving Zaminej, though. The idea of traveling is in my head all the time. But I don't have the heart to. But...let's see what happens. We'll see!"

Abbas didn't want to pursue the topic any further. Despite the fact that he didn't give much weight to Abrau's arguments, they did nonetheless prick at his heart. They didn't affect the roots of his convictions, but they shook their branches and leaves. They made him feel ambivalent and frustrated. They didn't change his path, but they bothered him all the same. So he didn't want to hear any more. He changed the topic.

"Why not head over to Auntie Sanam's house? I'll bet you there's a round of gambling going on there. Mirza Habib's made all the poor beggars into rich men."

Abrau said, "I'm not going to throw my money away on gambling. I want to buy some clothes for myself."

Abbas said, "Let's go anyway. You might end up changing your mind!"

"No, you go on your own."

"Come on, let's go as partners."

"No! I don't want to waste my money."

"Then at least come and sit by me as I play. You'll bring me good luck."

"No! I don't want to set foot in that place. I'll be touched by the devil if I go."

"Fine, let's just stop by there for a minute. Let's go and see if Morad is leaving tomorrow after all?"

As soon as he opened the door, Morad's wide and bony face broke into a wide smile. He presumed the brothers had come to say that they were joining him on his trip.

"Great. Welcome. Come in."

As they entered, Abbas asked, "Is there anyone else here?"

Morad said, "No! It's quiet here tonight. Ghazi's gone to sleep."

"You mean no one came by tonight?"

Morad laughed. "You're a real gambler, aren't you? You think all the guys who are planning to leave to go far away tomorrow are going to come to lose their travel money gambling?"

"So no one's...?"

"Two of the usual vultures did stop by with the same hopes, but they were disappointed. They stayed around and are hanging out inside right now."

"No doubt Ghasem Leng and Habib Kahi, eh?"

"Good for you. So you know your opponents well! They're still hungry. Ghasem Leng can't stop dealing himself hands from a deck of cards. If your money's burning a hole in your pocket, go ahead! They're just waiting for someone to come by!"

Abrau grabbed his brother's sleeve.

"Don't go! These guys will win the shirt off of your back!"

Abbas shifted his feet. Then he slid to the safety of the wall and, glancing at Abrau and Morad, slipped his hands into his pockets.

Morad said, "I know Abbas would be hopeless working with us, but I hope you're coming!"

Abrau said, "I've just arranged for some work right here. It's good work, too. Imagine! Working on a tractor, watching its iron blade cutting right into the earth! The same land that just last year we would slave away working on all day with just a pair of bulls. Or, if only they were bulls! No, donkeys! It's really exciting, don't you think?"

"It's exciting, but only if you have some claim on the land and the tractor."

"Of course, it's better if it's your own property. But it's exciting as it is. Have you ever heard the sound it makes? God! It sounds like a marching army, drowned in iron and steel. Its *vrroomm vrroomm* just makes your heart race! You know, if there were enough land and water, with ten of these tractors braying as they run down the valley, this whole place would be a heaven in two or three years!"

Morad said, "May its owner benefit from it! Is it true, as they say, that each tractor can do the work of a hundred men?"

"What's a hundred? The tractor they're bringing here has the power of one hundred and twenty *horses*. And you know, it's not even a big one."

Morad asked, "Where do they make these creatures?"

Abrau hesitated. He'd never thought about this before.

"And how much does it cost? It must need a pile of money from here to heaven!"

Abrau hadn't thought of this either.

"No doubt, they'll have to raise the money for these from the land itself, no? Just like the money from our own hard work goes in you-know-who's pocket!"

Abbas came over. He had an artificial smile, as if to hide something. Morad and Abrau were sitting in the alley, just by the doorway. The gate into Sanam's home was open; from there, three steps led down into a low yard. The building comprised a living room and a storage room. The living room was where Sanam served opium, and the storage room was used for gambling. Generally, Ghazi oversaw the storage room. The door into the room was half open and a thin, weak light shone from inside. Abbas set foot on the steps and said, "Let's go see how Auntie Sanam is doing!"

Morad and Abrau looked at one another. They both knew Abbas too well. There was no way to stop him. If Abbas began gambling, he'd be there until the morning. There was no point in trying to discuss it with him; it would only fall on deaf ears. Once he'd decided to join a game, he couldn't be dissuaded.

Morad said, "So far, there are a few of us interested in heading toward Shahrud, and some are going to go from Shahrud to Gonbad. Others will go toward Veramin. We might even try going to the capitol. We'll just go and see what it's about! If we can't own the world, at least let us see it!"

Abrau replied, "I also really want to see the capitol. Really! I swear on both of our lives, if this tractor hadn't shown up like this, and if my only option was to keep working in Ali Genav's bathhouse, I'd leave in a moment."

On hearing Ali Genav's name, Morad remained silent for a moment. Then, as he rose, he beat the dust out from the back of his pants.

"I hear they're going shopping tomorrow?"

Abrau swallowed his embarrassment and replied, "I don't know... So I'll see you by the roadside tomorrow?"

"Ah... who knows!"

Morad yawned and stepped inside the doorway. Abrau said, "Promise me you'll keep an eye on Abbas! I'm afraid these two vultures will skin him tonight."

Morad closed the door and said, "He's on his own! I'm sleepy."

The door shut on Morad's yawn. Then, silence filled the alley. Silence smothered the walls. Abrau was alone in the alley. He knew his brother would be in Sanam's house for a long time. He set out alone, walking close to the wall. He felt the waistband of his pants again and checked the money he'd hidden there. He wanted to go to Zabihollah's house to see Mirza Hassan and Salar Abdullah. But he didn't have the will to. What would be the point of sitting in doorway listening to Mirza Hassan speaking? Everyone knew that he was an eloquent, witty speaker. Abrau knew this from before, but it was a new sensation to have a desire to go and sit and listen to him speak. When Mirza began describing the gambling houses and brothels of the town, his stories were pleasant enough. But what Abrau enjoyed most was when he began speaking about pistachio farming with tractors and irrigation with deep wells. Abrau's eyes would be full of fascination mixed with excitement and his mouth would drop open. Mirza Hassan's descriptions illustrated something that seemed like heaven to Abrau. All of Abrau's dreams and hopes were realized in what Mirza Hassan would describe. But in any case, Abrau, only being a poor boy, couldn't just go to visit Mirza Hassan in the middle of the night without some kind of reason.

He turned toward home.

***

The lamp was still lit. It seemed Mergan had left the lamp on to mark an auspicious occasion. Abrau crept in the doorway quietly, thinking his mother would be asleep. He slid into a corner softly and quietly and lay down. But Mergan was not asleep. She was sitting with her back against a wall in the weakly flickering light, and she had Hajer's head in her lap. She was murmuring to her daughter and stroking her hair with her hand. Hajer had laid her head on her mother's knee like a lamb, and her eyelids grew heavier and heavier. Yet she struggled to keep listening to her mother's oratory, which her mother had begun early in the evening. She had begun to describe every detail that a girl should know on the eve of her marriage; everything her daughter should be aware of before setting foot in her new husband's home.

If alone, mothers are often able to speak to their daughters without exaggeration or metaphor, and by speaking, pull out what is most often left unsaid, like pulling a snake out of its hole. Indeed, this may be one of the most gratifying moments of her life: when she explains the duties and expectations of a wife in marriage. At these moments, the whispered sentiments of the mother, in fact, relate her own unfulfilled dreams. Her hopes and fears are held within these words, and the expectations she had once had that are now gone—but not forgotten—are mixed with an optimism for the future, overtaking her words and giving them an attractive hue. Her speech settles within the heart and her tone is sweet and light. At this moment, the mother grants her daughter the wisdom of her experiences—either pleasures or disappointments—drop by drop. And at the same time, the daughter is nourished by her mother's life, drop by drop, and she stores away the most valuable elements from it. So for both, such nights are as sweet as honey.

But with Abrau's arrival, Mergan went silent. Abrau was lost in his own thoughts, and Mergan treated him as a stranger. What she had been sharing with her daughter was not meant for his ears. So Mergan placed her daughter's head on the pillow and then lay down beside her.

The lantern was still burning on the lowest light. Abrau watched the light from the weak flame dancing on the smoke-stained ceiling. It was rare that Mergan would leave the lantern lit until morning. The only time she would do so was on the first night of the New Year. This only happened sometimes, and only when Soluch was still around. But Soluch's presence was not the only justification for keeping the lantern lit—it was only so when there was something to celebrate. So, the New Year's celebration only mattered when the winter was full of snow and rain. In some years, some seasons can be dry. So only on good years, on the first night of the New Year, the lantern would be left lit.

A weak memory was flickering in the depths of Abrau's mind. An image flickering in the weak light of the lantern, of Soluch from years past: a small man, with narrow shoulders and a balding head, taking off his shirt and lying down exhausted to light a cigarette. His entire mouth would fill with the smoke, and the cigarette would burn more brightly than the lantern. He'd roll on his side and place his elbow on the pillow to hold up his head, and he would remain in that position until the cigarette was finished. On those nights—the nights of the New Year's season—Soluch was often lost in his thoughts. So much so that once the cigarette was finished, it was often not easy to tell if he was still awake. Abrau himself would be falling asleep, even as he wondered if his father was still awake.

On those nights, the nights of the New Year's celebration, it was difficult to call the children in from the alleys. They'd never be finished playing. They'd all stay out until they were exhausted, and so Abrau would come home just in time to collapse into a deep sleep. Despite this, on the morning of the New Year, he'd still wake up at the dawn's first light to collect his gift coin from his father. Every year, Soluch would have somehow obtained a New Year's coin for each of the children and sewn them into the lining of his bag. Abrau remembered how on the New Year's morning, his father would sit smoking alone. On that morning, unlike most people, no visitors would be expected to pay their respects and to wish him a happy New Year. It was Soluch who would have to go to do so to others. Abrau could never solve the problem of this for himself: why was his father of lower standing than everyone else? He had learned that on the morning of the first day of the New Year, people would stay home until those of lower standing had come to pay their respects to them. But Abrau knew that there were indeed people of a lower status than his father—so why didn't they come to pay their respects then? He only now was beginning to understand why this was.

Early in the first morning of the New Year, Soluch would hand out the gift coins to the children, then sit and drink a cup of tea and eat a little. Then he'd rise, tie his waistband, put on shoes if he had them, and then bend over to walk out through the doorway. Where did he go? Abrau noticed how he would leave. Then it was time for the dried nuts and raisins, which Mergan would hand out to the children—each one would get a handful. Then they'd run out into the alleys—alleys full of children, the ground carpeted by springtime sunlight.

He shut his eyelids. He didn't want to think of his father any longer. It was not that he wanted to forget Soluch. No, rather it was that he simply didn't feel that Soluch signified the jumble of dreams and imagination that once used to attract him during moments of distress. Now, the sound of the tractor's chugging motor held his imagination much more. The possibilities ploughed through his mind. His body was tired, but his mind was racing. He knew that he would have to be well rested tomorrow for his first day of work. So he needed to sleep. But it was as if he'd lost his self-control. He rolled over and over and pressed his eyes against the pillow. Tomorrow the tractor would arrive. Tomorrow the ancient silence of Zaminej would be broken. Abrau would be standing on the running board; the wind would tousle his hair. He'd squint his eyes, cherishing the feeling of riding on the equivalent of one hundred and twenty horses. He'd be paid monthly at the beginning of the month. No more begging for the pittance he was getting: half a *man* barley, ten *seer* wheat flour, and seven *qerans* in cash! In this new job, his eyes would fall on four beautiful bills each month. From now on, everything would be by the book. One should know what to expect from his work and expenses. One can't live one's life hoping for a living to come with the wind!

Hints of self-regard were already taking root in Abrau; he had begun to look at himself in a new way. Small, worthless tasks had begun to grate upon him. He'd begun to pine for a different kind of work. Work with some kind of stature. Work that was defined. It was his good luck that of all the youth of Zaminej, he had been the single one to be given this job. Mirza Hassan and Salar Abdullah had chosen him. Abrau took this very seriously; there had been many others they could have chosen. Of all of his peers who were now making plans to migrate for work, would any have refused this job? And with it, the prospect of steady, guaranteed work?

The plan was that as soon as the tractor was finished ploughing the partners' lands, it would be rented out to plough elsewhere. Not only within Zaminej itself, but also in the neighboring villages. He expected that this would be the most enjoyable part of his work—experiencing new places from on top of the tractor. They said that the girls in the neighboring areas were more fun! From what he had heard, Mirza and his partners were planning to apply for a large loan from the ministry of agriculture. Once they'd registered the land, they would use it as collateral for the loan. For Abrau, it seemed as clear as day that their plans would entail further expansions. No doubt they'd eventually need one or two other tractors. By then, Abrau would have been trained as a driver; he'd sit at the controls of a tractor and wear his hat to one side. He'd be able to marry and get a house for himself. He'd go after any girl who took his fancy. By then, he'd be a man for himself.

Abbas stepped inside the house. Abrau couldn't see him very well. His eyelids were heavy. But even in the dark, it was obvious what had just happened to Abbas. He was tired and angry, swearing under his breath. As he set out his blanket, it was as if he was trying to tear it in half. Once or twice he spit a curse out from his mouth. Then he knelt beside the water jug and pressed his mouth against it. He drank water until his belly was full. Then he threw himself down, swore under his breath, and rolled over. Abrau imagined that his brother was biting on his pillow. But then he fell asleep.

* * *

In the morning, before the dawn, Mergan rose from her place and woke her daughter. Hajer sat up and rubbed her eyes, still tired and short of sleep. She felt heavy, and she couldn't keep her head up. She fell back and lay her head on the pillow. It felt as if her head was full of lead. Mergan returned to the room after washing up. Abrau sat up straight and looked around anxiously. He suddenly leapt up and ran to the door. The sky was already light outside. He turned back to his mother and asked, "Did you hear anything?"

"Hear what?"

"The sound of the tractor!"

"No."

Abrau relaxed a little. He went out, splashed water on his face, and returned. He took some bread, thrust it into his pocket, and rushed out the door. Mergan dried her hands and face and went back over to Hajer.

"Get up then! Your fiancé is about to come. He can't find you lying there like a corpse! Rise and splash some water on yourself! Get up!"

Hajer wanted to get up, but on spring mornings, sleep tends to weigh heavily on children of her age, holding them under its heavy wings. Mergan grabbed her daughter's underarms and dragged her outside, sitting her beside the well to wash her face and hands. Only then did Hajer begin to shake off the sleep. She sat against the wall while Mergan wiped her face with the edge of her shirt. Then she left to find her old wedding dress for Hajer to wear—a crumpled and creased red cotton shirt with a blue floral design, and a silk headscarf pocked with moth holes. Putting the shirt on Hajer, it was clearly too large for her; its edges dragged on the ground. The edges of the shoulders of the shirt fell on Hajer's arms, and her tiny hands were lost in its sleeves. The bosom of the shirt was empty, as Hajer's had not developed as yet. At best, her breasts were each the size of a walnut.

No matter! An oversized shirt is nothing to worry over...

Mergan found a needle and thread and brought in the wide neck of the shirt. Now she had to do something for the sleeves. The solution was to pull up the material on the upper sleeves and to fold it over and sew it, which she did. The shirt nearly fit now, but she also placed a pin at the neck of the shirt to hide Hajer's bony chest underneath. She felt it looked acceptable. But if she'd thought of it before and had done something to bring in the waist of the shirt a little, it might have been better. But it was too late now. She took the headscarf and placed it on Hajer's head. Folded over once, it was difficult to notice the moth holes in the material. Good...and here's a pin under the chin for the scarf. Let the extra material of the scarf cover her shoulders...That's more appropriate. And the corners of the scarf can just fall upon her chest. The bangs of her hair had to fall out of the scarf and cover her forehead until her eyebrows. And each tuft of hair had to have a gentle wave in it.

"That's good...May God let you grow old in peace and comfort!"

Mergan looked around and found Ali Genav smiling in the doorway. Hajer hid herself behind her mother. Mergan replied, "You and she can go together, God willing!"

Ali Genav said, "I hope so, God willing. Good...Fine...Now I'll go and saddle my donkey."

He stepped away to leave; the room again filled with sunlight.

Mergan grabbed her daughter's elbow tightly.

"You'd better stop acting the fool right now! He's going to be your husband. You're not a helpless baby. You're becoming a real woman. How am I going to get this into your thick skull?!"

Hajer said nothing. She only took a sharp breath. Mergan readjusted the scarf on her head and took her by the hand toward the door. She looked over her daughter in the sunlight. Hajer's face was so small it looked like a china saucer. Her eyes darted to and fro. She was upset, unlike her usual self—no one was better equipped to sense this than her mother. But Mergan didn't want to acknowledge this to herself, much less to discuss it openly.

"You look like the moon! A beautiful flower. If we had a full-length mirror so you could see yourself, you'd understand why I'm saying this. A crystal sculpture! May you be protected from the evil eye. I have to burn rue incense now. You'll have a wonderful future. May you avoid the eye of envy! Everyone should want to have a girl your age that they are marrying at this time of year. I hope they all drop dead from jealousy! I have to go and wrap a piece of bread in the bundle."

Hajer stayed where she was by the doorway while her mother went in, kicking Abbas' leg on the way.

"Hey, the sun's about to rise! Are you planning to wake up any time today? You can't take the camels out after the sun's already risen. You should be out in the fields by now!"

Abbas rolled over and growled. Mergan entered the pantry while Hajer leaned against the wall and looked outside. The yard was so empty. So empty! It seemed as if no one and nothing had ever entered it.

Mergan emerged from the pantry and tied a piece of bread into a measure of cloth, then shouted at Abbas.

"I'm with you, hey! The sun's up. Get up and get going, then!"

Abbas turned his head and with an exhausted face and closed eyes screamed, "Why all this shouting? What's it to you anyway? What do you have to do with my work? I don't want to go to take the camels out anyway!"

Just then, the footsteps of Ali Genav's cousin the camelherd owner—or Sardar—echoed from over the wall and into the house.

"Hey! Abbas...! When are you planning to take the camels out, then? Noon?! The sun's been up for a while! If you're planning on doing this job of looking after the camels, they'd better be out and grazing before the sun shows its face!"

The giant Sardar turned the corner of the wall and entered the yard, coming toward the door with heavy steps, seemingly filling the yard with his huge weathered body. Hajer pulled herself away from the doorway. Still only half-awake, Abbas collected himself, crumpled up the bedding, smoothing out his rumpled clothes.

"Coming, Sardar. I'm coming."

The Sardar's wide shoulders filled the doorframe. Abbas dashed into the pantry and grabbed his knife and thrust it into his leggings, threw some bread and his water into a sack, took his walking stick, and presented himself before the Sardar. The man's dark glare shone from beneath his thick, daggerlike eyebrows. He spit tobacco juice from the snuff beneath his tongue through his bushy moustache and beard, and said, "I just hope you didn't wager my camels in your gambling."

He turned away and began leaving. Abbas also left, following behind him. Hajer emerged out of a dark corner while Mergan circled around herself one more time. Then she gave a piece of bread to Hajer.

"Eat this."

Hajer's mouth was bone dry.

"Just try to chew it. If you don't eat, you'll faint before we reach town."

Hajer put the bread in her mouth.

"Ready to go now?"

It was Ali Genav's voice. Mergan replied, "Yes...there's nothing left to take care of here."

Ali Genav set his donkey's tether on the top of the wall and stood back. Mergan took the wooden case in one hand and grabbed Hajer under the arm with the other and headed to the door. As Hajer stepped outside, she sensed Ali Genav's breath on her cheek. He took the edges of the wedding chador in his rough fingers, so as to keep it from dragging on the ground. Mergan led the girl into the alley, while Ali Genav removed the tether from the wall and stood waiting for his bride. He had brushed his donkey, and he had thrown his only Baluchi rug over its saddle. Mergan and Hajer stood beside the animal. Ali Genav bent his left leg in front of Hajer, who was confused by this gesture. Mergan then took her under her arms and lifted her so her foot fell onto Ali Genav's bent leg. From there, she was able to pull herself up onto the donkey. The first thing she felt was the softness of the carpet. As soon as she was settled, Ali Genav drew the donkey's tether over his shoulder and set off.

Mergan followed behind to keep an eye on Hajer, who was grasping onto the back of the saddle with her hands, while her legs were tightly locked around the body of the animal. It was novel for a daughter of Zaminej village to ride a donkey this awkwardly. But this was due to the fact that even when Soluch had a donkey, the boys never gave Hajer a chance to ride on it.

As they passed the entrance to the narrow alley where Ali Genav's house was located, Mergan involuntarily glanced over at the door to the house. The house's entry was half-open, and his wife Raghiyeh was suspended in the doorway like an old tattered shirt, looking at them with her dead eyes. It was a look that shot like electricity through the very marrow of her bones. Mergan stole a look at her, and then hid behind the donkey as they walked on. She heard the crisp snap of the closing door, as if the woman had slipped to the ground sitting against the door as it closed.

Ali Genav was impatient. He thrust a hand into his pocket and brought out a handful of dried berries and walnuts and poured them into the loose edge of Hajer's shirt. Then he tossed a few nuts into his own mouth and tugged on the donkey's bridle.

Abbas was standing by the drain of the bathhouse and was tightening the band holding up his leggings. The Sardar was standing beside the drain a little farther down and was continuing to berate Abbas.

"A gambler's not worth a black coin! I know people who have bet their own herd of camels while gambling!"

Abbas finished tightening his waistband, and then slid his knife into it.

"Well, they had a whole herd to gamble, Sardar. But me, what do I have to lose?"

"You? What about the pants you're wearing? I've seen a gambler ante up his own ass in a game. So how much did you lose last night?"

Ali Genav was all too pleased to happen across his cousin, just to show off a little. He tugged at the donkey's tether and approached the Sardar.

"Good morning, cousin!"

The Sardar looked over Ali Genav, his donkey, and the mother and daughter with him.

"Good. Well, well, so you're heading out to town right now?"

"Need anything from there?"

"No, thanks. May you be blessed, and good luck."

"Goodbye."

Ali Genav continued on by Abbas and his cousin. Mergan stayed hidden behind her daughter, while Hajer shut her eyes as they went. But what for? Abbas didn't even look over at them!

The four of them continued on, and Abbas and the Sardar set out. The Sardar picked up where he'd left off before.

"Eh? Well you didn't say how much you'd lost!"

Abbas didn't reply.

"So how much did you win, then?"

Again, Abbas didn't reply.

"You think I don't know what's going on round here? Ha! Fine, I'll stop asking you. But be careful and keep an eye on the dark male camel. He has a bit of a spring fever. That's something to watch out for, I'll tell you!"

The black camel he was speaking of was standing stiffly apart from the other camels that had gathered in the wide yard and under the curving vestibule leading to the gate. He was scratching his neck against the sharp edge of the wall, his lips were covered in frothy spittle, and there was a wild look in his eyes.

The Sardar drove the camels toward the vestibule and gate by waving the edge of his cloak, which he wore both in winter and summer. Abbas stood by the gate and waved the camels on with his walking stick. The Sardar followed the camels out of the vestibule and stood beside Abbas. Beneath his breath, he measured up the camels happily.

"Go on. Go, and may you be blessed!"

Abbas began to follow the camels.

"I won't offer you any more than that, Abbas!"

"No worries, Sardar!"

Abbas said this and was lost from view in the bend of the alley.

The path was crowded. The young men who were leaving the village were sitting beside their trunks and sacks and were looking at the road ahead. They were still surrounded by their mothers and sisters, but no one was crying. Instead, the air was filled with a mix of excitement and anxiety, and both anticipation and hesitation flickered on their faces. What predominated, however, was the joking common to Zaminej's youth. They were invariably laughing, shouting, and swearing at each other. They had special jokes they played on each other in just these sorts of gatherings. Some of them would bear the brunt of the jokes and would become upset, but their anger would quickly be subsumed in the waves of laughter sounding from those gathered around them.

Ali Genav began to lead his donkey down to the path. But soon, he was trapped in the crowd. And so it was impossible to shake off Hajj Salem and his son demanding wedding sweets from him. But Ali Genav refused to even put his hand in his pocket to placate them. So the youths found a new pretext for their high spirits. They goaded Moslem to collect his share of sweets from Ali Genav. Moslem became more and more riled up as a result. Morad had also joined in the game. But Abrau was standing to one side, where he was focused on listening and watching the road.

Ali Genav finally put a hand into his pocket and freed himself of his obligation. He tugged on the bridle of the donkey, exiting the crowd with the blessings and prayers of Hajj Salem. Now it was the turn of the young travelers to follow tradition and to give something to Hajj Salem and his son before setting off. Hajj Salem stood in the midst of the youth and began reciting a prayer for them. The travelers all became silent.

The Salar's donkeys entered the crowd and mixed with the youth, while Abbas stood to one side. Morad approached him, and they said goodbye with an embrace. One or two of the others also came over to say goodbye. Hajj Salem was praying out loud, intoning a prayer for travelers. The mothers and sisters stood beside their sons or brothers and fought back their tears. Moslem approached Morad, who took off his hat so as to take up a collection of small change for Hajj Salem.

"Just give something, guys! Give a coin or two so we can get rid of him!"

Just then, Ghodrat arrived. The group was complete— twenty-one people. Morad started in on Ghodrat. "Do you think this is a trip to your auntie's house? The sun's been up

forever! And you want to find work in a strange land with useless shoes like those?"

Ghodrat carried a bag over one shoulder and his father was
following him, wiping his runny nose every so often.

"It's coming. It's coming!"

Abrau suddenly shouted and threw himself into the path.

"What's coming?"

"The tractor!"

First, a cloud of dust was visible in the distance. Then
something came into view. Then that sound, a sound entranc-
ing to everyone. But the group was about to leave. They were all
holding their sacks and satchels on their backs, and the mothers had just finished embracing their sons, the daughters
standing to one side with their lips trembling.

Abrau had his hat in his hand and waved to the tractor's
driver from a distance. The tractor approached with an increasing roar. The camels started to buck with fear. Abbas raised his
walking stick over his head and swearing in a continuous
stream at the tractor and its driver as he tried to gather the scat-
tering camels.

The tractor stopped beside the crowd, bringing with it a
cloud of dust from along its way. As soon as those gathered
extricated themselves from the dust, the young men began
walking away in a line along the side of the tractor. The
women gathered at a point on the path to watch their loved
ones leaving. Some of the young men could be seen to be
looking over their shoulders as they went, glancing back at
their mothers and sisters. But as they grew distant, their eyes
met less and less. The men kept walking, and the women
stayed in place.

Ghodrat's father was sitting on a rock. The tractor-driver half-glanced over at the women from beneath his lowered cap. Abrau leapt up to the tractor and put a solid foot on the running board. The driver asked about Salar Abdullah, and Abrau told him they'd need to look for him at his farmland. The driver started up the tractor once again, and on the far side of the machine, Abbas spit at the deep, dusty tracks it left behind.

**

The commotion settled. The women each went their own way. Only Ghodrat's father remained, sitting on the rock holding his head in his hands. Abbas turned and began walking toward the camels, which were following their habitual path to the outlying fields. Abbas was still in the middle of the settling dust, lost in his thoughts. All of his peers were leaving or had already left. Zaminej was emptying out. While they had been there, Abbas had rarely shared a feeling of camaraderie with them; indeed, usually he was at odds with most of them. But now that they had gone or were about to leave, he sensed their absence. Empty places, gaping holes, opened up in Abbas' mind. Like anthills in soft soil, spaces cut into the dirt.

Abbas crushed an anthill with his foot and marched on. He looked again at his feet and saw grass. The open fields. Fields streaked with green glistening beneath the soft warmth of the morning sun. Wide-open lands, tended fields alongside wild lands stretching out into the distance. To reach the distant wild lands where the camels would graze, one had to carefully direct them between farmed fields. He began to gather the camels..."Hey, ho, hey!"

The wheat had just begun to sprout, a green carpet over the fields. The camels were not to enter the wheat fields, as even if they didn't graze on it, they would crush and kill the plants beneath their hooves. The camels were still somewhat full from their morning provisions and so were not much tempted by the wheat stalks. They walked softly and calmly, free of their saddles, bridles, and gear. Camels are quick to sense this freedom, as is easy to see in their gait as they walk. Free of their saddles, they stride freely. They can choose to step lightly or heavily, in long or short steps, either trotting or walking. A camel can choose to stop in its tracks, turn its head over its shoulder, and look around; it can look anywhere and not just straight ahead. It can raise its tail and drop dung, unmuzzled and with nothing around its neck. When the camel's tethered in a train, with one camel's bridle tied closely to the next camel's behind, it loses its individuality. It acts as if it's bearing a load, even if there is none. That's what the bridle and caravan leader tell it: don't step out of line. Unless it is the lead camel, whose tether is handled by the caravan leader. Don't wander. Walk, walk. The leader will lead the way...

But they were free. The Sardar's camels were free in front of Abbas, untethered and without bridles, without anything, not even the bells or chimes that camels often wear. It was spring, and spring breaks the work habit of a camel. It may gallop or trot if it likes. It froths at the lips and there is a wild abandon in its eyes. Spring fever intoxicates.

Abbas had noticed spring fever in the camels over the past few days.

The black male was walking ahead of the others. It was not far to the grazing lands. By the time the sun was up three ticks, the camels would be in the wild lands. The sun was rising, and with it the daybreak's first heat was dissipating. The air felt milder and milder. Abbas began to feel that his shoulder was sweating beneath the sack he was carrying. The sunlight on the red earth reflected against the woolly coats of the camels. Abbas waved his walking stick over his head and called out, "Hey hey hey...you bastard!"

The black male had turned on a mare camel. Abbas ran forward and brought a blow down on the temple of the male, who had grabbed the female's throat in his teeth. Abbas brought down a second blow, and then another. The male let go of the mare and stared at Abbas. Froth was pouring from the edges of his mouth. With a shouted threat, Abbas pushed him forward and broke his stare. The black male camel fell in with the others and began walking ahead. Abbas walked along, calling at the herd.

Over the last few days, the look of the male camel had changed. He seemed unsettled, as if there was a trace of hatred or even anger in his actions. Abbas had sensed this. The male also disturbed the other camels. He would act aggressively toward them, biting at them for no reason. He would suddenly grab at them with his teeth, biting their legs or their ears. Abbas had been riled by this. He had to constantly separate this one camel from the others. With a few blows and by shouting he could eventually be made to let go of the other animal, but sometimes it would take forty blows to his head and legs before he would let go. Abbas was not so softhearted as to be bothered by hitting the animal. He was concerned more for himself in the situation, since this wasn't easy work. Separating two camels, one of which acts drunken and tinged with madness, made him tired and irritable. He would end up sweating all over. Alone in the desert, he'd be exhausted and had to eat more of his bread and drink his water quickly. As a result, he'd return home twice as exhausted as usual and collapse in his bed like a corpse at night.

With the ascending sun, the herd entered the grazing lands. The scrub was long enough for them to eat, green and moist. Other than in spots, these lands were covered by wild *shur*, a kind of plant that only camels can eat while still green, but that could be used for feed for cattle if dried. In the spring and summer, men would gather the *shur* into bundles for feed for their donkeys and camels, stacking it in bundles alongside the outer wall of their homes. The plant would slowly dry up and lose its toughness while taking on some moisture from the rain, making it suitable for their sheep and goats. Some would pound the dried plant to collect its seeds for use in laundering clothes; this was called *ajuvveh*. But as long as it was still green and in the ground, the plant was only suitable for the camels; only their mouths could pull the plant out from the roots and eat it with its salty flavor. The camel's store of water, perhaps, gave it a special ability to digest the plant inside its huge stomach.

Abbas let the camels go free in the field while he set down his sack and sat beside an ancient well.

This now-dry well was, as Abbas himself remembered, one of a chain of salt-water wells that were once connected underground. Before this system dried up, the water in it was used to power the old mill. Salt water is only useful for this, for turning the stone of the mill. But when the water level dropped, the mill also went out of use. And just before the old mill fell out of use, a new motorized mill was set up over in the village of Dehbid, taking over from Zaminej. People now had to take their wheat to this mill instead. So then the old salt-water mill's doors were closed and the miller, old Shahmir, had migrated to Dehbid. There wasn't much for him to do in Zaminej, and he'd gone blind by then as well. The times when Abbas helped his uncle Molla Aman with his peddling he'd sometimes see Shahmir in Dehbid, walking with one hand on a wall and a walking stick in the other, reciting old stories from the epic poems. If the women of Dehbid wanted, they would invite Shahmir into their homes for him to regale them with the old tales that only he knew from the poems.

Now Shahmir's old mill, far away from the village, situated at the end of the underground channel linked by the salt-water wells, had fallen into disrepair. Broken, dry, and crumbling, the mill was half-covered by sand and rubble and was a haven for snakes and mice.

Abbas reached for the water flask, put its mouth to his, and swallowed. The water wet his mouth and throat. He returned the flask to his sack, closed the bag, and lay on his back. Face-to-face with the sun, he brought his eyelids together, closing them. This was what was good about herding camels. You could set the herd loose in a field and then just relax. You could sleep if you were sleepy—it didn't matter. Before the evening prayers, all you had to do was get up once in a while and bring back any camels that had strayed too far away. The camels busied them-selves, and the camel herder was usually free to do as he wished. If he was ambitious, the herder could go out alongside the camels and gather a bushel of the scrub to bring home with himself at dusk. But those who shared Abbas' disposition would just while the day away until sundown, gathering the herd from the various corners of the field while there was still some sun, to bring them back to Zaminej. The evenings were the time for the young men to enjoy; sitting by a wall in the moonlight or gathering in the back room of Sanam's house—that was what Abbas lived for.

But where were the other guys now? All of the other youth, where had they gone?

Between his closing eyelids, Abbas saw his peers leaving...They were already gone. It was so quick. He shut his eyes. He had to forget them. Abbas didn't want to be the kind of man to let useless sorrow into his heart. Just like a young wolf that cannot afford to be swayed by regret or grief, he had to stay focused on eating his next meal and finding the next prey to ambush. No time for sentiments: let sorrow raise its head in some other place, far away.

This was all well and good, but something still bothered Abbas. All this coming and going would no doubt bring changes to the village. Some things were almost certainly going to be rearranged. But what would they be? He couldn't foresee them. He couldn't pass by the old ruins of the salt-water mill with his eyes shut so as to forget Shahmir's sad end. The mill that was now, at best, a haunt for spirits was not so long ago a warm and lively place. The people who brought their barley and wheat to be ground there would gather around its oven in the winter and tell stories and gossip. Abbas had gone there many times with Soluch to bring grain to be ground. Abbas rode on their donkey—this was before it died—holding a sack of barley between his legs while holding onto the bridle. The early mornings brought Soluch to the mill; for this reason, Abbas' memories of the path were usually of sleeping on the way, or of being on the smooth stone ground beside the mill's oven.

But now, the motorized mill of Dehbid could grind all the wheat and barley that was brought to it from all over, making more flour from the grains than one could know what to do with. And old Shahmir, whose eyes could no longer see, was left only with the old stories that filled his mind. He was left to tap his walking stick as he wandered, recollecting all that he'd heard and seen in his life, relating it to others in the weaving of his stories.

Could it be that the youth of Zaminej, Abbas' contemporaries, would never again return to the village?

Abbas was suddenly shaken. What if they didn't return? Some might never come back, since it had been said that after the group of partners set up their motorized water pump, there would be even less water in the cisterns. People were complaining that the pump would suck out the underground water of the surrounding areas. Abbas couldn't get his mind around it all— all of the changes that were beginning to occur. All the talk of pistachio farming. Pistachios. Even the name was unfamiliar. Abbas had never even eaten a pistachio. He'd heard it was something similar to the meat of an apricot pit. He had seen apricots, out in the foothills, while he was traveling with his uncle. But in Zaminej, all that came out of the ground was barley and wheat and cotton. There were fruits also, such as honeydew or watermelons, and in some places people planted tomatoes.

Abbas had heard that the water pump would reach down into the heart of the earth and bring up the water. Mirza Hassan and Salar had hired a few people to dig a well. When he heard this, Abbas thought of his father—himself a well digger. If he were still around, he could have become the overseer of the digging of the water pump's well. They'd not need to have hired well diggers from Dehbid. The rumors were that a few of the other landowners had gotten their courage up and had also invested in the water pump, so they'd be able to make use of it for an hour or two at a time. But most villagers had not only refused to invest in the pump, but had begun to give voice to their dissatisfaction about it as well. Their claim was that the pump would dry out the cisterns, and that if this happened all the other village lands would become dry and worthless. They'd say, "What it means is that once the pump is set up, we'll have to pack up our things and leave the village!"

Ignoring their concerns, Salar Abdullah and his partners expected the pump to arrive from the town any day now. Mirza Hassan himself had spread the word that he'd gone to the capitol recently and settled the business of the pump and that nothing would stand in its way. Today, the tractor had gone out to Mirza Hassan and Agha Malik's lands to plough the earth there. The lands that had previously been readied for dry farming and ploughed in a way to collect rainwater no doubt would be ploughed in a different way from today on.

Abbas thought, "That clever bastard Abrau really knew what he was doing when he jumped onto the tractor's running board! One day, I might find that he's even forgotten his own brother's name!"

Deep in his heart, Abbas didn't like Abrau. He felt like an abandoned fellow traveler, as if Abrau had gone and just left him behind. A dull and dust-covered grudge pierced at Abbas' heart. Just thinking about it made him grind his teeth.

"That son of a bitch! Like a clever dog nuzzling at his owner's stirrups, he's really got himself a nice little situation. But we'll see what happens!"

The lack of sleep from the previous night began to affect Abbas. Under the hot sun, his body began to go numb and his eyelids settled into the soft sands of sleep. The quiet of the fields and the wild lands settled like a weight upon his eyelids. Sleep overtook him. Then, all of a sudden, his body covered in sweat, he lifted his head from his sack and opened his eyes wide—the cry of one of the camels had filled the air. The dark camel had once again attacked the old mare. He had brought her to her knees and was sinking his teeth into her throat just beneath her jaw. The cries of the old mare took different shades, as if she were crying an old woman's lamentation. She waved her head to and fro, and then began to scrape and hit her head against the earth. She cried out in pain, but the dark male would not let go of her throat, as if he was set on her destruction. Abbas had to do something. If the old mare were injured, it would be his responsibility. Of course, even if Abbas couldn't be expected to compensate the Sardar for a lost camel, he would never find work again. They send a man out with the camels for a reason; and they expect you to be just that, a man!

Abbas grabbed his stick and leapt up. He reached the camels quickly. Their necks were bent into each other; the old mare was beginning to lose her breath. Abbas began beating the dark male on the neck, raining blows on him. He grasped the stick with both hands, unconcerned with where he was hitting him, on his head or nose or neck. He beat him, and with each blow his anger rose. He beat him and swore with each blow, cursing the camel and its owner, cursing him and the earth and the sky above.

Even with the most cold-hearted of people, when they are drawn to hit a beast in a moment of rage, there is still a sensation of pity that twinges in their heart. So usually a moment of realization will compel them to step back from their own wild violence. One sees villagers and camel herders or shepherds who, just after they have beaten an animal with a chain or stick or even rake or shovel, will begin to talk to the animal. They may shout at it, if only to give a reason or justification to the donkey or cow or camel for why they were drawn to lose control and take up violence, saying, "How else can I get it into your head, you beast?"

But in this case, the unequal clash between the old mare and the black camel had closed the door of pity in Abbas' heart. Abbas only knew that the black camel would have to be brought into line by force. So it was that he kept beating him with abandon, landing blow after blow upon his face and temple, like a rain of hail upon a black stone. Eventually the black stone cracked: the dark camel let go of the old mare's neck, bellowing in anger, and turned his gaze to Abbas. The old mare drew herself to one side on her knees and lay on her side. Now Abbas had to draw the dark male away from the old mare. But the wild look in the camel's eyes had frozen Abbas to his spot. The camel's mouth was frothing and its eyes were fixed onto Abbas' eyes.

Abbas was taken with fear. But he couldn't back down. One can never give ground to an animal. You can never show fear or it will attack you, throw itself on you, destroy you. He had to gather his wits!

Abbas shook his stick once. He did it again. The camel was supposed to lower its head and walk away. This was what Abbas had hoped. But the camel stayed put, and even began to advance on him. It picked up speed. Abbas backed up, and kept moving back. It was all he could do. He'd heard that one should never show one's back to a threatening camel. But this advice didn't work in the open desert. He recalled hearing how Yargholi met his end. On the road between Damghan and Rey, a crazed camel attacked him and had ripped his arm clean off, right inside the Damghan caravanserai. He was about to be crushed beneath the camel's hooves, but just as it was about to smash his bones, the other herders rushed in and pulled him out from under the beast.

But now? Where were the other herders? Their absence here could well be filled by death. It was death that was now approaching Abbas with long steps, in the form of the large black camel. He could no longer keep backing up while keeping his eyes on the animal. It was impossible to not turn his back on it. It was impossible. Impossible. He had to do something. He was at war. He roused himself and prepared for war. Face-to-face, he lay one blow on the camel's neck. The animal reared and cried out. Abbas attacked again, parrying then backing off. The camel then came at the boy, full of anger. Abbas recalled the old saying "A camel is late to grow angry, but woe to him who conjures anger in a camel!" Putting out the lake of fire that is its anger is no easy task. It will only burn itself out in a torrent of hatred. Its anger is like a thunderstorm raining daggers. Only the desert itself can absorb such a thunderstorm; but a single man, never. Escape. Now all he could do was run. He had to find a way to escape somehow. He needed an able body and quick feet. Be like the antelopes, Abbas! Run, run so fast as to leave even the wind behind. You'll have to run along with the wind, quick and lightly, because the gallop of a camel itself has the speed of the wind in it. Because it's death that is pawing at your back, now. And it's you who are running in the shadow of death; if only you had four feet instead of two!

Abbas wished he were closer to the ruins of Shahmir's old mill.

As he ran, he could feel the muzzle of the camel on his shoulder, as the giant shadow of the animal danced along his feet, rushing along the surface of the earth. Thirst. The moist breath of the camel was like the breath of a serpent that tickled the back of Abbas' neck, hotter than the heat of any desert wind. His shoulder and neck were wet with spit from the camel's mouth, but Abbas' own sweat prohibited him from being able to sense it. There was only a single step between him and death. A single breath. But death, when it nears you, puts its body upon yours without your feeling it. That is the moment when life dangles along the border of two opposing forces. That is the moment when weakness overpowers, after the climax of a struggle. It's the possibility of death that is so terrifying, not its actuality. And Abbas was already at the heart of death, and the intensity of fear had already drawn him to the climax of the struggle against it. He was now numb, and that fear that most often results in one's surrender was put out from Abbas' mind. There was no chance for him to even think, no chance for the kind of thinking that often leads one to surrender to the onset of death. For this reason, he could not even consider this possibility. Even to think, one needs a proper time and place. But Abbas could only run and run. This action was all that his body and soul would accept for him, and toward this end he deployed every ounce of power stored within his muscles and bones. His feet carried him on. The wind blew across an empty field, full of sunlight. Terror. Twigs and dried brambles. Winding shadows, the way of death in the approach of the camel. How unjust it is! A crazed beast grabs at the body of a man and knocks him with one hoof. The man falls. He tries to raise himself in vain, hoping against hope. But escape is impossible. His hope is in vain! The camel throws himself upon the man, dragging him beneath his chest. Just so he's positioned directly beneath the bow of the animal's chest. Then it crushes him, in such a way that as the sound of the man's breaking bones are heard, and as he cries out from the pain of his pulverized limbs, and as the crazed animal cries out as well, he dies.

This was what Abbas was facing, what he could be facing at any moment. His destiny. Oh no! The camel grabbed at his shoulder. He shook his body in defense, but the camel's teeth continued gripping his shirt and jacket. The flag of death was rising. Abbas sent the last of his strength to his knees, but it was already too late. The crazed animal was already like a tent above him. Now he grabbed at Abbas' head. The crazed scream of a human echoed across the fields. The camel was about to lift him and to throw him to the earth when Abbas pulled his head from its jaws and fell to his knees. Now the camel's hooves were upon him. Abbas slid and rolled like a snake on the ground. The camel dropped to its knees to try to grab him again in its jaws. This was Abbas' last chance. He raised himself to his knees and drew his knife from his waistband. There was no other choice so as to end the battle. But to slaughter a crazed camel is not something any man can do on his own.

Even the oldest and weakest camel of a herd needs to be tied down, and it takes six men with six lengths of rope around its limbs and body for the seventh to be able to slit the animal's throat at the jugular. And this itself isn't the end of the story. Even at this point the animal, in the throes of pain with its throat cut, can tear off the ropes holding it down and crush the men who are near to it. So what hope could there be for a single boy with no assistance and no rope to tie down the crazed animal to be able to defend himself with a single knife? To be able to slay the animal on the spot? To be able to kill it quickly and escape the death throes of the dying animal? Even if this camel is already struck by madness?

Abbas knew that he would have to thrust the knife directly into the jugular, just at the base of the animal's chest. He would have to do it without hesitation, and plunge the knife in to its handle. But this usually is done with the camel in your control, not the other way around. But then this was a battle, not the slaughter of a farm animal. Customs and traditions were irrelevant and were replaced by instinct and emotion. Mergan's son, his eyes swimming in sweat, with the sound of the sun beating in his head, began to stab at the animal hopelessly. He stabbed at its face, eyes, neck, and chest. The blade glinted in the crimson sun. His sleeve and shoulders and face were covered in blood. His nose, forehead, and eyes bloody. Drops of blood in the dusty sunlight. Streaks stained the earth, streaks on the dust, red reflections. The sunlight, the dirt, and the sand were purple and violet and yellow. The colors swirled together and yet also separated, pulled away from one another. Were not the earth and sky crimson from before? Breaths of air, breaths of wind blew. Wind, such a wind! A deed in one stroke, a battle

in one blow. Beneath the camel's neck. The jugular. A clean
stab, directly in the hollow of the camel's neck.

He pulled out the knife. Blood poured, a river of it. But
things were worse now. The camel was a thousand times more
enraged. It was now also a matter of life and death for the animal. And so if death was about to take it, was it going to just sit
and wait for it? But just then it seemed about to do just that by
lowering its head before Abbas.

Could it be that this river of blood had finished the camel,
broken it?

* * *

The camel suddenly reared itself again and threw Abbas to one
side, twisting upon itself with a cry of fury. Its mouth now
foamed blood, as it renewed its attack. Abbas collected his wits,
but his strength gave way. His only hope was the well—it was his
last chance. The old, dry, salt-water well. He dragged his body
toward it. Exhausted, spent, and in pain, helpless and hopeless,
he had one thought in his mind: in only a moment he could well
be dead. The camel also gathered its own strength, like a viper,
to pour the last cup of death into Abbas' veins. It leapt toward
him, but just before it reached him, Abbas threw his body into
the dry well.

With a flutter of birds escaping as he fell, Abbas felt something hit his head and he was unconscious.

When did Abbas awake? It was night... How late was it?
Abbas couldn't tell.

Above his head, he only saw a small patch of the sky. A tight,
circular field of sky dotted with white stars. Bits of constella-

tions shone, the Big Dipper. How the stars twinkled! They seemed to be panting, almost as if they were thirsty. Abbas' tongue was dry, as was his throat and entire mouth. He licked his lips with his dry tongue, and it felt as if it were a lump of sod. There was no moisture, so also his lips were dry. Even the stars seemed to be panting, panting from thirst!

Abbas moved his body. His entire body cried out in pain. The pain wasn't just in one limb; it coursed through the whole of his body. His hand was still grasping the handle of the knife. Conscious or unconscious, the imperative to defend himself had kept his grip on the knife throughout. He slowly lifted his hand from the powdery floor of the well. It was as dark as a grave, and nothing was visible. But he could feel that something was caked onto his hands, dried on them. He brought his hand to his nostrils and smelled it. Blood. His own blood, the blood of the camel. But where was he injured? It felt as if part of his shoulder had been torn. He felt at his legs and sensed that a part of the heel of one foot was gone. Where else? He couldn't recall what had happened very clearly. Only pain filled his mind. Pain where the camel's hooves had struck him, where he had been thrown against the earth, all over his back, his waist, his shoulders. His legs, his head. Pain all over. Exhaustion. Being pummeled. Thrown against the ground, rolling beneath the hooves of the camel. Struggle, a hopeless struggle for life and limb. Blows. Muscles beaten with blows. His joints felt as if they had been pulled apart. He felt as if it was impossible to even move.

And the well? He was just beginning to realize where he was. How tight it was! And deep, three and a half, maybe four lengths of a man's body. And the well was dug into soft sand. So even if he were strong enough to do it, there was nowhere to find a footing to pull himself up. As he was sitting there, a handful of dusty soil rustled down onto his head from the walls of the well. He smelled something.

And a sound, the sound of a camel's steps. The sound of a camel breathing. The cry of a camel's neigh. The dark camel, exhausted and injured, was still at the top of the well, crying in either anger or pain. It neighed and stomped on the ground. The dust that was settling on his head and shoulders had been shaken loose from the steps of the camel. The animal still wanted blood. It had been unsatiated, so it stayed at the mouth of the well. It had the natural capacity to wait in one place for nine days and nights without water or food, just to keep a hungry and thirsty Abbas trapped below. As for Abbas, he'd never be able to hold out for more than a couple of days. Even now he was desperate for a sip of water. He tried again to wet his lips a little. In the struggle he had waged beneath the sun, his body's water had been depleted. Now his tongue felt more like a piece of mud brick that had been baked in an oven. If only he could have a cup of water!

Abbas looked up. The camel's neck cut across the sky, separating Abbas' view from the stars. He blocked more than half of the constellation of Orion. Drops of blood still dripped from the camel's neck, dripping onto Abbas' dusty hair and temples. The camel wanted blood. For it, there could be no end to this other than Abbas' death. There was only one blind hope left, which was if the herd of other camels wandered back to Zaminej and the Sardar came out from the village looking for the missing black camel. And better if, along with him, Mergan and Abrau were also coming, with a lantern in hand. And if it had made it back to Zaminej, the wounded neck of the old mare camel could also be a sign of what had happened. That neither Abbas nor the black camel had returned to the village. The Sardar himself had remarked that morning that the black camel was showing signs of the drunkenness of spring fever.

But how could he know if the rest of the herd would head back to Zaminej?

Yet if they didn't go, that might even be better. Then perhaps the Sardar would be quicker to put on his shoes, take a walking stick and lantern, and collect some others to all come out to the open fields to look for the herd. This was the only hope, this and the outline of the mouth of the well which afforded him a view of the sky, and which brought in a little air for him to breathe. And the stars, how they seemed to be panting!

Another warm drop of blood fell on Abbas' face. The camel, angry and disturbed, now knelt at the edge of the well. He fit his head and shoulders as far as they could enter the well, and cried out. Another drop fell on Abbas' lips. He moistened his tongue and lips with the blood. Clearly, his knife had not been effective. If he had stabbed the camel in the right place, the animal would have been dead by now. The camel repositioned itself so that its chest and part of its belly covered most of the well. It rested a while, but this was even more terrifying. Now Abbas could only see one star in the sky, just next to the neck of the camel. Abbas now imagined that the camel would simply remain there until he died. He began to lose hope. If only he had a cup of water!

A soft rustling compelled Abbas to turn his attention away from the certainty of death, and from the camel above.

Rustling...A sound softer than a person snoring. Something like: *kurrrrrr, kurrrrrr*. Night filled the well in the deepest darkness. Where and how could he figure out the source of the sound around him? He'd need an eagle's senses, or rather, those of a bat!

Kurrrrrr...Kurrrrrr...

What kind of insect could be making this sound? He tried to sharpen his eyes; he placed all his senses into the act of seeing. Something flew, its wings slapping against the walls of the well. A handful of dust and sand poured down, and then the sound began again.

Kurrrrrr...Kurrrrrr...

A blanket of fear slipped over him, from whatever was silent all around him. A hesitant fear rising from uncertainty. If you know what it is that threatens you, then just by knowing what the instrument of your death is, you can try to prepare yourself. You can even choose just to give in to it. You may find no option but to go calmly. You might faint, and in a sense die before dying. You're relieved from the endless possibilities that your imagination can conjure up, stinging you with each fear. If you know what the instrument of your death may be, you are less anxious. Instead, all of your anxiety is focused on one thing. And what kills you isn't the anxiety, it's death itself. What Abbas faced in the struggle against the camel was simply to run, attack, strike, and to defend himself. There was nothing unclear about the threat to divide his fear into a hundred different possibilities. His opponent, the camel, was the essence of the danger. One may eventually forget pain itself, but one will never forget the threat of pain. The spirit flutters its wings, like a pigeon caught in an enclosed well. It's anxious; it flutters its wings against the walls. Fear overtakes, waves of fear. Something spreads through its body and soul. Again and again, without a moment's respite. The poisonous tongues of fear liquefy your fortitude little by little. You sense that you are slowly encompassed by the fear. Your inner focus collapses; it's at this very moment that your inner defenses crumble. An impossible hope pulls you: O sudden death, when will you strike? Why doesn't this well just collapse in on itself?

A rustling...

Then, a small, faint light. Like a night crawler, on the bottom layer of the well. It was as if it was inside a hole or sunken into the dirt. He tries to look. The sound is coming from these same spots. Small light spots are faintly pulsating. They're visible, then invisible. The sound stops and starts again. It seems something or some things are moving. It'd be impossible for anyone to see in such a deep darkness. But if you were stuck in the depths of the well as Abbas, you would feel that the essence of all human perception has been granted to you, just so that you can perceive what it is that is rustling beside you.

Oh, God...! Snakes...! They've sensed a new prey, inside their lair.

In some situations, it seems as if some people must die and be reborn a thousand times. This was Abbas' experience. He was circled by snakes. Desert snakes. Ancient snakes. If one was to breathe the fire of its breath at you, you'd be ashes.

So why was Abbas still alive?

That he would die inside the well now seemed a certainty for him. But to know when and how the snakes would come for him was something he couldn't know. He'd only heard scattered sayings about snakes from those who were snake catch-ers, herders, farmers, or older villagers with their own experiences of snakes to relate:

"A snake will never harm an innocent person."

"A snake knows the good of your soul."

"Never step on a snake's tail."

"If you see a snake move away, move away as well."

"A house snake is a blessing; don't bother it."

But none of this was of any use to Abbas now. He was not even able to ask himself what he could do. He couldn't even pin his hopes on some far-fetched possibility. His mind was simply empty. A silent terror had so thoroughly woven itself into him that he couldn't think at all. What should he wish for? What could he desire? Above, a merciless night. Beneath the night, the hell of the well. Between the night and the well stands a bloody and enraged camel. With his own battered body, Abbas couldn't ask himself how to escape? Whom to call to for help?

For one to begin to accept the need to give in, to accept the certainty of giving oneself to death, is certainly an extraordinary experience. And usually, when one happens to consider or give voice to such a sentiment, it is when death is in fact by no means a certainty. When death rears its head, one usually has no time to give a thought to surrendering to it. You don't have a chance to, either to surrender or to try to defend yourself. In a moment, you become a mass of particles that are all at once finished. Or one can say, it's like fire, or rather it's fire itself. You are entirely in flames. You burn quickly and are finished. Even if you're dried out, nearly dead already, even if you're at the bottom of the sandy walls of a well and you've aged a thousand years. Even if fear has frozen you, so that you can't move or allow yourself to hear yourself breathe.

Mergan's son was going to die, quickly and certainly. Even though it was as if he had been dead for hundreds of years and now it was only his ghost that was tracing a silent, hollow outline against the wall of the well before him, embodying something deeper than silence within itself. Oh... if only he could be certain that he was still breathing!

Is it possible for time to freeze in one moment? Of course not...However, a certain illusion sometimes leads one to imagining it has frozen. It is this very moment that ties you to the world by a thread of hair. In another moment, these experiences could be separated. For this reason, at the height of this fusion, one can only sense silence, total silence. But time has not stood still. The well grows slowly lighter by the crack beside the neck of the camel. If you had the strength to move, if you could look above yourself, through this crack, you would see that the sky was filling with light. The star, that only star you could see earlier, was losing its brightness.

The dawn was breaking. Hours had passed; many moments had given their lives. You could now see the camel's neck more clearly against the mouth of the well, but only once you find it possible to move your head upon your neck. When you've escaped your paralysis and the spell upon you has broken and your eyes are no longer frozen on what is just in front of you. What you were staring at, captured by, even as dust has settled on your eyes and draws webs over all you can see. Your gaze has exceeded itself, broadened itself, grown distant. In your eyes the particles around you are not what they are. They have been transformed. Dirt is not dirt. The wall is not a wall. Day is not day. You are transfixed, lost in your gaze. The snakes... two dark snakes, two old snakes, perhaps two vipers can now be seen more clearly. Morning has probably broken.

The snakes were looking at Abbas. But Abbas no longer exists. He has become ashes. One of the snakes moves, slithering slowly. It unwinds its coil softly. It grows longer and longer. It faces Abbas. If only it were possible to say, "Put me out my misery!" If only it were possible to say this sincerely. But this is now impossible; the soul is frozen. The snake approaches, puts its head on Abbas' knee, and slides over. It slithers softly and settles itself, coiling again and waiting. How long? Not for long, just as long as Abbas' life is spent, then it will no doubt move on. It slithers over his naked belly, slides over his chest, and on his shoulder begins to circle around his neck, passing through his hair. Then heading to the wall, it softly departs from Abbas' body and stops at the edge of the floor. Abbas no longer felt anything. He was blind, deaf, dumb, and numb. A corpse plunged into a cold sweat.

* * *

Hey...Hey...Abbas...Ahay!
Hoy...Hoy...Abbas...Hey!
Ahay...Aha...Abbas...Ahay!

The drunken cry of the camel sounded both near and far over the fields. The near and distant sounds of the field were caught in the camel's cry. Sounds, not those sounds that are familiar, but those that are confused, incredible. The onset of sounds, cries, wails, prayers, shouts. The long shadows of hawks, vultures.

How much time has passed? How many suns?

The sounds came from another world. The world that they spoke of, the Day of Judgment. The so-called day of the fifty-thousandth year. The blistering hot day that they say will find mothers seeking their children and not finding them, brothers seeking brothers, children their mothers and fathers. The day of fifty thousand years! The day no one is no one to anyone. Where one hand will not recognize the other, nor one eye the other. Abbas is dead, and he is dragging his battered body across the hot desert sands of the Day of Judgment. Abbas is dead and hears the lamentations of his mother, brother, sister, and father from within his grave. But then Mergan pierces a crack into the grave; Mergan's shouting and crying is heard. Mergan on the year of the fifty-thousandth year. The refugees of the hot desert, carrying the load of sins on their shoulders, beneath the hot sun. The sun of hell's fire. The dead have raised themselves from their graves and are silent. The day of reckoning. Hands are shaking in all directions. Hands and shoulders uncovered. Uncovered bodies writhe against each other, their mouths, tongues, cries, all silent. Fear and terror. Bodies in shrouds. Thirst. Panting from thirst. Fire rains from the sky. Abbas is dragged from the grave. He's uncovered, nude. The sun. The desert is panting. They encircle him; the camel is dead. Its body is bloated. The poison from the snake's venom has bloated it. The Sardar is beating himself with his fists. The camel lies to the side of the well; its legs are stiff. Hajer is hiding herself behind Ali Genav. Abrau cannot bring himself to look at his brother. Ali Genav cannot remove his eyes from the shock. Mergan can't believe it. No! This is not her Abbas! She comes forward. Abbas is at the edge of the well. He doesn't move. He's spellbound. Paralyzed. The sun shines. The hairs on Abbas' head are all entirely white.

The boy's sack falls from Mergan's hand to the ground. Mergan comes closer. No! How can one believe it? An old man stands before her. She comes closer. Her eyes are like the outlines of two dry wells. In the depths of her eyes, two old vipers are coiled. They are lost. The sun of hell shines over the fields and into Mergan's eyes. Her gaze is lost in the fields. She puts her hand upon Abbas' hand. His hand is in his mother's hand. Mergan begins to walk; everyone begins to walk. The Sardar remains with the body of his camel. They walk slowly. An old man is holding Mergan's hand. They are silent. Silence, sun, the sun of hell fire rains on the fields. Where is water?

4.

Karbalai Doshanbeh was used to sitting with his back to the wall. He would sit with his legs wide apart, the palms of his feet flat on the ground, and his elbows on his bony knees and he would finger his worry beads.

The cup of tea sitting before him had grown cold, and he was staring quietly into space. His silence was as heavy as a millstone. He was like a useless millstone leaning against a wall. Old and out of use, heavy and silent. He had plenty of reasons for making an appearance at Mergan's house, such as to ask about Abbas' health or to offer congratulations on Hajer's upcoming marriage. But more effective than these was the excuse of Molla Aman's presence in Zaminej village: this was Molla Aman, his old friend and the former herder of his camels. However, the actual motivation for his visit was doubtless the debt that Molla Aman owed to Karbalai Doshanbeh. It was time for Molla Aman to at least settle the interest that had accumulated on his loan so far. His host Mergan could choose to accept any of the possible excuses for Karbalai Doshanbeh's visit. The generous interpretation of his visit was the idea that he had come to see his old friend and companion Molla Aman, and was enjoying a cup of tea celebrating the marriage of this old friend's niece. The more jaundiced interpretation was the notion that Karabalai Doshanbeh suspected Molla Aman of trying to cheat him out of his dues and that he had shown up right then and there to begin such a row that the good news of the wedding would be quickly forgotten by all in the village. Mergan knew that both of these possibilities simply meant that he had at his disposal the ability to present different excuses, giving him the right to show up uninvited to her house in the morning over the next day or two: he could slide in and sit in a corner quietly, drinking tea, and, if possible, eating the bread and stew offered him, occasionally tossing out a suggestion or comment invariably tinged, as they always were, with sarcasm or a veiled insult. This was his nature and in fact the story of his life, and the residents of Zaminej had come to just recognize it as the way he was.

Since Molla Aman was in a tight spot, he had no choice but to act obsequious and deferential to Karbalai Doshanbeh. He had to let pass most of the more insulting insinuations and had to find a way of coming to terms with his old friend. At heart, he simply wanted to find a way to bear the next two days, since he didn't have much keeping him in Zaminej. He was only there to give Hajer's hand to Ali Genav before taking his donkey's tether and heading back out on his way. As for Abbas, it was clear that there was nothing to be done for him.

Abbas sat in a dark corner, quietly staring at the floor, as if in shock. No one bothered him, and he interacted with no one. He was silent and sullen, with lips shut and eyes open. Eyes that had not yet seen sleep. Yet no remedies were offered him, no prayers said for him.

"Just wait a few days. A few days have to pass first."

This had been Karbalai Doshanbeh's suggestion. Ali Genav had nodded his head to this. Molla Aman had to respond in turn, and said, "What's done is done. Now things just have to return to normal. Ah...life is full of these twists and turns!"

Hajer was hiding herself somewhere. It seemed the event that had befallen her brother was not an auspicious sign for her.

Abbas' sudden aging was interpreted most simply and persuasively by Ali Genav.

"I myself spoke to a *dervish* in front of Shazdeh's caravanserai that somewhere in the Mount Shahjahan region the same thing happened to another boy, but that after a few days he'd returned to normal. These worries are just a stage; they will pass. You can't get wrapped up in them. Eh, Uncle? What do you think about this?"

Molla Aman looked over at Karbalai Doshanbeh.

"Karbalai Doshanbeh is much more worldly than I!"

The response came, "Just wait a few days. A few days have to pass first."

Molla Aman had agreed earlier, and then agreed again.

"Yes, well...What else can we do? It's just the way of the world!"

But Mergan was on fire, burning like incense. It was as if smoke was pouring from her eyes.

"Auntie...Auntie..."

Ali Genav had begun calling Mergan "Auntie." Mergan walked out of the room and joined him where he had drawn himself against the outside wall.

"Everything is ready now. I've cleaned the house as well. It's ready."

Mergan replied, "Very well. Come tonight and take your wife's hand in yours and you can take her to your home. What else should I tell you?"

Ali Genav asked, "Is everything set with her clothes, bedding, shoes...?"

"They'll be ready."

"Fine, good. So I'll go and make the rounds, now. And listen, I've made arrangements for dinner to be ready there tonight. You come and bring Uncle Molla Aman with yourself. Afterward, you can bring back a couple of bowls of meat for Abbas and Abrau as well. Okay?"

"Fine. Okay."

Ali Genav left and Mergan returned to the house. Karbalai Doshanbeh and Molla Aman were still sitting against the wall. Mergan passed by the stove, under Karbalai Doshanbeh's gaze, and entered the pantry.

"I need to have a word with Hajer. I need to tell her a few things!"

Karbalai Doshanbeh's gaze followed Mergan and then crossed over to Molla Aman, whose head was lowered. Karbalai half-smiled as he said, "So go make Mergan a bride! Why don't you marry her off?"

Molla Aman raised his head and was about to open his mouth when Karbalai Doshanbeh spoke again. "I wish I would die! I smashed my own wife like she was made of crystal! My neck could break from all of the gossip they told about me! I wish people's tongues would fall out!"

Molla Aman said, "Don't start all over, Karbalai. What's happened, has happened."

Karbalai Doshanbeh said, "The hurt is still there. She was like fine crystal, that woman. But the gossip! She gave birth in the seventh month, and the gossip began. Disrespectful mob! They kept saying, 'That girl was pregnant before she entered her husband's home'!"

"The innocent girl! After all, would I know better, or them? But I smashed my beautiful crystal with my own hands. I wish my neck would have been broken instead! After that, even water was too bitter for me to drink. I beat that girl like she was a beast, and kicked her out. In the cold of winter, with the babe in her arms. And I don't know where she ended up! How could a seven-day-old baby survive the cold winter outside? The poor child! It's all the fault of Abdullah's mother, my first wife. She was the one who began all the gossip. Evil woman! She didn't want to see a shepherd's daughter on God's Land. And if I'd kept her at home, she might have done her in herself. In any case, she wanted me to be without a second wife. Although I can say I also was able to make the life of Abdullah's mother hell. From that day on, I ended any real marital relationship between us. Absolutely! And it's been twenty years. That's what she gets for her gossiping. But...but, now the old woman's beginning to win the fight. She's kicked me out of my own house and left me in the old storage shed. Well, her son's now become a man for himself. *Salar* Abdullah! He provides for her. What does she need me for? She refuses to even wash my laundry. She won't even offer me a glass of water to wet my bread in. If I were in the throes of death, she wouldn't so much as open the door for me! It's as if we're not husband and wife, as if we never were! But I understand...She's getting her revenge. But...but, I wish my own neck had been broken rather than my having made my beautiful crystal of a wife homeless as I did. I broke her myself."

Molla Aman again said, "Don't start all over, Karbalai. Don't renew the pain!"

"But it's still there, Molla Aman. Its pain doesn't grow old. Unless...unless someone were able to fill her place...Molla Aman, you need to make her a bride. Mergan needs to remarry! Her husband's dead. Soluch didn't have the constitution to survive the difficulties of living far away from here. I've done it myself. I've seen how it is. I can tell you, he's dead. No doubt, he is dead. I promise you, I've heard so myself. And there is a legal basis for it. You just need three reliable witnesses to say that Soluch is dead, and then Mergan can remarry. There is another way, too, in the law. If a man leaves home for some months without any word—I'm not sure how many—his wife gains custody of the household. You see what I'm saying? It'd be good for you and me to become family. We've traveled far together, as friends, companions. We can settle our accounts with each other as well. So, have a word with your sister. How long does she expect to go on without someone's protection? And she's still a young woman; she's in good health. It's just the bad luck that she's had that has twisted the poor thing a bit. So do something so I can take her in hand and help her. And God will surely repay you for the good deed it is. I'm sure this is what the prophet would have wanted himself."

Karbalai Doshanbeh rose and shook the dust from his pants.

"These children need a guardian as well. You can't be keeping an eye on them all the time. But tonight I'll come to Ali Genav's for dinner."

Molla Aman accompanied Karbalai Doshanbeh to the alley and returned.

Mergan was standing by the door with a look full of anger.

"What was he talking about now?"

"Nothing...Let's go inside."

They went back into the house together.

Hajer was sitting by her box and was sorting through her things. Abbas was still in the same place, silent against the wall, with his big eyes, his disheveled white hair, his hollow cheeks, his crooked teeth, his gaunt face. His white hair, white as white.

Mergan sat on the floor angrily. She hid her face in her hands and plaintively said, "What does that man want, coming to my house?!"

Molla Aman said, "He's an acquaintance. What can I say?"

"What kind of acquaintance? The kind that can go to hell! Karbalai Doshanbeh is no acquaintance of mine! He just shows up out of the blue when you're here for a day or two."

"So you're upset that he comes to see me?"

"Not that he comes to see you, but that he uses you as an excuse to come here. And you can't stand up to him, since you owe him money!"

"So what do you want? Shouldn't I come here to see you?"

"Not at all. Why're you saying that? You're my brother, my older brother, but you're giving this bastard an excuse to come around here. And then others will start whispering about it. Ever since Soluch has gone, this man has been sniffing around this house, scratching at the door. And how he likes to put on airs! Even snakes hate pennyroyals like him and would rather coil up somewhere than deal with one."

Abbas trembled for a moment, as if tremors had passed through his body, and then he was calm again.

Molla Aman said, "Yes, and he's gone so far as to invite himself to dinner as well."

"Dinner? Where? Here?"

"No, at your future son-in-law's."

Mergan raised her voice. "He's a fool if he's invited himself! That pathetic beggar. And everywhere he goes, he expects a reception."

Molla Aman said, "He says he has witnesses who say that Soluch is dead."

Mergan replied, "Fine! If he's dead, he's dead. God rest his soul. But what's it to him?"

"Maybe Soluch owed him money?"

"He can take the debt to the grave. I'm too busy with my own affairs to be caught up with the little chirp-chirps of the likes of him. I've moved on, and it has nothing to do with me. Let him run after other people's bad luck. I don't need to take on something that will put me in a cage with a wild dog!"

"But if Soluch is in fact dead..."

"My worries are that I have two sons to care for. What am I to do with them? And with one in the state you see him in! Can't you see him?"

Molla Aman looked at Abbas and said, "He's not asking to marry your sons. He wants to take you to his house."

"And how does he propose to help my sons? Wasn't he just saying they need a guardian?"

"That was just talk. Your daughter's going to go to her husband's home. And your sons are almost old enough to leave the nest on their own. And so you would go to his home."

"His *home*! You're a real simpleton, aren't you? You know he's living out in the storage shed. Which home does he expect me to go to? I even hear that there's trouble between Salar Abdullah and his wife. Because she's being tortured by this black-mouthed, big-bellied, old man hanging around their house. You really believe him? You'll see, in two days he'll be slithering over here with a blanket to shed his skin in!"

Molla Aman said, "You know what's going on better than I do. I'm just telling you what he's said. I'll leave it in your hands from there."

Mergan rose and said, "I don't want a husband. Maybe Soluch's dead, and maybe he's still alive. But I'm too busy with my own work now!"

***

The evening stretched out. If Mergan began her errands now, they'd take until the dusk call to prayer to complete. She'd taken Hajer to the baths. Now she had to do the rest. She had purchased a bit of rouge and face powder. But she had to pluck the hairs on Hajer's face first. She brought out an old broken mirror in a wooden frame and set it by the door against the wall. Then she brought over a box and set it by the mirror and took her daughter's wrist and sat her by the mirror as well.

"Nothing to be afraid of! Every bride has her face hairs plucked!"

She had laid out the threads to use for the task beforehand. She hooked the threads onto her fingers and began running them in a cross pattern across Hajer's small face. The girl pulled her head away from the threads that were ruthlessly tugging at the skin on her cheeks. Mergan berated her and told her to hold still for a little. Hajer tried to stay calm, but the pain and burning she felt on her face was too much. She was just about able to stay still, but couldn't hold back the tears, which slowly filled her eyes. But Mergan showed no mercy and kept tugging at and burning the girl's dry skin with the threads, and Hajer's face became more and more scarlet from the friction, as if she had been slapped, or even as if she'd been bruised.

"All the better! You'll have a bit of life and color in your face now. You can't go over there looking like a corpse!"

Mergan was clearly distracted. Her only worry was to find the nonexistent little hairs on her daughter's lips and face and to eradicate them. So what if it hurt!

"The first time always hurts. All the girls feel the same burning when they thread their faces for their wedding!"

"It's burning me, mama. It's burning!"

"Now, that's better."

Megan pulled Hajer's face into the light and examined it closely. There was nothing left; her entire face was now scarlet and irritated. Like a beet, nearly bruised. It was time for Hajer to splash some water on her face.

"Now, get up and quickly wash and come back!"

Hajer ran outside. The bucket was half full of water. Hajer thrust her entire face into it.

Molla Aman rose and made as if to leave. He stood by the door and said, "If you want the truth, I've heard myself that Soluch is dead, God have mercy on him."

He didn't wait to hear Mergan's reply; he stepped out and left. Mergan had nothing to say; she just felt numb and dizzy. But she gathered her wits quickly and cried out at Hajer, "Are you taking a bath out there? Come back, it's getting late!"

Hajer thrust her face into the bucket one last time, then rose and returned to her mother.

Mergan had prepared the rouge and face powder. Her look had become softer, gentler. As if she'd just remembered not to snap at her daughter—it was her wedding night, after all. Why direct her anger with Karbalai Doshanbeh at her daughter instead? Hajer was innocent, even though Mergan did not reckon herself a culprit either. It was just that they wouldn't let her rest for even a second. She would escape from the cage they set for her like a wild animal, and before she'd realize it she'd have bit some person—her children were the most common victims of her anger. And this would in turn only distress her more.

And now, what had happened to Abbas came to be the greatest blow yet. His sudden aging, his injuries, his silence had all affected her terribly. Her hands had begun to tremble, and her eyes would dart from place to place. She would say one or two words and then be choked by tears that were welling in her eyes. It was as if she had lost her self-control. She'd go into a rage over nothing. She was sleepless and distracted. Her thoughts tormented her, depressed her—thoughts about Hajer's wedding, which deep down Mergan knew better than anyone was an ill-considered, inopportune deed. Thoughts about losing the bit of land they had had, about her sons having turned on her, and now, about the pain Abbas was in. Add to that the marriage proposal from Karbalai Doshanbeh and Mirza Hassan's skill at taking their land...and now, Soluch's death!

But could it be true? Was Soluch dead?

***

"Oh yes...look at that! Look at that!"

It was Ali Genav, whose body blocked the light. He was smiling. Hajer turned away and covered her eyes with the edge of her headscarf. Ali Genav pursed his big lips and looked at Mergan, who gestured at him to leave. She didn't want Hajer to be affected by her fear of him.

Ali Genav turned to go, unhappily but still happy. Mergan finished applying the rouge to Hajer's face. She rose, filled a cup with water, and set it beside her. Raising Hajer's headscarf, she wet a comb in the water and drew it through the girl's hair. Her hair was clean, thin, and fine, and it shone with its blackness.

Mergan combed her daughter's hair with a hint of sadness, and the girl rested her head on her mother's arm and looked at the ground with a deeper sadness. She stared at the earth. She was engaged now! That's that. Marriage!

Hajer could not help but think about how easily everything had been handled when they went to town. The cost of making the engagement legitimate was even clearer to her than to her mother: the pair of red shoes, two silk scarves, a shirt, and a chador for praying. After the purchases, they took her from the bazaar into the alleys and through the alleys to the caravanserai. There, Ali Genav bought some bread and sweets. They sat by the walls of the cavanserai looking toward the coffeehouse and ate the food. Then Ali Genav went over to the coffeehouse and brought three large teas back to them. They drank the teas. Then Ali Genav went to the caravanserai stables and put a bit of food out for his donkey there. Then it was time to go, so they left. The alley behind the caravanserai connected to the central mosque. The lower door of the mosque led into the courtyard, which they crossed and exited through the higher door. Ali Genav led them across a street and back into narrow alleys. They passed by a cistern and entered a very narrow alley: Twisting and turning, it became more and more narrow. So much so that Hajer began to feel dizzy. All she remembered was that the surface of the ground was cobblestone, which she could remember from the sensation of the stones pushing at her feet through her leather shoes. At the end of the alley, they stopped beside a low door, lower than the alley's surface. You had to descend three steps to the door, through which you reached a small courtyard. Next to the shallow pool in the center of the courtyard, there were six pomegranate trees. Ali Genav took the women up a set of stairs onto a veranda. They had Hajer sit there by a door while Ali Genav and Mergan went inside. Hajer never saw the cleric; she only heard his voice, which was interrupted by his constant coughing. He sounded old. He asked Hajer to say "I do," which she did, and the job was done. Now Ali Genav could take her hand in his, which he did and he brought her down the veranda stairs. Then they returned in the same way: alley, street, mosque, alley to the caravanserai.

Ali Genav took his donkey out of the caravanserai stables, placed the bridle on him, and took the tether in hand. He paid for the stable, and left. Hajer and Mergan followed behind the donkey. Outside the town gates, Ali Genav stopped and again knelt for Hajer. Mergan grabbed her under her arms and she got onto the donkey. Ali Genav held onto the tether for a while, but after some distance, he tossed the tether on the donkey's neck, pushed the tethering nail into the saddle, and walked alongside Hajer's leg.

Mergan followed them and was lost in thought. Once, she sat down on the side of the path to adjust her shoes. Ali Genav had bought her new shoes, which she hadn't yet broken in. Her feet were sweating in them. Once they reached the outskirts of Zaminej, Mergan walked about a hundred paces ahead of them. She was far enough ahead that Ali Genav was able to pinch Hajer's leg two times. Hajer tolerated the pain of his pinches and acted as if nothing had happened. She was afraid to speak to Ali Genav. As they went, it was probable that he had spoken to her along the way, but she didn't remember anything. She remembered much better the road itself, between Zaminej and the town. Morad's shadow seemed to follow them everywhere. When they reached the gates of the village, he had passed by them, carrying a bag on his back, without so much as looking at Hajer. It was not that she was secretly in love with him. No. But now that things had ended up in this way, she thought about Morad often. He had become a kind of pillar of support in her imagination, a kind of refuge. But she was too young to actually have fallen in love with a young man like him. But she didn't understand why it was that she kept thinking about the grimy back of his neck, his torn collar, and his sweat-covered shoulders?

And could it be that by now he was riding away in some automobile and was gone, truly gone?

Mergan tied the silk headscarf over Hajer's brushed hair, and then artfully arranged her bangs over her forehead. She then took the girl from in front of the mirror and set her beside the trunk. She took out the cotton shirt Ali Genav had bought and put it on Hajer. Then she took out a pair of black trousers and gave them to her daughter, who took them to the pantry and returned a moment later wearing them. Mergan knelt and straightened out the waistband, pulling them up. But the legs were still too long, so she rolled up the bottoms. She thought to herself that now the pants looked good. She brought out the shoes. Hajer was afraid to put them on, but she had no choice. Mergan placed her daughter's feet into the shoes, and she told her to walk around. Hajer walked with her face contorted; it was difficult for her to take steps with them. With the shoes on, she felt as if she had hooves, and it was difficult to keep her balance. It was as if her feet had been carved out of wood. She walked stiffly, jerking her feet as she went, in small, broken steps. With every step, she would bend at her knees. But she had to try. Mergan grabbed her elbow and began walking her around the room.

"Don't be scared. Take a step. And another. Yes, another. Now just keep yourself up like that. You're not a cripple, my dear. You can do it!"

Hajer walked in circles around the room. Then she suddenly sat down. Rather, she threw herself down and began to cry.

"My feet! My feet hurt! Why do I have to wear shoes at all! I don't want to...I don't!"

Before replying to her daughter, Mergan ran and quickly shut the door. She couldn't let the sound of Hajer crying be heard outside. She then came and sat with her knees against her daughter's, put the girl's head against her chest, and calmed her. Hajer slowly stopped crying. She knew what her mother wanted. Mergan took her daughter's head from her chest and carefully wiped the tears from her eyes before they could spoil the rouge on her cheeks. But it was difficult to see Hajer's face, as the house was dark. Abbas' white head, set on his bony shoulders, was all that could be seen, quiet and motionless.

Mergan suddenly rose, ran to the door, and opened it. Molla Aman was standing in the doorway. Calmly and clearly he spoke, "Why is the door closed?"

"I was dressing Hajer."

"It's night already. You're not ready yet?"

"We're nearly done."

Mergan ran to Hajer, took her hand, and pulled her toward the light from the open door. She took another look at her face. Oh no! Her tears had made streaks in the rouge and powder that Mergan had applied to her face. Mergan carefully and calmly wiped under Hajer's eyes with the edge of her scarf. Hajer's tears were about to drip from her eyelashes.

Molla Aman said, "Why don't you bring in a lamp for this house?"

"Honestly, I just forgot."

Mergan went and brought out the lantern. A gray light filled the room. But now things could be seen a little better. Molla Aman sat leaning against the wall and looked over at Abbas, who was sitting quietly, not moving at all. Molla Aman wanted to speak to him, but couldn't. What could he say? He rose from where he was and went to pour some feed in his donkey's trough.

Mergan was done. She felt as if she should sit for a bit, but didn't feel as if she could stay in one place. Instead, she kept circling around herself, coming and going, for no particular reason. She went to the pantry, then into the yard, then up to the alley and back to the house again. Then she thought she would put a bit of incense in the fire, and the smoke from the incense filled the room. Molla Aman shook the bits of hay off his sleeves, then stepped in the room, intoning a prayer. Hajer remained sitting against the wall. Molla Aman sat to one side and lit a cigarette.

Where are they? Why haven't they arrived yet?

This was what his eyes seemed to be saying. He finished his cigarette, put it out under his heel, and then left the house. Night had begun to spread. Molla Aman stood for a while by the alley, then came back. He was anxious. He stood by the door and said, "What do you say we go over to the groom's house to see what is going on?"

Mergan said, "That's just not done. How would it look? They have to come to seek the hand of their new bride and take her, not the other way around."

"I'm just worried that woman...Maybe she's pulled some sort of trick?"

"No! Wait a second. What's that sound? Ah...I hear something..."

Molla Aman ran out to the alley. The light of a lantern was accompanying shadowy outlines. Molla Aman stepped forward and then suddenly stopped. He saw Raghiyeh, Ali Genav's wife, limping ahead with a crutch under her right arm. But it seemed she was also holding something in her left hand, a tray. In the middle of the tray was a copper bowl, shining with a dim light emanating from inside it, the light of embers. Beside her was the groom himself. Ali Genav was carrying the lantern and was walking slowly to keep pace with his wife. Behind them, Karbalai Doshanbeh, and beside him Hajj Salem followed. At the back, Moslem was following behind his father. As they arrived, Karbalai Doshanbeh stepped beside Raghiyeh and took a few seeds of incense from the tray and placed them into the embers. Hajj Salem called out a prayer. Molla Aman went to greet them; he was very clearly pleased. If all went well tonight, he would be able to load his things and leave first thing in the morning with a clear conscience.

They came into the narrow yard of the house. Mergan brought out her lantern. Raghiyeh stood leaning on her crutch. Mergan also poured a few seeds of incense onto the embers. Molla Aman entered the house, took Hajer by the hand, and brought her out. Hajer was walking with difficulty. She could hardly even stand up straight. Mergan held her by her elbow as the group turned to leave the house, lit by their two lanterns. The surface of the alley was uneven, so the shoes of the bride were that much more unwieldy. They moved slowly; in a way, it was good that Hajer could not walk fast, as Raghiyeh was also pulling herself ahead only with difficulty. That was why they had been late even traversing that short distance to the house. Once they arrived, Mergan took Hajer into the pantry of Ali Genav's house. The nuptial bedroom was to be there. Ali Genav had prepared the bed already. Hajer took off her shoes, and

Mergan came out. The guests sat in the room just beside the pantry. Raghiyeh did not join the guests; she was standing by the oven holding onto her crutch. Mergan went to prepare the dinner. Raghiyeh was silent, but despite this Mergan was still uneasy. As a woman, she understood her perfectly.

God forbid it were I! I should bite my tongue!

Mergan could easily imagine a day when this weak and broken woman would try to harm Hajer.

The meat was cooked. Mergan took the pot and brought it into the room. Ali Genav had laid out a cloth and had set the bread and yogurt on it. Moslem and his father were on one side. Molla Aman and Karbalai Doshanbeh were on the other side. Ali Genav and Mergan were to sit on another side. Raghiyeh stayed outside.

The dinner did not take long. Ali Genav quickly cleaned up afterward. Everyone knew that the wedding dinner is usually a different kind of assembly, but in this case it was proportionate to the situation at hand.

"May the blessings of your table be increased. May God bless you!"

"Amen. Amen."

Hajj Salem had intoned the first prayer. Karbalai Doshanbeh offered the Amens.

Molla Aman found an excuse to break up the gathering, and so helped up Karbalai Doshanbeh to take him outside. Ali Genav pressed a coin into the hand of Moslem and helped him up as well. The men went out and Ali Genav accompanied them to the alley and then returned. As per tradition, Mergan was to stay behind, but Ali Genav also encouraged her to leave.

"Don't worry, Raghiyeh is here...If we need anything..."

Why does the bride's mother usually stay behind? To confirm her daughter's good fortune? But what else could she want?

"Take the leftover stew and give it to the boys. Don't leave them at home all alone!"

***

Mergan's sons were sitting in the darkness, silent and blind. Mergan relit the lamp that had gone out in the alley. Abrau was leaning against a wall. It looked as if he'd just come back from work. These days his clothes were, head to foot, covered in oil. He spoke much less, as if he had suddenly aged. He had grown serious. He acted older than his age. It was as if something had been added to him, something that Mergan didn't want to know about. She simply sensed that now she was dealing with a man rather than a boy. A man who in some ways was trying to become a stranger to her. There were aspects to Abrau's life that were no longer in Mergan's hands. They were now in the hands of others. It was as if he came from somewhere else. He was a stranger to Mergan, but strangely also a cause for her to feel proud. What can be more pleasurable for a mother than to see her son become a man? Even if this son, this man, has in a sense also stabbed her in the back by selling her portion of their land in his name.

Mergan placed a bowl of the meat stew before Abbas and then called Abrau over. He moved over and she brought them dry bread, which they broke and sprinkled into the stew. Abrau asked about his uncle. Mergan said, "I have a feeling he's gone out with Karbalai Doshanbeh."

Abrau said, "Mirza said to say hello, and that you should come by to get your money from him whenever you'd like."

Mergan replied, "Tell him to save his money. I won't sell!"

Abrau said nothing more. Abbas was eating the food in large mouthfuls.

Molla Aman came in.

"This guy just won't leave me alone. He's a real bastard, you know!"

Mergan didn't reply, and didn't raise her head. She didn't want to discuss Karbalai Doshanbeh in front of her sons. She busied herself with some task.

Molla Aman sat beside the pot of stew and began to eat as well.

"He didn't even let me have a real dinner! It's as if we're living in a famine; half of my stomach is still empty! So...good for you, our hero, my boy! Tell us, what kind of a beast is this tractor anyway?"

Abrau didn't take his focus off of his competitors for the stew from the pot, replying, "It starts a racket and just keeps going!"

"Well, well, the times have changed. Who would have expected it?"

Abrau said, "When you head up to the higher villages, ask around. If anyone has land they need ploughed, they can hire us. We just finished ploughing God's Land this afternoon."

Molla Aman replied, "That's not bad. Let's see what'll happen. And will I get a broker's fee?"

"From just saying a few words?"

"Well, yes. These days, even husbands have to pay their wives compensation for work. So you want me to do work for

Mirza Hassan for free? Why? Because you think I like the look of him so much?"

"It's not for Mirza Hassan; it's more for me. The tractor shouldn't be left unused for even an hour, you know? As long as the *chug, chug* of the tractor is going, I'm working. If there's no work, and the tractor goes quiet, I'll have to pack my bags like the others and leave the village. You see these pants I'm wearing? I bought them for twenty-eight *tomans*. You have to spend money just to live!"

Molla Aman said, "Let me see! How many pockets does it have?"

Abrau rose and turned around himself, while still licking his fingers.

"Four of 'em. And it has a little pocket right here, next to the waistband!"

"Good. So you can fit all your extra money into the pockets! It seems Mirza Hassan's paying you a decent wage?"

"He does, and why not?"

"So that's all right. Have you borrowed from him as well?"

"Ah... not that much, but a bit. He gives me enough for food and clothing and..."

"Does he save the rest for you? Or does he hold it in escrow?"

"Escrow for what?"

"Nothing! I'm just kidding around. So, do you have a bit of change so we can play a game of dominoes?"

"No, and even if I did, I don't want to gamble. I have to sleep pretty soon. In the mornings, I can hardly get up since I'm so tired. Mama, can you clean this up!"

Abbas licked the bottom of the bowl. Mergan took the empty bowl and the leftover bread. Abrau rose to set out his bedding.

Mergan and Molla Aman also set out their beds and lowered the wick of the lamp. Eventually, everyone was lying down but Mergan, who was still sitting. Her brother was leaning his head against the wall and smoking a cigarette. As soon as he was finished smoking, he went to sleep. Abrau began snoring.

And Abbas? Abbas was somewhere between sleep and consciousness. He was lying down quietly. He could have either been asleep or awake. Like every night, he was lying with his eyes fixed at the ceiling. Actually, he hardly slept at night. Near dawn, he'd finally fall asleep, until his hunger would wake him in the morning. When the sunlight poured onto his hands and feet, he would wake up and limp awkwardly out the door to wash up. Then he'd come back and sit in his place quietly as he always did, just in the corner of the room. Hajer or Mergan would bring him a piece of bread and a cup of tea, which he would eat without moving. He would, on occasion, leave the room and go out to the old clay oven in the yard—to the same spot that Soluch used to occupy. He would sit there, hugging his knees. He would rarely speak. If he did say a word or two, he'd do so listlessly, dispassionately. His voice had a strange quality, like a dog's yelp, as if his vocal cords had been stripped apart. His face had also changed, and it was now marked with a peculiar effeminacy. One couldn't imagine his being able to grow a beard now. It seemed as if the soft hairs once on his face had been burned off. In short, Abbas had been completely transformed.

Mergan remained seated in her place. Her eyes were dry in her gaunt face. Her head was full of voices, and her heart was uneasy. She was anxious. Her limbs and body felt out of her control, and without even realizing it, her eyes were fixed on the door. Her lips were moving, perhaps in prayer, perhaps as part of a dialogue with herself. Whatever the reason, she was not about to fall asleep. She couldn't even keep her head on her pillow.

How can you think of sleeping with an easy heart? You've just sent your daughter to her nuptial bed.

Shrieks filled the air, like a spear that penetrated the heart of the night. Hajer's terrified voice echoed in the alleys of Zaminej.

***

"Mama...Mama, no...Help me!"

Mergan dashed into the alley. Hajer was gripping onto her pants as she rushed down the alley, like a field mouse escaping from a hawk. Ali Genav was running after her. He was running as he tied the waistband of his pants. Hajer hid in her mother's arms, losing herself in her mother's embrace. It was as if Mergan were holding onto the wind. Tears, crying; her broken sobs were cut through with a deep sense of fear. Intermittent cries sounded out by the girl's thin voice. She was shirtless, with her bare feet and her uncovered head. Ali Genav arrived. Mergan pulled her daughter to the edge of the wall. Genav entered the house. As quick as a shooting star, he'd woken up Molla Aman and Abrau. Molla Aman left the house shoeless and without a head covering. Abrau stood in the doorway. Hajer tore herself from her mother and dashed into the house and into the pantry. No one spoke; no one could speak. Ali Genav was frothing at the mouth. Molla Aman went over to him. Mergan entered the room, as Abrau asked, "What's happened?" Mergan knew what had happened. Abbas was sitting in his place. Mergan went into the pantry, and Hajer began to scream.

"Mama, I'm scared! I'm so scared! I'm going to die! Who did you marry me to? Who is this? Why did you give me to him? Why? Mama, I'm scared!"

Mergan held her daughter's head against her chest. She had to say something. She had to console her. But what could she say? What was there to say? Was she supposed to say something like, "I'll die for you, my love!" But Mergan couldn't find it in her to say anything. At times, the mind simply freezes.

Molla Aman pulled back the curtain to the pantry.

"Come on out, girl. Come and go back to your husband's house."

Ali Genav waited no longer. He stepped around Molla Aman's broken shoulders and into the pantry. He took ahold of Hajer's wrist and began pulling her out. Hajer held onto her mother and would not let go. Mergan also held to her, and she was pulled out from the pantry with her. Hajer dragged one heel on the ground shouting, "I don't want to, by God! I don't want to! I don't want to marry...Oh, God!"

She began to lose her breath. Her face was darkening from screaming. Ali Genav didn't want to let the scandal continue. He began to pull Hajer harder and he dragged Mergan along with her daughter. At the door, Abrau leapt onto Ali Genav's arm.

"Hold on! What do you think you're doing? Is she your prisoner?"

Molla Aman pulled his nephew off Ali Genav and pushed him to one side.

"Don't interfere, you! He's taking his wife to his home!"

Abrau pulled himself up in front of his uncle.

"What are you talking about? She's my sister!"

Molla Aman responded to Abrau by hitting Hajer's neck with his closed fist.

"C'mon, get ahold of yourself and go back to your house, you troublemaking girl! C'mon!"

Somehow, he peeled Hajer off of Mergan, grabbed her under his arm, and tossed her out of the house. Hajer dashed toward the clay oven and then made a quick dash toward the wall. She was about to pull herself up onto the roof when Ali Genav reached her and grabbed her from behind. Hajer began to shriek again, kicking and bucking. Ali Genav covered the girl's mouth with the palm of one broad, rough hand and set his path toward the alley.

"I've had enough of playing! You want to cause a scene? Shut up and be quiet, you!"

Hajer's voice was muffled by Ali Genav's palm. But she continued to kick and squirm. Molla Aman peeked over the wall and saw something that looked like a one-winged bird being dragged in the dirt alongside Ali Genav. Hajer was now silenced. Raghiyeh arrived, looking lost while navigating on her crutch. Molla Aman returned into the house. Mergan, who had been left holding her daughter's twisted pants, ran outside with them stuffed under one arm. She reached Ali Genav and put a hand on his shoulder.

"Ali, my dear! Ali, let me bring her to you myself. I'll bring her, Ali dear! But let her breathe! Don't smother her, Ali!"

Ali Genav didn't pause a moment. He kept dragging Hajer

along, like a lion that has taken a lamb from its mother. Mergan had no choice but to return. But how could she? Helpless, she walked behind him, begging.

"Ali dear...Ali dear...I'd sacrifice myself for you...Just have mercy on my daughter...Have mercy...Ali dear!"

He didn't bother to respond to Mergan. He entered his house and shut the door behind himself. Mergan waited at the door. She was still holding the pants. She sat down, and Raghiyeh approached her. She also waited, and then sat down facing Mergan. She leaned against a wall and stretched out her broken leg. Mergan took her head into her hands and her body began shaking by itself in a gentle motion, moving from one side to another.

"Oh, my Lord. Oh, my Lord!"

Then a sudden scream. Not simply a scream, an electric bolt of a shriek. A cry that was extinguished. Hajer must be unconscious now!

Like someone struck by lightning, Mergan leapt to her feet, frozen. How long? She couldn't tell. Then suddenly she transformed her hands into fists and began raining blows upon her own head, and then began hitting her head against the door, over and over.

"You've killed her! You've killed her! Murderer! You've killed my daughter!"

The sound of voices rose from the homes of the neighbors. The voice of a woman, perhaps of Moslemeh: "You brought your misery on yourself, Mergan!"

More voices of the neighbors. A voice of a girl, perhaps Zabihollah's sister: "Are you surprised, Mergan?"

Again, more voices. This one of a woman, perhaps Mergan's mother from the grave: "You'll never see good come in your life, Mergan!"

Now just the sound of a woman, the sound of Mergan. Sitting by the door with her hands on her head. Something inside her was exploding. The silence of the alley swallowed her sobs. Her sound was no longer that of crying, but rather that of mourning. Her voice echoed in the alley until the dawn. Raghiyeh had fallen asleep. In the dawn's light, Ali Genav opened the door. He had his bath supplies under one arm. He didn't speak, just passed them by with his head lowered. Mergan attributed this to his shame; she hoped he was overtaken by shame. But it was unlikely. The gesture could just as well have been a sign of his lack of concern for her. Isn't a husband a king for himself? Mergan rose and came to his side.

"How is she, Ali dear? Ali!"

"She's fine!"

He walked on. Mergan ran back to the house. Raghiyeh was sitting, readying herself for her prayers. She said, "She's asleep!"

Mergan lifted the curtain to the pantry. A body resembling a small fish lay upon the dried blood of the mattress. She's weak, very weak; her skin, the pallor of death. Is she dead? Poor small fish, fallen onto the earth! No, her heart was still beating. Her eyes were closed; her eyelids had the hue of a shadow. Her eyelashes were clinging together. Just over night, her cheeks had become sunken and hollow. Her hands, thin and fragile, were like two harmless snakes moving this way and that. Her shirt was bloody; her hair was matted together. A piece of cloth was still tied around her feet. This was a clear indication of what had happened, but Mergan couldn't accept it, despite its simplicity. She crept into the pantry quietly, like a strange cat, not wanting to awaken her daughter from sleep. She made out the marks of blows on Hajer's neck, scrapes and scratches. They were the marks left from slaps or punches. Or perhaps not; even her hands had the same marks, red and swollen. The blood was either from the scratches or from the cuts on her skin. Cuts like the mark of a yolk on a sheep's neck. Mergan suddenly realized her daughter had been tied up, like an animal.

My daughter... Oh! My little girl, who couldn't move. Like a turtle turned over on its back. But she struggled. She must have struggled. Her head must have hit the pillow so many times that her cheeks were bruised. Her neck is scraped from the friction of the shawl around it. Her fingers have lost their color beneath her fingernails. Her fingers had been grasping at the mattress, at the ground, my daughter.

Hajer, your mother should die for you!

Mergan rose. She had to go find ointment, the same ointment she had procured for Abbas' shoulders and his legs.

Raghiyeh was sitting by the wall, saying her prayers. Mergan passed her and left the house. It was as if there was no alley, as if she simply didn't see it. She reached home and saw Molla Aman putting the saddle on his donkey. He was preparing himself to leave. Abrau had already gone. In the middle of the night, he had just gotten up and left the house. Abbas was still in his usual place, staring into space. Mergan couldn't bear to look either of them in the face. Her tongue was dry in her mouth, like a piece of sod. She was anxious and couldn't stay still. She flew to and fro, like a pigeon caught in a well. Molla Aman, when he was younger, used to go to the mouth of a well and sleep in a tent there over night. In the morning, he'd crawl to the mouth of the well from the tent and would catch pigeons in the well. On returning, he liked to describe to Mergan how the pigeons would flutter their wings. She didn't know why the memory of these pigeons, and how Molla Aman would catch them, had just now come back to her. Molla Aman was oblivious to what Mergan was thinking and readied himself to leave. Mergan didn't know what to do. She would sit down and then stand up and walk in circles. She gripped her own hand with her fingernails and swallowed with difficulty. It was as if her throat had become narrow and was closed up. Or as if something like a handful of hay was blocking her throat. At the edges of her lips, white spittle had dried up. She was lost, confused. Why had she come to the house, anyway? And why wouldn't the sun rise, damn it!

***

"So, Mergan, I'm leaving now. Goodbye."

"Thanks for coming. You're always welcome here."

Mergan came outside. Molla Aman had the tether for his donkey in one hand. He pulled and led the animal into the alley. Mergan walked with him to the alley. He hadn't gone very far before he turned and gently spoke to his sister.

"I'm considering heading over to Shahrud this trip, and maybe I'll buy some sheep oil there. I'll also stop by the mines there and see if I can't find out something about Soluch for you. Don't worry yourself too much! You'll just end up sick from it, and that's no good! Say goodbye to Ali from me as well."

He raised one leg up and pulled himself onto the donkey, riding it down the road. His long legs were not far from the ground. It looked as if the tips of his shoes were scraping against the dirt. One last time, he called out, "Goodbye!"

"God protect you."

Then he disappeared down in the alleys, all but the tip of his hat, and then that too fell out of view.

Mergan returned to the house.

Abbas was sitting on his feet now, and he spoke up suddenly, "May God forgive the Sardar for his mistakes. Amen!"

Abbas sounded like a yelping dog. Mergan waited, looking and listening in the hope that Abbas might continue and say something more. But he fell silent. He leaned his head back against the wall and shut his eyes. Mergan stayed there staring at her son, wondering what he was thinking, how he was feeling. Where did his thoughts take him, her suddenly aged son?

Oh, if only it had been your mother and not you, Abbas!

What was the wall that had arisen between mother and her son, between their hearts? It was impossible to relate to him, to speak to him, to listen to him. An ancient fortification had arisen around Abbas, an old, ancient rampart. What had happened to him?

Oh God! My son left the house a boy and returned an old man. I don't understand it. Why won't he speak?

He was silent. Abbas said nothing, as if he were locked shut. On the rare occasions that he did speak, the sound of his voice and what he said were so strange that they only increased her confusion. Some people came on the first day or two, staring at Abbas before leaving. Some of the older villagers suggested he was in shock, but they too left right away. They left, everyone left, and Abbas remained behind, in the house. Silent, like an owl. He stayed there with Mergan, a burden to her, but also lodged in her heart. Quiet, old Abbas, sitting in the corner. Isn't this what they mean by being homebound? Abbas was now homebound. He would hardly ever even stand up. Isn't this what they mean by being an invalid?

The spring had passed and summer was coming on. The time for cotton ginning and harvesting. And so Mergan always had one foot inside the house and one foot outside. She couldn't leave Abbas to himself. But she had to work as well. Harvesting and picking work was available. She had to go to the fields for gleaning. She couldn't just leave the land fallow, but she had no hopes that Abbas would suddenly stand up and take care of himself!

Mergan, you fool! You were going to go and find medicine for your daughter. Why are you just sitting here instead?

"May God overlook your faults, Sardar!"

Abbas rose in the dark room, taking his cane and leaving the house. He walked slowly, step by step, down the alley, leaning from time to time against a wall for support. The sun was peeking into the alley, over the walls, and onto the rooftops. There was no sound to be heard, and no sign of life to be seen. Abbas continued, walking with his back hunched and knees bent. He held himself up with one hand against the wall, moving slowly, like a turtle. He looked ghostly. His hair had grown long and curly and was matted like a piece of felt. Mergan had once tried to cut his hair, but was scared away by the look in Abbas' eyes. So the hair had grown longer and longer. And the longer his hair grew, the larger his head seemed and the smaller his face appeared within it. His face had seemed to shrink smaller, giving his eyes and nose a resemblance to those of a field mouse. Within their sockets, his eyes looked dry, wider—profound but also disturbing. His hunched back, prominent nose, and his eyes—which were both frightened and frightening—all made him look more and more like some manner of rodent.

In the empty alleyways of Zaminej, Abbas walked slowly, without shoes, his gray shirt torn and his head overflowing with white hair; he looked like a strange creature. He was headed to the house of the Sardar, out on the edge of the village. The wall behind his house divided the barren wastelands from the village proper. Although the Sardar's house was not very distant, it seemed to Abbas to take forever to reach it. In truth, it was well before noon when he arrived; the sun was still shining at an angle.

The camel's gate was the only entrance into the Sardar's home. Abbas entered the vestibule. The camels were scattered around the yard. He walked straight ahead to the Sardar's room, the door to which was open. The Sardar lived alone with his camels. A half-finished bowl of buttermilk and some leftover dry bread was scattered beside the wall. Flies covered the bowl and the bread. The Sardar himself was asleep, using his shoes as a pillow. Abbas entered the room, walked quietly over, and knelt beside the man's sleeping body. He sat there, like a statue. He was silent except for the sound of his breathing, inhaling and exhaling.

How long he was sitting there, he couldn't say. But eventually the Sardar seemed to sense the sound of another's breathing. He lifted his forearm from his eyes and opened his eyelids, seeing Abbas sitting beside him. In normal circumstances, the huge Sardar was not the kind to be frightened by the appearance of someone like Abbas, but the time and manner of the boy's appearance beside him clearly brought a shadow of fear around his heart.

Unconsciously, the old man pulled his limbs together and pushed himself back against the wall, staring at Abbas' eyes for a moment. Abbas did not react, other than to continue looking back at the Sardar. The man slowly began to emerge from his confusion between sleep and wakefulness. He eventually regained his composure, and with a cough that seemed unlike him, he glared sharply at Abbas with jet-black eyes.

"Well, what do you want? In the state you're in, and under this hellish sun, what've you come here for?"

Abbas responded in a broken and sad voice, "My pay. I want my pay."

When the Sardar comprehended Abbas' request, he leapt from his place, saying, "Your pay? Fine, if you want that, go bring your mother and I'll deal with her myself!"

A moment later, Abbas rose and limped out the door, heading toward the vestibule. There was a jug of water by the wall. Abbas knelt and struggled to lift the jug, then raised it to his lips and drank deeply. Then he set the jug back down with a struggle—the same jug he once could raise with one hand. As he rose, he saw the old mare camel stretching its neck toward him with a look of warm familiarity in its eyes. Abbas suddenly felt the pain in his shoulder and leg return. There was something about the look of the camel and the feeling of standing in the sun. The sun, the camel, the fields, the well. The snakes...A tremble passed through Abbas' battered body. Despite the fact that Abbas had overcome his terrifying memories enough to walk all the way to the Sardar's house, the sight of the old mare had rekindled the pain still caught within his body.

He held to the wall as he stood. The sun and the long walk had exhausted him. It was exactly noon, and the empty paths of the village at midday were burning his feet. Sweat, both from the heat and the effort it took to walk, was pouring down his face. His large head was too heavy for his thin neck. He couldn't control his head; it swung from side to side, making him dizzy, and his vision would go black. His eyes were lost in the dust, in the dusty sunlight. He felt weak, but he had to return home somehow. Even if the sun was not very hot, it felt as if it was sucking the blood from him. He began walking, but with great difficulty. He dragged his body, hunched and broken as it was. His legs had lost their strength, his heart felt weak, and his eyes were covered with dust. No, he couldn't go on. He simply couldn't go on. He felt his strength wane, so he leaned his back against a wall in the alley. His knees gave way. His body folded, crumbled, and fell onto the ground. He lay in the sun. The sun was hot; the earth was hot. It had never seemed so hot before. But perhaps it'd always been like this. Abbas had no further strength to draw upon; he felt like he was nothing. He felt he was evaporating. Little by little. He seemed like light; he seemed like dust.

Oh no, Mergan. Your son has fainted in an alley somewhere while you were grinding herbs in your pestle to use as an ointment.

Hollow, Abbas' body was hollow. Light, lighter than it should have been. His bones seemed to have become crumbled. Mergan may have exhausted herself running in the sun-drenched alleys, but she did not falter in raising Abbas' body. She lifted him and leaned him against a wall. Then she put her back to him and pulled his arms over her shoulders. She knelt with one knee in the dirt; then, like a man lifting a bundle of wood, she rose while pulling Abbas over her back. She slipped her long, bony arms under his dried-out legs and stood. It was difficult to run with this load on her back, but she took her steps with care and determination. As she walked, she could hear water sloshing to and fro inside Abbas' belly.

Abbas himself felt numb. Even the shaking of his bones as they went left very little, if any, impression on him. He only felt something distant and hazy, something fleeting and indistinct. It felt like riding on Gabriel's wings. The movement was regular and soothing. His hands had fallen over Mergan's shoulders and against her chest. His head was like the head of a dead bird, rolling against her back. His eyelids, like dried leaves, were still half-open.

Mergan placed her son on the ground and lifted off his shirt. She ran to get water. Abbas had crumpled on the dirt floor of the room. His head was to one side, his arms to the other. A bit of spittle was dripping from one side of his mouth, and his heart beat an uneven drumbeat within his ribcage. Mergan returned with a bowl of water, and then took off her headscarf and wet it in the water. She wet Abbas' face, forehead, and lips with the wet scarf, then rubbed the dripping cloth against his chest and belly. It had an effect on him. Abbas' bedding was set out by the wall, and Mergan dragged him over to it. Abbas placed his head on the pillow and struggled to open his eyes. But before he was able to look around or see anything, his eyelids fell shut again.

No, Abbas was no longer Abbas, and he would never be him again. He was now a broken corpse, as broken as if he were an old man, left fallen beside the wall. Mergan slid to one side and leaned against the wall, staring at him in this sorry state. What should she do? What could she do? Abbas had been transformed into a misfortune. A misfortune dear to her. If your heart is injured, you can neither erase the injury from your heart, nor can you throw it away. The injury becomes a part of your heart. If you lose the injury, it means you have lost your heart. And if you truly wish to be rid of the injury, you are in fact willing yourself to lose your heart. And how can you lose your heart? So you go on, with the injury and your heart as one. Abbas and heartache were now one. They had become as one. Would it be possible to separate them? Abbas was himself the pain in her, and vice versa. The two were united and were indistinguishable. They were an injury on Mergan's heart. An aching in her heart. And she had no choice but to love the injury and the pain. She went to Abbas. She had to hold him, this very moment. She wanted to kiss his eyes. She knelt beside him. But no. She couldn't. Abbas was not the child he had once been, nor was he the young man he had become. He was now a man, an old man. An old man with wrinkles covering his face—where did they come from?

Mergan couldn't kiss her child. Something was preventing her from taking him in her arms, even as she was overflowing with love for him. There was a wall between the two, however dear they were to each other. A separation between their hearts. She couldn't grant her kindness, her deepest treasure, to him.

Oh Mergan! Your love is only apparent in your most ancient of aspects, your tears. And you are burdened with the task of having to cry until the Day of Judgment. Crying, so that your mother's tears are like still waters within you. Dig a well and let it flow; let it flow from within you. Let yourself flow. You can cry with the tears of all mothers, a storm of cries and laments and tears. Oh dormant sea!

But no, Mergan had become a fortress. Although her mother's tears had become a still water within her, other inclinations had built a rampart around it, holding it locked within her. Let this still water become putrid! Let it dry out. Dry, autumnal, silent, and cracked. Burnt, borne on the wind. Autumn, the yellow leaves of fall. The howling of the lost winds. She was like an evergreen in autumn. Mergan had lived through many autumns. But no, the ancient evergreen does not cry out. It never cries. Let all this crying end. Be gone! What of anger? A dam of fury set on a river of the oldest anger. A scourge on the ancient still waters. A flood on the face of the rain. An uproar, tumult. Unforgiving, a kind of cruelty meeting cruelty. An outcry against pain. Not a lament, but an eruption. Clawing at tear-filled eyes. She has had an illegitimate child, the illegitimate child of lamentation, mourning, surrender. Let go, set free. Set yourself free, Mergan! Free of all the life-sapping pain! Let fury and knives and blood rain without pause! Mergan's heart, the essence of the naked shame in Lot's desert.

A shadow! What is this shadow? Who is it? Who?

"What do you want, eh?"

"Bring over that bit of bread, so we can sit and finish our deal!"

"Eh? Mirza Hassan! No, I won't give you the land!"

"I'll just have to take it then!"

"I'll never give it to you. It'll be my grave!"

"I've already registered the deed. The company's given us a loan with that land as collateral. I'm mechanizing farming in this area. You don't even understand what this means! Mechanization! So it's all in my favor; everything's backing me. I'm telling you nicely. I don't want people to say that I'm fighting against a woman. That's not how I work. Let's make an arrangement, come to terms. I have plans to do important things in this area. Cotton farming, pistachio farming. Do you understand what I'm telling you? I'm going to make this area green! You see, I just want to come to terms with you. Despite the fact that you're only Soluch's wife and don't have any claim to his lands. So even if he had registered a deed to that land, you'd not have any claim to it. But I just want you to be satisfied!"

Mergan's eyes were like daggers. "Get out, get out!"

"I'll go. But just know one other thing. I've bought your daughter's claim as well. Your son-in-law brought the contract to me with his two hands."

"I'm telling you, get out!"

"Fine. I'm going."

The shadow departed. Mirza Hassan was no longer there.

Mergan walked up and down the room with long strides. She came and went like a lioness in a cage. Her lips were firmly shut, her eyebrows furrowed. Her head was bare, her feet bare. She didn't even realize that she hadn't bothered to cover her head before Mirza Hassan. Her hair was limp, thin, dark. Her eyes were wide; her look cut like a knife. Her hands were fidgety, but her steps were firm. She was drawn and taught, like an arrow in a bow.

Abbas was mumbling deliriously, "May God overlook my faults."

Mergan spit and left the room. She took Soluch's well-digging shovel from the stable and walked to the alley. She walked quickly, winding like the wind from alley to alley. She reached the outskirts of the village, the open fields, and made it to the wild lands beyond. Shortly, she was at God's Land. The lands there had fallen, like someone's prone body. They were tired, flattened. Mergan had never seen them in this way. She had always seen the lands as alive, fertile. Now, outlines in the land had been erased, but despite this she could still see how it used to be laid out. If you divided the plot into six sections, one section belonged to her. Abbas and Abrau had each sold their two sections, four sections in all. Hajer had also sold hers, her one section. These divisions followed the traditional rules of inheritance, males inheriting twice what each female inheritor can. So, the remaining one section was all that was Mergan's. She measured out the section and separated her one section by drawing a line in the earth with the shovel. She outlined the four corners of her land with piles of dirt and sticks, and set stones onto the piles. She then picked up the shovel and stood straight. She was done. She wiped the sweat from her brow.

It was dusk. The shadows from the thistle bushes were long on the earth. She left the field and turned to look at the watermelon plants. The plants had been upended in the dirt. Most of them had dried out. No, nothing would be harvested this year. What harvest? What work? Mergan, all alone and between her various jobs, had come and planted seeds and left them. But that was it. She'd not had the opportunity to tend to the patch. She had to go. With regret in her heart, she turned and left.

***

Zaminej was sinking into the dark embrace of dusk. Shadows came to and fro. Women walked, carrying containers of water on their backs. Men passed in small groups, walking shoulder to shoulder. A donkey, with no saddle, stood looking lost. A dog passed slithering alongside the wall. An owl sat in a ruined house.

Mergan walked along the wall. She was lost in thought, walking in the dark alleys. A silent darkness. In the old village, even intimate friends would fail to recognize one another. Mergan walked with her head lowered. Her home was not in the alley she had chosen to walk along. This alley led to the Sardar's home. The back alley. Mergan was worried about Abbas. But she had decided that she would have to ask the Sardar to give her his pay. She felt that if she at least was able to collect his pay, it might have some effect on her son's poor health.

The Sardar's camels were scattered here and there. Sitting, standing, lying. The Sardar was sitting, busy tying up his tools and rope in the light of a lantern hanging from a nail in the wall. It seemed he was readying to take out the camels at the break of dawn. Quietly, softly, Mergan entered the yard and walked toward the Sardar. He had finished tying a knot and looked up. Mergan was standing before him. He wiped the flecks of hay that were stuck to his beard and eyebrows with the palm of his thick hand and set his big dark eyes on Mergan.

"So. You've come then. What do you want?"

Mergan said, "Just Abbas' pay."

"His pay? What pay?"

"Just the pay for his work. For herding your camels. We can't get any work now. He hasn't even been able to take my hand and go work. I went to see my land and..."

"Aha! So...pay! Ha! Fine. But what about my camel? Who will pay me for that?"

"I don't know! What does it have to do with me?"

"You know it was worth a hundred *toman*?"

"Why should I know?"

"That camel was my best animal. Your son killed it!"

"Why do you say that?"

"Well then, who killed it?"

"Snakes! It was bit by a snake!"

"Well, fine, it was bit by a snake. But your son was responsible. Why do we send a herder out to watch the herd?"

"Your camel was crazed. You should have had it tied down!"

"How should I have known? You think I have second sight? Or that my mother was..."

"You knew. You knew. How can you call yourself a camel breeder and not know something like that? Your job is to know everything about them!"

"Yes, fine. Okay. My job. But if a camel gets spring fever, what am I to do?"

"You don't have to do anything right now! I just need to know what I can do. My son's turned into an old man. From working for you, he's become an invalid! What am I to do with him? How am I to feed him? I've lost my young man. What do you think I should do?"

"What do I know? God will provide."

"I'm not here begging from you, for you to say that God will provide! I just want my son's pay."

"Your son killed my camel, and you still want me to pay him? There were forty knife wounds on his head and neck!

Didn't you see? I couldn't sell the hide for half the usual price, since it was full of cuts. Were you blind or didn't you see the field was full of blood? How do you think I found your son that night? By following the footprints in the blood, blood that was on the earth, the blood of my camel!"

The Sardar rose and began to walk toward the stables for the camels. Mergan hesitated, then said to him, "Sardar, you'll never be able to rest. My son will be a curse on you!"

The Sardar stuck his head into the stables and said, "You go on then. The cat's prayers won't bring rain!"

Then he was lost in the darkness of the stables.

Mergan waited by his sack, hoping that he would come out again. But it seemed he wasn't planning on coming out anytime soon. So she went to the stables. There was too much left to say! She stood by the door. The Sardar had lit an oil lamp and had busied himself with mending a camel shawl. She leaned in the doorway and stared at him. He looked like a huge ghoul fixated on his work.

"Eh! So you're still here?"

Mergan said with a broken voice, "Sardar, we're relatives now. My daughter's married to your cousin. You can't leave us like this! Tradition..."

"All right! Go fetch me a cup of water to drink and we'll see what we can do!"

Mergan was familiar with the homes of everyone in the village. She went, took a bowl from the pantry, filled it with water, and brought it back to the Sardar.

The light only illuminated the face and knees of the Sardar, where he had laid out the camel shawl he was mending. The rest of the stables remained dark. It was a wide room with a high ceiling, where the camels would stay during the depths of the winter. The smell of wool and hay and cottonseed, and the odor of the mud-brick walls, filled the air. She walked slowly toward the Sardar with the bowl of water, then stood before him. He raised his large head, and before he took the water from her, he fixed his eyes on her. There was something strange fluttering in the depths of his eyes. It was frightening, wild, and barbaric.

Mergan blinked. He had the same look, persistent and penetrating. Her hands began to tremble. The water poured from the edges of the bowl. A few drops poured onto the Sardar's hand. The cup was clearly shaking in her hands. A crooked smile cut a crack through his beard and moustache. Her heart beat faster, feeling like a bird caught in the sights of a viper. She was caught in the spell; something was growing within her. A new and terrifying world seemed to open up.

Until this moment, Mergan hadn't thought to make a mention of the Sardar's wife, who had run away from him. This was twenty years ago, and he had not yet remarried. Since then, he'd lay his head on his pillow alone each night. During his camel-herding days, he had brought his wife—who was still no more than a girl—back from Yazd. Within a year, she had run away. Her brothers and uncle, who were traveling to Kashmir, had come to buy wheat in the village and had taken her away with them while he was gone. So, she had run away with her own relatives. When he returned, the Sardar couldn't bring himself to go looking for a new wife.

The water was pouring from the bowl. Mergan was trembling. She was frozen and trembling; she didn't know how to escape. Oh God! She dropped the bowl and leapt toward the door of the stables. She ran. Just then a camel stepped into the doorway. She stopped, and before she knew it, her leg was in the clasp of the Sardar's rough hands. He pulled her back to the darkness at the end of the stable.

"Where do you think you're running to, my little bird?!"

"No! Not this... Not this!"

He paid no mind to her cries. The camel shawl and bridle were tangled up around her head. These lands had been left fallow for too long.

She gave in. Enough!

When she pulled off the camel bridle and shawl and threw them aside, the Sardar was gone. First, she took a breath; the suffocating thought that she was about to lose something had overwhelmed her. This was replaced by incredulity, disbelief. She waited a second in the darkness. Then she leapt up, like a bird with its head cut off. A camel was looking at her. Her mind felt beaten, kicked to a pulp. She grabbed her breeches and went into the yard. It was quiet there. The camels were still as they had been. She heard the chains of the door being shut; she saw the Sardar shutting the door. She put on her breeches quickly. He entered the yard; his eyes and lips were still trembling. It was as if she were seeing him for the first time. She came to herself. Terror. She was filled entirely with a sense of terror. She covered her mouth with one hand to stop herself from screaming. The scream was caught like a bullet in her throat. The Sardar stood still; he didn't move. But Mergan sensed he was coming closer. Why was he facing her now? She walked backward until she hit the wall. The stairs to the roof were behind her. Still covering her mouth, she began backing up the steps, using her other hand as she went. She was on the roof. He kept looking at her; his eyes watched her. Mergan pulled herself over the rooftop. Open fields, the other side was only open fields. She jumped down and into the fields. She threw herself into the night. She leapt and took her hand from her mouth. The fields were full of cries, and the night full of wailing. Like the cries of the jackal. The howling of the jackal.

*　*　*

She went home.

"Auntie Mergan! Tomorrow night there will be a mourning ceremony at Zabihollah's house. He's asked for you to come and make the arrangements."

5.

"This is from the Sardar. He says it's Abbas' pay!"

Tired and sweaty, Abrau tossed the shovel to one side, lowered a sack of flour from his shoulder, and leaned against the
wall. Then he beat his hands together and shook the flour out of
the sleeves of his shirt. Mergan sat, silent and shocked. She
looked at the shovel that she had left behind at the Sardar's
house. She kept staring at it. Abrau sat on the ground and said,
"He told me he'd set the flour aside for a whole month for you
to come and pick up. Why didn't you go earlier?"

Mergan said, "I was busy. Anyway, I thought I'd go and get
it closer to the winter, when we really need it."

From the corner, Karbalai Doshanbeh said, "Good for the
Sardar! Good for him! It seems he's become fair in his
accounts. It used to be that it caused him pain anytime one of

his herders came to ask for his wages. Well, God bless him! He's finally become a man!"

Abrau had become more conscious of Karbalai Doshanbeh; a moment before, as he was lowering the bag of flour, he saw him but did not want to display any reaction. But now he had no choice but to look at him. He was sitting, as always, straight against the wall in the spot he always sat in, with his head lowered. When he was quiet, it was possible to forget he was there at all. He would still be there, but quiet and introspective, a heavy presence. He would sit against the wall, his elbows on his knees, with his hands busy fingering his worry beads. This man, this old man, did always have a kind of presence. But his silence was as if he were absent, and one could imagine that he could stay in his position against the wall for years, fingering his worry beads. He was short of words, but his words always had an impact, and now he was mocking the Sardar. It was of no real importance to him that the Sardar had sent a bag of flour to Mergan. Anything the Sardar did gave him a pretext for a clash, and so he would invariably attack. Whatever the cause, he would attack. But Karbalai Doshanbeh didn't attack anyone in particular. He had the temperament of a scorpion and walked like a tarantula, with his bowed short legs and his long and crooked arms. His shoes were torn. His scarf was oversized and stained. His pants were too short, and when he walked, his overcoat's edges blew to and fro. When he began to laugh, whenever he had shown up someone, his cheeks would turn red and his eyes would fill with tears. He was an old man, and he looked like he'd seen both good and bad in his lifetime. He was proud of this, proud that he had lived in places far from the village, and also that he had spent time in prison.

But others who knew him well considered his experiences outside the village, and the episode of his imprisonment, as a point of disgrace for him. The story was that he had been wrongfully arrested in Eshghabad, and in fact on the day he was to have been released, someone else was mistakenly released in his place. The story was that the officials had mistaken Karbalai Doshanbeh for one of the affiliates of Khabir Khan, the famous profiteer and smuggler, and had arrested him. It was nearly a year before it came to light that he was not the person they had been seeking. When the wardens called his name in the prison to release him, by the time he heard them and reacted, another convict had quickly presented himself by that name and had been released. So Karbalai Doshanbeh remained in the Eshghabad prison until the day that they called someone else for release. The person they named wasn't there, but the officials found Karbalai Doshanbeh lying in the far corner of the prison looking at them silently. Only then did they realize what had happened. They picked him up and dragged him out. One of the local officials slapped him on the back of the head, and then they threw him on the street.

This version of the story was told by Karbalai Doshanbeh's old traveling companions and the people who went out in caravans with him, people like Molla Aman and the Sardar. But rarely did he tell his own side of the story from beginning to end. Mostly he'd make elusive comments about the experience, and if he discussed it, he would only speak in general terms. There were a few people who had heard him tell the entire tale, but they were very few in number.

Abrau had become used to seeing Karbalai Doshanbeh, as recently he had begun to come by their home more and more often. He would sit, drink tea, and mutter comments under his breath, occasionally saying a couple of words out loud. If lunch or breakfast was offered, he'd eat. Eventually he'd get up slowly and then just leave. He clearly had begun to see himself as part of their family, or as one of their closest friends. At times, he even would make a joke or lightly poke fun at something, just to have a laugh. Even if, in the end, he was the only person to laugh at the joke. In any case, Abrau saw that the old man's feet were leading him to their home more and more often. He didn't approve, but he had no choice but to just bear it quietly and not say anything. The main reason for this was that Karbalai Doshanbeh was Zabihollah's uncle, and Zabihollah was a close partner of Mirza Hassan's. Abrau was, at this point, significantly indebted to Mirza Hassan. The issue at hand was Abrau's livelihood and his relationship with Mirza Hassan; all it would take would be for them to fire him from the job with the tractor and his life would be over. So Abrau felt he had no choice but to accept the indignities and not say anything. Abrau's inability to say anything, and Abbas' continued silence, not to mention Mergan's confusion over what to do, all gave Karbalai Doshanbeh an arena to continue to make his advances unchallenged. All that was left was for him to go and put his bedding on his back, bring it over, and move into Mergan's home permanently.

Let's just see what will happen...

This was what Abrau told himself.

But what about Mergan? What was she thinking and feeling?

Mergan acted indifferently, as if she didn't care if the world were washed away in a flood. When you're caught inside a typhoon, you don't worry if you've remembered to button up your collar or not. You don't worry that dust is getting into your eyes. You're in the middle of a typhoon; you can't be worrying about whether or not your throat is dry. You've just endured a deep dishonor, and you're going to get upset that Karbalai Doshanbeh is practically moving into your house? If he decides to, so what? Why worry about it? Let others say what they will. What can they say? Nothing. They can't say anything. Mergan is the only person who can say something about this situation. Freeing yourself from others is actually quite easy. What is difficult, perhaps impossible, is to free yourself from yourself. That's why Mergan was unable to find an answer for herself. It wasn't out of a fear of what others might say. What worried her was not that the word would spread that Karbalai Doshanbeh had made himself comfortable in Mergan's home. No, the looming disaster was that Mergan's own confusion made it difficult to even consider her own feeling about what others were saying. The weight of Mergan's thoughts, and the opinions of others about her, were so far from each other that she had somehow lost herself in between the two points. She was lost, rudderless. She kept hitting her head against her frustration, and she wished she could tear off the skin of lies clinging about her with a single scream.

Ah! You're all wrong, fooling yourselves!! The only thing that's true is what I am saying—this is the truth. Mergan, don't wallow in lies either! Your heart is right here; see where it is. So why are you shooting arrows at a fantasy of your own making?

To have screamed this out loud may seem easy enough, but Mergan couldn't see herself doing so. How could she thrust the knife of hostility into her own chest? What would result from this? Will others set aside their ideas about you? If they do set aside their fantasies, will your spirit truly be at peace? No, of course not! It will seek out some other excuse. Your spirit will just become more adept at finding excuses to be unhappy.

What if I don't say a word?

This feeling will still torment you. It won't let you be. The only hope is to try to forget. But is it possible to try to forget? To forget everything? No...Especially since you're held back by the sack of flour. So, no, it's not possible to forget everything. It may be possible to forget your poverty, but the clash of two inner instincts, no. The violent clash of two trees breaking in a typhoon. No, there's no easy solution. It's impossible to digest it. It's not a knot that can be easily opened, whether by hand or by teeth. The more you think of it, the less clear it becomes and the less you can discern it. It becomes more convoluted, and if you try not to think about it, it exhausts you even more. It's like a tack that sticks in the sole of your foot. It incites you. It calls you to itself. It makes you dizzy. It cuts your breath. It fogs your eyes, agitates your look, your face. You look but don't see. You laugh, if you have laughter left within you, but you don't know why. You feel you could have cried instead. You're turned upside down. But if you do think about it, you're no better off. The pain comes from the fact that you have not been able to face what has been unleashed within you and come to a decision about it. To have a clear idea about it. To either brush it off, or to feel victimized by it. To drive it away from yourself, or to accept it within you. You're pulled from all directions. You don't know which direction to turn, where you are going. You're caught in a dead-end facing the unthinkable. A violent pleasure has overrun you. A violent pleasure has planted the seed of a wild violence within you. You're caught in the middle. On one hand, you're a woman; on the other, you're supposed to be chaste, pure. You are free and tied up at the same time. At peace and yet tortured, open and yet closed. The two are caught in one thought, which twists in the nooks and crannies of your mind. At the same time, need and desire also flicker within you, evident despite the mighty struggle that tries to repress them. They twist within you. In the recesses of your mind and in your deepest thoughts, in the unspoken, hidden, and undiscovered moments of your life, desire moves and even tries to break down the walls of social propriety with its horns. A cow overflowing with a lust and desire is ramming its horns within you. You are a woman. There is no escaping this. And a mother; again, no escaping it. You have a man, and yet you don't. Soluch exists, and yet he doesn't. His shadow and his face come and go, but neither is actually him. They aren't Soluch. Is he alive or dead? Will he return or not? The flames, questions made of flames. Where is there an answer? There is no answer. The struggle of two lives in one. The Sardar, Soluch. Torment, desire, and rejection. Struggle. The lashes that scourge your spirit. You've been ploughed through and through, oh dry earth, oh barren land. They've ploughed you and pillaged you, oh earth. But you are both the land and the land's protector, the guardian of the land. And the land and its guardian are two different things. A fertile land is ploughed, and that is what it desires, in its essence. But the land, Mergan, has been pillaged. Plundered. Ravaged. So where was she, Mergan, the guardian, to protect Mergan, the land, from her pillager? What sort of protector has she been? Shame and a sense of dishonor. What is dearest to you has been plundered!

This was what was tearing Mergan apart inside. This was the division within her. The fabric of her soul was torn. A fabric that before had only been marked by work and pain had now taken on a new color. This new color that tinted the fabric of her soul had cast a shadow over her actions and thoughts, over her face. An unspoken color, however new it was.

Abrau could not understand any of this, other than to note it. *She's different now; somehow she's changed!*

Yes, she had changed. She was uneasy and often lost in her thoughts. But not thoughts about a decision. Clearly, something must have happened to her. But what? One could surmise almost anything, anything but the truth, which only Mergan knew!

"See what it's doing?!"

This was Abbas. He had risen and, like an insect, was trying to pull the sack of flour toward his corner in the room. It was as if he wanted to spend a night in peace, sleeping beside the sack of flour. However difficult it was, he dragged the sack to the edge of the wall under the eyes of his mother and brother. His forehead was covered in sweat. He knelt beside it. Weak, he fell to panting. He set his elbows on the sack of flour and held up his forehead in the palms of his hands. It looked as if his head was spinning and his eyes had gone to black. His hands shook and it seemed as if his neck was holding his head up only with difficulty. His fingers scampered like little crabs through the mass of his hair, scraping at his scalp.

Abrau was sitting across from his brother, leaning on the opposite wall. The two brothers had not spoken a word to each other after that night. Abbas had fallen into his own silence, and Abrau didn't know what to say to him. He was hindered by the question of whether or not he could speak to him at all. He felt he couldn't. The wall that had gone up between them was growing taller and stronger day by day. So much so that it would seem that soon they would be unable to see one another over it. This had driven Abrau to take his own course in life, to some extent. It was the sense one has when one has lost something and wants to make up for it in another part of one's life. So he became more and more committed to his work. He would spend more and more time working with the tractor of Mirza Hassan and his partners. He had become a part of its nuts and bolts. Eventually, riding on the tractor's running board, he'd seen all the farmlands of Zaminej from the machine. Along with the driver from Gonbad, they would plough sections of the land and take the money they'd be paid and hand it to Mirza Hassan. Although the farmlands of Zaminej were owned by different landowners and weren't all the same, still Mirza Hassan's tractor had ruined the market for ploughbearing cows in the village. Farmers who had been able to secure a loan that would simply cover the rental of the tractor had thrown away their old yokes and ploughs. So it became rare to see cows, donkeys, or camels that were pulling a plough with an old man walking behind. The slicing blades of the tractor cut the heart and belly of the earth out, transforming wild grassland into a field of rubble. Even the strongest cows from Sistan would never be able to do this. In Abrau's estimation, Mirza Hassan's tractor was omnipotent.

Eventually, Abrau was allowed to sit behind the wheel of the tractor on his own. For different lengths of time, sometimes for half an hour, sometimes even an hour. At least long enough for the Gonbadi driver to smoke a cigarette or wet his mouth with water. Sometimes long enough to drive the tractor to and from somewhere. Mirza Hassan had also given Abrau the hope that he might give him the job of driving the tractor sooner rather than later. He told him it could happen as soon as the water pump was installed. This would give enough time for Abrau to be trained. Mirza Hassan didn't want to lose the Gonbadi driver just yet, but it was clear that his time in Zaminej would be temporary. He was already homesick for his own town and area. He didn't have the heart for the weather in Gorgon and the desert here; someday he would be leaving. So Abrau was an asset for Mirza Hassan. He would do the same work for less pay, and he would be less likely to complain or make demands. In fact, he loved the work. The only thing was, he lacked experience. The tractor wasn't just a hulk of dry metal that could be driven by one's fancy—it needed expertise. While he learned, Abrau kept his eyes open for any sign of the water pump's arrival.

"So, Mr. Driver, when do these new lords of ours plan to bring their little water pump our way?"

Abrau didn't answer Karbalai Doshanbeh's question. In addition to harboring a deep dislike of the man, he feared opening himself to injury by his sharp tongue.

This sarcastic, biting delivery was just part of Karbalai Doshanbeh's mould. In general, this delivery would become more acidic and poisonous when attacking something that was new or novel. It was as if he could not believe in anything that didn't fit his own desires. He acted as if the new instruments and tools were so many useless toys. This was why, although his own son Salar Abdullah was a major investor in the pump and tractor, he himself had avoided any involvement, and indeed was waiting for the day when the partners would show up at his doorstep—the day when they were too ashamed to go to the government for further loans. If Karbalai Doshanbeh had loaned the partners the same amount of money they had just borrowed, who knows how much interest they'd have to pay annually?! He didn't have such a substantial amount on hand, and even if he did, they would never be able to offer a collateral that would be appropriate. Before all of this, before the emergence of what Karbalai Doshanbeh called "the new lords," all the landowners borrowed from him. But now, new options were available to them, new paths. The system had changed. There was a new clique in charge. These new arrivals were now borrowing from the government itself and selling their harvest to the government as well. Of course, when they were unable to meet the terms of their loans, they had no choice but to sell their harvests off to the government. It was simple: the value of their yield would be used to compensate for the cost of the interest they owed. They accepted this and didn't want Karbalai Doshanbeh to eye their debts. It hadn't yet occurred to him to do as the government and to collect on his debts by buying the harvests of farmers at a price he would set. It was unlikely he could have pulled it off even if he had tried. In any case, his business had fallen off dramatically, since the petty landowners were now looking to the government's coffers, and the only people dealing with Karbalai Doshanbeh were people who couldn't even claim a single star within the seven skies. The landless, homeless people. People like Molla Aman and a few others who didn't have anything to offer for collateral. So the money that they would borrow from him was never enough to return him much of a profit. This made Karbalai Doshanbeh even more venomous in his treatment of others around him. He had hunkered down in a fort of arrogance and indignation, shooting arrows at whomever approached him, whether friend or foe.

Somewhat involuntarily, Karbalai Doshanbeh had actually given his son, Salar Abdullah, some assistance and help in becoming a major investor in Mirza Hassan's project, thus allowing him to make a large claim in the tractor, the pump, and whatever harvest came of it. Despite this, his nature and character were clearly in conflict with his son's. He would never confront his son, however, and in public he only would say to him, "You know best." But in his heart, he did not approve of his son's work. In any case, Karbalai Doshanbeh's narrow mind and limited imagination were not of a quality to challenge what was happening in the village. The scorpion ends up trying to sting anything, from stone to iron to human bodies. He no longer even tried to assess the situation before attacking. What was worse, it was unlikely he would ever change; his mind had become thick and inflexible, and for a long time, it had been unable to accept anything new. When a new idea was voiced to him, he acted as if he hadn't heard it. Many had made themselves hoarse by trying to tell him, "Don't perform your ablutions in running water!" But he would still insist on doing this. Any time he had to perform his ablutions, he would stand right in the middle of a stream and would begin to wash himself in the water that was directed into people's water jugs just a few dozen steps downstream. And he would always spend half an hour performing his ablutions; he was incredibly finicky about the ritual. It was as if he considered himself to be inherently impure, and so a sense of religious purity came to him only with great difficulty.

But here, in Mergan's home, Karbalai Doshanbeh began to feel as if he had been stung; he felt a burning sensation on the leathery surface of his heart. The sack of flour that had been sent to Mergan by the Sardar stung him. But he also felt stung by the partners that owned the water pump and tractor. At this point, this seemed even more important to him; it distracted him from the matter of the sack of flour.

"Eh? So you don't have an answer for me, Mr. Driver? When is the water pump of these novices arriving? For two or three days now my Abdullah keeps talking of slaughtering a sheep in celebration. So I'd guess it's coming soon, eh?"

Abrau uncomfortably answered, "Yes, I would think it'll reach Zaminej any day now. Mirza Hassan's gone to bring it here."

It's not necessary for someone to have killed your father for you to have a grudge against him. There are people whose walking, talking, or even their laughter incites hatred within others. Karbalai Doshanbeh was one of these people; at least that was how Abrau saw him. To begin with, on numerous occasions he had made insulting comments concerning Soluch. Even the bits of copper that Salar Abdullah had taken from their home as collateral, or the welts he'd had from the lashes that had him twisting in the cottonwood field like a snake, all led back to Karbalai Doshanbeh. Added to this was now his heavy, suffocating presence in their home—this had been going on for much more than simply a day or two. It had now been some months since he first began finding excuses to come and sit in their house. Sometimes he would not even bother to invent an excuse, and he would just sit and make snide comments, or sit silently like a sentry to the gates of hell. To understand the psyche of Soluch's younger son, one has only to place oneself into his shoes. In the folds of Karbalai Doshanbeh's calm and unemotive face, a kind of impudence and cheekiness shone through. Something that was not easy to rub off and clean away. This shadow cast itself over Mergan's entire life like a dark cloud. And perhaps Karbalai Doshanbeh's self-confidence was overstated, as if he needed to feel confident regarding the Mergans of the world as a consequence of his own failures. Whatever the reason for it, his presence was an insolent insult for Abrau. He couldn't stand seeing the old man. How many times had he imagined himself tearing off the old, stained kerchief from around his throat? His presence in the house was suffocating him. It was like a slap in the face. In the company of the old man, he'd been unable to hold his head up at all, or even to look directly at his mother. He was in torment, a life-sapping, constant torment. It wasn't something that just stung him and let him be. It wasn't just a kind of pain. It was something living, something that had been born within Abrau's soul, and was always with him. Something he couldn't shake, even if for a moment, even if just to have a breath of air. The constant jabs and insinuations only made the situation more intolerable.

"Ha! I've heard you're packing away your daddy's shoes!"

"I've heard you say, 'Yes ma'am' to a flea!"

"Abrau, my boy! When will I see you carrying my bath things and following me to the bath house?"

"Don't worry. He's bound to have found a place to lay his head down somewhere!"

"It's not what you've heard! Karbalai Doshanbeh's not one to give up a fight with the angel of death!"

"Look, it seems Mergan's appetite is increasing!"

"Mergan was never really one to skip a meal, even back when she'd eat thirty-five *seer* in a sitting!"

These barbs were always followed by laughter. Laughter that brought spittle to Karbalai Doshanbeh's mouth, with his long tongue, his bulging unkind eyes, his terrible teeth. And worse, no one else knew what Abrau was enduring. It felt as if he was confronted with a barrage of insinuations and insults as soon as he lifted himself from his bed in the morning. What could he do? Once, he had stopped Salar Abdullah and said, "Salar! You have to tell Karbalai not to come to our house like he does. It's not right."

Salar Abdullah had replied, "He's my father, not my son! How can I prevent him from doing what he wants to do? He's his own boss."

And he had stepped aside and walked away.

What more could Abrau do? Their house didn't have doors or rooms to be able to find a bit of privacy from visitors. Karbalai Doshanbeh would just tuck his head down, cough at the door, and then walk in and sit in a corner of the house. It didn't matter when or what time of day it was, either breakfast or dinner. Once there, he would drink their tea and eat their bread. He would even pick at the bottom of a bowl and lick it, before sitting back and saying, "Thank you, God! You have the goodness. You have our thanks!"

Recently he'd begun to bring raisins with himself. When Mergan would pour him a cup of tea, he'd fish around in his pockets, bringing out a few raisins and handing the others two raisins each. Wild raisins from the mountains. But no one would take the raisins he'd set out for them. But as soon as he'd walk out the door, each of them would take the raisins he'd set out for them and eat them, even Abrau.

During the entire time that Karbalai Doshanbeh would be sitting there, Abrau would be trying to guess what Mergan was thinking. But it was impossible; he could never make out anything clearly. Mergan herself would not visibly react to the man's presence. She would just sit and do her work, sewing a patch or washing up. She was busy with repairing clothes, or standing by the stove, or coming and going, managing the affairs of the house. She showed little interest in Karbalai Doshanbeh; she seemed to just endure him as if he were something hung on the wall. It was clear that tonight, her agitation was unrelated to his presence in the house. She had been anxious before his arrival. She had also broken two glasses earlier, at the mourning ceremony at Zabihollah's house. This was unlike Mergan; she was not a woman to be clumsy in the work she did.

The Sardar rarely made an appearance in the weddings or funerals held for people in the village, but he was sitting against the wall in Zabihollah's home. Mergan was busy with bringing and taking the tea, sugar, and tobacco from the kitchen and was trying to act as if the Sardar was not there. But the eyes of the Sardar, like two arrows, were provoking Mergan. Her anxiety and agitation rose until the booming voice of the Sardar intoned, "At least bring me a cup a water, won't you, woman!"

Mergan was shaken. Her toe caught in the leg of her pants and she tumbled onto the floor. Two of the cups fell on a stone and were smashed to bits. Mergan felt dead and brought to life: she would never forgive herself for losing her composure like that. She had struggled to complete her work that night, and when she returned to the house, her face was pale with agitation.

Abrau couldn't imagine that something had happened between Mergan and Karabalai Doshanbeh, though. Let those who gossip say what they will. He just simply couldn't imagine it. He wouldn't even allow the thought of it into his mind. But why was Mergan ill at ease in her own skin tonight? Why was she jittery and unable to stay still? Why was she busying herself with chores for no reason?

Abrau was baffled.

Karbalai Doshanbeh spoke up, just like a cloud that occasionally rumbles with thunder.

"If Soluch, God rest his soul, were still alive, he could probably work for these new lords as a well digger for their new pump. At least that would have been work for him!"

Abrau remained silent, but inside he felt as if he was tied into a knot. He waited for his mother to say something, but Mergan instead chose to get up and go outside. She ignored Karbalai Doshanbeh's barb, but the old man grinned a poisonous smile, and exclaimed, "Hmmmm!"

Abrau felt his whole body convulse. His young heart was beating against the wall of his chest. He felt his lips had become dry as mud-brick. He'd had to fight numerous fights as a child, and he'd heard many things said in each. He'd sometimes replied to these things in kind. Sometimes he'd been beaten; while sometimes he'd given his opponent a beating. But

Karbalai Doshanbeh was something else. He was another level. And Abrau didn't have expertise in this kind of game. This old opponent! What could he do? Everyone has to take a fall and be beaten at one point or another. At least once in one's life. So it was time for Abrau to take a risk. With a shaking voice marked with the fear and anxiety of youth, he spoke up.

"What bastard's told you that my father's dead?"

Karbalai Doshanbeh didn't so much look at him with his eyes as with two lizards, saying, "Uh oh! Look who has a tongue in his mouth!"

Then he fell silent. He turned away from Abrau. He looked at the ground and began fiddling with his worry beads.

Abrau leapt up like a flame and ran out the door. Mergan was standing outside by the clay oven, her calloused fingers to her lips.

Abrau dashed to his mother and stomped a foot on the ground.

"Why don't you throw that man out of the house?"

What could Mergan say to this?

Abrau expelled all the rage that had been caught in his chest through a single syllable.

"Eh?"

Mergan took the boy's elbow and led him into the stable. It was the only place where one could have a private conversation. But the sound of heavy steps at the door of the stable stopped them before they could speak. They could feel that a man had rounded the wall and was coming to the house. They both turned; a giant was facing them. The Sardar! His teeth shone white in the midst of his bushy beard. Abrau sensed the trembling that had taken over Mergan's body through her fingers, still holding his elbow. The trembling of a bird in the trap of a viper. He sensed that she had gone pale. The Sardar began laughing, approaching them. He had a handkerchief filled with something. He set the handkerchief between Mergan's chest and arm, and he turned and entered the house.

"How's my old friend there?"

Abbas was silent, all eyes. He stared at the Sardar as he had stared at Karbalai Doshanbeh. He didn't reply to the Sardar's inquiry, but the Sardar hadn't expected one anyway.

"Don't worry about him! I lost my camel to him, but there's always more to have in the world, eh, Mergan?"

Abrau and Mergan stood in the door, watching this uninvited guest standing in their home. Mergan saw a black look in the Sardar's eyes. She lowered her head in silence. The Sardar pulled a pipe from his cloak, sat on the mortar, and took out his tobacco. Seeming as if he'd just noticed Karbalai Doshanbeh, he exclaimed, "Well! Karbalai is here, too!"

Karbalai Doshanbeh had not moved from his place. He'd not move for the Sardar or for God Himself. He hadn't even raised his head. This was not just here; that was how he was everywhere. Whether in mourning, or at a wedding, or at any gathering for any reason; it was just the millstone that he was.

The Sardar's pipe smoke rose, and Karbalai Doshanbeh looked at him from the corner of his eyes.

"So, you say you've come to see how your old friend here is doing, eh?"

Karbalai Doshanbeh's question gave light to a suspicious presumption, which did not escape the Sardar's notice. It was the kind of suspicion that the person who says it is aware of, and the person who hears it is aware of as well. Old opponents understand each other's speech. This understanding between the Sardar and Karabalai Doshanbeh was not recent; they had known each other well for some thirty years. When the Sardar was young, Karbalai Doshanbeh was already a man. They would lead their camels together in caravans. Head to tail, they would comprise a single team. During their travels, they would rarely be apart. The Sardar was the front leader of the caravan and Karbalai Doshanbeh would be responsible for overseeing the entire team. But it would be wrong to think that their familiarity with each other was a kind of friendship. This was because Karbalai Doshanbeh was rarely a friend to anyone. The sense of companionship he shared with some people was simply borne out of need. These were needs that arose from having to cross a dangerous pass in the deepest winter snow, or in having to cross the desert in the summer heat. For him, companionship was simply a solution to the problem of being alone, either to face the threat of wolves in the winter or to find protection from jackals in the summer. Everyone knew this. But you can't kill someone for being self-preserving. Goats have hair, and sheep have wool.

"Will you smoke a pipe, Karbalai?"

"Um...yes...I'll smoke."

The Sardar offered his pipe to Karbalai Doshanbeh.

"You'll suck it up even if they were giving it away for free! Ha ha! You've been smoking pipes for a hundred years, but I've never once seen you take out a bag of your own tobacco from your sack."

Karbalai Doshanbeh exhaled the smoke from the pipe and said, "A hundred years? More like a hundred and twenty years!

Just go and bring my death shroud, won't you? Do you think you're a spring chicken yourself? Don't judge by your beard, just because it's still jet-black! How old do you make yourself to be, anyway?"

"How old do you think I should be?"

"You tell me."

"Fifty. At most, I'm fifty."

"No. Start at twenty! You're still innocent and haven't seen the world, eh?"

"So you think I'm older than fifty?"

"I told you: you're twenty!"

"If I'm older than fifty, why don't I have a single white hair?"

"What does white or black hair have to do with anything? A goat's hair is black! Is that an argument? White hair runs in the family."

"So your beard went white while you were still a young man?"

"Ahmmm…"

Karbalai Doshanbeh wrapped his lips around the pipe, and the Sardar looked at Mergan with a gleeful smile.

"You don't want to bring us a cup of tea and a date?"

Mergan was still holding the handkerchief full of dates. She didn't know what to do with them.

"Put them somewhere by the cabinet. Just put them over there. They're delicious dates."

Mergan put the handkerchief by the cabinet. Then she looked at Abrau, who looked away from her. Mergan went to put the kettle on the stove.

"Hey, Abrau! Where are you, boy?"

Salar Abdullah's voice rang in the alley. Abrau ran out. He couldn't bear the thought of Salar Abdullah coming inside and filling the room with his huge frame as well. He met him and stood chest-to-chest with him, his back against the wall.

"Yes, Salar?"

"Run! Run and bring the ram over to the road! Mirza Hassan is coming. He's bringing the water pump. Everyone's gathering at the road. We need to celebrate by killing a ram! Now, go. Run!"

Mergan was standing with one foot inside and one foot outside of the house, listening to what Salar Abdullah was saying. She listened to her son's footsteps and those of Salar Abdullah until they faded into the distance. Then she returned to the room.

"So, they've finally brought it!"

Karbalai Doshanbeh was speaking to himself.

Megan sat beside the stove.

The Sardar asked, "What does this new group want to do with their water pump, Karbalai?"

As always, Karbalai Doshanbeh waited a few moments before offering a few words.

"No doubt they want to draw water up from the earth! Ha ha!"

"But from dry earth?"

"What do I know?"

"But if our land had water, it wouldn't be dry. If it had water, our canals wouldn't be drying out every day."

Karbalai Doshanbeh saw that the Sardar and he shared the same view in this matter.

"They say the water in the canals is so low there's no point in re-dredging them."

"Well, let them dredge them again, if they want!"

Karbalai Doshanbeh began to laugh silently.

"What? Dredge them? Who'll take charge of that? You have an active imagination! This group can't manage to drink a glass of water without someone telling them what to do. They can't get anything done without the threat of the stick! When there used to be one or two real leaders in this village, the landowners used to collect money to have the canals dredged. Soluch himself, God rest his soul, used to make a month's living every year from dredging them. But now that our former leaders have gone to live among strangers in town, they don't bother with the canal waters any more. So this is now in the hands of the petty landowners. They've spent all their money for the land and irrigation on buying and selling. So the canals have fallen into the hands of this group of new lords! And they each think they should be in charge, since none of them trusts the others. Each of them considers the promises of the others as worthless. They each say, 'What do I care? I only have a foot of water myself. Why don't the others do anything about it? What's it to me?' The other issue is that the value of grain has fallen. That's the most important reason, actually. They have to sell their wheat for less than three *tomans* per unit. It's not worth it to the petty landowners to farm more than what they'll use themselves. So now everyone who has some land and a bit of water only plants enough for his own use. During the harvest, how much pay can you set aside to hire gleaners? And those who don't have land have to buy their wheat from the market. So, they need to get money from somewhere. Where will the landless in Zaminej make money these days? From the small landowners? The small landowners are already in a tight spot. That's why Zaminej is falling apart now. The young men are leaving to sell their labor elsewhere. Many may not return. That's why the canal's been forgotten. Everyone's forgotten about the canal. And the canal's like a person, or, if you like, a camel or a sheep. If you don't care for it, if you don't feed it, when you don't care for it when it gets sick, it falls from its feet. It becomes ill. It gets worse day by day. Its throat tightens; that's the water level dropping...and it will get still worse than it is now! You've not seen anything yet! Mirza Hassan will show up and hire a few simpletons to help dig the well for this pump. But what will be the end of all of this? I don't see any good coming from it. And I say this while my own son is a partner in this plan!"

The Sardar asked, "So is the pump supposed to do the work of the canals, then? Will I still be able to get water for my camels, or will I eventually have to pay for it?"

"It's all new for me, so I don't know!"

"The pump, as you say, is owned collectively, no?"

"Yes, like the canal itself. There are two or three primary owners, and the rest have allotments allowing them to use the water for an hour or two at a time."

"So the owner is now actually Mirza Hassan, yes?"

"Ah...that's what they say."

"And he's planning to take the role of the overlord of the village, yes?"

"Probably. Most likely! But this is where he's stuck! What lands will he be the lord of? The barren wild lands? Ha! That's a difficult job. His eyes are on the lands owned by my son and by my nephew Zabihollah, but he's stuck there as well! The lands aren't all contiguous. There are bits and pieces here and there. You want to know how much it will cost to distribute whatever water they manage to pump to these scattered bits of land? A water pump! All of the village's money was collected by these three or four people and they've thrown it all at this heap of scrap metal—and let's not forget the money they borrowed from the government! We'll see a day when they can't afford the pants on their legs!"

Right or wrong, Karbalai Doshanbeh was mixing his hopes for the future into his predictions, which were no doubt stained by both envy and spite. They were wishes for the failure of others. If these others were to fail miserably, then he would be able to protect his sense of superiority. There are those who establish their own standing through the misery or degradation of others. In a thousand ways they say, "Don't move, so that I can stay ahead of you even if I'm standing still!" These kinds of people, given that they're stuck and frozen at a specific point, can't imagine any way ahead. Full of spite, they're like snakes sitting on the road. And although sometimes the road may indeed end in the point that they have predicted, one cannot consider their predictions as perspicacious. What they foresee is essentially a reflection of their envy, even if it contains scraps of the truth as well. What lies in their hearts is jealousy, enhanced by the fear of losing their position.

To Karbalai Doshanbeh, it was as plain as day that his position was being eroded. He had been comfortable as long as people were in need of him. But whenever and however people found or established a different source of hope for themselves, he sensed a tremor shaking the ground beneath him. The grounds were shifting. He'd been feeling it again recently. The government loans were putting him out of business. And he had neither the instinct nor the craft to find another use for his money. He also lacked the courage to change his ways. Earlier, his lack of spirit and his narrow mind had prevented him putting his money, which he had raised from selling his camel herd, to productive use. He hadn't even bothered to buy a drop of water from the canal, nor a handful of land. His son, Salar Abdullah, had inherited the land and water that he owned from his mother, in addition to a half-day allotment of water from the water lords. Slowly, Karbalai Doshanbeh had become like an old viper curled on the top of an ancient jug of money. His view perceived nothing but the handful of people whose lives were somehow caught up with his, the poor souls who were compelled to go to him to borrow a bit of money, the interest of which would eventually weigh on them and bend their backs even more.

But the situation was still changing. The larger landowners had, for one reason or another, sold their lands and water and had moved to the nearby towns. Many of the landless people had also set out on roads leading to distant towns and cities, and so were now no longer in need of Karbalai Doshanbeh. All that remained were the small landowners and those who had been able to continue to provide for themselves. These were the ones who were now making an effort to take up the roles of being landlords and leaders. They wanted to stay in the village, and to move up there. They wanted to clear a new path, and head out on it. There were others who were left in the middle.

Those who, due to the low prices on the harvests, and the expense of paying for labor, had no choice but to make use of the tractor and thresher and the water pump in their fields. These people were tied to the land and had no choice but to stay. These were the people who had to struggle to make ends meet. But even they were no longer in need of Karbalai Doshanbeh's services. They'd found a new saint to protect them. A new saint had been offered them, and they now sought their protection from it: the government. And Mirza Hassan was on the vanguard of this new idea and worked day and night for it. He ran from one governmental office to another, and from one governmental official to one or another bank. From one city to another, from one province to another. From Gonbad to Gorgon to Mashhad and back to Zaminej, across the desert. He was like a sword that cut through everything, engaging with people far and wide to get his work done.

"You remember when this newcomer Mirza Hassan used to be a sugar thief, Sardar?"

"Of course I remember!"

"Even though my own son is now his partner, I can't tell a lie about him! No, I'm no fool! Whose rope is he using to pull water from the well?"

"So why don't you join them? You could put all your money to some use! Why not partner with them? After all, you don't want to take your money to the grave with you!"

"What money? Ha! Money! Are you kidding me? Do you think I have any money left?"

Mergan set the teacups on a tray and took the handkerchief of dates from beside the cabinet and brought them over.

The Sardar said, "And put a cup out for Abbas!"

Karbalai Doshanbeh sipped from his cup and sucked at the date through his useless teeth. He took out the date seed, sized it up, and said, "That's a nice date, Sardar! Top grade! You still eat dates like this?"

"I get a batch every month. Haji Mashi sets them aside for me himself. If I didn't have them, I wouldn't be able to keep up with my camels! That's why I always have a batch of the best kinds of raisins, or the best grade of currants."

"That's good, very good! What memories!"

"And what do you eat, Karbalai? Dry bread and water, or do you chew on gold coins like a mouse?"

The Sardar wasn't concerned about offending Karabalai Doshanbeh with something he had said. At heart, he wanted to hurt and to drive the old man from Mergan's home using nothing but his sharp tongue. So he continued.

"Even during your days as a camel herder you never ate much! You always could find enough on other people's plates to fill your own belly. You would drink your tea with the sugar or currants you were offered from the traders. You would butter your bread with the stock you were transporting with your camels! But what do you eat now? You don't have the same people to go to as before. We don't have the bankrupt landowners that you used to visit during meal times to ask them about their payments. So what can you be doing for food? It must be that you're keeping yourself nourished by breathing the sweet smell of all your money! I've never known you to use even two *seers* of butter to soften your bread. So how much dry bread can you eat, man? Don't you injure your intestines with all that dry bread you must be eating?"

Karbalai Doshanbeh retorted, "You're sitting all high and mighty, blowing hot wind out your throat! For me, I've never heard of the poor shoeless Sardar having anything with his bread but watered-down yogurt! But friends and enemies alike both know that Karbalai Doshanbeh has one portion of the best sheep's fat with his food every day!"

The Sardar spoke under his breath, "In different people's houses, no doubt!"

"Why in different people's houses? Nowadays, no one has anything to spare. I eat in my son's house. My own son's house!"

"Oh, so you eat in your son's house? One would have to be deaf not to have heard that his wife has kicked you out of the house and that you're living out in the storage shed!"

"His wife? You think his wife can kick me out of my own house? She'd never dare to! She knows that every day I expect her to prepare three full meals to put before me. Each week I eat eggs and molasses cooked with yellow oil seven times."

"If so, where's your fat ass?"

"You want to arm-wrestle me over this?"

Now this was completely reckless. Karbalai Doshanbeh blurted this out from frustration, all at once. Something instinctive had compelled the old man to say this, or rather, to let this slip out. It was pure bravado. If Mergan hadn't been around, Karbalai Doshanbeh would never have spoken so foolishly, not even in a hundred years. But it seemed that Mergan's presence, and the fact that she was the audience to their verbal sparring, had agitated the old man. He was now heading for a confrontation with the huge Sardar, which would no doubt have a sorry end for himself.

The Sardar began to roll up his sleeve and prepare.

"What's the bet?"

"You decide!"

They both clearly understood the reason for their resorting to such bravado and, now, tests of their manliness. It was also clear to them that Mergan had sensed the reason for all of this as well. So the Sardar quickly said, "The bet is, whoever loses can never show his face in this house again!"

There was no place for backtalk or negotiation in these terms. The Sardar had thrown down the gauntlet, but was confident of winning. Before Abbas' wide eyes, and Mergan's quietly shocked gaze, the old hero Karbalai Doshanbeh rose calmly from his place against the wall and came to the lowered floor next to the hearth, standing before the Sardar. Short and compact, he was quiet and serious. He set his left knee on the ground, and set his right foot in the ashes of the hearth. The Sardar did the same before him. The two old men took their positions facing each other. It was now time for them to grip each other's palms and to try to break the other down. This ritual to test men's strength was brought by the caravan drivers from Kerman province as a gift for the people of Khorasan. They each grasped the other's right hand. Karbalai Doshanbeh's fingers were short and thick, while the Sardar's were each like a cucumber. In this test of strength, their hands were to be locked together and their elbows set onto their raised kneecaps.

Mergan didn't know what her role was in all of this. In fact, she was the most worried of all. She didn't want to be a part of this game. She stood and watched the battle from the edge of the room. Two ogres had made their way into her house, had imposed themselves on her and her household, now she could find no way to extricate herself from the predicament they had laid out before her.

"Okay, let's see how strong you really are!"

"You begin. I'm waiting for you to start!"

"No, both together!"

"Okay, together...Go!"

Each directed all of his strength into his arm and toward his fist. The contest was simple, gauging the strength of two men's arms, pushing in opposite directions, as two sources of power. The veins in Karbalai Doshanbeh's neck began to bulge. The Sardar's eyes began to widen. The struggle proceeded quietly, slowly. The pressure moved in waves through their muscles and nerves, focusing in their hands. The veins in the backs of their hands were visible. The two hands had become one; the two men, one body. A body set alight. Blood rushed to their temples. Their cheeks and eyes were contorted. Stones in the slings of two fingers. Their teeth bit their lips. They could each taste blood in their mouths. Necks stiff and thick. Beards trembling. Nostrils wide. Bodies shaking as if feverish. Their bodies looked as if they were breaking down, nearly collapsing.

It was clear that the Sardar could, in one sudden motion, break the grip of Karbalai Doshabeh's fingers. But he didn't, on purpose. He wanted to play with the old man, exhaust him, cut him down, and lay him out for dead. He mercilessly pushed on, intending to completely destroy the old man. But Karbalai Doshanbeh held his ground. It was as if he was finding strength from each of the days he had lived through. He found the spirit to defend himself as if with claws and teeth. Blood began to trickle from his lower lip into his beard. The capillaries in his eyes were red with blood. The vein in his forehead was about to break. But he didn't want to back down. He couldn't bear the insult of defeat. He was looking for an opportunity to play one last card. The Sardar gave him room to keep looking for a way out, given his complete confidence in his own strength. So as to give some hope to the old man, and to drag out the game a little, he began to shake his wrist on purpose. Karbalai Doshanbeh couldn't help but believe that the tide was turning, and his hopes were raised. He summoned all the strength he could gather and in one sudden move broke the pillar of the Sardar's hold, causing his hand to shake in a way that was now out of his control. He gained momentum and mercilessly pressed down, so much so that the angle of the Sardar's grip fell to a point that made it impossible for him to recover his initial advantage. Karbalai Doshanbeh made the most of the dead end that his opponent had now found himself in, and he brought one more final surge in his grip. Crash! The Sardar's four fingers broke backward. The sweat-covered palms of the two men's hands broke apart, and the men each fell back, bathed in his own sweat.

The pain was immense, but the disgrace was much worse. What does a man have other than his own word? The Sardar raised his body, holding his injured fingers under his arm. Without looking at a soul, he exited, under his opponent's triumphant glare. Mergan followed the outline of the man's broken shoulders as he disappeared into the darkness with a hint of pity. The miserable, wretched man!

Karbalai Doshanbeh dragged himself to the edge of the wall, leaning against it as he always did. He busied himself with massaging his fingers, without saying anything or looking at anyone. He sensed Mergan's silent surprise, but he felt it improper to ruffle his old feathers before her any more than he was doing.

Abrau entered the room, his sleeves rolled up and his hands covered in blood. He was holding a horn from the head of the goat that had just been sacrificed to celebrate the arrival of the water pump. With a glance at the flushed face of Karbalai Doshanbeh, and another to his mother's pale visage, he tossed the horn to one side. He pulled a knife from his waistband and, standing just before Karbalai Doshanbeh, he thrust the knife into the wall. He turned and looked the old man in the eyes and leaned his body against the wall. The bloody knife was in the wall just above his shoulder. This was the first time that Abrau had slaughtered an animal. This may have been the reason for the new color and disposition in his eyes. He opened his lips and growled, "Up, Karbalai! Get out of this house!"

The weight of the words was such that Karbalai Doshanbeh's arrogance was shattered at once. The old man put one hand on his knee and half-rose while saying, "Not a bad idea... I was just thinking of... leaving!"

He rose and walked to the door. He paused and asked, "So, it seems the water pump's arrived without a problem?"

Abrau didn't respond. He shut the door behind the old man, threw the latch into place, pulled the knife from the wall, and turned to face Mergan.

Who would believe it? Could a son kill his own mother? Abbas' large, worried eyes were staring at them. No, Mergan couldn't believe it!

Abrau, under Abbas' anxious gaze, stood before his mother, looking directly into her eyes.

"Tell me the truth, mother! What the hell are these beasts doing in my father's house? Are they here to try to take his place? Eh? Did you lose your tongue, then?"

That was right. Mergan had simply lost her tongue.

* * *

"Auntie Mergan, Auntie Mergan! Moslemeh wants you to come to their house tomorrow; they need help with the clay oven! Aren't you at home, Auntie Mergan?"

BOOK 4

1.

Fall marked the coming of the water pump, and the return of the boys of Zaminej.

Only Ghodrat didn't return.

"But why? Why only him?"

"He said, 'Why should I return?' He said he'd just have to go back again. 'That's a fool's game,' he said. 'One needs to just go and find a place for himself.'"

"He didn't give you a letter or something to give me?"

"No...He didn't give me anything."

"But where is he staying?"

"When the work as a field hand was done, he made his way to the capitol and sent word that he found work in a bakery there. But he said that working as a baker wasn't his destiny. He was sure he'd find better work soon!"

"But what about me, his own father?"

Morad laughed and said, "He said my father can go to hell! I didn't bring him to this world so as to now owe him something—he brought me here!"

Ghodrat's father pulled away from Morad and Abrau and stood by a crumbling wall. There, he said, "Ghodrat, my boy! You're tearing my heart out! I hope nothing will happen to you, my son! I hope that wherever you end up, you'll have bread to eat and you'll be healthy, my son!"

Abrau and Morad walked away from the weary, wretched old man. The sound of his lamentation faded as they left him behind. Morad's pocket was full of money, and he was walking on clouds. He had no patience for sadness. He wanted to walk all around Zaminej in one go, showing himself off to all the people of the village. He had a new set of tight clothes on, and he walked as if parading for anyone who saw him. His left hand was thrust into his pocket, and he shook the change in the bottom of the pocket to make it jingle. Abrau took every opportunity to assess Morad's clothes, if only to find some fault with the length or the cut of them. In Abrau's mind, the clothes were strange. The pants were cut short and their crotch was too tight. The sleeves of his jacket also didn't come to his wrists, and it seemed as if at any moment his sturdy shoulders were going to tear the jacket in two across his back! But Morad had no plans to take off the clothes before each and every inhabitant of the village had seen them. Morad was in love with the brown stripes that caught the eye as they crossed against the khaki background of his jacket and pants. Although Abrau had an impulse to try to buy the clothes off of Morad, Morad was not willing to consider selling them until the clothes lost some of their splendor. And Abrau would just have to eat his heart out waiting!

"So what do you say?"

"They're not for sale, man!"

"But they look terrible on your body!"

"So it looks bad! Don't look at me then!"

"Fine, I won't!"

"Fine, then don't!"

Shoulder-to-shoulder, they walked along with few words exchanged between them. They headed to Mergan's house so Morad could visit Abbas. But neither Abbas nor Mergan was at home.

"Where did they go to, so early in the morning?"

"What do I know? None of us knows much about what the others are up to any more."

"Are you fighting with your mother?"

"We don't really speak. What is there for us to talk about?"

"What about your sister? How's Hajer?"

"I hardly see her. The bastard won't let her leave the house! Even if she just goes to fetch water, he watches her with four eyes instead of two."

Morad reflected for a moment, and said, "Well, then...!"

Abrau changed the subject. "Mirza Hassan has started up the water pump. Let's go and see if he has some work for you!"

Morad said, "What would I do that for? He'd have to beg me to even consider it. You think I don't have enough? I have savings that will feed me until the next New Year without needing anything from anyone. And if on the day of the New Year I find my pockets are empty with nothing but some fleas in them, I'll pick up my bag and put on my boots. And who knows, maybe this time I'll go and not look back—like Ghodrat! What about you? I guess your work's not too bad then?"

"Me...ah...no. My work's not bad."

"If you only could see all the tractors that are everywhere in the next province over! They're like ants! No one there ploughs with cows any more. They even harvest the wheat with tractors as well. We can't get work as harvesters, you know. Now we can only work on the summer planting. The summer planting has to be done by hand, so the tractor's no good for that. And over there, the summer work pays really well, since you're so close to the capitol. The harvest gets to the market in two hours. Nothing goes bad before it's sold. But that's honeydew for you! Each one is three or four *man* in weight. Sweet as honey. If you eat one, you're full till sundown. It's really something!"

"What about the work? Is it hard?"

"Work's work, you know? Have you ever known it not to be hard? You have to pick and dig at the same time. And that's under the hot sun, with flies and salt water. You can imagine the rest. You start at dawn and end at dusk. Either the landowner or his brother or his son is standing over your head. If they're not there, you still have the foreman to deal with. If you're not in good shape, they can be ruthless! Ghodrat himself ended up going to the capitol mostly because he wasn't strong enough for the summer work. That's why he went to find some other nook or cranny for himself. I didn't want to tell his father this, but I heard he had fainted a few times while working. I was working somewhere that was not far from where he was. I heard they had to drag him out of the field into the shade and they threw a bucket of water on him. The problem is that once something like that happens, you're stuck with that reputation. You become known as lazy or weak and then no one will hire you any more. That's why Ghodrat saw the writing on the wall and decided to find some work in the city. If you're a good worker, you'll get a good name, but if you're a bad worker...If you work well, the owners will sing your praises, but if you don't, they look at you as if you're worse than a dog."

"How about you? With this fancy outfit on, you must have gotten a pretty good name, no?"

"I worked as hard as a Sistani bull for people who were totally ungrateful!"

They'd reached the outskirts of Zaminej. Mirza Hassan's tractor was parked beside the wall. Abrau made a half-circle around the tractor, kicked the tires, and then checked its oil. He climbed on top of the machine like a professional and fit himself onto the seat.

"Jump up!"

"What? You're going to take it for a spin?"

"Why shouldn't I? You think I can't?"

"You mean in the time we went and came back, you've become a driver?"

"Are you surprised?"

"No...No...But...!"

"No buts! You went and came back and in that time I've gone and ploughed about half of the lands of the villages around here."

Small-boned Abrau was in the driver's seat and Morad, with his tight clothes, climbed on board with difficulty and sat next to his friend. Abrau acted as if he were riding on the back of a hawk. His hands moved quickly and confidently. He gripped the wheel in his hands, turning it smoothly from one side to the other. With every movement he answered Morad's inquiring look.

"This is the gear. You see! Now it's in its place."

Abrau held onto the steering wheel with his left hand, and with his right he moved levers that Morad did not know the use of.

"When you move this, it brings the digger down. This one is for the plough."

Morad didn't understand anything. He was confused and at a loss for words. This gave Abrau confidence to puff his feathers out a bit and show off even more. He looked into the distance and tried to talk less, with the steering wheel in his hands. He answered Morad's questions with short, compressed answers. That was all fine, but it seemed to Morad that Abrau was overstating the importance of his work. Perhaps he actually felt this way, but Morad didn't appreciate the fact that Abrau had obtained the work with difficulty and had to appreciate its value.

"This is a tractor, not a sack of potatoes! How many thousands of *tomans* do you think has gone into it then? It's not a shovel or a hoe that they're letting me take care of! It has the power of a hundred and twenty horses! You should see how much work it does in a day. All this brings in money!"

Morad accepted most of this.

"Well, yes. Driving and working anything isn't easy. That's why Mirza Hassan wants you working for him! But tell me, if it has some kind of problem, do you know anything about how to repair it?"

"I can take it apart into ten pieces in a blink of an eye, and then put it back together just as quickly. But of course, you need tools. So sometimes you can get caught in the middle of nowhere. Those are the times that drive you crazy. You don't know what to do! Then it has to go to the repair shop. And where's that? You have to take it to town. You know how far away that is! And how can you get it there? It's like torture. You leave it in the field, and you go to the repair shop. And the guy there is probably busy. So you have to beg and plead to even have him listen to you. If your boss' name is one that they know, they might send an apprentice out to the field with a few nuts and bolts and a hammer. But it's like trying to pour water into a cracked jug! Before you know it, you've fallen behind ten days. Then the bill is sent to Mirza Hassan and he loses his temper and starts swearing up a storm. And of course, one or two people end up getting the brunt of it. But what can you do? You have to let it go!"

"So maybe it's not worth all the trouble then!"

"Worth it? Yes, it's worth it. This tractor's been working for six months, now. In these six months, it's done about ten to twenty thousand *tomans* of work. But Mirza Hassan says that the expenses come up to that much. That is, considering the pay for the driver, the gas, the oil, and the repair expenses. But he's lying. The expenses are much less. It's had two major repair jobs and a few tune-ups."

"And it loses its value, doesn't it?"

"What did you expect? For it to gain in value each day?"

"That's all I'm saying; it loses its value. So how much did he pay for it?"

"The Gonbadi driver said it cost twenty-two thousand *tomans*. It's secondhand, you know."

"If it brings in twenty thousand *tomans* a year, and it costs some seventeen or eighteen thousand *tomans* to run, that leaves you with two or three thousand at the end. And every year, the tractor probably loses two or three thousand *tomans* in its value. The more it works, the more worn-out it becomes. The more worn-out it becomes, the more it costs to fix it. And on the other hand, it brings in less income because the older it becomes, the less you can use it for work. So day by day, its costs rise and its worth drops. And the older it is, the less valuable it is. What are you left with? Just the harvest that you gathered from the land with the tractor. So, what's the harvest?"

The tractor had made a circle and the whistle of the autumn breeze was mixing with the tractor's roar.

"Mirza Hassan and his partners have done the calculations better than you and I can. You don't need to worry about them."

"Now where are we going?"

"To God's Land!"

"God's Land?"

"You heard right!"

"What for?"

"We're going to marry off your mama! What kind of question is that? What do you take a tractor out to a field for? It's obvious! We're going out to plough. I need to first smooth out the uneven land there."

"What has Mirza Hassan been doing all this time, then?"

"He was holding your mama's head! What's he been doing? He's been going crazy getting the water pump, registering the land and everything."

"It's taken this long?"

"What do you think? You think it's a game? Anyway, if he hadn't been so clever at this, it wouldn't have been arranged by now."

"They're saying the water pump isn't pumping very much water!"

"It's still just at the beginning of things. Wait a bit and see. If God helps us, Zaminej will turn into a garden."

"The elders are saying the pump is taking water from the canal system."

"Let the old men say what they want to. And who cares if it does? The canals are drying out anyway, so it's good if it takes the water from them. What difference does it make? The small landowners who use the canals are all partners in the water pump. And if they're not, they can buy into it. If they don't get fed from the trough, they can eat in the manger! And it's not like you or I need more water than what we need to drink, do we?"

Morad changed the subject.

"Who are those people over there?"

"Let's see!"

A group had gathered on God's Land. Mirza Hassan was towering over everyone else, standing beside a short, stocky Zabihollah. Behind them, the Kadkhoda and Salar Abdullah were both standing, speaking to each other. The father of the Kadkhoda and Karbalai Doshanbeh were also both there; the two old men were sitting on a pile of dirt, chatting. Ali Genav was there, standing near Mirza Hassan. Both of them were smoking cigarettes. There was a stranger beside Mirza Hassan who looked like an official from the Land Registry Office. He was accompanied by policemen, representing the law.

The tractor stopped by the group. Morad first removed himself from the stuttering metal machine. Then Abrau leapt off in a single movement and walked over to Mirza Hassan. Abrau couldn't understand what was happening.

Mirza Hassan said, "Once again, this foolish woman's making a scene! She's sitting over there and refuses to move. She's dragged that poor, sick, old child over here as well. In any case, you know how to speak to your mother better than we do. Go and say something. Don't let her cause a disgrace. I don't understand what this woman wants! She didn't listen to her own son-in-law. You go and try to get into her head that she doesn't have a claim to this land any more!"

Abrau silently walked over to where Mergan was sitting. Only her headscarf was visible, as well as the white of the tufts of Abbas' hair. Mother and son were both sitting in a freshly dug ditch. It was clear that Mergan had just dug the ditch in order to sit there with her son. Abrau stood beside the ditch. Mergan was hugging her knees. Neither she nor Abbas spoke.

Abrau suddenly screamed at his brother, "What the hell are you doing here, Shaggy?!"

That was the nickname that people had recently given him.

Abbas looked up at his brother, saying nothing.

Abrau shouted again.

"You've already gone and sold your part of this little scrap of dirt, didn't you? Don't you remember? Didn't you go and take the money from Mirza Hassan and then gamble it all away in one night? Wasn't that you! Wasn't it you who lost the money in Sanam's house? Here's a witness, right here!"

Morad was standing by Abrau's shoulder. Abbas looked at him as well. Abrau continued, "Up! Get up and get out of here! Get out, you son of a bitch!"

Abbas was about to scurry out of the ditch like a frightened dog with its tail between its legs when Mergan grabbed his ankle, pulling him back.

"Sit down. He doesn't know what he's talking about. Just sit down!"

Abrau stared at his mother and said, "What's wrong with you, then, woman! Don't you understand anything? What are you trying to prove? Why are you causing a scene like this? This isn't your land that you're sitting on, in any case! Is this just because you're stubborn?"

Mergan didn't reply to her son.

Abrau slid into the ditch and then grabbed his brother's hollow wrist.

"You get yourself out of this disgrace! You'll do what I tell you! Go!"

Abbas surrendered and let himself be dragged in any direction his brother pulled him. But Mergan intervened, grabbing Abbas' waist and pulling him back.

Abrau said, "Don't be so stubborn, woman! I'll put you under the dirt, right here!"

Mergan looked away from her son, as if she didn't want to see him. She quietly put her head on her knees.

Ali Genav approached them.

"Why are you rolling in the dirt like that, you foolish woman! What's come over you? Why is it nothing seems to lead you back to the straight-and-narrow path? This was wild land. It's not something you inherited from your mama! That man's gone and registered it and has a government official with him. So why are you causing a scene...?"

"You come down here. Come here!"

Ali Genav went into the ditch. Perhaps Mergan wanted to have a private word with him? Instead, Mergan spit at his face and said, "Now go, you!"

Ali Genav leapt out of the ditch, reached into his pocket, and pulled out a length of chain, as if to beat her with it. But Morad moved quickly and wrapped his arms around Ali Genav's belly, holding him tightly. Ali Genav tried to push forward, swearing. But Morad held his ground. Eventually, Ali Genav managed to pull himself free from Morad's grip, turning to face him.

"What's with you?! You want to lock horns with me, pip-squeak? Itching for a fight?"

Morad ripped his jacked off and said, "You sorry bastard. You think you can fight me? Think you can raise a finger against me? I'll shit on your pimping daddy's head! Go on! Take a swing!"

Before Ali Genav could swing his chain over his head, Morad had tucked in his head and thrown himself at his body. He forced one shoulder beneath Ali Genav's body and began to lift him up and suddenly with all his might threw him to the ground. He grabbed the chain from his opponent's hand, and— as if he was putting a muzzle on a horse—he pushed the chain across Ali Genav's mouth.

"You want to talk fancy with me, you fool?"

Ali Genav couldn't reply in kind. He was beating his legs and arms against the ground and foaming at the mouth. The village men and the officials ran over and pulled Morad off of Ali Genav's chest. With a bloody mouth, Ali Genav leapt up, picked up his hat from the ground, and took up a fighting stance. Mirza Hassan grabbed him by the arms and pulled him aside. The fight had to be contained. He passed Ali Genav over to the elders of the village and came over to Mergan.

"See what a mess you've started, Mergan?!"

Mergan didn't reply.

Abrau grabbed Morad by the collar and said, "You go get Abbas out of there! I'm not my father's son if I won't bury that woman under dirt today myself. But you get that innocent fool out of there!"

Then he ran to the tractor, jumping in the driver's seat and starting up the motor.

Mirza Hassan ran over to him, shouting, "Don't do anything foolish, son! We don't want blood to flow. If you do anything, only scare her!"

Abrau didn't reply. He took the tractor's shovel control in one hand and pressed on the gas pedal. The tractor stormed over toward Mergan. The officials were circling Mirza Hassan, and the crowd moved forward. Morad had pulled Abbas out of the ditch. Mergan had let go of Abbas but was remaining seated inside the ditch. Abrau drove the tractor forward. Steel has no conscience! It roared and moved ahead. The tractor's shovel rested on the edge of the ditch. His mother remained there seated: her face, leather; her eyes, coals; her lips, stone.

Abrau shouted from where he was sitting.

"Get up or I won't control myself, mother! I don't want to hurt you, but you'll be torn up under the teeth of this shovel!"

She remained silent. It was too late for talking.

Abrau threw himself down, and by the edge of the ditch, on his belly, he nearly began to plead.

"Get up, mother. Get up! Don't let me go insane. I'll kill you, I swear!"

She still didn't respond. Abrau let forth a bestial cry and threw dirt at her eyes.

"Just stare at me! Just stare! Why did you ever give birth to me!"

Mergan just blinked.

Abrau jumped back onto the tractor, and the machine began to roar again. It began to back up, and he waited for a moment. Then he pressed on the accelerator. It advanced. It was as if the teeth of a giant began to press into the dirt on the edge of the ditch. The crowd began to shout, screaming and swearing. But the hubbub was lost in the roar of the engine. They waved their hands; the old men waved their cloak ends. But what could they do? Mother and son were of the same cloth. Mergan was the mother of this boy, and Abrau was the son of this same mother. But at the last moment, Mirza Hassan managed to climb onto the tractor and switched the ignition off.

Abrau, looking injured, sour, and unsettled, leapt off the machine and into the ditch and threw himself onto his mother.

Had Mergan turned to stone? She didn't even open her mouth to swear at him. Abrau dragged his mother's body from the ditch and pulled her over to the tractor. He struggled to tie her onto the tractor with a rope. He sat cruelly in the driver's seat, and again he started up the metal beast.

The deed was done. The crowd stood seeing what the outcome of the reunification of God's Land meant. What was the tractor doing?! What was Abrau doing? Was the cruelty acceptable? Mirza Hassan lit a cigarette for himself and then untied Mergan from the body of the tractor.

Mergan had collapsed in a heap. Abbas had as well. Mergan took Abbas' hand—they held each others' hands. Morad followed the two of them. The mother and son were unified. Mergan had aged. She didn't walk as she used to; now she matched Abbas' broken steps. They walked like two ants. Morad walked to the same rhythm, quietly and calmly. It was as if the earth had been emptied and only these three people were walking on its tired back.

What color was the sky? And the earth? The earth was so strangely silent! Was there so much as a bird in the fields? No...the earth was empty, the sky was empty, everything empty. But Mergan faced down whatever they had put upon her.

"Don't worry, my son. Don't worry. You'll live a long life yet!"

At the cusp of dusk, Mergan and Abbas reached home.

Morad stood outside the door. Then he sat against the wall and held his head in his hands. How many years had he aged today? He felt as if he had become heavy, like a mountain. He didn't want to speak a word to anyone. He didn't know anything; he just didn't know anymore. He felt dizzy and at a loss for words. He didn't feel like leaving. He didn't feel like standing. He didn't feel like sitting. Everything seemed meaningless. How meaningless were these new clothes on his body! The only thing he felt like doing, that his heart would want to do, was to take off the clothes. But why now? His questions remained unanswered. He rose and went into the stable, emerging only wearing his undershirt and underwear. He entered the house and tossed the new clothes onto a pile of blankets and sat in a corner.

Three people, three corners, quiet, exhausted, weary. What flame will rise again in you, oh friend, oh brother, oh mother?

The dusk set, and the air grew dark. But with a light heart, one can see in the dark. When your heart is darker than the night, what color can the night have? Let the darkness fill you, penetrate you; let the night come on. Eyes can no longer see other eyes. People no longer see others. All the better!

"Why don't you light the lamp, Mama?"

It was Hajer's voice. She slid into the house. All was silent again. Hajer lit the lamp. In the shadows of the lamp's light, Morad raised his head from his knees and looked at Hajer. She paused for a second. Then she ran outside, as if she'd seen a ghost. She looked back inside, and the same eyes were still looking at her. Then she left. Morad put his head back on his knees. It was as if the silence was not meant to be broken. It was as if sound was an injustice that was imposed on people.

"Oh God... Oh God... Why have you forgotten me?"

Was this Mergan's voice? No, she wasn't speaking. So who was speaking? It had to be Mergan. Could it be her spirit speaking?

Hajer entered the room.

"What happened, mother...? Morad, tell me! What's happened?"

Hajer was speaking to Morad. He raised his forehead from his knees and looked at her quietly. He couldn't answer. He spoke to her under his breath.

"I brought you a bracelet. Hajer, I brought you a bracelet!"

Ali Genav's voice echoed in the alley.

"Where did you go, girl! If you're at your mother's, you're really going to get it!"

Hajer left quickly. Morad again set his head on his knees.

2.

Raghiyeh had lent her crutch to Abbas. It had been fashioned out of a branch from a knotted and twisted old tree. She could now walk on her own, holding herself up with one hand against a wall. She'd cough, curse, or cry as she dragged herself across the dirt like a leech. No one disturbed her, and she was unable to be much of a bother to anyone else. She no longer cursed anyone in particular. She cursed, but her target was everyone and everything. Despite her misanthropy, she'd given her crutch to Abbas. Could he have escaped being a target of her anger? After all, as they say, misery loves company.

Abbas was able to get around with Raghiyeh's crutch. He didn't need a crutch to help him with a limp. No, it was simply that his legs and body didn't have the strength to bear him, and the crutch helped him remain standing. It held his weight up, just enough that he was able to walk around the empty alleys like a strange animal. The small children were terrified of him, and as soon as they heard the sound of the crutch, they ran home, shutting the doors behind them while screaming, "Shaggy! Shaggy!"

No one called Abbas by his own name any longer. In the village, both young and old now called him by this new name, so much so that he had begun to forget his own name. The name didn't take hold all at once; it took some time to spread. First, they called him "Shaggy-haired Abbas," then "Shaggy Abbas," and finally "Shaggy." Eventually, it settled on just that one word. The word seemed enough on its own, and the name "Abbas" simply disappeared!

However, Abbas had stayed the same all along: wordless, confused, weak. It was clear that there would be no going back to his days of good health; even Abbas never thought about those days any more. It seemed as if he couldn't even remember the days before his work as a camel herder. From the way he acted, it appeared that he saw himself as the way he had become, and he had deeply accepted this new "self" as himself. It was as if he had been born as he was, with this new name. Before he began speaking again, others couldn't tell what he thought. When he did eventually begin to speak again, he never said anything that shed any light on his state of mind. The less compassionate used him for amusement. Abbas usually ignored these people, or just distanced himself from them. Often a Good Samaritan would come along and defend him, extricating him from the difficult situation. On these occasions, Abbas would just put his head down and walk away, tapping his crutch. He liked to go looking for gambling circles; this was the only apparent vestige of his former self. He liked spending his time in these circles, because he always had a role to play. In those games, he was treated like a lifetime member of the club, even while not participating in them, and each gambler had a specific feeling about his presence. Some thought his presence brought them good luck, while others thought he brought them bad luck.

"Don't stand behind me, white-eyed Shaggy!"

"Come sit by me, Shaggy, my friend!"

Shaggy would be pushed from place to place, but he held on. People would kick him, but he held on. They'd sometimes take his crutch and throw it aside, and he'd crawl on his hands and feet and get it; but he held on. Snide comments, jokes, attacks, insults—he endured all these, and he held on. Whatever happened, he held on. They couldn't do anything about it. He was there to stay.

Moslem, Hajj Salem's son, was no less persistent. He and Abbas had become like a knife and butter. Both loved to spend time in the gambling circles. Those who didn't like to see Abbas hanging around would try to incite Moslem against him. Eventually Moslem would leap onto Abbas and beat him. But Abbas held his ground.

"Run, Shaggy! Moslem's coming!"

The sight of Moslem truly made the hairs on Abbas' back stand on end. But he wouldn't run away. Abbas had come to depend on the gambling circles as much as he needed air to breathe.

"Come here, Shaggy; these two *qerans* are a gift for you. Put them somewhere in your pocket for safekeeping!"

At home, no one bothered him, and he minded his own business. He had made a place for himself out by the clay oven. He was comfortable there. With some stones and dirt, he'd managed to make a refuge for himself. He filled the holes in between the stones with bits of cloth and tin and hay. He would sit at night and look at the stars and the moon, the sky. It was then that he felt most refreshed, as if he could spend a hundred years looking up above him. And before he put his head on his pillow, he would once again count the change he had collected from people in the gambling circles.

"Twenty-two *qerans* today. Eighteen more *qerans* and I'll have twenty *tomans*!"

He had no friends or companions. Abrau no longer came to the house. Mergan was busy with her own work. Abbas only glimpsed her shadow from time to time. Sometimes, a bit of bread, a cup of tea would materialize by the oven; apparently these were from Mergan. Only Raghiyeh would sometimes come out and sit by the clay oven. At times, she would speak, sometimes not; sometimes she listened, sometimes not. Sometimes she'd get a *qeran* or two from Abbas to go and buy herself some chewing tobacco.

If given the means, someone like Raghiyeh would likely become an opium smoker. Or at least a smoker of tobacco water pipes. But Raghiyeh couldn't afford the cost of these luxuries. Her fear of Ali Genav was such that she would never dare to try to take some of his money for these ends. Instead she'd go to Abbas and try to get enough change to buy some chewing tobac-co. Two *qerans* worth kept her satisfied for a week. She put one pinch under her tongue and kept it there for an entire day. The lime in the tobacco had begun to irritate and injure her gums.

But the tobacco was Raghiyeh's only pleasure, as it made her a little dizzy. Before sleeping at night, she liked to also put a pinch under her tongue just as she was going to bed.

In the midst of this, Abbas was becoming a local oddity. His coming and going, his sitting and standing, his work and rest, his refuge, his den, his crutch, his hair, his torn clothes, his silence, his speech, his face, his eyes, the way he looked at things, his bones, his crooked walk—these all had come together to comprise a person with the name of Abbas, son of Soluch, now called Shaggy. Adding to this was Abbas' bizarre appearance, which had made him a sort of legendary character; stories of him passed from person to person.

On his own, Abbas had become "other." His separation from his mother, and his new place by the clay oven, had made his singularity even more pronounced. No one understood why Abbas had moved to this new place all of a sudden. Why did he make his home away from Mergan? Even his mother didn't understand. The only thing that occurred to her was that Abbas had wanted to stand on his own two feet, even if helped by his crutch. He wanted his existence to have its own color, to carry its own burden. Perhaps the ordeal had left one thing of Abbas behind; himself. A "self" with whatever face it had. And perhaps Abbas was instinctively struggling to find these scraps, these scattered shards, so as to put them back together as one. In this way, he somehow had to try to understand his own life. He had to see himself alone, without relying on others, to seek his self out, to sense and feel it. To do this, he had to emerge from beneath his mother's wings and present himself. Until he did so, his being would always be submerged, if not simply a burden. Led on like a pony, but worse, as an invalid—which he was. Even if each finger was endowed with a different kind of skill, in the eyes of others you are only seen as a transplanted branch, as something the existence of which is dependent on something else. They say, "Your mother takes care of you, your brother pays your expenses, your sister washes your clothes." In this, they can only make mention of you in relation to some-one else. And if you speak of your "self," it's only in vain, as in their eyes this actual "self" doesn't really exist!

One can't be certain if this was what led Abbas to separate himself from the household, but it may well have been. What other hidden power could have led him to leave the house and to build a den for himself out by the clay oven?

Perhaps it's not right to say that everything about a person is mutable.

Abbas was sitting in his usual place by the clay oven, and as was his habit, he was looking at the night sky. This habit had followed his injury, from his experience seeing that sky from the bottom of the well. From then on, he looked at the night sky in such a way that it seemed he was looking for footprints that were imprinted there. Forgotten footprints. Abbas' solitude was broken by the sound of approaching footsteps out in the alleyway. These footsteps were not familiar—he was now most used to Raghiyeh's soft footsteps that were always accompanied by her broken lament. There were other sounds that he heard in the alley, but Abbas mostly listened out for her footsteps, and these were not hers. The sound stopped.

"Abbas! Abbas...Are you asleep?"

He looked where the sound came from. There was a shadow against the wall. Abbas coughed to indicate that he was awake. The shadow approached him. It was Abrau; he stood facing

Abbas. Abbas looked at the cigarette burning between his own fingers. Abrau stood beside the wall of the oven. Abbas couldn't imagine what he wanted, so he waited to see what Abrau would say. But his brother remained silent. A moment later, he came over and sat down. The wide mouth of the oven separated the two brothers.

"Here! I'd heard you picked up smoking, so I brought you a pack."

Abrau fit the pack of cigarettes into the heap of stones beside Abbas' hand. Abbas watched his brother's movements, but didn't say anything. He didn't know what to say.

Abrau continued, "I know I should have come a long time ago. Too long has passed. But I couldn't come back here after that day. And now...I waited until night fell to stop by. It's better in the dark. I can't show my face around here in daylight. I really lost my mind that day. What a cursed day that was! It was as if I wasn't myself when I did those things. I've not seen our mother since then. I couldn't see her after all of that. I did try to send her some money, but she sent it back. How is she?"

Abbas tossed the butt of his cigarette into the oven, and quietly, with a muffled sound that had become his particular voice, said, "I don't know. I don't see much of her! She's probably in the house right now."

"How is she for food and water?"

"I don't know! I split the sack of flour with her. But I don't know more than that!"

"I really was bad on that day; it was really bad. How terrible! What son acts that way toward his own mother? But what can I do now? I've been sleeping out beside the tractor this entire time. But it's getting really cold now. That dry winter cold is setting in! This evening, the Gonbadi driver shut down the tractor for the season. When he shut off the motor, he took it out and took it with him. I don't think he'll ever bring it back. He may just try to sell the motor in the open market, to make up for the back wages they never paid him. God's Land is all ploughed, and we planted the pistachio saplings. But we have to wait seven years for the first fruit. And the major work of the tractor is done. All that we can do now is rent it out, which isn't really worth it. The expenses of the tractor kept getting higher, day-by-day. Mirza Hassan might have no choice but to sell the tractor off. They're saying that it costs more than it brings in. And you can't work the tractor all year round...! By the way, Abbas, do you know how pistachios come to bear?"

Abbas didn't know. Even if he had, he wouldn't have had the heart or interest to reply to Abrau's question. Abrau understood this, but had no choice but to keep talking. These words had become a burden on his heart, and the only person he could unload them onto was his older brother. Abbas' reaction wasn't of great concern to Abrau; loneliness had taken its toll on him. He felt like an outcast, separated as he was from his home and family. This made him anxious, and so he'd come to pour his heart out to his silent brother in the depths of the night.

"I had thought that Mirza Hassan was planning to plant wheat as well as pistachios and cotton. But he didn't sow a single seed of wheat. When someone mentioned this to him, he'd say, 'You think I have a donkey's brain to want to plant wheat? What on earth for? How much will I have to pay the gleaners? And who is here to glean, anyway? Once I harvest it, how much can I sell it for? How much do you think the company will pay me for it? They'll pay less than three *tomans* for each *man* of wheat! If you do the math, you'll see it won't pay for even half of its costs. What sensible person would do such a thing?' If I think about it now, I have to admit he wasn't wrong. Planting wheat and barley these days isn't even close to being profitable. Mirza Hassan also used to say, 'The government is importing tons and tons of it from abroad!' But that's why I'm worried that the tractor won't be put back to work. The planting land here is all in bits and scraps. This cursed tractor is made to work on digging up big tracts of land. Here, if the land is really a large plot, you're still done before nightfall. Then you have to drive three *farsakhs* to go find another plot of land to lower the blades on and plough. Just getting around wastes all of your time. You start to figure out the costs of these things slowly. There were many times when we didn't have more than one hour's work on a person's plot of land. How much to you think we could charge for one hour's work? And then think of how long it took to get there and back! That's why I'm worried this tractor might end up being passed on and sent to some other province. Somewhere like Gorgon Valley. That's where it was before. Or who knows, maybe Neyshabur Valley. And that's if the Gonbadi driver actually repairs the motor and returns with it! You see, he set up the water pump and drove the tractor, but now the tractor's out of service. And Mirza Hassan's up and disappeared. They're looking for him from the government's Office of Agriculture. I don't know! What should I try to do? I can't go back to doing odd jobs. But there's no other tractor for me to find work on. What a fool I was to have raised my hopes as much as I did!"

Abbas said, "How much does a pack of playing cards cost, anyway? Do you know?"

"Abbas, you're still awake!"

It was Morad's voice. Abbas turned to look where the sound came from. Morad peeked over the wall.

"Oh, you're here as well?"

There was a hint of shame in his voice. He walked around and into the yard.

"Come on up next to us. There's plenty of room."

"I'm fine here."

"Come on! Come here!"

Morad could sense clearly that Abrau was desperate for someone to talk to. He sat at the edge of the oven and asked, "So what's new? I hear the Gonbadi driver's up and left? I saw the tractor over by the graveyard, gathering dust! They say the driver took the motor on the excuse of repairing it and he's disappeared! Ha! You must know all about this; was the motor really in need of repairs?"

Abrau said, "I don't know. I don't know! However it is, it looks like the tractor's a goner!"

"You don't think the Gonbadi driver took the motor to make up for the pay they owe him?"

"Who knows? Maybe."

"Definitely! A hard-working person doesn't accept to have his pay delayed until the harvest! People like that aren't easily fooled by the likes of Mirza Hassan, either! The guys from Gorgon have had ten or twenty years' experience with all of this. But where is Mirza Hassan now?"

"He's disappeared. That's what I was just telling Abbas. There's been no word from him for about a month! And each of his partners is more clueless than the next!"

Morad mockingly said, "Hey...you're such a simpleton, boy! That Mirza Hassan shows one face, but he has a hundred hands working under the table. What did you expect of him? You thought that someone like him would really take on the work of sowing and harvesting? He sent his brother up to the higher villages to gather workers to take to town. They're planning to level the old caravanserai and put a shopping arcade in its place...Real estate! And the water pump turned out to be a farce. Now the newcomers who had opened their mouths in expectation of the money they'd make from selling water are left holding the bill! The small change that they'd worked so hard to save, they invested in this water pump. Mirza Hassan took the money from them and pocketed it and left. The pump cut the canal water in half and doesn't bring up any more water than we used to get from the canals. Where did they expect to find more water in this desert? So now we have to leave the village earlier than ever before. What's funniest is that Karbalai Doshanbeh's minding the machine!"

Abrau spoke out loud to himself, saying, "So what was all this fuss about?"

"You know, they don't give out loans from the Office of Agriculture just like that! You have to have something to offer as collateral!"

Abrau, who suddenly had the air of someone who has only just realized that he's the loser of a game, spoke loudly.

"So you people who knew all of this all along, why did you sell your lands to them with your two hands held out like beggars?"

"Our lands? Ha ha ha, lands! You say the word as if we all had major plots to offer. What lands were there to speak of? If

you used all of God's Land, and if it had water—which it does-
n't—it still wouldn't serve to feed five families! One needs land
to get one's bread from it, not just to play around on it. If Mirza
Hassan hadn't shown up and paid us to give it to him, we'd
have eventually just forgotten about it ourselves. You can't say
that God's Land was real farming land! Mirza Hassan didn't
buy the land to actually use it. He just needed a stretch of open
land to show to the government officials. As for you and me,
our families never made their living from farming. So, whoever ends up with control of the farming lands, we're not the
ones who'll ever benefit. Our claim here is wage labor, and it'll
always be wage labor. Before this, we were gleaners and
ploughmen, for a wage. And now we'll do some other kind of
work, for a wage. Before I leave for the next season, I'm actually considering going up to town to work on Mirza Hassan's
arcade. Even if his brother's not yet come to Zaminej to find
workers, I know he'll let me work on the job. I'll go there and
be a wage laborer, so that at least each night I'll have a couple
of bills of money in my pocket to show for it. I'll just sleep
there, in the corner of the caravanserai... But what about you?
What do you think you'll do?"

   "I...For now, I don't have the hands or the heart for
laboring."

   "Abbas! What about you, my friend? Have you thought
about this at all?"

   Abbas quietly murmured, "Thought? Thought! I...think!"

   "Do you think you'll leave?"

   "Leave? Are people leaving?"

   "They have no choice."

   "Leaving? Going to...?"

"What do I know? Anywhere. Somewhere!"

"No...no, cousin. I...no...not going...I...no...strength for traveling...no..."

Morad once again turned to face Abrau.

"What about you? You still don't know what you'll do? Are you sitting here waiting for Mirza Hassan to come back?"

"No, no. I don't know. I don't know yet!"

Indeed, Abrau didn't know anything about his future. He was dizzy and confused; he felt lost. Things had happened, events had taken place, but Abrau had no understanding of what they meant. He was in the middle of the action and couldn't make out the bigger issues. Perhaps others, such as Morad, could see things better from the outside. But Abrau was unable to. He felt that he had to have some time to himself to understand the implications of these recent changes. He had to be alone and in peace. He was still confused by the excitement he'd felt. He was still caught up in the storm brewed by Mirza Hassan, and he couldn't see a way out. He couldn't see what he would do if the storm were to dissipate. He was in the middle, in the eye of the tornado, the howl of which was still ringing in his ears, the dust from which was still filling his eyes.

When you leave the scene of the battle, you're still caught up in the battle. The battle is still raging inside you. The struggle, the fight was still inside Abrau. It was caught up in him, and he hadn't yet cleansed himself of it. He believed, or wanted to believe, that Mirza Hassan was going to return. That he would return to complete what he had made others believe he would do for the village. But he couldn't accept what seemed to have happened. He didn't want to believe his dreams were based upon a set of lies and fantasies. No, this couldn't have all been a game. There had to have been some element of truth to it. Abrau had devoted his heart and soul to something; he had believed in it. And it wasn't so simple for him to break the chain linking his heart to this project, the exciting work that had been begun. He also couldn't and didn't want to believe that he'd been taken advantage of. Abrau had done his work with the dream of turning Zaminej's fields into a lush green garden, and in doing so had nearly destroyed everything he had previously had in his life. He had worked day and night, giving up sleep and forgoing meals. He'd walked long distances in both heat and bitter cold to obtain a nut or bolt for the tractor, or a gallon of oil. He'd endured insults, and he'd sold off the bit of land that was his inheritance. He had worked. Worked like he'd never done before. He had sacrificed his body to it. The work had torn him apart. And in the end he had attacked his own mother like a savage dog, or something worse than that, in fact a hundred times worse. The shame of this fact was now eating away at him.

But what was now left to show for all of Abrau's sacrifices? What was left for him? Mirza Hassan had disappeared all of a sudden. He had taken the money that he was supposed to spend on the scheme and just vanished. The tractor and the water pump were now left to the partners, as was all the debt Mirza Hassan had run up on purchasing them. The tractor was now out of commission, and the water pump barely managed to bring a trickle of water out from the well. The canal water was drying up. The petty landowners had fallen to infighting. Those who hadn't bought into the water pump and who were relying on the meager water left in the canal had registered a complaint with the provincial governor's office. They claimed that Mirza

Hassan's water pump had dried out the canal waters. Those who had put all they had into the water pump were split into two groups. One group had tried to confront the complainants and the other group had begun to give up hope in the water pump and wanted to re-sell it. There were some who had already stopped paying dues for the pump to Mirza Hassan's older brother, who was in charge of collecting them. The dues were meant for buying oil and gasoline for the machine. And there were some who had invested both in the canals and in the pump and were now caught in the middle, uncertain of which side to take. It was not yet clear which side was most beneficial to them. In the middle of all this, the Office of Agriculture was still demanding the monthly payment on its loan!

On the surface of it, it seemed clear that everything had fallen apart. What had to be destroyed was clearly losing ground, but what was taking its place wasn't what it should have been. It was being replaced by confusion, by a loss of direction.

Although Abrau hadn't lost very much materially in these events, he still felt lost in the storm. He felt stranded in the desert. He didn't know what his role should be, what he should hope for in his work. As a result, his disposition had been upended, and his temperament and nature had changed. He no longer saw things as he once did. The earth, his home, his brother and mother, these all had new meanings for him. Something had collapsed under its own heavy weight, imploding, and its bits and pieces were scattered in the shifting dust and smoke. The scattered pieces were no longer recognizable. They were part of the original object, but had lost their original mass. They were now scattered, lacking identity. Each of them no doubt sought a new identity, but Abrau couldn't recognize them. Among the pieces were Abbas, Abrau, Hajer, Mergan, and—perhaps—also Soluch. These were the elements of their family, but none of them comprised the family on their own. They were all individual elements to themselves. Also, the people of Zaminej were individually still the same people. But as a people, they were not the same. It was as if an infestation had spread into everyone's clothing. The landless people had set out on the roads to town, and the small landowners were hiding in various corners of the village, still trying to make out what was to be won and lost in this new game. Zaminej was being torn apart. The previous stillness that blanketed the rubble of the village had been overtaken by a new struggle, a struggle inevitably leading them into a new battle.

No one could try to imagine where and in what city, province, or location Mirza Hassan might show up next.

"I had come to ask about Auntie Mergan as well!"

Abrau came to himself. He started in his place. Morad came down from the oven and began heading to the house. His heart pounding, Abrau quickly leapt down and grabbed the edge of Morad's jacket.

"Take me with you. By God, please take me with you! Will you?"

Morad removed the edge of his jacket from Abrau's hand and said, "You can come on your own. Who's stopping you?"

He didn't wait for an answer, and he stepped over to the threshold of the door. The house was as dark as a grave. He stood leaning against the doorframe, trying to get used to the deep darkness of the room. He couldn't see anything. He took a match from his pocket and asked, "Are you asleep already, Auntie Mergan?"

"No!"

Her voice sounded broken. Morad drew the match to light it and stepped forward. He could see the outline of Mergan in the trembling shadows cast by the light before the flame died out. Mergan was sitting, just sitting quietly. The flame went out. Morad went to the cabinet and lit the lamp there with another match. A layer of dust, as though it were one hundred years old, covered the outside of the lamp. It was as if Mergan never used the lamp. Morad wiped the dirt from the glass and turned up the fuse a little. The room was illuminated by a dim light. Morad turned around; he could now see Mergan clearly. She was sitting with her back against the wall and had her chin resting on her knees. She sat motionless, frozen, and silent. It was as if she had been in the same position for a thousand years.

Morad walked forward, holding the lamp. He set it down and sat before Mergan, looking at her. Her eyes were set deep into their sockets, a strange look caught in them. A peculiar, frightening look. This stopped Morad from opening the conversation with niceties, and he was at a loss for words for a few moments. Suddenly he wondered, why had he come? He didn't regret coming, but he was disturbed to be there. The problem of what to say and how to explain why he had come at this hour, and to have a good excuse for having come at all, now stymied him. He was stuck, trying to find a way to move this mountain, wondering how to raise it. Something suddenly occurred to him.

"Abrau! Auntie Mergan...I've brought you Abrau! He's sorry for what he did! Auntie, do you want to see him?"

Mergan remained silent. It was a heavy and profound silence, one that seemed impossible to break with a few words, especially uncertain ones. It was a silence that portended a forty-day vow of silence by Mergan. A forty-day meditation, the kind that seeks new avenues into the soul. A silence hinting at living through a distilling experience, twisted and terrifying, passing through pain to a summit. A forty-day vow that becomes one of forty thousand years. An old, even ancient vow that ends up as something entirely different from what it began as. It casts a new mould, takes a new structure.

A forty-thousand-year vow by Mergan, or a forty-day vow by Morad.

How can a mere infant speak with the old mother of the earth? He can't converse with her; it would be sheer impudence! But how can this infant now escape the field of Mergan's disbelieving stare? Morad felt short of breath. He had to find a way to release himself of this situation. His forehead was bathed in sweat, and he felt as if his shoulders were bound tightly and his legs were paralyzed. The feeling was like death. He wondered, what kind of woman was this? What kind of woman had Mergan become? Was she made of stone? Of dead earth? Was she death itself?

"Ahh...Auntie Mergan, shall I bring him? He's come to kiss your hands."

He no longer expected an answer. One couldn't expect an answer from this Mergan. So this was his avenue to escape. It was as if the silence was frozen in ice. He had to make a move. And to make a move, he had to say something. So he spoke, not for her, but just to speak.

"Let me bring the poor boy in from the dark!"

He ran outside and grabbed Abrau's elbow, dragging him in with himself.

"Come on. No need to feel embarrassed! You've said yourself you ate shit for what you've done. Your head was full of air
that day. Now you're sorry! So come on!"

In the doorway, Abrau pulled his elbow out of Morad's grip
and stood by the wall. He felt like he did when he was a little
boy. He had thrust his hands into his pockets and looked at a
spot on the floor. On his face, below the skin, an abundance of
feelings mixed to make an expression that was unintelligible.
Did it signify pain and love, regret and arrogance all at once?
And this was not the full burden that he now felt lay upon himself. A thick smoke had wrapped the young flame of his soul
into itself. It was a smoke that exhausts, that makes you listless,
that smothers you and makes you want to claw at your collar and
tear your shirt open to your belly.

While the cells in his body were enflamed, Abrau just
stood there silently. It was as if his entire existence had been
awakened. He felt as if covered by a thousand scorpion stings.
Stings stung upon other stings, all venomous. Abrau felt filled
with this venom. It rose within him; it poured over. It poured
forth like a fountain, from his eyes, and his breathing, the
helpless breaths that come and go, carrying a torturous world
upon themselves. This venom pours like a fountain—from the
cells of the skin of his face, from his forehead and his eyes. A
fountain of the soul's poisons. Is it the blood rushing in his
veins that beats within him so anxiously? It is his jugular
pumping, or is it the feckless beating of the wings of a pigeon
whose head has been ripped off by hand? Why don't these
veins rip apart, then?

"Okay...I've brought him...Auntie Mergan...! Here...
finally...finally...Well, okay!"

Mergan sensed her son, but didn't look at him. Abrau was still standing in the same place. He'd grown up! His voice, most likely, had dropped? She didn't know. Maybe his facial hair was beginning to sprout by now. That day—how many months ago was it?—the day he took her out of the ditch? That day, she'd sensed that his arms had gained the strength of a man's arms. Bless you, my boy! He'd pulled her out of the ditch in a single motion. He must be a man now. Thank God! She finally knew that she had brought one of her children into adulthood. But what of the other two?

I wish my back would break! I wish your back would break, Mergan!

If she had been able to bring the other two to this same stage, she would have had no sorrows in the world. But they'd been wasted along the way. Each was trapped in a different predicament. Her sorrow no longer centered on the question of why Abrau had turned out the way that he had, but why the other two had turned out as they had.

I'd sacrifice myself for you, my son!

But Abrau was now of age. He was a full person. He could fly away, or work. He could work without being tormented. He could even fight with her, with Mergan!

Come here, my son. Come here!

No, but Mergan couldn't do it. She couldn't. It was not that she couldn't forgive him; she could do that easily. She had already forgiven him. Mergan no longer had a sense of herself, although she knew herself. Things had been shifted; some things had been unified. Her "self" was no longer separated from the "self" of her children. Mergan "was" as they were. Her inability to speak was not as a consequence of her difficulty in forgiving him. She could forgive. But she didn't want to fill the house with lamentations by opening her mouth. If she opened her mouth, she felt, fire would shoot out, a store of smoke and fire and pain. She would be crying, wailing. Tears were better left for solitude, especially if they were going to make your throat ring like a piece of copper. She didn't want to release the unending pain from its binding within her heart. There would be other times to cry. But not here, not now. Abrau had not come to mourn. He had come to make peace. His man's shoulders need not be made to tremble. He need not cry! He need not drown himself in lamentation. This was not the role of a man, and Mergan's son Abrau was now a man.

My son, be strong!

"At least say something, Auntie Mergan!"

She didn't say anything.

"So you come forward, Abrau. You say something!"

Abrau looked at his mother. Was she looking back at him? No...it seemed she was both in her own thoughts while also almost looking at him. She was like stone, like crystal. Abrau approached and stood by Morad. Mergan remained sitting in the same position. Abrau had to say something. But what could he say? He stood there.

Morad again began speaking.

"Kiss each other on the cheek then! The world is the place to forgive. So go ahead, kiss each other!"

He grabbed Abrau's wrist and pulled him into a kneeling position.

"It's the night before the holiday, as well. So make peace with each other. Come on, Abrau!"

Abrau threw his arms around Mergan's neck. His cheek pressed against his mother's bony cheek, and he stayed in that position for a moment. Their eyelashes were blinking. Their hearts were beating. Abrau turned and sat on the ground.

Morad said, "Good! Auntie Mergan...good...You can set aside your anger now. You, Abrau, act like a decent person now. What was that you did? But let's forget it now! Okay, let me go and set the kettle on. We can drink a cup of peace tea, no? Where is it? Where is...?"

Morad was looking to light the stove and prepare the tea. The blinking of Abrau's eyelashes slowed a little. He pulled himself to the edge of the wall. Mergan sighed. The air was broken. Each one, by the movements of their bodies, or with a glance, broke the dark icy silence, which was thrown into confusion. The first to strike at it had been Morad. Once he had begun to speak he didn't stop. He busied himself with preparing the tea, and kept talking. He said nonsensical things, as he had become a prisoner of his own stream of words. He talked and talked and talked, and when he thought he had said something that made no sense, he just tried to make up for it by saying something else. This led to further binds; nonsense begat worse nonsense. But Morad wasn't trying to just say sweet things, or trying to have his words produce a specific outcome, or bear a specific fruit. He didn't think of these things at all. His only desire was to fill this house of ghosts with sounds, the sounds of voices. He wanted to rend the curtain and try to take things back to where they had once been. He didn't hesitate to add flourishes to what he was saying, and even spun unrelated tales—some true, others not—about his work and life outside the village.

"... so now it was almost dusk! We were going to go to wash our hands to think a little about what to do for supper that night. We brought up some water from the well, and all of us made a circle around the well. There were eight or nine of us! Guys from Kashan to Nahavand, and from around here, too. All that was left of the sun was a sliver the width of a single tooth from a winnowing tool. I turn my head, exhausted and tired, and I could see that someone was coming toward us from far away. He looks tired, too. He's limping. He has a shovel in one hand as well. I tell the guys, look at him! They all turn. We're all looking at him. When he sees us, he begins to slow down. It's clear he's hesitating. When he comes closer, we see he's a stranger. None of us have seen him anywhere in the area where we were working. He comes closer. We see that his clothes are all torn up. Nothing on his body is in one piece. One of his sleeves is torn right off; one of them's only hanging by a thread. His arms are bare up to the shoulder. But what muscles he had! His shirt was torn from the collar down to his belly. His arms are bloody up to his elbows. There are scratches on his forehead and on his cheeks. The blood on his face and chin is dried. He had cuts on his chest as well. One of his pants legs wasn't torn; that was the leg that was limping. I thought maybe he'd been hit with a stick or a shovel. He didn't say anything, and neither did we. One of the guys from Kashan—Rizaq, what a great friend he was—took him a bucket of water. The man kneels at the bucket like a thirsty camel. I think to myself that it looks like he's not had a drink of water in ten days! He puts his face and lips in the water, and it seems like an hour before he takes them out. The sun's set by the time he gets up from beside the bucket. We thought he'd just wash up and then rest with us and tell us what had happened to him. But he just takes his shovel, and without looking at any of us he leaves, vanishes. We were just left there, completely baffled...I'll go get the kettle off the stove. The tea's ready. Shall I pour you both some?"

Abrau was also helping out. He brought out the cups and went to get the kettle. Mergan pulled the lamp over to the wall. They sat in a circle. Abrau brought the kettle and put it beside his mother. Mergan took the kettle and poured the tea. Three cups of tea. It was time for them to sit back and drink the tea. Mergan took the cup before her, took a block of sugar, stood up, and walked out the door. Out by the clay oven, she set the cup and the sugar beside Abbas and then returned and sat down.

Abrau slid his cup of tea over toward his mother, saying, "We'll take turns!"

Morad lifted his cup, and while he blew to cool it, said, "Don't worry about it, Auntie Mergan! That land wasn't really any good for anything. You could burn yourself out working on it and still not end up with a bit of bread from it. Let it go in the wind! Let's see how those who were fighting over it do and what they'll harvest from it. Mirza Hassan's planted a handful of pistachio saplings and took the rest of the money off somewhere where even the wind can't find him. It's not clear how and where he ended up with the money! Just a little while ago I was saying that those lands are nothing but a burden on whomever owns them! If someone knows he has nothing, it's better than driving yourself crazy over something you own! What's the point of becoming the master of something worthless? You need to stand on something that has some value. I've figured out what my life and work will be. My heart's not tied to anything here. All I have in the world are two hands, whether I'm here or somewhere else! I can go to Tehran, Mashhad, Ghuchan; anywhere I go, I can work and make some money to feed myself with. I'm trying to convince Abrau to come with me as well. Over in other parts, you find as many tractors and other machines as you can dream of. They're everywhere. And there are more and more by the day. Abrau's already learned a skill for himself. He's good at these kinds of things. So what's to worry about? We'll go and find work. We have our health. Our hands and arms are strong enough. And this country, thank God, is rich enough. We'll find a corner for ourselves in the end, won't we?"

Mergan didn't really understand the details of what Morad was saying. But she comprehended the overall message. Despite this, she couldn't answer. She couldn't align her yesterday and today the way that Morad did. She felt she had chains around her feet, such as Hajer and Abbas. How could she tear herself from her children so easily? Her children were the same as her. So she remained silent and hesitant. There were many things that could compel her to leave the village, but there were many things that bound her to stay. This tug-of-war went on inside Mergan. It was not just a consequence of Morad's discussion, but he had taken root in her from the very moment that Soluch disappeared, when half of her wanted to just pick up and leave. But why should Mergan speak of something that she has no confidence in? Uncertainty appeared in her heart that was already split in two—no, in many—different directions. She couldn't lie to herself, could she? Did she not sometimes have a desire to fill the jug of water at the Sardar's house again and bring it to him? Yes, she did. Are there not many things that blossom within a person that will be taken by them to the grave? As a woman, this was clear to her. It was clear that her desires as a woman would be going with her to her grave; her baneful, seductive desires. It was something that would be lost in the dirt, in the earth. Despite this, could she deny its existence? No, it is and is and will be! Is it possible to forget the most colorful flower that you were ever given, even if hatefully, and drive the memory from the house of your soul? It is something that is left within you. You take it with you wherever you go. You take the good and evil of it with you and leave it in you. It's there, wherever you go. You try to expel it from your memory, if you don't actually gain strength from the memory! It's not just you who are trying to overcome it; it also has its own presence. It sometimes tickles you. Sometimes it stings. Sometimes it makes you ashamed. And sometimes in overthrowing all of these feelings, it boils up within you. You're still a woman, even if you're Mergan!

"We don't have anything to lose. We've never had anything to lose, mother. What do we have? I've been thinking about it for a while. We were born naked and we're still naked. We don't even have clothes on our bodies that someone can't take from us! I've got a skill. I will use it for work. Mirza Hassan's tractor has broken down, but even if that's broken down, the world's not broken down. My body's still healthy. That's enough for me. I'll go with the others and leave the village."

Abrau said this and tried to stop the trembling in his trumpet-shaped lips.

Mergan looked at her son. She looked at him openly. She felt that from her roots she wanted to once again understand him; she wanted to understand her own son Abrau, to believe in him. But was this the same Abrau? Was this the same boy who used to speak openly and honestly? Was this the same boy she had given birth to? That she had washed and dried as a child?

My son, my boy!

The sound of Abbas' crutch turned Mergan's head to the door. Abbas was standing there—he put the empty teacup by the door and turned and left. The sound of the crutch receded, died out, faded.

Morad rose, picked up the cup that was left by door, and said, "Don't worry about Abbas, Auntie Mergan. He'll take care of himself."

Mergan was all eyes, ears, and imagination: that's right. He's able to take care of himself! That's easy enough to say. But others like Abbas have been worn down, become dispirited, become listless, and have died. The distance between these stages, from being worn down, to becoming dispirited, and from that to listlessness and death can be quite short. Abbas could take care of himself, true, but how? What kind of work could he do? What skills did he have? Work! Work was the key to keeping all of Mergan's children on their feet, even if it had been forced or cruel work. They always had to first lift a hand before they were able to put food in their mouths. So yes, Abbas could take care of himself, but she didn't know how he would. Perhaps Abbas himself would know!

All of a sudden Hajer threw herself into the room, quickly, violently. She was trembling; she had run all the way. She was upset and her voice cracked in her throat. She hadn't noticed Morad.

"Mother, uncle's come! I've seen him!"

So what? Why should Mergan care?

"Mother, Karbalai Doshanbeh stopped uncle's donkey in the alley and took the animal to his own house!"

Again, so what! So what if he took it?

"He's keeping it there until someone comes and vouches for uncle. No matter what people say to him, Karbalai Doshanbeh's not listening!"

Mergan looked at her daughter and a faint smile began to take shape on her lips.

Abrau shifted and Morad coughed. Hajer sensed Morad and so left the house awkwardly. At the same time, Morad noticed that Hajer was pregnant, and only just caught himself from saying something under his breath.

The sound of Molla Aman's steps and his cursing voice echoed in the alley.

He and his kind can go to hell; let him take what's mine! It's more of a sin than for him to have eaten dog meat! He thinks he'll live another hundred years! How much does he think I owe him, anyway? It's just theft, that's what it is! What else can you call it?"

The edges of his cloak were wrapped around his legs; his collar was open and disheveled as he entered the room. Once inside, his voice rose even louder. His cursing increased. Without looking at anyone, he made several circles around the room before sitting angrily against one wall. He took his cigarette out of his pocket and struck a match with his shaking hands. A moment later he breathed out a pillar of smoke.

"The miserly fool! He finally poured out his poison; he finally struck! Oh God...! He took my donkey and my goods as collateral. He tore the edge of my cloak! He ripped the cuffs from my sleeves. It's just evil to do that, no!?"

No one seemed to be listening, or at least, no one responded. Molla Aman spat and began addressing an absent Karbalai Doshanbeh.

"You want a woman for nothing? Come on! You're not worthy to sleep beside her. Aha! You shameless man!"

Mergan rose, went beside the stove, and sat down again.

Molla Aman continued, "May your hovel burn down, you pathetic man! I finally will tell her the truth. Soluch! Soluch is alive! I've found him. He's not dead. Our man is alive!"

Mergan looked at her brother's face. She knew that lying, to him, was as simple as drinking water. But why would he lie about this? And if Soluch were still alive, where was he?

"He's near Shahroud, in the mines!"

What? Mines? In the mines?

3.

Where are you?

Where have you been?

Where are you, Soluch—you, whose name is the song of the bells of a caravan in the far reaches of the hot deserts of salt?

In what dark cloud have you been hiding? In what haven?

With what fabric have you hidden your face? In what sands have you been swallowed?

How did you melt to water and penetrate the dirt? How did you transform into dust and blow away with the wind?

It defies imagination how you lost yourself in the mountains and hills, you who were a man of your home.

Your name! Your name has assumed a narcotic songlike quality. Your name was swept away by water; your name was blown away on the wind. Your name—Soluch—is the song played by bells tied to the camels of a caravan lost in the hot desert!

You grew distant, were lost, disappeared into nothing!

Your story, Soluch, is an echo in the expansive valleys of an ancient night. How late you came!

The song of your name, dear man, is still not clear. The sound of your being is muffled, is rendered wordless. It's a wordless sign in the midst of smoke and sun and dust.

Where are you?

Where have you been?

My hands and face are outstretched to you; my steps are held hostage to you.

An ancient pain shoots like an arrow from the taut string of my bow.

You can't hear the cry of my pain, Soluch—in the bow of my back!

***

Mergan straightened her back. Somehow, there was news. News tainted by dreams, news of Soluch. She had a new strength within her. There was a movement in her veins. Blood was still pushing against the walls of her veins, as a heart cannot but keep beating. The old pattern of breathing had been over-turned. Waves of confusion beat against her head. Particles of memory were awakened. A new life, a new spring had begun.

Mergan straightened her back and rose. She had to set out, once again. The past had been a heavy load, but looking to the future compelled her onward. Is it possible to stay frozen in one place? How long can you continue to sulk in your hovel like a beaten dog? In this immense world, there is, after all, a place for you. There is, after all, a path for you. The door to life is not blocked shut by mud!

But Mergan still could not decide what she should do. She was still unsettled by the blows she had absorbed. Nonetheless, she had to collect her wits. She tied her chador around her waist and left the house. Abbas wasn't in his usual place. Abrau had risen early in the morning and left. Molla Aman, who was trapped in Zaminej for now, had left the house. He had gone to see if he could strike a compromise with Karbalai Doshanbeh. In the alleyway, Raghiyeh was sitting in the sunlight beside the wall, sewing the pocket of Ali Genav's vest. When she saw Mergan, she looked away and stared at the ground. Mergan stood beside her feet. Raghiyeh continued her work and acted as if she had no interest in conversing with her. Despite this, Mergan couldn't pass by her without speaking. She sat before Raghiyeh's knees and asked about her health.

"I'm fine!"

There was nothing more to say. Mergan rose; it was clear that Raghiyeh's heart would be set against her until Judgment Day. But Mergan didn't want Raghiyeh to be hurt even more by her disregarding her. If she were able to help Ali Genav's wife in any way, Mergan would do so with all her heart. But the ramparts that Raghiyeh maintained around her did not give Mergan a momentary opportunity to breach her walls. The only thread of relation that Raghiyeh kept with Mergan's family was through Abbas. And to continue this relationship, Raghiyeh did not feel it necessary to show kindness to Mergan's heart. Anytime the need or desire struck her, Raghiyeh simply went and sat by the clay oven, commiserated for some time with Abbas, hobbling away only after having gotten a couple of *qerans* from him. She paid no mind to Mergan's comings and goings. It was as if she wasn't Abbas' mother at all. And Mergan in kind tended to pay no mind to her. For a long time, she didn't speak to Raghiyeh at all. So now, it was useless for Mergan to try to win over the dead heart of Ali Genav's wife. Without saying anything further, she moved on.

Mergan walked around the alleys of Zaminej with no purpose or direction, saying hello and asking about the health of each person she encountered. She would knock on the doors of some houses, going in to sit and talk for a little. She laughed and made pleasant small talk, offering to help with the laundry and washing if there was any, or finding a broom and sweeping the house a bit before leaving. It was as if she were trying to tie up the loose ends of work that she had not finished in the village. Also, it was as if she were trying to see everyone in the village for one last time. It was, one might say, a kind of farewell. She was tearing her heart away from the village and was now caught in a limbo, between the feelings of hope and despair.

They say that some people grow suddenly kind just shortly before their death. Could it have been that Mergan was anticipating the day of her passing? But no; it was not as if she could have been considered unkind before this, could she? For whatever reason, she was now going to sweep up the dust from people's homes, as if she felt a debt hanging from her neck that she wanted to be freed from. Whether or not people gave her a little in compensation for the work didn't matter. Poverty has its own kind of generosity. An empty hand can still come with a full heart.

"What are you up to, Hajj Salem?"

"Sewing the crotch of my pants, my sister. I'm going to go to the water pump today. They say there's something going on there! But this needle shakes too much in my hand, and my eyes no longer see right. I feel I'm on the threshold of death, Mergan!"

"Give it to me. I'll finish it."

She sat in the sunlight by the wall, taking the pants and needle and thread from Hajj Salem's hands. He had wrapped himself in a torn old cloak, but here and there parts of his bare body were visible. But even so, what did Mergan have to worry about? She finished the sewing in the blink of an eye and handed it back to Hajj Salem before rising. Moslem was on the other side of the ruins, playing a game with some cow dung he'd retrieved from the stable. Hajj Salem carefully pinned the needle into the hem of his cloak. Then he rose and put his pants on, keeping his back to Mergan. He was tying his waistband when he noticed Mergan was leaving.

"Let God not take you from us, Mergan! The house that you whitewashed last year is still shining like the skin of a chicken's egg."

Mergan left the ruins, running into others on the way.

"Where are you headed to, Mergan?"

"Nowhere in particular!"

"This year since my children's mother died—may God rest her soul—I've not shaken out our blankets. Now they're infested with lice. Could you do us a favor and delouse the blankets? I'm going to the water pump myself. They say an inspector is coming from town today."

"Why not? I'll come to help."

Shortly, Mergan's fingernails were covered with the blood of lice. She wiped her hands on the ground, washed them in water, and then rose to leave.

"Mergan, before you go, there's a piece of bread for you here!"

"You eat it yourself, Zebideh dear! It's not yet noon, and I still have other work to take care of."

Mergan stood in the alley.

Halimeh's mother was chasing after her daughter, cursing as she ran. Halimeh had put her two little hands on her head and was screaming as she tried to escape.

"Get her, Mergan! Get the little devil!"

She caught the girl in her arms.

"Don't cry, my dear. Don't cry!"

Halimeh's mother pulled the girl from Mergan's arms.

"She keeps acting up, the little shrew! You'll see! She's ten already but her head's still an empty void! She'll have to be married in a little while, but all day all she does is scratch her head. Her disgrace of a father just pretends that he's not left this little beast in my hands. It's as if it wasn't his seed that was thrown into the well! Day and night he's caught up in this water pump. This morning again he took his shovel and left to go to the pump."

"What do you plan to do with her?"

"I'm going to pour bitumen in her hair. I'm not going to rest until I cut off her hair. She's driving me crazy! Come and help hold her hands and feet, otherwise I'm liable to kill her with my bare hands!"

***

466   Mahmoud Dowlatabadi

The sound of Halimeh's cries still echoed in Mergan's ears.

"Hey Mergan! Where are you off to with your head down like that? Could you help throw some dough in the oven and take it out when it's ready? My son's crying up a storm and I can't leave him!"

Mergan stood out by the oven, covered her face up to her eyes with her chador, and busied herself with baking the bread.

By the time the mother had put the boy to sleep, Mergan had finished baking the bread.

"Here, take this piece of bread and give it to your children for their lunch!"

"God repay you. Thank you."

Mergan walked down the alley with the bread.

The Sardar was carrying two jugs of water and was going to fill them.

"You're going to fetch water yourself?"

"Who should I send to fetch it?"

"Give them to me!"

"Bring them back to the house."

"Of course. I'm not going to leave your water jugs at someone else's house!"

She lowered the full jugs off her shoulders in front of the vestibule to the Sardar's house.

The Sardar was sitting out on a bench. Mergan leaned the jugs of water against the wall and took her bread from his hands.

"Don't you dare look at me like that! Ha! I'll tear your eyes out of their sockets!"

"What look? Wait a second! I need you for something!"

"Well, I don't need you for anything!"

Mergan was at the graveyard, next to the tractor. She stood beside Abrau and placed the bread on his lap.

"You're still sitting here? What are you waiting for?"

"I tell myself that the Gonbadi driver might still come back to return its motor!"

"If he had any intention of doing that, he'd have come back by now!"

"I don't know. What do I know? I don't know anything. And everyone's going out to the water pump! Half an hour ago a Jeep came in from the city and went up there. I'm sure it went out to where the water pump is. It looks like things have come to a head. It seems those who don't have a share of the water pump have had their complaint heard by someone, finally. I just hope it won't lead to a fight."

"Is Mirza Hassan there as well?"

"What do you mean, Mirza Hassan! He's disappeared into thin air!"

"So, he's really vanished!"

"Morad was in town until yesterday, demolishing the caravanserai, and he didn't see Mirza Hassan in those parts. Only his brothers and the foremen were there. No one knows. His partners here have been left out to dry. You see what the Gonbadi driver did when he caught wind of all of this! Even Mirza's older brother's stopped minding the water pump because he's not been paid either. Now Karbalai Doshanbeh's trying to run the pump, but all he can do is to hit the pump with one fist and hit himself in the head with the other! Salar Abdullah's running from one place to another like a wild dog. He's been camping out by the doors of government offices! I think that was him riding in the Jeep. He went to get the authorities. It'll be good if no one comes to blows today!"

"Now let me just sit here with you and let's see what happens."

Mergan split the bread as she spoke. She gave Abrau one half and began eating the other.

"Isn't that Uncle Aman, coming from up there?"

"You're right. Why is he running like that? Is someone after him?"

With each step he took, Molla Aman's long strides made the black wings of his cloak flutter in the wind, making him resemble a hawk in midflight. Without pausing beside his sister for a moment, he continued past them, leaping across the dry stream, dashing between the gravestones, breathlessly saying, "The Sardar's camel...! His old mare has fallen into the main well of the canal system...! It's blocked up the water for the whole system...! Things are happening...! I'm going to go tell him now...Who knows, it might have been someone's doing!"

"It might be someone's doing?"

Abrau swallowed a mouthful of bread and said, "It must be Zabihollah's doing! He wants to blame the Sardar's camel's body for the low waters in the canals...Damn him!"

Shortly, Molla Aman returned from the village with the Sardar with him.

"It must be Zabihollah's doing. It's clearer than day to me, Sardar! And behind it is that old dog Karabalai Doshanbeh. Don't think just because he's silent he's not involved! He's a cunning old fox!"

The Sardar pounded his walking stick on the graves as he took longer strides to keep up with Molla Aman. But Molla Aman kept his lead, speaking to the Sardar over his shoulder.

"It's been a month that the old dog's kept me here in his trap. I'm constantly struggling with him. I go to his shed, and I sit and talk from morning to night; but do you think he listens to me one bit? Do you think he responds to me at all? He only nods his head and looks at me like a donkey looks at its owner! And he's tied my poor animal in the corner of his stable in front of an empty trough; its ears are drooping from hunger! He thinks he's become the new owner of my poor donkey. So he just sits and stares at me, and I look back at him and sigh. What am I to do? May God strike him. He doesn't even give the poor animal a single strand of hay to eat. Woe is me! My donkey used to eat half a *man* of barley each day; now its stomach is drying out! And he's taken my peddling goods and tossed them under him!"

They passed through the graveyard and by the tractor. Abrau looked at them and shook his head. Mergan rose and began following behind them. Abrau turned to watch his mother as she left.

"Where are you going, now?"

"I'm going to see what's happening!"

"What's it to us?! Who are you to have anything to do with all this?"

Mergan followed, keeping pace with Molla Aman and the Sardar.

Molla Aman was continuing his monologue.

"...and now he doesn't even let me into the house. His son's bride, Salar Abdullah's wife, doesn't even open the door for me now. Yesterday evening I had a hankering to go out to the fields. I told myself, I'll go out in the fields to clear my mind a bit, to shout, scream! If I can't shout in the open air, I'll just put

my head in a well and shout. What do you know! I was in that
state of mind when I happened by the main canal well. What do
you think I saw? Ha! It was Karbalai Doshanbeh, sitting by the
canal well looking like he was reading the future in the water. I
said, hello old man! He suddenly leapt up and screamed. He got
up and moved away from the well. He shot a glance at me and
one at your camel. And your camel herder, the son of Sadegh
Jal, was lying on a boulder, asleep. The old man didn't give me
a chance to say anything. But suddenly a sentence popped out of
his mouth; he said that since they took the cover off the top of
the well, who knows what kinds of dangerous things might happen. And look, he said, the Sardar's camels are just wandering
freely all around here!

"I didn't say anything. I just waited to see what he was going
to say! Then he added, the old mare's also blind in one eye; it
could easily fall into this well! I still didn't say anything. He
ended by saying, the Sardar's brain must be in the heel of his
foot, as he's given a boy of twelve the job of looking after ten or
twelve camels. Then, when he saw I was looking at him suspi-
ciously, he headed back down to the village. I followed him. I
could see he was nervous about me. He kept trying to slip away.
When I saw that he was frightened, I just stayed quiet. He was so
nervous he turned and promised me that he'd give me back my
donkey and peddling wares. That's when I saw Zabihollah heading up in the opposite direction. Karbalai Doshanbeh shot off
in the direction of his nephew. I stayed where I was. I saw that
they exchanged a few quiet words, and then Zabihollah set out
again, this time walking faster. But how was I to know what they
were planning? I was just following my own complaint with
Karbalai Doshanbeh because I could tell the old man was soft-

ening up a bit. I came by last night myself to tell you about it, but you weren't home. I stayed at your home until late at night, until Sadegh Jal returned with the camels. But one was missing: the old mare. The poor boy didn't know what had happened. He had decided the old mare must have headed in the other direction toward the desert. He had cried so much his eyes were totally red. He had stayed out there late last night. I asked about you. He told me you'd gone to town. So I came back early in the morning and I helped him take the camels back out to graze. Then I came back again and waited for you at your house. The sun had come up, but you'd not returned. I was worried, so I went back to the fields to see if I could find out what happened. I saw that a group had gathered around the well. I didn't waste a moment; I turned right around and came back. I decided if you weren't home, I'd go straight to town to look for you. And now the canal waters have dried up, just overnight. Come! See! That's how people discovered that the mare had fallen into the well. Look! There's no water in the canals! The well is dry!"

Molla Aman pulled the Sardar to the edge of a canal, and the Sardar looked at its moist bed. There was only a thin stream of water trickling down the center. The Sardar pounded his stick into the half-dead stream, making a hole in the bed as deep as a fist-sized rock. By the time Mergan caught up, the two men set out again in a hurry.

***

Small groups of men were standing or sitting in the center of the canal system. It was something like a mourning ceremony. Most of them were the poor villagers who had small stakes in the canal waters. Hassan Yavar, who had a larger claim than the others, and who had made the complaint against the water pump owners to the governor's office, was not among them. He was likely with the officials at the water pump itself.

As the Sardar arrived, the men rose and encircled him. Ghanbar Shadyakh, the father of Halimeh, pounded his shovel before the feet of the Sardar and said, "May God take account of you if you don't testify to say that the water of the canals was already low before your camel fell into this well!"

Hamdullah Kanaan, a stout short-tempered man, dug his claw into the Sardar's shoulder, saying, "These are some right bastards, Sardar! We had to deal with a hundred obstacles before we managed to get the officer and the inspector to come out here, and then today they've blocked the canal water like this! They took your poor defenseless camel and threw her into the main canal well just to claim to the auditor that the low water level of the canals isn't caused by the water pump!"

The Molla of Zaminej, who was standing there, was muttering, "Judgment Day! Judgment Day!"

Ali Yavar, not addressing anyone in particular, said, "The fields are baking from the lack of water! Baking! If our fields don't have water in a day or two, the next harvest will be destroyed!"

Molla Aman and the Sardar walked the path up to the well, with the others following behind them. Ghanbar Shadyakh was holding his shovel on his shoulder as he ran between the people, saying over and over, "God will take account, Sardar. He'll take account if you don't testify about the water!"

Hamdullah also kept murmuring his own curses. "These are a bunch of bastards all right! Real bastards!"

Morad approached the Sardar and Molla Aman.

"Here they come, Sardar! Zabihollah's brought the inspector to look at the main well. He's telling them why the water's backed up. The Kadkhoda's also written up an affidavit and is having it witnessed. He's over there. It seems he's taking their side on this."

Molla Aman said, "But the traitor has a stake in this canal himself!"

Morad said, "The poor son of Sadegh Jal is sitting by the well and crying."

A group was standing around the well. There were tire tracks from the Jeep imprinted in the dirt. Standing on the running board of the parked automobile was the driver, a broad-shouldered young man with tight curly hair who was the only person standing apart from the circle surrounding the well. Two policemen were walking back and forth next to the crowd. Three other strangers, the inspectors and officials from the Office of Agriculture, were standing apart from the others and were speaking among themselves. Salar Abdullah was standing by the group of officials. The son of Sadegh Jal was sitting by the edge of the well with his face hidden in his hands. Zabihollah was pacing to and fro with a nervous look on his face. Kadkhoda Norouz was standing behind the group of officials holding a sheet of paper in his hand. Hajj Salem and Moslem were milling about the group of people. Ali Genav was sitting to one side smoking a cigarette. The various smaller investors in the water pump were standing around with no obvious purpose, every bit as worried as the major investors who were all there.

Morad went straight up to the head officer and pointed out the Sardar.

The Sardar pushed aside the crowd and stepped up to the edge of the well. He looked into the well and heard the weak whine of his camel emerge from the bottom of the well. He knelt over and leaned farther into the well, calling out in a broken voice, "My poor animal! My poor animal!"

When he pulled his head from the well, his big eyes were full of tears. He looked around himself. Zabihollah was standing near him, looking askance toward him. The Sardar stood up, turned around, and parted the crowd as he made a beeline toward Zabihollah. Before he could duck into the crowd for cover, Zabihollah found himself face-to-face with the Sardar. Mergan gasped and the Sardar's walking stick went up. Zabihollah jumped and began to run, heading toward the open field. The Sardar pursued him. Zabihollah, unarmed as he was, kept running. He was younger and had strong legs. The Sardar was already tired by his walk from the village. But he was more surefooted on the terrain. With two leaps, he managed to catch up with his prey. Desperate, Zabihollah grabbed a rock in his hand. But it was too late. With one blow by the stick to his leg, he fell, holding onto his leg with both hands. His forehead was crumpled and his eyes were shut. The worst pain always comes in the first blow. So the next few blows that the Sardar inflicted before some of those in the crowd managed to separate them did not add much to the pain that the first blow had already sent coursing through his body.

The police took custody of the Sardar from the crowd, and Mergan sat beside Zabihollah. The Sardar tossed his walking stick to one side as he approached the Jeep, getting into it. One officer remained with him, and the other came over to Zabihollah to take him away. The men picked up Zabihollah and carried him to the car. One officer sat between the men. There was fire in the Sardar's eyes, while Zabihollah's face was chalk white.

"Why'd you hit me, man?"

"Why'd you throw my camel in the well?"

"Me? No! No! Not me! I had come to cover the well, when...Oh...People! Come help me!"

The Sardar had tried to jump from the car, but the rifle of one of the officers was against his chest in a flash.

"Sit down. Where do you think you're going?"

The other officials also got into the Jeep and the automobile set off.

Zabihollah asked painfully, "So, sir, what happened? What have you decided?"

One inspector replied, "You'll need to change the position of the water pump!"

"What?!"

The Sardar's camels were scattered around the field and he could see each of them, whether close or far, from the Jeep's windows as it drove off. Two of his camels were standing near the drain for the water pump, and Karbalai Doshanbeh was standing by one of the animals, watching it drink from the water. The Jeep stopped beside the pump, and one of the inspectors and one of the policemen got out, walked over the pump, and shut the machine off. A moment later, as Karbalai Doshanbeh watched them in shock, they reentered the Jeep.

"We've signed and sealed it!"

Karbalai Doshanbeh walked a few steps toward the Jeep and then stood aghast in the dust that rose from the wheels as it drove off.

The two camels had stopped their drinking of the water and were looking at him. He turned and faced the animals, then sat by the pump drain grumbling.

"Imagine that I was planning to be the caretaker of the pump! Isn't it a shame? Isn't this clear water a shame? It was pure enough for your ablutions! Why did they shut it down? Working here saved me from that hovel, that shed! I spit on this life and the next!"

"Get up, Papa! Get up. They're ruining our means of living!"

It was Salar Abdullah who had reached the water pump along with the crowd of partners and shareholders in the machine.

"Get up, Papa! Our property's gone and turned to smoke!"

Karbalai Doshanbeh looked at his son. If there were a word to describe crying without tears, one would use it to describe Salar Abdullah.

"You see them? They're going to get a rope to pull the camel out of the well. Two of them have gone to get a well digger. They won, Papa! You see them?"

Karbalai Doshanbeh rose, shaded his eyes with one hand, and looked. A group of men were walking from the edge of the well toward the village. They had shovels on their shoulders as they walked. Another group was also approaching, scattered as they were. The shareholders in the water pump were walking scattered through the field like the Sardar's camels. Karbalai

Doshanbeh lifted his hand from his eyes and said, "No! They've not won. They'll never get that camel out from the bottom of the well. No way! Are they taking Zabihollah to town, then?"

"They're taking him and his broken bones to town. Go get your torn blanket and let's leave."

"No! No, I'll stay here. I'll stay right here!"

Karbalai Doshanbeh said this and went into the shed housing the pump's motor and shut the door behind himself.

He grumbled to himself, "I'm staying. I'll stay here. I have nothing left to return to Zaminej for."

The group reached the pump one by one, gathering around the drain. They sat around it as if they were at a mourning ceremony. The trickle of water from the drain pained their eyes.

Molla Aman, Morad, Mergan, Hajj Salem, and Moslem were in the midst of the group. Moslem went to stand in the shade of the wall of the pump housing. He removed his clothes one by one and ran naked toward the drain pool, throwing himself into the water.

Hajj Salem looked at those gathered in exasperation. "You see that beast?"

Mergan turned and set back out toward Zaminej. Morad and Molla Aman also set out following her. They were silent and didn't look around as they walked.

***

Abrau had fallen asleep by the tractor. Mergan didn't have the heart to wake her son up. Morad sat down in the shade of the tractor and waited, as Mergan and Molla Aman walked away across the graveyard. Mergan looked at her brother. Molla Aman turned his head and averted his eyes from hers. Mergan asked him, "It wasn't your doing?"

"What? What wasn't my doing?"

"You were out until the middle of the night last night! This all wasn't your doing?"

"What are you talking about? What wasn't my doing?"

"The camel! Did you throw the camel into the well?!"

"You're crazy! Sister, you're insane!"

Molla Aman didn't continue. He turned to go toward Karbalai Doshanbeh's home and said, "I'm going to try to find a bit of hay to give to my donkey! And maybe a bit of water!"

Mergan didn't watch him as he left, and she set out walking on her own path.

Raghiyeh wasn't in the alley any longer. Mergan looked into Ali Genav's home. Her daughter was sitting by the mortar and was grinding something inside it. Hajer's pregnancy was now showing. Mergan entered and stood before Hajer beside the mortar.

"What are you grinding?"

"Some herbs. Ali brought it for me from town. He also brought some other bits and pieces. Some herbal flowers also. He's so happy! Nothing's happened and he's already brought back some leather for me to make his son a vest! His son! Ha!"

"Good...Good...Hajer!"

Hajer raised her hand from the pestle and looked at her mother.

"Yes?"

Mergan took the pestle in her hand and busied herself grinding the herbs in the mortar. She was about to say something, but before she could open her mouth, Ali Genav came barreling into the room.

"Where are the ropes? Where? I had put them here somewhere!"

Hajer asked, "What do you want the ropes for?"

"We need to gather all the rope we have in the village and tie it together. It's not a baby goat that's fallen into the well!"

He looked for the ropes, finding them in the pantry. He didn't say anything to Mergan. He tossed the coil of rope around his shoulder, and as he left he said, "The baths need water. Cattle need water. Crops need water. We can't live without water!"

He went to the alley, and silence once again spread its blanket inside the house.

Mergan quietly continued to grind the herbs in the mortar with the pestle.

Hajer asked, "What's happened?"

Instead of replying to the question, Mergan said, "We're leaving."

"Where?"

"We're going out to the province where your father's been seen."

"All of you?"

"All of us? I don't know!"

"Will you come back?"

"I don't know."

"What about me, then?"

"You…you have a house and a life here. You have a husband. Now that you'll be bringing him a child, he'll love you more. What are you worried about?"

Hajer was shocked into silence. Then she said, "But if you go, who will I have? If I need some help, who will be there? Who'll cut the umbilical cord for my newborn baby?"

Mergan couldn't give in to the compassion she felt in her heart. She said, "You'll have people here. Someone will help you. I've not done anything bad to these people. They won't refuse to help my daughter!"

Hajer's lips began to tremble. Mergan couldn't let herself be affected by her daughter's tears. She rose and changed the subject. "You have a rash on your face!"

Hajer replied with a broken voice.

"That's exactly what I'm worried about. Some of the neighbors are saying having a rash is a sign of the child being a girl!"

Mergan had heard this said as well. But she didn't want to worry her daughter. She raised her head and said, "Let them say what they want! Are they in touch with God?"

She couldn't take it. She turned, leaving Hajer sitting beside the mortar, and left.

Raghiyeh was sitting by the clay oven in the yard of Mergan's house, knitting a small shirt, something for Hajer's child. Abbas was sitting next to her on his knees, with his crutch close by. He was counting his coins out separately and was putting the coins he had counted back into the purse that hung from his neck. Mergan untied the remainder of the bread that she had kept tied into her chador, set it by the oven, and went inside. She didn't usually spend very much time with Abbas and Raghiyeh. She knew that they did not enjoy her company. Ali Genav didn't much concern himself with their relationship either. This was because it was well accepted in the village that Abbas was burnt out, such that he was not considered a man. This was due to both his inner and outer self. He'd not grown a beard; his voice was still high and thin. His manner- isms were androgynous and he was uninterested in women; he never spoke of them. He didn't have a fancy for anyone at all. He never joked about such things. It wasn't as if he had even an interest in female donkeys! And overall, there was no sign of the usual desire and impudence of a young man within him. All this indicated to the people of the village that Abbas was burnt out. And Mergan knew this more completely than anyone.

Raghiyeh's fate was not much better than Abbas'. She was a bundle of sad bones, with a voice that rose only with great dif- ficulty, with a curse close at hand. She was a creature who seemed to emit only curses and complaints. Raghiyeh the nag! That was the name that some had mockingly given her. So there was nothing to worry about: let the two sterile freaks keep each other company.

"So add it up again. Two two-*qeran* coins make four *qerans*. So we have four here!"

Raghiyeh held up four fingers separated widely.

"That's four *qerans*."

"Here are three five-*qeran* coins; so that's fifteen!"

Raghiyeh repeated, "Fifteen *qerans*."

"Add those together, and we have...nineteen *qerans*!"

Raghiyeh added, "So we're twenty-one *qerans* short."

And here we have twenty-five ten-*shahis*, which makes...Let me put them in pairs together. Here! One, two, three...It's twelve *qerans* and ten *shahis*. So, add this twelve *qeran* and ten shahis to the other nineteen *qerans*, we have...Let's see! Ten over the nineteen becomes twenty-nine *qerans*."

Raghiyeh said, "Thirty, minus one *qeran*."

"And over here I still have the two and a half *qerans*. I'll put one with the twenty-nine; that'll make thirty. So what's that in total?"

"Thirty *qerans*, plus an extra one *qeran* and a half."

"Okay, so here! These thirty *shahis* are for you."

Raghiyeh took the three ten-*shahi* coins from the ground.

"So how much do you have there?"

"Thirty *qerans* all together!"

"Good. Thirty."

Abbas said, "Now hand over the bread so we can eat it. I nearly killed myself to collect this much money. And in the old days I'd see a thousand *qerans* blow away in the wind!"

Raghiyeh brought the piece of bread that Mergan had left on the oven for them and set it before Abbas.

"Do you want me to take these thirty *shahis* and buy yogurt or molasses for us to put on the bread?"

Abbas filled his mouth with a bit of bread.

"No, no. That's for you to keep. Go buy tobacco for yourself. God's already prepared the bread for us. We'll eat it as it is. So eat! We need to be frugal to be able to get what we want. Everyone's leaving!"

"You mean Mergan?"

"Mergan and her son! They're not infirm or tied to anything. I'll take over the house. And I know what to do with it. A shop! I'll sell so much during the winters that I'll be able to earn a living for us for the whole year."

"What kind of shop, exactly?"

"I'll begin by having gambling circles here. Then, maybe I'll have the stables fixed up and cleaned and put a grocery shop in it. If you're here, we'll run it together. If Mirza Hassan's tractor is working, we can load it with a few large sacks of flour that I can sell here to the locals in small quantities. Or perhaps we can rent Ali Genav's donkey. But we need to be able to make a living for ourselves. It's a shame neither of us has any use for our limbs! Otherwise we could start a bakery as well. But for now we'll just have to bring small wares and junk from town and just line them along the wall."

Raghiyeh said, "Let's see what'll happen! If this bastard has a bit of mercy and agrees to a divorce, then I'll be free."

"You need to come to an agreement with him so that you will give up your claim to the dowry you're due. But if only he doesn't come around here in a few weeks trying to claim that his wife, Hajer, has a stake in these four walls as well! You understand? You have to pin him down. Ali Genav's a cunning man!"

Raghiyeh said, "I know him well enough. But I doubt he'll object to the divorce. He's actually waiting for me to suggest it. But one thing!"

"What thing?"

"I want to have an opium cafe. You know how much income that brings in? Look at Sanam! She's free and doesn't need anyone!"

Abbas tied the string to his change purse and carefully placed it beneath his shirt, then said, "It's not a bad idea. I'd not thought of it before!"

Raghiyeh put a piece of bread in her mouth, rose, and said, "I should go then! It's dusk. Maybe I can go and lend a hand to your sister. She's in the last month. Why do my bones hurt so much?"

Abbas also rose and slid over to the edge of the oven, lighting a cigarette. The sun was fading behind the rooftop.

Mergan came out with two cups of tea and brought them over to the oven.

"I'd just poured her a cup of tea!"

Abbas exhaled the smoke from his nostrils, saying, "She left!"

Mergan placed the teacup before Abbas and remained standing there.

Mother and son both had sealed lips. Abbas smoked his cigarette, and Mergan trained her eyes on the edge of the roof. They both knew they had to speak to each other, and they knew the subject as well. But neither was able to initiate the discussion.

Abbas tossed the end of his cigarette into the oven and took a cup of tea, sipping it softly. Mergan sat down by the oven and put her back to its outer wall. Now they didn't have to look at one another. Abbas was on one side, and Mergan faced the other. Mergan, in the shadows of the dusk, put one hand under her chin and sat there. Abbas was sitting upright, with his long drawn face and wavy white head of hair, staring into nothingness.

"So what are you planning to do, Abbas?"

"What do you mean, what am I planning to do?"

"Are you staying or coming with us?"

"I'm staying."

Mergan couldn't bear it any longer. She rose and stood face-to-face with her son.

"I don't know what I'm supposed to say to you! If I told you to come with us, I don't know what would happen. But if I say stay, I still don't know what would happen to you! I feel cold, hot, wet, and dry. My heart's uneasy. On one hand, I see that your brother, who is now our breadwinner, isn't happy and can't work here any longer. He's become used to a kind of work that he can't do here. On the other hand, in whose hands am I to leave you here if I go? At the same time, I'm hearing news about your father. Oh God! This son, that daughter, that son, my husband, myself. Oh God! Why are we all splitting apart? I don't understand it at all! I feel like I can see what has happened, but I can't understand it at all!"

Abbas said, "You have a right. You miss your man!"

"No! Don't make those heartless insinuations! That's not all. My heart's been torn into pieces! Each of you...I feel each limb's been pulled in a different direction. And then nailed down!"

Abbas replied, "You're going to go looking for a man who left us disgracefully. He's dishonorable!"

"You're calling him dishonorable? No! If among all those who have left, one of them were to be called honorable, that would be your father, Soluch! Many others left and were never heard from. But not with your father..."

"Very well, it really doesn't matter to me either way. I'm not trying to stop anyone. I didn't try to stop him, and I won't try to stop you. Go then! Go, and farewell!"

Mergan was hurt. She said, "I don't want you to speak that way, to tell me to go and farewell! It's not the pilgrimage to Mecca I'm going on. Where I'm going is no heaven. I don't even know where it is! They say he's in the mines. But I don't even know where they are! I just know that I should go. It's not in my own hands. In fact, it's more like I'm being taken. But my heart breaks when you...It's as if you think I'm going to the garden of paradise that you're so cruel to me! Oh God! God, why are you tearing me apart like this?"

Abbas picked up a half-smoked cigarette and said, "There's no need for you to beat your chest like this for me. Just go! I've not said anything to you, have I? So, just go!"

"Go! Yes, I'll go! But I don't want to go with your tears and curses following me. I don't want to be hurt by you more than I already am."

Abbas said, "If you don't want my tears following you, just don't forget about me!"

"Of course I'll not forget about you! How am I supposed to forget about my own son?"

"I don't mean you should sit and cry in my absence!"

"So what do you mean?"

"Send me money! Help me with money. I'm still a living person. I breathe; I have to eat. But you see I can't use my arms or limbs for anything. So I have to find a way to make a living. I'm thinking of opening a grocery or a flour shop. So that one day I can order a bushel of dates, four boxes of tea, and ten *mans* of flour, and to have had five *seers* of bread to eat before that. You can't start with an empty pocket! With empty pockets you can't even raise dirt."

"Okay. Fine. Accepted. I promise. I'll send you some. I'm not one to avoid working. I'll work. And I'll send you something when I have it. What else?"

"Nothing. Nothing, really. When you do see my father, if you really want me to think kindly of you, have him send a letter bequeathing me these four walls here. I'm not in a position to have to confront Ali Genav tomorrow if he starts demanding part of it from me. It's clear as day to me. It's as if I've read it in the palm of my hand: in a short while, Ali Genav will come around here demanding his wife's share in this property. And if he wants it, he'll get it! I'm just a bag of bones. How am I to stand up in front of him? He'll come and put a line in the yard, take the house for himself, and put me in the stable! What'll I be able to do?"

"You're right. He's capable of doing anything you can imagine. Fine, I'll somehow obtain a letter for you and will send it. What else?"

"Nothing. That's all. I do want one piece from the copper that you've hidden. I'm only human. I want a bowl to drink water in."

"Fine! That large bowl that we use in the house, I'll leave for you. What else?"

"Nothing, nothing, nothing!"

"Good! So why don't you get up and come into the house? Why are you staying out here by the oven?"

"Don't worry! I'll come in; once you're gone, I'll move my things into the house."

Mergan took the teacup and said, "Do you want me to pour you another one?"

"I wouldn't mind it if there's some left. My mouth is dry."

By the time Mergan had gone to fetch the second cup, Abbas lost himself in a reverie. He was leaning his head against the wall and had a cigarette hanging from his lips with his eyes shut.

The dusk was so pleasant!

A voice rose from the alley: "They can go to hell! We're going. Let them gather all the ropes in the village and weave them together to see if they can get the old mare out from the well. Ha! Do you know how deep that well is?"

"Ninety-eight lengths of a body!"

"I still remember when Abrau's father Soluch used to say it was more than ninety-eight lengths. It's the main well, after all! No joking!"

Molla Aman, Abrau, and Morad turned from the wall. Abbas opened his eyes to look at them. The men were speaking among themselves with excitement. Molla Aman and Morad didn't let each other complete a sentence, and each would cut the other off by talking about what they had seen and what they had thought about it. Abrau was caught in the middle, lost for words, watching their mouths as they spoke. From the grave-yard to here, he'd slowly pieced together that matters concerning the canals had descended into a quarrel. He'd seen the groups of men who had returned to Zaminej anxious and worried. He'd heard that the authorities had taken Zabihollah and the Sardar to town. But despite this, his mind wanted more new information, and this was not to be found in the banter that continued between Molla Aman and Morad.

Molla Aman took a cup of tea from his sister's hand and gulped it down in one go, saying, "Ruined. Everything's ruined. Fallen apart. The death of everything... My poor donkey's dying from thirst and hunger in his stable! What a hell!"

Morad said, "I think that many of these people who were living off a goat's sip worth of water from the canal system will now have no choice but to leave!"

Molla Aman handed back the teacup and said, "If they don't now, they'll have to eventually. The heaven or hell we're left with will be on their hands!"

Abbas raised his head from his place by the oven. Abrau sat

beside it and Morad went over to the water jug.

Abrau said, "You think things will be improved if they change the place of the water pump?"

Molla Aman laughed and said, "Maybe!"

Morad said, "Don't be so naïve! Where is Mirza Hassan to come in and roll up his sleeves and try to set things right? Do you know how much it would cost to move the pump? Ha! It's not just a waterwheel that you can pick up and set on a donkey to take it somewhere else! It's a thousand *mans* of iron! Maybe more! Who has the expertise to do that? They'd want to be paid the price of their father's blood. Not just anyone knows how to do this. You'd have to go out to Gorgon or the capitol itself and lure a couple of experts out here with a pile of bills. Do you think they weren't paid a pretty penny to set it up in the first place? And how quickly they came out and shut it down! But what about Zabihollah!"

Molla Aman, using the same mocking tone he'd been using all day, said, "The best thing to come from this was that! I loved it!"

"The Sardar really has a way with the stick, no?"

"I doubt Zabihollah will be walking anytime soon!"

"I really doubt it."

"They can go to hell!"

Ali Genav's voice rose from the alley.

"Hey! Don't you want to come and help get the camel out of the well?"

His head appeared at the edge of the wall and stayed there.

Molla Aman said, "Help for what? You think I'm eating bread for free to go and put myself to work like that? That same Karbalai Doshanbeh who's locked himself into the pump house has taken my donkey and is starving it to death! He's made me wretched! So I'm supposed to go and help open his son's canal system! Whoever has land needs that water. Whoever needs that water can go and do the work. Why am I supposed to go and kill myself to pull that camel from the well? If I'm injured, who's going to pay for my stay in the hospital?"

"What about you, Morad?"

"I'm busy. I have to go and get my things ready to leave. We're leaving."

"And you, Abrau? They have the ropes all ready. Everyone's going."

Abrau said, "I've done plenty for them! No more! They can go to hell!"

As Ali Genav turned away, Mergan ran out following him.

"Wait a minute. Wait. Let me come with you. After all, a body's a body."

Morad looked at Molla Aman. Abrau looked down at the ground.

Molla Aman said, "It's not in her hands. She has no self-control, this woman. She's a fool!"

4.

In the end they failed. They failed to pull the camel from the
well. They motivated themselves, used all their strength, but
still they failed. All of the village's ropes were brought to the
task, and the experienced well-diggers of Dehbid went down
into the well with them. They passed the rope beneath the
camel's body, wrapped it around its neck and legs, and then
pulled themselves up the rope like snakes. They shook the dust
from their bodies and clothes and said, "Go on! Pull!"

The rope had eight ends; the rope made of all the ropes of
Zaminej village had ended up with eight ends. Ten men took a
hold of each of the eight strands—eighty men's strength all
together!

"One, two, three—God's help!"

The camel's body rose from the mud and earth in the well.

Eighty men, together! The camel's body began to ascend the earthen wall of the well.

"Wrap the ropes around your waist. Ha...go! It's coming up!"

"It's stuck! It's stuck! Wait a minute! Hold yourselves. Plant your feet into the dirt."

The men held on with the ropes wrapped around their waists, digging their feet into the earth. Their bodies leaned back; their feet were set forward. They were like narrow trees bending in wind. The two master well diggers were standing at the edge of the well and were looking over the edge into the well.

The rope was also twisted around Mergan's body.

"Its neck is caught against a pole in the well. Right in the middle of the rod!"

"What shall we do? What can we do? Our hands and waists are being cut through!"

"We have no choice! Pull. We have to keep pulling. We can break its neck and then bring it out. Pull!"

"Pull! With God's help!"

They pulled with all of the strength they could conjure from their bodies. But the animal was still stuck.

"Pull!"

"No! Don't pull!"

Two of the rope strands went slack and tore. Two of the groups fell back onto each other. The body slipped down and six groups of men were pulled forward with their strands of rope.

The well diggers shouted.

"Slowly, slowly, pull on the ropes! Slowly!"

"Slowly, now let the ropes go loose! Slowly!"

The body suddenly tumbled back down as the wall of the well collapsed onto itself, and six strands of rope, like six dragons, leaped into the mouth of the well.

"Oh no! Worse! The spring in the well will be blocked by all the dirt!"

A billow of dust rose from the mouth of the well.

"Oh no! Much worse!"

Covered in dust and sweat, the men stood there.

"Now what do we do?"

The well-diggers sat down.

"We need tools, implements. And better rope."

"Ah! I have an idea!"

"Okay. What is it? Tell us!"

"Let's cut the animal into pieces and bring them up one at a time!"

"That's a great idea, Khodadad. You always know what to do, old shepherd!"

"Let's get to work! Who thinks they're up to it?"

The shepherd and the well-digger volunteered.

"Bring the well wheel! Sharpen your dagger, Khodadad!"

"Who's going to explain this to the Sardar!"

"I'll do it!"

"We'll all do it!"

"All that's left for him is the price of its hide!"

They brought the well wheel to lower down the men. Khodadad the shepherd and Mohammad Kazem the well digger took off their boots. Khodadad thrust his dagger into his waistband and went toward Salar Abdullah and the Kadkhoda.

"I'm taking my life in my own hands by going to the bottom of this well! I'm expecting to be paid. One hundred *tomans*!"

It was no longer necessary to have everyone there at once. Those who had a role to play and those who had a share in the waters of the canals stayed. The others began wandering back to Zaminej.

But no, they failed to pull the camel from the well whole. Ali Genav went to collect the grazing camels for his cousin the Sardar. Mergan was also worried by the thought that the camels would be lost.

"It's a shame, those camels! They shouldn't be lost in this way!"

* * *

The moon had risen by the time Mergan returned home.

Only Abbas was still awake. He was sitting and looking up into the night. The others, Molla Aman and Abrau, each had put something under his head and fallen asleep.

Mergan was exhausted, so she should have gone to sleep as well. But how could sleep come to Mergan's worried eyes? Without sitting down, she began to pack whatever possessions she had. Possessions...one might just say a few shirts and a pair of leggings and a shroud.

Those people who have roots in the old ways generally accept that at the first opportunity, whenever there's enough to feed oneself for a bit, one should then think of obtaining a death shroud. A couple of lengths of cloth; it's not expensive to procure one. And once in her life, Mergan had found herself with such an opportunity. A shroud, the only piece of clothing that a person will wear only once. She packed the shroud separately in a trunk, setting it aside. She also wrapped some bread, sugar, and tea in a separate package. She collected some bits and pieces to leave for Abbas and put the trunk with the shroud on top of them. Then she went over to the bag of flour; there was less than one *man* of flour left. She also put that beside the bits and pieces for Abbas. Only one thing remained, one task she still had to do. She looked at her brother and her son. They were both asleep. She tiptoed outside. Abbas was still awake, and the light of his cigarette shone in the darkness. Ignoring him, she went into the alley.

In the late-night alleys of Zaminej, it's impossible to even see a bat flying. The darkness can be deep, the silence profound. But the uneven ground was familiar to Mergan's bare feet. Walking from alley to alley, from hovel to hovel, she quickly reached the outskirts of the village. The fields and the night filled her lungs, both immense and yet compressed. She paused. Not from fear, but from doubt. She turned and walked back toward the village and went straight to Sanam's house. The door was shut and everyone was asleep. She knocked on the door. Morad, sleepy and confused, opened the door.

"Eh? What's happened, Auntie Mergan?"

"Bring your shovel and bag and come with me. I'll explain."

He took his shovel and bag from the edge of the wall and latched the door behind himself quietly. The two were in the alley together. Mergan walked in silence, and Morad couldn't bring himself to ask about what they were doing. He walked behind her quietly as she traversed the various winding alleys to the outskirts of the village. She stopped there and turned to face Morad, who stood beside her. She asked, "You're still coming along with us?"

"I told you myself! I'm coming. Why would you think otherwise? I'm not meant to stay here. So what if I leave a month earlier than I'd planned? I was going to go in one direction; now I'm going in another! What difference does it make?"

"Good, okay...Now listen up, then! I've buried something out here somewhere, and I have to dig it out. Just follow me!"

Mergan walked ahead.

"I would trust Abrau as well, but I'd be afraid if someone else caught wind of it. But I feel I can rely on you. I think of you as one of my own sons. Come this way!"

Morad walked through the empty field behind Mergan. He asked, "How are you going to find anything in this darkness?"

"I'll find it. I'll find it. Just come! I just hid my possessions from these thieves. But I'll find it. Come this way."

Mergan suddenly turned around.

"No one noticed us, did they?"

Morad said, "At this time of night, everyone's asleep dreaming of kings and princes. Who has the heart to go out walking around in the darkness?!"

Mergan froze in her place.

"This is it! It must be right here! Start digging here. I'm sure it must be here."

Morad brought the shovel down from his shoulder and busied himself with digging the dirt. Mergan knelt on the ground and dug with her hands as well. But it was in vain. Mergan had chosen the wrong spot.

Morad asked, "Are you certain this is the right place?"

"I'm sure; I'm certain. I did the calculations."

"Let's take a minute so you can remember. What was the marker of the spot?"

"A rock! A large rock. I'm sure, I remember. It was a large rock!"

"But there was no rock here!"

"I don't know. Maybe I'm losing my mind!"

Mergan sat up and grasped at her knees with her hands, like a mother wolf who's gone to give birth in the desert night.

What if she couldn't find what she'd buried?

She rose and took Morad's hands in her own and said plaintively, "Morad my dear, you have to find it! Find it for me...My heart will break if you don't! Morad dear, please!"

"Yes, okay. But first, calm down. Just sit here. Tell me, how did you measure where it's supposed to be?"

"It's a straight shot from the wall of the Sardar's home. I took a thousand and nine steps from the edge of his wall to the big rock. I dug a hole next to it, and when I was done I pulled the rock over it to cover it."

"Fine, just stay here and don't move. I'll go back over to the Sardar's wall and will count the steps. You won't be afraid here, will you?"

"No! Go on. Just please find it. Those few bits of copper were going to pay for our travel costs. I only have you to help me!"

Morad went back and Mergan watched as he faded into the darkness. Then she was all alone, alone with the night.

Who could have dug up the earth and taken Mergan's things? Other than Hajer, who knew about what she had done?

No one. But could her innocent daughter have come and dug them out from where they'd been buried? Could Ali Genav have made her do it? That's all she needed! But Mergan didn't believe it. No, Hajer couldn't have done it.

Or could she have? No. She couldn't imagine it.

"I think I found it, Auntie Mergan! I found it! Come here!"

"Where are you, my son! Where are you?"

"Here. Can't you follow my voice?"

"I hear your voice but I can't see you. I can't see!"

"Just follow my voice. This way!"

"Oh God! I'm so lost! Help me, God!"

"Come this way. Why are you going in the wrong direction?"

"Which way?"

"Stop! You can't seem to get your bearings. I'll just dig them up and bring them to you."

"Should I just stand here?"

"Stay where you are!"

Mergan and the boy were in the night fields, apart from one another. Mergan was standing in her place like a bush or a tree, shaking. She was excited, worried, frightened. The sound of digging stopped and the field was again filled with silence. Mergan held her breath.

Had Morad taken what she'd buried and left?

God damn you. Why are you so suspicious?

Mergan bit at her lip with her teeth. Morad emerged from the darkness. He planted the shovel in the earth and took his bag from his shoulder. Mergan peered into the bag and in the night's darkness began to feel the copper plates with her fingers. They were all there! Her copper! She calmed down, then rose with a prayer, "May your youth be blessed, my boy! May my dust give you life. Let's go. You want me to carry the bag?"

"No, you can carry the shovel."

When they reached the middle of the village, Morad asked, "Shall we take them to your home?"

"No, I'd rather you kept them safely. I'll sell them in the morning when we reach the town."

"Should I come to your door tomorrow morning?"

"No. Stand by the stream just outside the village. On the path to town. We'll find each other there, before the morning prayers are called."

The mother and the boy separated. Morad went toward his house and Mergan toward her own. Mergan entered the yard quietly and went toward the door of the house. She hoped that everyone was asleep, but stopped upon hearing Abbas' burnt-out voice.

"Good evening!"

Mergan turned to the boy, trying to get herself out of the predicament she found herself in.

"You're still up?"

Abbas said, "So where's your loot?"

"What loot?"

"The copper!"

"What are you talking about? What copper?"

Abbas said, "I'm still your son. It would be nice if you were to have left me one of the jugs to make buttermilk in during the hot days of summer!"

Mergan didn't tarry any longer. She walked toward the room, saying, "I hope dust fills your envious eyes, my child!"

For some reason, Abbas didn't bother to continue the argument. He lay back in his place, set his head back, and looked up at the stars. The night was like any other night.

That night, what was left of it, Mergan didn't sleep. She lay there with no feeling, but she didn't fall asleep. Instead, something—a kind of dream—surrounded her. Wordless images ran across her mind, caught against one another, broke apart one another, appearing and disappearing. The images would fade away, only to attack her once again. Her physical exhaustion and her mind's confusion were in a battle with each other, and from this battle nightmares were emerging. The images were continually reborn, renewed at every moment. They came together, then tore apart, ghosts that would become entwined and then would be pulled apart. Images that had no substance or language. Some of them were entirely unknown to Mergan. Images that she had never experienced before, never seen before. Some were fantastic. The outlines of strange faces. What sorts of creatures were these, then? What connection, what relation did they have with each other? Where did they come from and where were they going to? Mergan's mind was an endless desert, an endless sky. With no beginning or end, with unknown shooting stars, with flames in motion, with bats and night birds in flight. What were these images that were presenting themselves to Mergan? Had her mind been plundered? Why did these thoughts run riot in her mind? Why were their beginnings and ends unclear? Whose face was this that was visible in the darkness of a well, that was transforming itself from moment to moment? Whose visage was this? Why was it expanding, filling the entire darkness of the well, and then giving light to thousands of other images which would collide and be shattered, like thousands of eyes? Then they'd grow smaller and smaller, collapsing into dots. Each dot would then become a star.

Who was this man who was standing in the threshold?

Who was this woman whose hair was down?

Who was this man, standing in the threshold, who was speaking and speaking, but whose voice could not be heard?

Who was this woman with her hair down who was screaming and screaming, but whose voice could not be heard?

How wrinkled were the breasts of this woman! Look at her eyes. Her eyes! In the depths of her eyes, were those children whose heads were the heads of humans and whose bodies were the bodies of lambs?

Why can the man's voice not be heard?

How wide are the eyes of this woman!

How is it that the heart of the sky is punctured from time to time? How do the walls come together from time to time? Lamentations ring out! Then the sounds of drums and cymbals! Is a wedding made into a funeral, then? The canals. They're opened; perhaps they've been opened. The sound of a horse neighing! It's a stallion dashing across the desert! A black snake has planted its tail in the earth and is standing straight under the glare of the sun. A dry tongue has fallen to one side within a mouth opened wide. Look how the sun spreads its chest out across the earth!

"God, dear God! Why can I not calm down? Do I have a fever? What have I lost...? Rise! Get up! Morning is breaking. Wake up!"

Mergan rose. Her brother was also up. And now Abrau, by Molla Aman's feet, also rose. Mergan took the small trunk from beside the wall and carried it outside. Molla Aman and Abrau also folded up their sheets and came outside. Abbas was half sitting up in his usual place. Mergan went to the oven. Abbas looked at his mother with tired, sleepless eyes. She said to him, "Here, the house is yours! Now take your things and go inside!"

Abbas was silent. Abrau was wrapping up the blanket he was taking with himself. Molla Aman splashed water onto his face. Abbas came down from the roof of the oven. His mother approached him, grasped his head onto her chest, and whispered into his ear.

"Don't worry, you won't starve, my boy! You'll be okay! I'll send you money, and until then others will look after you. I've always done well to others here. I've been a mother to everyone. They won't let my boy suffer. I trust them like my own eyes. May you live a life of perfection, my son!"

She grasped Abbas' dry, aged head and pressed it to her chest as if gripped by a kind of madness. Then she suddenly let him go, as if she didn't want the waves in her heart to overflow. She couldn't let them. So she let him go.

Abrau, himself now ready to go, had wrapped the straps for his satchel around his shoulders and was carrying his blanket on his back. Mergan looked at her boys. The brothers were drawn together. Abrau, with a load tied to his back, began moving toward Abbas calmly and—for some reason—with a hint of shame. Abbas, with his head overrun by white hair that seemed almost to be scraping against the dark morning sky, had turned toward his brother as well. The brothers paused a moment as they grew nearer, but then Abrau extended a hand toward Abbas, who suddenly threw himself into his brother's arms. His shoulders were overtaken by a wave of shaking and trembling. A muffled sound that was akin to an injured dog's yelp caught in his throat. Despite this, he began speaking with difficulty and in a broken voice.

"I'm afraid...that I won't live long enough...to see you...to see you again...brother! Don't...don't...forget me...will you?!"

Abrau held Abbas out and shook him.

"Calm down! It's no good to be crying just as we're setting out! You never cried before!"

Abbas leaned against the wall and wiped his nose with his sleeve.

"No...only...only...Forget it...! Nothing...! Just go then...! May you travel in safety...I...won't say any more!"

Molla Aman was already in the alley and shouted over the wall.

"Come on then! Are you preparing to go to battle or something? Let's go!"

Mergan, and Abrau behind her, walked through the opening in the wall and out into the alley, following Molla Aman's footsteps.

Abbas came to the alley, walking with his crutch, and poured a cup of water in the footsteps of the travelers for good luck. Abrau turned once again and waved his cap at Abbas.

As Molla Aman and Abrau walked on, Mergan's footsteps faltered at the door to Ali Genav's home, and she stopped. They continued on. She opened the door and stepped inside. But then she stopped inside the doorway. She didn't want to wake her daughter. No, it would be better if she didn't know and didn't see them as they left. Also, she didn't want to see Ali Genav while she was leaving. So, caught between two impulses, she stood where she was.

A moment or two later, Raghiyeh came out, like a mouse leaving its hole. She was quiet and calm. The sound of the door couldn't have woken her. Mergan imagined that Raghiyeh hadn't slept the night either. She came toward Mergan limping quietly and passed her by, as if Hajer's mother wasn't standing there before her. She went to the alley. Mergan turned and followed her out.

"Raghiyeh dear, Raghiyeh! I'm leaving my daughter, Hajer, in your care, and I leave you in God's. Raghiyeh dear, don't bother her. She's just a girl. If she's done you wrong, or if I have, don't do wrong to her!"

Raghiyeh didn't look back. She didn't answer, and under Mergan's gaze she limped over to Mergan's house, now Abbas' house.

Mergan watched her until she reached the wall of the house, walking softly, with determination. Then she shook herself—her brother and son were far ahead by now. She looked one last time back at Raghiyeh, then set out walking quickly, reaching Molla Aman and Abrau at the outskirts of Zaminej.

The tractor was still sitting by the graveyard. It was like a corpse that had been pushed out of its grave. Wrapped in a shroud of red desert dust. Morad was sitting by the tractor, next to the stream, one hand in the water.

Water?

"It's blood. Do you see the blood?"

They sat. There was blood in the water. Molla Aman lit a match, "Water stained by blood! They must have cut up the old mare's body, then."

They rose, all but Mergan. She remained sitting by the water, looking down the stream. Someone was coming. A man was coming. Somebody was coming. A person covered in a bloody shroud. He had a shovel in one hand—Soluch. With a muddy shovel. He had emerged from the canal drain. He must have opened the canals himself. His face was not visible. Beneath the shroud, blood was dripping from the cloak he always wore, the cloak made from the hide of his donkey. The blood left an unbroken trail in his footsteps.

"What kind of place are the mines? How are they...? Is there work for women there as well?"

***

The night was breaking.

The night was breaking on the trail of blood.

—1979